LOW

RENT

A

Semi-Autobiographical Novel

By

Thomas Edward Jordan

———

The following is based upon true events from the author's life; however, all of the names of the characters and some of the identifying details have been altered in order to protect those involved.

————

————

ISBN: 978-0-578-12866-5

————

———

Fourth Edition

Ω † ¢ $ ♫ § ☾ 🐵 ♫ £ π ♪ Δ

For those of you who share these
memories with me.

I - Prologue

Long curling gray hairs protrude from each of my ears and pour from my nose in the world's shortest race against the unkempt yellow nails hanging on for dear life to my withered pointers. A disheveled gray crown with matching stubble conceals a decrepit mind that is lost in the simplest of memories, erroneously calling my grandson by the name of his cousin. No, I say to myself, I refuse to live in such a future. Luckily, none of this plagues me quite yet, and I should hope not, I'm only twenty-seven years old. Yet there are beads of sweat that have formed upon my forehead, and though I feel empathetic for those who have been swallowed up by the weathering of old age, I sense the weight of time pressing upon me to rise from the couch and accomplish something more than just abstaining from the bottle and the boob tube. Though I fear being incarcerated for eternity in the misery of my own nostalgia, I can't help but feel the need to exist in at least one other place than my head stone which will read, "For a Good Time, Dig Here ↓." That other place where I feel I belong immortalized is a place one only arrives at through the strokes of pen and key.

Just the same as the next guy, I deserve a chance to successfully release what may, if I'm lucky, make it around the camp fire, but is otherwise doomed to be quickly forgotten and fade into the Syd Barrett's and Daniel Johnston's Mothers' basements. I fear my chance will prove to be a beautiful fake, a trailer hitch on a Geo Metro, a long road that just leads back to where I started. I can easily disappoint, missing my mark with remarkable ease, yet I somehow manage to survive most expectations of me, even ending up on top from time to time. Successful or not, once this damn thing is finally finished I'll be on the tip of the top of somewhere of my choosing.

I've found an escape hatch where I am able to observe life through eyes other than my own. I see a different you, me, now & then, this place & that place, our living world in a frenzied twist. Yet even on the outside, the air is heavy with regret, and I am still haunted by Nostalgia. Nearly all of the places I escape to include water in some form or another, whether floating down a river, soaking in the tub, or lost at sea, the beauty and tranquility found in the movement of the water evokes the wistful longings for days gone by that threaten to drive me mad. The sounds become smells, and I breathe in the feeling of lost love's touch. In these worlds I inspire whiskey bottles to teeter dangerously on edges of tables with sideway eyes that cease to pour clear blue lakes and the cold gray rain clouds that follow me around like sad little stalkers remind me, yet again, of lost opportunities. If I had only given it one more chance, if I had let her prove to me that her Love was worth my time, what if I had worn a condom and never had to go through that abortion, or better yet, what if I never had sex with her in the first place? If I had only done this or that differently, life may have turned out… Though painfully trivial, the what-if's have had a relentless grip on me for some time. The only good that comes of it is the reinforcement of certain notions: that it's not all my doing; I was neither raped nor was I the rapist; but what it does remind me of, is that destiny and its ally, fate, play just as an important of a role as the rest of the driving forces that have steered me to where I am today. I know, however, that dwelling on all of this is a waste of my time and emotional energy. Yet I can't help but lose my time, and the shittiest part is that I often over indulge these notions, both the pleasant and the repellent: the shitty commute to work in the morning, the most dreadful drive of the day for way more reasons than I can cover in any introduction, and the night drive from work once I'm off for the day is almost equally as brutal because I'm rushing home to get either drunk or high to forget the day; the dog; the cat; the car; a woman I fancy that frequents the same bar as me, and despite the fact that on any given night there is typically less than five dreary souls haunting the place, I still haven't grown a pair and said the slightest thing to her, not even a simple "hi" or "excuse me, do you mind if I steal this from you," gesturing towards an ash tray in front of her or a seat next to her hoping that after we've both spent a few hours a day in the same place for over six months she might have noticed me by now (what's her name again?); finding a little bit of self worth in the fact that the bartender remembers my name, though she does work for tips. Are these banal features of American life truly the extent of the universe we've created for ourselves? Well, they've been mine before, but they haven't always been able to pin me to the same city, job, home, billing, shipping, or email address.

————————————

The older I get the more I learn not to take most of what I do or have for granted, yet I still can't help but over analyze the life I lead today, and harbor disgust for how uneventful and unrewarding life can be at times. Youth was no picnic either, with the constant insecurities, self-deprecation, and shyness. Though I must admit, I was allowed a certain flight from the life our parents groomed us for, the life most of us lead, Plan A. The time between birth and treading the first steps on the path towards Plan A is the defining period where anything is possible, and the choices you make may determine whether you take that main path, stray off down another path entirely, or make an entire new path of your own. Before I steered myself back toward the path of Plan A, or espoused myself to the idea of something similar to it, I was running down so many paths at the same time, I had devastated the whole forest floor. Though in retrospect there was but a few trees and bits of shrubbery left by the time I was back on the main path, I wouldn't change a thing about the choices I made or the way in which I went about them. And even though there is this uprooting nostalgia that stabs at me like a rock in my shoe, the memories beckon me to search out a valid reason for my existence, or at least a reason to be. What I see is one foot in front of the other, but only a few feet away from where I now stand, and those few feet are as far as it seems that I can get beyond my present self, pathetic really.

I'm trapped within and outside of my own imagination, and I am unable to imagine myself any further down the road. I see the ghost of me pacing around the same block for eternity. I become jealous of the five year-old, crayon in hand, drawing what they want to be when they grow up, four stick figures, Mommy, Daddy, Brother, and themselves in a spaceship, the five year-old sitting at the controls eating ice cream, all of them smiling. Envy doesn't even begin to describe what I feel, while the child is able at any time, on demand, to awaken light years away in a day dream with thousands upon thousands of different possibilities, I'm afflicted with this crippling inability to regain that childhood world in my head. However, my biggest fear, other than not being known posthumously, is that as time goes by, I'm forgetting more and more of the many great stories from my life. It is with the self-portrait that follows that I aim to kick start that quadrant of my brain, and forever be rid of my nonexistent dreams, and to always remember, to immortalize my life, even if I can't remember every great tale. I have come to terms with the fact that life is finite and the end is already determined for all of us.

Subsequently, the real question now plaguing my thoughts is do I want to be standing tall when it comes, or on my knees begging for forgiveness? Though I'll have my reservations just like any other human being, I will most definitely be standing lofty and tall because I have already learned to accept the inevitable. One such reservation is that I'm deathly afraid that I'll be accused of being just another withdrawn, introverted old man once the AARP letters start flooding my mailbox and Ronnie McDonald serves me discounted coffee. Whether it is the beautiful shades or the ugly shadows from the portrait of my life, the fear has developed even further to include the complete disregard for my past altogether, favoring one that was much more grandiose that I will conjure up as time wrinkles on. Thankfully, I've had what I believe has been a pretty magnificent life that many people could only dream of.

_____

My father once told me that "Love ain't free, it'll cost you plenty kid," crushing the romantic ideal of what future loves and relationships would be like for me. Seeing as how he wasn't around much when I was a kid, I consider myself quite lucky to have had that conversation with my father when I did because Dad was right; Love is expensive, taxing both your wallet and your stash of emotional valor. This gave me a great perspective on the difference between freedom and being free, living cheaply and being cheap. I quiver at the thought of obsessing over a woman or the storybook love affair that never came to be. I've seen too many people lose their freedom to the idea that the romantic ideal created by Hollywood can be theirs. Once the reality of this twisted world gets its grip on them and they realize that sex and love are nothing like what they saw portrayed as in the movies, they become crushed and embarrassed by the awareness of being taken for a fool. Feeling helpless and losing all reason to go on with life once these ideals have been instantaneously decimated, some feel driven to take a fully loaded, semi-automatic pistol to their school or office, and kill as many of the people that actively play a part in making the world less than romantic. I believe it's what we do with our freedom that define us, and if we're headed for a Dystopia, which really isn't too farfetched a future to believe in the way things are headed, then I must rush to the blank page while my liberties are intact, because for me, I am only as free as the pen and key allow me to be.

_____

Though I'm still a young man, thus far my eyes have seen too much of what could be considered hell. Like Dante's levels, I'd venture to say I've taken four giant leaps in and out of various hells, and I've seen what the demons have to offer: dried up wishing wells; highways so full of garbage and road-kill that they have become impassable; and winter nights where, for no good reason, birds are mysteriously awakened from the deep sleep of hibernation and can be heard chirping in bitter anguish. Enough hells that it would take up more of this book than I care to write about. Now it's time to entertain and to let those of you who are on the outside, in.

_____

II - A Few Moments Ago

The story goes that a legend has it, so I've been told that once upon a time there was an old Storyteller that had forgotten all of his tales one day. Every single one, from the firsts to the lasts, all the way through the only times ever… He'd forgotten them all and died with nothing worthwhile to say upon his death bed. I'm afraid I'm bound to get lost in the here and now, and forget about the important moments that have shaped and defined me, doomed to a wordless last breathe like the poor, oblivious old Storyteller. Up until now I have lived my life thrusting a knife into a socket with one hand, holding a half full glass of water in the other, and blowing troubles from a mouth that never seems to relent.

At twenty-one years old I was by no means living any sort of dream, or cliché for that matter. I was doing what I wanted, when I wanted, and there was no one there to tell me I had to live my life any other way than my own way. There was nothing cute about it though, not a single thing the commonwealth could've benefited from in the particular light I was living. In fact, there was no light to speak of, it was downright evil, a living night terror. The worst part about it was that I often profited from the more malevolent, unethical elements. For instance, while those who bought my drugs became addicted and poor, I became that much wealthier. Beautiful women surrounded my wristwatch, and rode with me in the many cars I owned, tributes to my success. I parked them throughout the city at various apartments I had rented out, each serving a specific function in for my day to day Business, not to mention what a tremendous help it was with dating multiple women simultaneously. I had brought a dream to life and surrounded myself with guns, girls, dope, cars, all sorts of fancy material possessions, and plenty of loot to pay for it all.

I was living the life I had wished for, ironically however, the lifestyle was killing me. Everything was moving so fast that I had lived quite a long life in an alarmingly short span of time. I truly believed that if I hadn't already come into this world with an old soul, I sure as hell was leaving with one. I saw myself as a rising phoenix that had been born less from the ashes and more from the still burning needles, beer bottles, trash, and wannabe's. One moment was caressed by long laughs lost over beautiful views, and the next was a series of nightmares ritually pushed through tiny holes in my arms, ankles, and wrists. Juvenile delinquent, prolific graffiti writer, hobo, drug dealer, felon, college student, artist, ordained minister, junkie, white collar worker, Godfather to my nephew… Where I've been is no place at all, and from my visits I quickly learned that the halo has very little to fall to become either a necktie, or a noose. I wasn't sure which was worse, but I knew I didn't want to stick around and find out. From then on I was destined to wear horns and never a halo, thus my search for a vehicle to convey my dirty little secrets began.

Any man who does not accept the conditions of life sells his soul.

– Charles Baudelaire

III - A Few Moments in Now

There's a hooker in my basement. Yes siree, a real live whore. Step right up, step right up! See the onerous, devious, devilish, deceitful dame from Sin City. She flew in from Vegas almost a week ago, and she'll be gone long before her story ever sees print. Glorified. She's the antithesis of a high school sweetheart for my roommate, Mark Death, who told her that she "should do us all a favor and just kill yourself." He demanded this of her not just once, but on a daily basis when they were in school together, and frankly, I'm amazed the abuse didn't drive her to do so. She kept repeating it to me after she had blown a few lines from the gram of coke I had sold her earlier in the day. Apparently, she really took it to heart, which MarkD said "only strengthened her resolve to be even more of a piece of shit."

I refer to this poor, tormented Vegas whore on a sojourn trip through my basement as "Caribou" because she's a big, ugly, nomadic, beast of a slut. At least that's what I thought of her at first. A layer of ever-apparent grime appears to be alive on her skin. As well, an equally dirty mind with a mouth to follow, and a sense of humor, one of extreme filth, one that is frighteningly similar to mine, are what struck me most when confronted by her presence.

After a few days of quick quips caught out of the corner of my eye, her berating of MarkD on such a personal level really began to grow on me, but don't get me wrong, I have not, and will not even consider Ms. Caribou as a possible lay. No thanks. I would slice my dick off before it ever got anywhere close to that cum filled abysmal germ-hole. Yet this disgustingly hilarious whore is in my basement, and the scary part is that we're not all that different from one another.

The house I live in is over one hundred and twenty years old, and it has one of those grimy unfinished basements closed in by cracking cement walls with streaks of yellow and brown running down them from rain water that seeped through once upon a dreary. The landlord does a walk-through every six months or so to check in on the house and how we've been treating it, and every time he goes into the basement he asks us to stop letting our cats down there because he accused us of letting our cats use it as a bathroom. He vehemently denies what numerous neighbors and even public record has confirmed to be true: the basement stinks like cat piss because a previous tenant was using the basement as a meth lab just a few years prior to our arrival. Dumb-dumb luck. Legally, the landlord is obliged to maintain the home as a vacant crime scene, condemning it for another few years until the toxicity has dissipated to safer levels. Needless to say, our landlord is a total piece of shit.

MarkD calls the basement home, a dreary place he pays a measly $100 a month to live in. The basement or what he refers to as the 'Pain Cave,' is where he keeps all his worldly possessions, which are really just some clothes, a dilapidated mattress with no frame or box spring, a record player, and a pretty awesome record collection. Somehow, MarkD has been able to bring women down there, and they haven't come screaming up the stairs, running for their lives. During her short stay with us, Ms. Caribou has even managed to have a threesome with MarkD and some other poor girl in the Pain Cave. They woke me up with their groaning and drunk babbling which gave me nightmares for the rest of the week.

Tonight I'll go home, and there will still be a hooker in my basement, but I suppose there have been worse things down there.

When I arrived home from work tonight Caribou was sitting in the living room watching TV by herself. It was seven o'clock and the Simpsons were just coming on. I was no more than five steps in the door when a can of beer came flying in my direction. I snatched it out of the air, and in the same motion I twisted the cap off and brought it to my lips.

"Thanks Caribou(gulp, gulp)… awwwwwwwwe," wiping the foam mustache from my upper lip. "You here all alone?" taking a seat in the reclining chair opposite her, next to the TV.

"Sure am. No one's here and I have no idea where MarkD is. How was work, Business Boy?" she asked, followed by a short chuckle, and a long pull off her own bottle.

"It was alright," adjusting myself in my seat.

"Well?" she smiled.

"Well what?" confused.

"Well what did you do today?" she inquired.

"If you know me well enough by now to know that I like to drink beer right after work, then you should also know that I hate to talk about work right after I get off?" I grumbled.

"Oooook, I guess I don't know you well enough then huh?" she laughed awkwardly as she stared at the beer in her hands.

A few minutes passed and I finished my beer before reluctantly apologizing, "Hey, I'm sorry, I'm usually pretty grumpy when I get off work. Thanks for the beer."

"You're welcome," she said softly.

We continued watching the Simpsons and when the show was over and I had finished four beers, I stood up and said, "Hey I'm gonna go to the corner store and get some more beer, you need anything?"

She rose to her feet as well, "I'll come with you," following me to the front door.

"Yeah alright," I said as we walked out of the house, and turned right at the bottom of the front stoop. "So Caribou, what's your plan?" I said a few steps later.

"Not quite sure yet, I'm kinda waitin for my man to wire me some money before I do anything, otherwise…"

"Your man?" I interrupted.

"Yeah, ok… If you must know, he's my Pimp. Anyway, if he don't wire me the money, I guess I'm gonna have to pull a few tricks from your hood here so I can get back home," she said, obviously a little perturbed. "Anyways, what's your plan?" she inquired.

I pushed the button at the crosswalk as I replied, "My plan? Tonight? Well I gotta work early so…" The electronic sign changed to a white stick figure, indicating it was safe for us to cross the street.

Before I could finish, she stepped in my path, spinning around to face me, "No, I mean the big TommyJ plan, your life plan," she said as she walked backwards.

"Shit, um…" laughing as I searched my head for some semblance of an answer. "I think I got what you'd consider a career now, but other than that, I have no idea really. I guess I'll just take it easy for a while. I feel like I've done all there is to do… What I mean to say is, that I've been through a hell of a lot in the last few years," I answered. We arrived at the corner store and I followed Caribou in the front door.

"You've been through it all huh? Bet you haven't pulled any tricks have you?" she smirked as she nudged me in the side trying to tickle me. She was slightly successful and I jerked away clenching my forearm to my rib cage. "Well... since you don't seem to know what you wanna do, or where you're goin, why don't you tell me where you've been?" she asked as she pulled a forty ounce of Mickey's Malt Liquor out of a cooler.

"Uh, I don't know," I replied. I was reluctant to indulge her, so I decided to turn the line of questioning back in her direction, "what about you?"

"Oh nuh uh, I asked first. Come on, since you seem like such a badass," she said mockingly, "why don't you tell me one of your badass stories?" she asked, laughing.

"Whatever, let's just get our shit and go watch TV?" I pleaded. I really didn't feel like I should try and impress some prostitute with stories of my sordid past.

"How bout I tell you one of mine first, and then you can tell me one of yours?" How could I refuse? It took the spotlight off of me, and maybe she would get so into talking about herself, she wouldn't stop until it was time for me to hit the hay for the night.

"Go for it," I reluctantly agreed.

We exited the store and stood near the entrance for a moment, each of us taking the first swill from our beers in brown bags before she began her story. "Right before I came to Portland, I decided to take a few days off work because of a really shitty trick I got stiffed on," she explained as I snickered at the pun. "Hey!" she exclaimed as she hit my arm. "Ha ha, very funny! Anyways, this guy not only didn't pay, he knocked me around before he split. You see, I was supposed to meet him at a Starbucks because I always meet my clients at a public place so I can kinda…" she said trailing off for a few seconds, "Get a feel for them before I agree to do anything else with them you know?" she asked rhetorically. But this guy had a bullshit story about how he was partially crippled that he was in a lot of pain that night, and he claimed he couldn't meet me anywhere other than his motel room downtown off the strip. So of course, being the trusting, naïve girl that I am, I went up to his room. Yeah sure, the asshole was crippled, he was missing a leg, but the fucker wasted no time at all hopping around the room chasing me, swinging his prosthetic at me." We both laughed before she continued, "Apparently, he gets his rocks off by slapping around little girls." She quietly stared at the ground for a moment as we continued to walk home, "So, there's my story, now it's your turn."

"Geez, I don't know if I could possibly follow that amazing story," I said as I laughed.

"Hey! Give me a break," she frowned.

I began to search my memory for a really good story of my own, one that would put hers to shame. Unfortunately, however, I was shooting cognitive blanks. "Hmmm, I'm trying to think of just the right one to tell you, but I'm coming up empty. Not because yours was so great, but because I just can't think of one. I have the shittiest memory, I swear."

"Well, why don't you… Hmmm, why don't you tell me a story from your college years? You went to college right?" she inquired, trying to lead me towards something, anything.

"Yeah, but I never graduated," I said as we arrived at my house. We walked through the front door into the living room and sat back down in the same spots we were sitting at before we left for the market. I suppose it was somewhat more of a desire to show that I indeed had some pretty fucked up experiences than it was this prostitute's provocation that drove me to dig deep and recall the perfect story to share with her. "Ok, not because I want to, but because I feel it's my duty to show you how to tell a story, I'll indulge your curiosity…" I said as I began my story.

---

4. Dead Wind

Stagnant, putrid, unmistakable, yet Dead Wind often remains unacknowledged. The last breath, the last words, the absolute last trace of a life is what gives us Dead Wind, and I have had the unfortunate opportunity to witness the secretion and subsequent presence of this sad, but beautiful force.

A ninety-five degree day had me laid up watching Hitchcock's *Rear Window* whilst perched upon my love seat just a few inches from the air conditioner. At full blast the little fan inside was whistling a soothing melody into my ears. I suppose I will forever associate whistling machines and the sense of relief from obnoxious heat with black and white thrillers, and a three dimensional, high-def, real life story about a young man's death. Movie over, I jumped into a cold shower in my claw foot tub, shedding the sweat I had acquired in the few short minutes since I had strayed from my cool resting spot. Out of the shower, dried, dressed, phone calls made, skateboard and keys in hand, the buzzer from the front door of my building rang. I had a beautiful antique wall phone that had the sole function of buzzing my room from the front door of the building. I walked over to it, picked up the ear piece, and put it to my ear.

"Ellow?" I said in a stoutly but muddled cross between a British and Australian accent.
"Eh mate, it's Geverz, I gots me board, and two forties, one with your name on it," my Aussie friend Geverz said in his genuine Aussie accent.

"Oi, good on ya mate, I'm on my way down," I said before I ran out of my apartment into the hallway. I locked the door, flew down four flights of stairs, and was out the front door into the courtyard in less than a minute. We said our "ellow's," Geverz put a fresh forty ounce of *211 Steel Reserve* in my hand, as well as a big smile upon my face as we walked to the street. My malt liquor induced jubilation was short lived, however, and just as quickly as I had been delivered my smile, a frown was forced upon my face with a similar abruptness. As I peered down the length of the bottle I was sucking on like a kill in my cross hairs, I could see a guy in the distance I had met earlier in the day. His name escaped me, Frankie, Eddie, I don't know, some greased up name like that. It would have been of little concern to me had he been pacing madly somewhere else, but the fact that he looked like a freaked out canary in a coal mine in front of the building next to mine made me twitch with nervousness...

I lived on the corner of 14th and Clay Street in downtown Portland, which is on the southwest side of town. The building I lived in is situated next to numerous other turn of the century apartment buildings, and various Victorian homes scattered about the neighborhood, many of which had been converted for business use or had the bedrooms divided into separate apartments. The University campus was also just over the freeway interchange a few blocks away. At the end of my street was a high-rise dormitory for the college that numerous friends and clients called home. I also knew someone from just about every building on my street, and I was constantly meeting new people in the hood through friends and by simply skateboarding & walking the streets. I also met quite a few of my neighbors at the local bar, The River City Tavern. This is where I met the man who would become my dealer for quite some time, ReggieJ, and he conveniently lived in the building right next door to mine. He didn't actually live there, he only slept there if he wasn't staying at one of his girlfriend's places, or at one of the many other apartments he rented throughout the city.

The only thing separating our buildings was a narrow alleyway that had an imposing security gate guarding it. It was over fifteen feet tall and came dressed in stainless steel barbwire meant to glimmer in the sun and into the eyes of any would-be burglar with the hope of stopping him in his tracks, but if that weren't enough, if one were brave enough to try and scale this prison worthy behemoth anyway, they would be met with a 20,000+ volt jolt once they touched any metal part of the gate that was over the eight foot high mark. I often used the alley to gain access to ReggieJ's place by climbing down the fire escape on my building which led to the end of the alley.

———————————————

I had to pay ReggieJ a visit earlier in the day before I went skateboarding with Geverz, so I dropped by just a few hours before the Aussie showed up. Once I had reached ReggieJ's front door I knocked lightly, "Hey, it's TommyJ," I said as I backed away from the door enough to be seen clearly through the peep hole. The door opened and ReggieJ was standing there with his left arm extended out leading me into his living room.

"Here you go," I said as I handed him a wad of cash.

"And here you go Mr. TommyJ," ReggieJ said as he handed me a half pound of Coke in a large sandwich bag. Though Blow is usually bought and sold in Kilos, ReggieJ and I agreed to do our trade in pounds since this was America and we don't use the metric system here, plus we sold the shit in divisions of pounds: grams, eighth ounces, ounces, etc. "Sorry man, that's only a half pound. It's all I've got right now, but you can come by tomorrow and grab more ya hear?" ReggieJ explained. After that I thought I'd be out of there lickidy split, but ReggieJ wanted me to stick around for a while so it wouldn't look so obvious to the neighbors that he was selling drugs. He had a valid point since I had come over empty handed and what the neighbors would see would be me leaving just moments after arriving with a large bag in hand. Plus the more often I paid quick little visits to the place, the more likely they'd become suspicious. "TommyJ, meet my new friends, this here is CalC, MikeR, and MikeR's girl LaceyJoe," he pointed to each of them as I thought, great, just what he needs, fresh faces.

"Pleased, Pleased, I'm sure," I made gestures of my own.

"Take yourself a seat and indulge me… and of course my new friends here," ReggieJ said as he motioned for me to sit on the couch. I sat, like a fool. A few lines of this and that powder were poured upon the table in front of me and straws were made from dissecting ball point pens. Thanks to the blow, I made nice with the new guys. CalC was a local in our neighborhood, and like me, he was selling for ReggieJ to the local college kids. Then there was the other guy MikeR, he was a complete and utter mess. He was CalC's hippie dippy friend that just got back into town after following the band Phish around on a six month long tour. Following a band around seemed pretty lame to me, especially one as 'cool' as Phish.

The hippie, MikeR, was mumbling and maundering to himself, constantly eyeing the bathroom door as if looking for a way out, obviously in way over his head. His girl, LaceyJoe, just sat there nodding out periodically. She didn't say a word the whole time I was there which was fine by me because I assumed she probably didn't have anything interesting to say anyway. I began to feel twitchy and thought to myself that the coke was strange this time around. "Hey," I called out to ReggieJ, "that was just coke in those lines right," as I wiped the snot that was beginning to drip from my nose.

"No man," ReggieJ said as he laughed, "I threw some crank in there for an extra kick."

I knew I could handle the mix just fine, but it was obvious that this MikeR kid couldn't. He was teetering dangerously close to the edge.

"Now we gonna take a cab huh?" skinny little MikeR blurted out louder than the NWA tape that was playing on the stereo, louder than our thoughts even.

"No MikeR, wait a little bit, KimmyK's still coming over," CalC said shaking his head. I tried to keep MikeR in the real world with conversation, but talking to him was like a phone call with bad reception. I could tell that he had been gone for months, and no one was really home.

"I…I… Love," MikeR slumped over in his seat whiter than Snow White herself, out like a light. Out for good. We all laughed. Moments later the kid was still in the same slumped position with his chin to his knees, his right arm extended, almost pointing to that bathroom door he kept staring at, and his left hand was under his leg like he was reaching for something in his back pocket.

"Hey MikeR," CalC said as he nudged his friend with the toe of his Converse. "Miiiiiiike!" CalC nudged him again. Nothing. I decided it was time to go and so I gathered my bag of coke, concealing it in the inside lining of my coat.

"Well good luck with uh…" I said stumbling over my words, "that guy," I went on pointing at MikeR, and then I walked over and opened the front door.

"See ya," ReggieJ said just as MikeR suddenly got up from his seat, and as I shut the door behind me I turned around just in time to see the stupid Hippie fall on his face, and I felt the air go still around me, but I thought nothing of it at the time.

―――――――――――

I ran over to my house where I weighed out twenty or so smaller bags from the bag of blow I had just picked up. I proceeded to sit on my ass and watch another movie while I waited for my girl, MishK, to come home. Even with the air conditioner on, I sweat profusely from the sun beaming through the window as I tried to get into the movie in order to pass the time. The high began to wear in and out, until finally she arrived. It seemed to have taken her forever.

"I need your Dick," she exclaimed, the door flying closed behind her, tongue on lips, hell in her eyes.

"I made something for you," I stuttered, almost frightened by her horniness as I got up and walked away from her towards the back of the room.

"Sorry, Hun, not right now," she replied, "I wanna fuck!" she demanded as she tackled me with a couple of beers in her hand, the big couch, she leaned up, shook one real good, and lifted the tab letting the beer fly as she ripped my shirt off. We rolled around and fucked for what seemed like hours. I came so many times that I lost track. My memory also fails me when I try to remember all the parts of her body that I searched out with my tongue, seeking the sweat salty beer that covered her every inch. It's too bad really, I'd like more of that memory, the memory of the best drink I've ever tasted. From time to time, while drinking beer in the sun, with the taste of sweaty, hoppy froth on my lips, this heated moment will come to mind and bring a long dark smear of a smile across my face and a tightness in my jeans. After licking her dry and fucking the everlasting lust into submission, we both gave into our exhaustion and fell asleep.

A few hours later the buzzer rang on the antique phone. I walked over and picked up the receiver, "Ellow?" I said in a stoutly but muddled cross between a British and Australian accent. It was Geverz on the other end waiting down stairs for me to go skating. So I grabbed my skateboard, ran down the stairs, and met up with Geverz out front my building. Geverz handed me a beer and as I chugged it, I saw CalC pacing like a mad man out front of ReggieJ's place.

"Check it out," I said as I nudged Geverz. The two of us then walked down to where CalC was.

"He's gone, I mean... we gotta go… I just don't know what to… What to do, I mean..." CalC sounded agitated as he mumbled and puttered around his car which was double parked right there.

"You alright man?" I asked after waiting until he had turned back my way with scared, yokeless eyes.

"Yeah, yeah," he said regaining some equanimity. "I'll be fine," he went on as he slowed his pace to a mere twitch of his leg, it was quite awkward really.

Geverz and I exchanged looks of confusion, nodded to CalC, stepped on our skateboards, and skated off down the hill. We ended up skating until the summer sun came down over the cityscape surrounding us.

22

I came home and fell into bed with MishK, and all I wanted to do was fall asleep, but my quest was abruptly interrupted by the pissed off shrills of my girlfriend, "Where the fuck have you been? We were supposed to hang out all night and you left after just one fuck!!!" she screamed as she jumped up off the bed sending the sheets flying.

I rose to my feet, "You were out like a light, and I had forgotten that I made plans to go skate with Geverz. I'm sorry, I didn't think you'd be back up from that last fuck for days," I said followed by a light chuckle, careful not to piss her off any further, unfortunately I was unsuccessful.

"Oh fuck you, ya asshole!" she continued screaming as she sent one of my Dead Moon records flying at me. It hit me square in the jaw and shattered into tens of pieces falling upon my feet. It was times like this that made the mad love I had for her grow even crazier. I walked over and grabbed the next record out of her hand that she was planning to throw at me.

"I'm sorry sweetheart, I honestly didn't think you'd care, or even wake up to care for that matter. C'mon baby, let me make it up to you?!?" I said as I set the record down on the nightstand, and put my hands on her waist. She tried to squirm away from me, pulling her arms to her chest as she tried to push me off of her. I kept apologizing but I fucked up by laughing so she turned her head so that I couldn't kiss her though. This worked to my advantage because the neck was a big weakness of hers, so I kissed and bit it gently. Jumping on this vulnerability of hers this and every other time I was trying to smooth things over between us seemed to work like a charm. She became Jell-O in my arms, melting into my lips, falling off my tongue, and losing to my words. "You believe me don't you baby? I didn't mean to hurt your feelings, I knew I would be back just in time to catch you waking up so we could snuggle," I pleaded, kissing and licking her between every few words.

"Oh baby… I believe you," she said, shivering as she softly gave into me. I had tamed her with my tongue, and in order to make up for this one, I knew there had to be more where that came from, so I gently slid her panties off and slid down her, kissing her breasts on my way down. I kissed her navel, then down to her thighs where I treated them much the same as her neck, kissing and biting gently on the inner sides, and then finally delving my tongue and kisses into her center sending more shivers throughout her body that I could feel on my ears as she wrapped her legs tightly around my head. "Oh baby! Yes, yes, YES!!" she screamed as she quickly came to her climax. With her wetness dripping off my chin onto my chest, I wiped it with one hand and took off my pants with the other. As I came up to kiss her, I wiped her on my cock to get it wet just before I put it in.

The following day I was low on my resources and I needed to re-up again, so I rang ReggieJ on his cell. I was expecting a quick conversation like, come on over, make a moment with me, something to that effect, but this was not the case. The phone rang and rang but there was never an answer. I must have tried him ten times over the course of the day. I ended up watching a few movies while I waited to get a hold of him. I also needed to stick around my place because

I had a few of my customers coming over to pick up some blow themselves. I was in dire straits by about four in the afternoon when I had been completely cleaned out. I had about six different people calling me every twenty minutes wanting to pick up, but I still couldn't get a hold of ReggieJ, A few movies, a few episodes of Dexter, and many text messages later my phone rang, finally it was ReggieJ "TommyJ, come out front and jump in the Camino!" he said sounding less than elated.

"K, I'll be out in just a sec," I said as I scrambled to grab a few thousand dollars out of one of the three safes I kept at my apartment. I kept one half of my cash and drugs in one safe, and the other halves in another safe. I put rocks wrapped in hand towels in the third safe to give the effect of having the same contents as the other safes. Anytime I left my apartment I made sure to lock all of them up, putting the two with the drugs and money behind a false wall in my closet, and leaving the third one out on my coffee table. The idea was that if someone were to break in, they would grab the safe that was out in the open, and get out of there before I came back or someone saw them. If you knew me well enough to know that I had that shit in my apartment, then you knew me well enough to know that I always carried a gun with me as well.

After putting the safes in their respective homes and my pistol in my waistband, I flew down the stairs, not wanting to miss out on re-upping from ReggieJ. Luckily I made it out of my building quick enough to be in his El Camino within a minute of talking to him on the phone, otherwise I feared he may have flown off with his paranoia as he was somewhat of a flake. As soon as I was in the passenger's seat, he peeled out and off we went.

"Hold on tight little buddy. We have to go somewhere and talk, where shall we go? You always know the best places," nervousness dominated ReggieJ's tone.

"Shit, um, how about the River City Tavern," I said as I pointed to the right, in the direction of the bar.

"Right... right, good choice," he said as he quickly turned the corner. Within seconds we were pulling up in front of the bar half way in a loading/tow zone and half way in front of a fire hydrant. We got out of his Camino and as he walked around the car to the sidewalk, I was standing there with a funny look on my face looking at him, then at the car, and then back at him.

"What? Shrugging his shoulders and holding out his hands.

"Did you happen to notice where you're parked?" I asked as I pointed to the tow sign and then the fire hydrant.

"Um, in front of the River City Tavern, duh," he replied half smiling and shaking his head at me as he walked into the bar.

Yeaaaaah, he's out of it, out of this planet, I thought as I followed him. At ReggieJ's suggestion we sat down at a table near the jukebox which was blasting a Beatles tune. I couldn't help but wonder what kind of high he was on, and what kind of trouble he was about to involve me in this time.

After situating ourselves at a table, our waitress came over, and before I could tell her what I wanted, ReggieJ had already ordered me a forty ounce of Pabst, served in a tin bucket full of ice. He also demanded that she get a couple of those little umbrellas and put one in my forty and another in the Martini he ordered for himself.

Other than a few motoring mumbles on the drive over, ReggieJ hadn't made so much as a peep until our drinks had come and were loitering under our chins. "Ok," he said as he sighed, and what ensued wasn't quite as awkward as I expected, rather it was pretty funny. He took a long drink and finally spoke, "I smelled death the other day, breathed it really." This was followed by another long pause as he looked at me expecting a "what," or even a "why" from me, but I was too used to hearing him spout all kinds of bullshit, that his strange comment didn't carry the shock value he was expecting it to have, and I could tell he was slightly agitated that I just sat there staring at my beer. Peculiar, sure, but it was nothing new, and anyways, everyone knew that a peculiar ReggieJ, was a calm ReggieJ.

"You stupid on the Pot boy?" he nearly shouted at me trying to be heard over the loud song on the Jukebox. Of course half way through his shout the volume was cut in half, and everyone in the bar heard him holler "Pot Boy!" That got a few stares from around the place, and even a few laughs.

From behind the bar our waitress stood with a remote she must have used to make the jukebox quiet down, "Oh sorry, I was turning it down so you two could talk," she explained with a little chuckle as she turned around and set the remote on the bar. I laughed so hard it almost sent beer shooting out of my ears.

"Hey," ReggieJ said as he hit my arm, "this shit ain't funny man," abruptly becoming pissy. I could tell now that something was really bugging him, and I quickly realized that he had sat next to the jukebox so no one could hear our conversation. Albeit a situation I didn't ask for, he was pissed that I wasn't taking him seriously and equally pissed at the waitress for fucking up his clandestine little plan.

"I should be getting paid more for this kind of shit," I said, laughing somewhat sarcastically.

I took another drink from my beer, and as I sat it down. He leaned in and whispered sharply, "I'm not fucking around here!" sending spittle onto my face on the "f," causing me to flinch and reach instinctively for the landing zone. He retracted a little but his piercing stare-down never ceased.

Wiping my face with a napkin, I nodded, "Alright, alright, I just never know when it's Homeland Security code Red or Blue with you," I said stoically, refraining from even the slightest chuckle this time knowing that if my comment didn't seem threatening to one of his egos, then I'd be ok. This was the same approach I used with any other eccentric I ever dealt with, kind of a defense mechanism of mine, like I'm speaking a dialect of their language where I feel safe sharing air with them and there's no risk of a lack of oxygen.

"You remember the other day…" ReggieJ said, pausing a second to take a drink, and during which time I had to refrain from not shouting the dialect before he continued, "…when you were over…" he said as he coughed.

"Jesus! T-T-T-Today motherfucker!" I mocked his incontinence, I couldn't help myself.

"The other day when you came to pick up weight and I had those college boys over, and I made you stick around for a bit and get fucked up with us?" making a lot of unnecessary gestures with his hands, pointing at the table, at me, and then in the air like a mad man.

"Yeah, sure, and I have to ask, who were those douche bags? I mean really, c'mon! What a couple of Nickelbacks man, but seriously, what the fuck were those guys doing at yer place, I mean, do you need the business that bad? What I mean is that they seemed too young and, well, pretty sketch as well. Not to tell you how to do your business but those are the types I'd never sell to." I was comfortable enough with him at this point to tell him just that, "…dude, you gotta be a little more careful with who you're selling to," putting his stare to shame with my half-drunkard, fatherly advice.

The next thing to come out of ReggieJ's mouth was utterly sobering, and I wanted to take a break halfway in between his first sentence and the rest of the story, get up, leave the bar, go down to Burnside, and find some black diacetylmorphine to calm myself down with. I knew the seriousness in his tone was genuine because this was only the second time I had ever heard it, and both times it felt exactly the same. "You're absolutely right," he nearly shouted as his fist hit the table, not enough to spill the beers, but enough to bring the foam up a few inches in my bottle. "I never should have had that fucking kid over. I mean…" ReggieJ said as he sighed deeply, shoulders slumping. This nearly brought both a tear and a laugh to my eye.

"What the fuck are you talking abou…" I started to say, stopping short as I suddenly remembered walking past ReggieJ's place with Geverz a few days prior, and seeing CalC pacing outside.

"You didn't see, I mean, you weren't there when that kid went down were you?" he asked me as my squinted left eye tried to meet up with the cocked up corner of the left side of my mouth while I tried to squeeze out the memory of that day.

"Ummm," I began to say, squinting harder as if it was helping me remember. "Yeah," I lit up a smoke, "that's right, that stupid kid who'd been," pausing to snicker. "It was the kid who'd been following that awful band Phish around on their tour. Anyhow, yeah, I did see him go down. He was slumped over passed out on the couch for most of my visit, and as I was leaving I saw him get up and trip or something sending him on his ass. I only caught a glimpse of it through the crack in the doorjamb as you shut the front door. I laughed my ass off the whole way home, so hard in fact I could see my breath even though it was ninety degrees out that day." I explained.

"He fell over alright, fell over and died, died right there on the floor in front of us," eyes wider than a screaming, eye-lidless banshee, yet he was quieter than a cop on a wire tap. He slumped further into his seat as he continued on, "The air, it just went, well, kinda still, and then there was a distinct scent in the air, a weirdly soft and…" he trailed off. "It was, was a kind of… uh… an iridescent smell I guess, like how blood tastes like metal because of the iron in it," he said sinking a little more into his chair like the shipwreck he was. I was so fascinated by ReggieJ's use of a word I didn't think he could even spell, and the fact that he remembered how to use it in the proper context, that I had almost forgotten about the dead hippie. Thinking back to that day, I did recall a strangeness to the air that I noticed just as I was leaving the apartment, I just couldn't place it.

"What do you mean by scent in the air? Did the odor from the kid's dirty ass Petrulli oil get stronger or ya breathe it in and taste the nastiness or somethin?" I said as though I was thinking out loud, a babbling of thoughts that eventually developed into a more sound inquiry. I think he's actually telling the truth for once in his life. By god this might actually be for real, I thought without the further involvement of speech. Not just another one of his paranoid delusions brought on from a combination of sleep deprivation and drug use. This may very well be the truth. The hippie's dead and ReggieJ smelled his death, perhaps Death himself.

"No you asshole. It was fucking weird… When he got up from the couch, I think to go to the bathroom or something, took about two steps, and did a face plant," he explained, slapping his hand on the table.

"Yeah, when I saw that happen, I thought he was just ridiculously wasted…" I shook my head and took another drink from my beer as ReggieJ interrupted me.

"Well he was wasted, beyond wasted. His girlfriend and I tried to revive him for like twenty minutes with CPR and shit, but it was too late, he was gone, he'd turned blue and his eyes had rolled to the back of his head. They looked like glass, glass marbles," shaking his head. "It was fucked up man, LaceyJoe went berserk, cryin and shit and she wouldn't let go of him, so CalC and I had to literally pry her off him. After we finally got her off of him, CalC started freaking out too. I think the reality of the situation finally set in, and he began sputtering out gibberish as he cried like a loon. I didn't think he was ever gonna come outta that trance, and it's kinda fucked up to say, but I almost laughed at his freak out dance. He seriously sounded like the transient bag lady that always asks me for my spare change when I walk Fitzy," his Pit-bull, "by the supermarket she loiters at on 33rd." ReggieJ finally smiled, easing the overall tension that was gripping our table.

I laughed as well as I muttered out my words, "So what the fuck did you do? Better yet, where the fuck've you been the past few days? I tried calling and texting but I never got as much as a text back?" I asked him wide eyed.

ReggieJ adjusted himself in his seat, letting out a little laugh before continuing, "Then I couldn't believe it, the girl was the one who came to her senses and suggested that we take her boyfriend's body to the hospital, and drop his ass off at the front door of the emergency room. I wanted to just drop him off at a park with a blanket around him, but his LaceyJoe hated the idea of leaving him all exposed to the world like that, so she demanded that we take him to the hospital and drop him off so at least we would know he'd be in good hands. We had some other ideas we were tossing around, but LaceyJoe wasn't having any of it, she said either we took him to the hospital or she'd call the cops, Bitch. So CalC and I loaded the kid in CalC's car…"

"Huh, that must have been right after Geverz and I saw him out front of your place," I interrupted shaking my head, "crazy!"

"The three of us, CalC, the girl, and I all piled into CalC's car and drove over to Providence, you know, that hospital over on the east side? Anyway, as we pulled up to the Emergency Room entrance LaceyJoe started to really freak out. I mean screaming and flailing around like a crazy person," he said flailing his arms around before abruptly pulling them close to himself as he leaned into tell me something quietly. "CalC and I looked at each other and we both were thinking, fuck her you know? She's the one who wanted to take him to the hospital so badly, so she should be the one to take the body in right? Yeah well, once we were parked in the loading zone in front of the ER, we all jumped out real quick and after we'd determined that there was no one else around, we pulled MikeR out of my trunk. I was holding him from his armpits, and CalC was holding his feet as we dragged him to the entrance. We laid him down and I said, ok let's get the fuck outta here, but LaceyJoe just couldn't leave him."

"Jesus, that's fucked up! I understand why she was having a hard time with it, but come on, what a dipshit," I said as I shook my head.

"I know, I know, but can you imagine, there I was, outside the emergency room standing over a corpse with two hysterical people by my side. If a bystander had seen us, the whole scene would've looked like something straight out of a horror flick," pausing to take a drink, "like zombies hovering over a fresh kill or something," he finished saying which was followed by an even stronger, more distressed laugh from the depths of his diaphragm. "CalC and I had to cover her mouth to keep her from screaming as we tried to drag her back to the car. It didn't matter though because it was too fucking late," scoffing before he continued. "Apparently, there was a cop stationed to the parking lot of the ER that night, and he saw everything," he said, shaking his head.

"Oh man, shitty! You're fucking with me right?" I said loudly at first, finishing the question at a mere whisper.

"They arrested us on suspicion of murder and mishandling a corpse or some shit like that, but they only got me and LaceyJoe," he said pointing to himself and then out the window as if LaceyJoe were standing right outside the bar.

"Mishandling a corpse, I've heard of something like that before… Corpse Abuse is what they call it, I think, but what about CalC, why didn't they arrest him?" I said before looking at the jukebox which, even though no one had put any money into it, it started playing Frank Sinatra's "Close To You" out of nowhere, and based on our earlier interaction with the bartender, I was inclined to believe that she was trying to help us cover our conversation.

"Well, because CalC's a fast runner, that's why. You see, we were kinda hovering over the hippie's body and all of the sudden we hear this car peeling out on the far end of the lot, and wouldn't you know it, it was a cop. CalC said fuck it, and ran his ass off towards 45th street which wraps around the hospital, and I guess he got away. Me and the girl just sat there like, fuck it, we ain't running, plus where the fuck was CalC thinking he was goin? His fucking car was sitting right there in front of the ER," speeding up his story, ReggieJ's tone grew excited.

"Diiiiiiiiiiiiiiiipshit!" I squealed in a voice that sounded more like that of a cartoon character than my own voice, which made us both laugh.

"So they took us to the downtown precinct, and began questioning us separately," snickering. "What they didn't know was that we had worked out a story in the car on the way to the hospital way before we met those pigs," he said, smiling broadly.

"Smart thinkin!" looking solemn yet concerned.

"Exactly, and after being interrogated for six hours by those fucks, I finally got released," he said as he took a sip from his martini before continuing. "You see, we told em that we'd just met the kid, alive of course, and that we still didn't even know his name. We said that while we were sitting with him in a park, he suddenly fell over, turned blue, and he was just, like, dead. Anyways, a few hours after bein released I get this call from LaceyJoe saying she had stuck to her story and she'd been released as well."

"I can't believe you walked away from that without some sort of felony charge." Just then ReggieJ looked over to the front entrance as the door opened which drew my attention as well, and in walked a chubby, short, hippie looking girl with dreadlocks, grit, and the whole Hippie bit.

"That's the fucking girlfriend LaceyJoe right there, no way! We gotta get the fuck out of here man!" he bellowed as he quickly threw $40 on the table. I took his queue and began to chug the rest of my beer as fast as I could. Meanwhile, LaceyJoe had made it up to the bar to order herself a drink. Luckily, we were able to stealthily slide out the back door before she noticed us. ReggieJ would later tell me that he thought it best if she didn't see him because it might have brought up bad memories for her, creating an awkward situation for them both. Out of sight, out of mind.

I sipped my drink while a long, foreboding silence ensued. Caribou stared at me expecting more, "So what the fuck?!?" she snapped from the edge of her seat.

"What the fuck what?!?"

"I mean what else happened? Was it in the newspaper or on TV on the News? Did you get jail time? I mean you can't just leave the story hanging like that!" she was genuinely intrigued.

"Nah, nah, nah. I can't, for many reasons, including the statute of limitations, in good conscious go on with this story," I said, laughing whole heartedly.

"Fine then what can you, in good conscious, go on about?" mocking me with a funny imitation that made us laugh. "You're a really good story teller! So go on! Go on!" she slapped me playfully on the knee, "tell me another!"

I'll tell another, but only as long as it doesn't appear as though she's becoming attracted to me, I thought as I searched for the next story to embellish, because as soon as I recognize the slightest hint of interest for me in her eyes it's quitting time…

_____

5. Forerun

Early February, 1960, the Chicago winter was in full swing. Walking through the financial district all bundled up, save his face, was my father's father, Grandpa Bob. As he briskly strolled down the Chi-Town streets he was whipped in the face by the city's cursed winds. With temps dropping well into the negatives, the winds were brutally bashing him like sucker punches from a fist made of ice. He stopped at a corner diner for coffee which he took to go, continuing on his walk from his hotel to the Democratic Convention which was in its second day. As he walked down the street he stopped periodically to take sips from his coffee which was steaming hot when he left the diner, but his cup quickly grew cool as he trekked along. After only a few blocks his cup had been beaten by the same wintery blows he himself had sustained and now all it held was a coffee ice cube. Slightly perturbed by his defunct purchase, he looked for a trash can where he could throw the cup away. Three or four blocks closer to the convention, my grandfather spotted a public trash can across the street from him on the corner. He opted to cross the street in the middle of the block, a jaywalking that he would regret for the rest of his life. Half way across, after seeing a quickly moving blur in front of him, Bob was suddenly drenched in a thick warm liquid. By the time the liquid, like the coffee, had begun to freeze and make his clothing stiff, my Grandfather realized what had just transpired. Grandpa Bob stopped dead in his tracks in the middle of the street, vomiting profusely after realizing that he was covered in the blood, flesh, and bones of a man that had just departed the 24th floor of the building across the street, just as my Grandpa stepped off the curb. By the time Bob had collected himself enough to stop puking and get his breathing under control, cars had stopped just before the spot where the man had liquefied on the pavement. Various bystanders came to his aid with napkins, newspapers, and anything else they could find to help him wipe what was left of the jumper from his face and clothing. Thereafter, considering coffee bad luck, Grandpa Bob refrained from drinking even a single of the black evil for the remainder of his life.

Elvis Presley, JFK, J. Edgar Hoover, or Ethel Merman: I would love to write you a romantic story where one of these famed icons is a Great Uncle, Grandmother, or second cousin, but it just isn't true. According to my living elders, there was never any famed blood running through the veins of anyone even remotely related to our family. Though, this of course depends upon the assumption that my elders' memories are true and accurate. Furthermore, the accuracy of such genealogy is limited because we have no idea what became of the members that lost touch with the rest of the family, and apparently they were numerous, especially around the early to late 1800's when many of my ancestors immigrated to the United States. However, I recently heard from my great-aunt that we're possibly related to the great aviation pioneer, the father of the famous infant that was kidnapped and subsequently murdered, Charles Lindbergh. It has been speculated that his wife, Anne Morrow Lindbergh, is related to a great-uncle of my grandmother, but it has never been confirmed.

"So Caribou, though it's extremely absorbing to me, my genealogy will likely bore you to tears, nevertheless, I am compelled to present as much as I know about my roots. I'll reprieve you from the boring hum drum of the entirety of my family's history, and I won't cover every family member. I promise I'll only tell you about the best parts. Sound ok?" I asked her before taking a long drink.

"Oh yeah, please go on, I'm honestly quite intrigued," she smiled, looking genuinely interested.

On my father's side, the trail begins in the county of Cork in southern Ireland. My great-great grandparents emigrated from Ireland, like some million other Irishmen and woman, during the Great Potato Famine that began in 1845. The famine was a result of a disease, commonly known as the Late Blight, which decimated the potatoes of Ireland whose population was reduced by over 20%. 10% were deaths, and the other half, like my family, left the island for the promise of a better life, or for that matter, a life at all. Most of these Irish expatriates came to America. However, what they didn't count on was the awful persecution they would encounter once they got to the states.

My great-great grandparents settled in Manchester, New Hampshire on a farm they named Irish Hills. My great, great grandfather, B.G. Christopher, was born in 1895, a birth which killed his mother, and drove his father mad with grief. So mad in fact that shortly after her death he left his infant son with some friends of his, and he was never heard from again. His adopted father was the town Blacksmith, a trade which B.G. Christopher would later pick up himself.

In 1910, they moved to St. Paul, Minnesota where they lived a lower middle-class life until 1919, when B.G. left his family and home in St. Paul, and moved to Portland, Oregon. Shortly after moving to Portland he met a woman by the name of Nell Hobbs who he was quickly wed to. She was from an Irish Catholic family that immigrated during the potato famine as well. Her parents homesteaded their land in Indiana turning it into a flourishing farm. Many years later they did very well in real estate which made them quite wealthy. They were the first to have electricity and the first glass front door in the entire state of Indiana. A strange story to be passed down, but in their time, it was a big deal to have such commodities soon after they were made available. B.G. and Nelly had my grandfather, BobJ, in Portland in February of 1920.

After High School, BobJ worked various jobs to put himself through Law School, and soon after graduating, just after the onset of WWII in Europe, he enlisted in the United States Army, where he achieved the rank of First Lieutenant. He had unspecified health issues which kept him from going overseas and seeing any real action during the entirety of the war. He remained in the states training new Army recruits.

One day during a training exercise, while at the shooting range, a young draftee was in a latrine that stood near the range where he put his rifle in his mouth, and pulled the trigger. My grandfather, BobJ, was near the latrine and was unlucky enough to have the bullet graze his ear. The man died immediately, and for the rest my grandpa's life, he had hearing problems in the ear that heard the bullet's whisper.

While in the service, his orders were constantly being changed and he had to relocate to several different Army bases throughout the U.S. which put a strain on his marriage to his new bride BettyJ. However, after his service in the Army, they remained married until their deaths in the 1990's. After some five years in the military, BobJ and his family, which included his wife BettyJ and three boys MichaelJ, DennisJ (my Father), and PatrickJ, settled back down in Portland, Oregon. All of the men on this Catholic side of my family were named after Saints, my brother AndrewJ and I included.

In Portland, Grandpa opened a law firm with a good friend of his on the eastside of town. He later became a Judge for the Multnomah County Judicial Court, where his biggest case was a murder trial. His son, my uncle MichaelJ, and his partner's son, who recently passed away, would later obtain their law degrees and join their fathers to carry the practice, and the Firm's name, into the 21st century. While my grandpa BobJ was a young man he became quite involved in politics, the Democratic Party to be specific. During John F. Kennedy's campaign for Presidency, which began in 1959, BobJ was the leader of the Democratic Party for Multnomah County. My grandfather met with JFK on many occasions from 1959-1960 during the campaign, and even had him over for dinner at their less than majestic home in NE Portland. My uncle PatrickJ was even charged with driving him to the supermarket so that he could purchase a few items he had forgotten to pack for his trip from Boston. On the wall in my father's office hangs a large frame matted into three sections. In the center is a photo of JFK, on the right is a letter written to my grandfather from JFK whose actual signature is under the closing salutation "With every good wish, I am sincerely, John F. Kennedy." To the left of the photo there is an invitation to his inauguration to the Presidency on January 20th, 1961, unfortunately, BobJ was unable to attend.

As I recall, my grandfather was a thin, tall, teddy bear of a man that was quite successful in his endeavors, and a model to aspire to. Any real depth into his character, from my perspective, is regretfully lacking because I only knew the man when I was a child. He was marvelous in his range of character from the constantly humorous, gentle giant, to the super affectionate Husband, Father, and Grandfather that we all love and miss tremendously.

———————————

My great-grandparents on my mother's side were a couple of real Aces in their heyday. Between two children at home, a bar, and a restaurant to run, you could say they were playing with more than a full deck. They always managed to put smiles on each other's faces and those around them, a great way for them to distract you from the fact that these Aces had aces of their own tucked neatly between their sleeves and their overworked wrists.

In 1965 the construction of my great-grandparents' new bar, which today is known as Club 21, had been completed just a year prior when business really began to take off. The bar was tucked into a little sliver of a corner lot where five streets shook hands making for one crazy introduction, and an even crazier time for drivers because the city, which was broke at the time, could only afford three of the necessary five stop signs, making it a popular place to crash a car. One of the five streets was a main thoroughfare that ran west into nearby downtown Portland, and east four miles or so out past the airport. Known today as Sandy Boulevard, this busy street was a prime location and it helped keep the place buzzing every night of the week. At any given time, in the late 60's through the late 70's, you could find my great-grandfather, LouieA, behind the bar serving drinks, and my great-grandmother, MaryA, waitressing on the opposite side of the bar. The club became a local sensation almost overnight, and it was all thanks to MaryA and her unique approach to her job. Rather than the usual title of Cocktail Waitress, she preferred to be called a Champagne Waitress. Their club, in her eyes, was a sort of Cosmopolitan destination that reflected who she felt she was, not just as an Owner or Hostess, but with respect to every aspect of her life. My great-grandmother was more than just hip for her time, she was a staple of the posh scene of the time. She was so hip in fact, that she was considered not just a local icon, she was also nationally recognized for her ability to not only predict what the next big thing was going to be in the world of fashion, she would also be one of the first to completely embrace and absorb it. She would be wearing the fur before fur was in; long chains of pearls before it was prominent on every woman in the bar; she had the runway dresses before the fashion designers that created them had even been potty trained; portraits that hung on her wall had acquired pounds of dust before the artist or their movement had ever been recognized; and just about anything and everything that would grace the pages of the next quarter's fashion, art, and culture magazines my grandma MaryA was already hip to. This sixth sense of hers, if you will, was a magnificent radar for Pop culture, including: fashion, music, film, and art. In fact, it wouldn't be fanciful of me to say that she herself caused trends and sensations in the limelight that followed her around. There were many write-ups on her in the local newspapers where she was often referenced and used as a barometer of sorts for the fashion and design world. Frequent appearances in the local media prompted national attention which landed her an interview that was published in an issue of The New Yorker, attention which culminated in an appearance on the Tonight Show. She was so well received by both the paper and Johnny Carson that she was asked back for follow-ups, appearing in both about a year, and a year and a half later respectively.

MaryA was an only child to lower class, Gypsy parents that were constantly on the move throughout much of Eastern Europe and the western states of the U.S.S.R. Some believe that the nomadic life of the Gypsy is a result of the socialization to a life of itinerancy. This suggests that it is just as natural for the Gypsy to move around as it is for the majority of the population to stay put in one place as they were born and raised to do. The Gypsy's proclivity to constant travel, often referred to as "wanderlust", was a passion MaryA did not share with the Gypsy community. The life just didn't appeal to her for various reasons, and at the age of sixteen, she had had enough of her family's lifestyle. She made a plan to run away to the West, which she hurriedly carried out late in the summer of 1911. She left with the clothes on her back, a double-edged knife, a small cache of hard bread & salted pork, and a few hundred Deutsche Marks. Her plan was simple: make it out of the God forsaken east, and into the thriving, cosmopolitan cities of the West.

My great-grandmother's first destination was Paris, but her ultimate goal was to arrive in New York City one day. She jumped on freight trains and hitched rides on the back of horse drawn carriages across the Ukraine, through Poland & Germany, and finally through eastern France to Paris. Once there, MaryA quickly found work at a few taverns where she served drinks by day, and performed in burlesque shows of her creation every Friday and Saturday night at two of the taverns. She gained local notoriety for these shows and became an overnight sensation in Paris, as well as quadrupling the profits the taverns had previously been making on weekends. It seemed as if she had found her calling, however, after only a few short months, she found herself growing bored of her new life, and knew that she would remain unhappy if she continued on in Paris. Once again, she found herself planning to run away from a life she disliked. No sooner had she exclaimed her distaste for the life Paris had to offer her, had she heard of a newly built ship that was supposed to be the most magnificent vessel to ever grace the seas of the world.

It was January 1912 when MaryA had first heard the buzz about the Titanic, and the ship was not due to leave for the United States for at least three months. This afforded MaryA plenty of time to save money for a ticket, finalize her plans to leave Paris, and plan for a new life chasing the American Dream. The Titanic was making her maiden voyage from Southampton, England, heading to a few stops in England, Spain, and Ireland before she would be off to her final destination of New York City. MaryA wanted to be there when the shipped cast off from port for the first time, so she planned to board the ship in Southampton.

During the few months before she was leaving, she met my great-grandfather LouieA. MaryA had already purchased her ticket for the Titanic and was determined to be on the ship when it left for America, but what she hadn't counted on was falling madly in love with LouieA and agreeing to go to the U.S. together at a later date. Fortunately, LouieA wasn't able to purchase a ticket for the great Titanic, so MaryA decided to sell hers, and thank God for that decision! I can only imagine their astonishment when they heard that the Titanic had sunk just five days after casting off from the Southampton harbor. They both felt it was fate that brought them together and kept MaryA from the plight of the Titanic, and though it was a tragic event, it had the positive effect of not only strengthening the resolve of my great-grandparents' relationship, but ensuring my family's existence. By late that summer they were finally prepared to leave Paris for New York and beyond. The first thing they planned on doing when they arrived in the U.S. was to travel out west where they would start a family once LouieA had acquired gainful employment. One cruise ship; three subway trains; one passenger train; two hotel rooms; and many cities and states later but only one of concern: Portland, Oregon.

Within the first year and a half after arriving in America, MaryA gave birth to a son and then a daughter, my mother's mother. MaryA stayed home and raised the children while Grandpa LouieA drove a Wonder Bread truck which he sold and delivered bread out of, for over twenty-five years until he retired at the fairly young age of fifty. By then, their children had each married and started families of their own. MaryA and LouieA had also become quite wealthy through a combination of hard work and brilliant financial investments. Most of those investments were in real estate, primarily residential, but they dabbled in commercial properties as well. They would buy property that they would initially live in, fix up, and sell a short time later, known today as property flipping. Moreover, as time passed and the money began to pile up in their savings, they were allowed the luxury of holding onto multiple rental properties that they collected rent on. As they got older, they began to sell off most of their real estate assets making for a plush retirement plan.

It also afforded them the opportunity to purchase several restaurants and bars around the city.

I love my family dearly, unfortunately it took me nearly twenty years to realize this, and of course by that time, much of my family was either dead and gone, or split up. Every family has its secrets, quarrels, and dark times, but every family also has its shining moments such as marriages and the birth of new members. The way I look at it is that you have but one family, so make the best of the one you've got.

The sad thing about my dad's side of the family is that his two brothers haven't talked to one another in over twenty years. From what I understand, their relationship went sour when there was a quarrel between the two brothers stemming from the divorce of the eldest brother, PatrickJ. Exactly what they were fighting over isn't clear, and honestly I don't think they even remember what it was all about themselves. Once their parents, BettyJ and BobJ left us, the family really ceased to exist as a whole, breaking off into smaller families of which some haven't talked to the others for years. They cannot for the life of themselves man up and forgive one another, and it's simply because they can't let go of their decades old grudges.

My favorite family members are easily my parents, all four of them. They are my closest friends and I am very lucky not only to have them in my life, but also to have them as such great friends. My father and I make a point to have lunch together once a week, and I also make a point to try and have dinner with both sets of parents once a week. My Father and Step-Mother recently moved back to town which has been quite nice since I get to see a lot more of them. I'm also blessed with three step-siblings that I consider just the same as blood. I was recently asked by my sister, KatieC, to be the Godfather of her newborn boy, JavierC. I'm not only honored, I was completely caught off guard.

Hands down though, the best part of the family to me is my Brother. He is the core of the family to me, and without him I don't believe I'd have anything to do with the rest of my family at all, save my parents and step-siblings. Unlike me, he gets along a lot better with the rest of our family, and that may be because he has been away so long in the Navy, or the fact that he more reflects their "normalcy", but kudos to him, because ultimately, that's what I would want if I could have it. And even though the two of us have our differences, unlike some of our other family members we have had the maturity and a lack the arrogance enough to look past these differences and leave them in their corner pockets when we are with each other. This is because, simply, our respect, admiration, and love for one another is genuine. With great confidence I can say that this love and friendship that I share with my brother is everlasting, and I know that no matter how greatly we disagree or piss each other off, we will always overcome these differences and forgive one another. We can both see the big picture, that in the end we have only each other to count on. That is what Brotherhood and family is all about, and this is my brother, AndrewJ.

"Ok Caribou lets back up a little," I said to her as I sat up in my seat. "I really should back this whole thing up. In order to truly understand the timeline of my life, you gotta understand that there are these chunks…"

"Chunks?" Caribou interrupted.

"Chunks yeah, chunks. Anyhow… There are chunks of time that are… well… simply missing, you know? Missing pieces… I guess you could say they're missing pieces to the puzzle, the whole puzzle, and by puzzle I mean my life," I said as I tried to lay out for her why my memory may get hazy here and there with the various stories I'm sure too be telling over the course of the night.

"So was this drug induced, or is this simply selective memory at its best?" she inquired.

"Honestly," I say in overly combative tone which I caught myself doing after the fact "sorry," I said before looking at my feet remorsefully.

"Yes, honestly," she said making a funny face which made us both laugh.

"Well," I said as I waved my hands in the air in a goofy way to further lighten the mood, "honestly, a little of both. Let me explain as best I can…" I continued as I hunched forward, placing my elbows on my knees.

_____

6. LOST TIME

Before I continued with my account of my accountless time, my first experience with blacked out chunks of time came as a brief wisp fluttering through my mind, that of a boy name Kessler. This was a kid I met my senior year of high school, and I'll never forget just about every time I ever hung out with him for one reason, and one reason alone: he was a notorious liar. I had heard this from various peers before I was ever properly introduced to the kid, but knowing how rumors work, especially when you're at that age, I never put too much stock into them. Such judgments I left up to my intuition. And Holy Wow were the rumors more than accurate: the very first thing I heard this kid spew from his mouth was more than just a lie he was perpetuating in order to impress those around him, it was a more serious infliction. The truth was that this and all his other lies, for that matter, were lies he had convinced himself were true by repetitively telling them to others and to himself, because his aspirations had grabbed a hold of his nut-sack so hard that they had successfully squeezed out what little truth remained leaving only lies to lead the way.

And if I wasn't convinced enough by my own common sense telling me that he was often full of shit, the first time I met his Mother was all I needed to confirm that he was in fact a pathological liar. A few months before this meeting, according to Kessler, he had rolled his car over ten times on his way back to a party after getting beer in a town called Newbergervilla. He had drank well over a half rack of beer to himself in a short period of time, so in his eyes, the road forked around every turn. On one such turn he chose the double vision induced apparition of a road, and ended up rolling his car down an embankment and crashing through a fence. Yet according to NathanielJ who was the passenger in the car at the time of the crash, the car only rolled twice, and there weren't any fences that the car went through. Passenger NathanielJ also made sure to point out that Kessler had conveniently omitted the part of the story where he pissed his pants during the crash. The Kessler version of the story wasn't all that great by itself, but the whole thing took on epic proportions as I juxtaposed the two stories in my head. I knew the excessive drinking Kessler claimed to have caused a drought with at the party before leaving for their date with the car wreck couldn't possibly be the cause for his pissy pants, because NathanielJ also confirmed that Kessler was only two beers deep when they departed for Newbergervilla for more beer. I had to do everything in my power not to bust up laughing, or making piss pants jokes around Kessler after hearing the passenger's account of their crash. This was a common occurrence with Kessler and the many lies that I and others would catch him in. The best Theatre of the day for my friends and I was watching girls catch him in lies and then confront him publicly. The best times were either at school in the halls or at house parties on the weekends. Anywhere where there was a sizable audience really, the choir of laughter made for a great, comedic moment in a not-so-great moment for Kessler.

He was still without a car when my buddy JakeH and I came over to his Mom's house to pick him up to go swimming with some girls on a notably hot July day, and that's when I met his Mother. First of all, I can't continue on to the relevant part of the story without first mentioning that this woman put the grrr in Cougar, she was

HOT, and man-o-man did we let Kessler know. We teased the living
hell out of that kid, and I have to give it to him, he really took
it in stride. So JakeH and I were greeted at the front door by
Kessler's mom, and after introductions were made, she informed us
that he was still in the shower getting ready, and then she showed
us to the living room where she offered us both something to drink.
To my amazement, she brought us both beers before sitting in a
recliner across from the couch JakeH and I had sat on. She then
produced a small metal pipe which she loaded a little nug of weed
into and began to smoke. I couldn't help but stare in awe at the
pipe, the low cut tank top which revealed her D cup tits, and the
fact that she seemed so laid back. Though both JakeH and I had to
roll our lips up off the carpet a few times, we managed to keep each
other's gawking and chin dropping in check just enough so that
Kessler's Mom either didn't notice or if she did, it didn't weird
her out.

Once we had gotten the customary how-do-you-do's, and nice-to-meet-
you's out of the way, she began to ask us odd personal questions:
what do you think of my son; is he a good boy; do you two do as well
with the ladies as my little Kessler does; and other such questions
along those lines. How do you answer such questions? Well you sure
as hell don't want to tell someone's Mother the truth, no matter
what end of the spectrum they may be on. So we did what any good
friends would have done in our position, we lied. She immediately
called us out, laughing and saying that we were bad liars. "But you
know who's a good liar, well not so much a good liar as he is a
pathological liar?" she asked as she laughed again. JakeH and I
shrugged our shoulders in unison which threw her into another
laughing fit, which she finished by answering her own question, "My
son, Kessler of course…But I'm sure you two already knew that, or at
least had an inkling right?" laughing less intensely this time. "I
bet you're wondering why, as his Mother, I would be telling you such
a thing? Well the answer is simple: the kid loses friends like
they're going out of style, and from what he's told me about you
two, you seem like friends he shouldn't lose. What I mean to say is,
is that you two are likely a better influence on him than most of
the guys he brings over here, guys that typically ogle my tits," at
which JakeH and I both laughed, making her laugh as well. "Don't
think I didn't notice your wondering eyes either," she whispered
with a big grin on her face as she pointed at us both, "but you're
just healthy, straight teenagers, so it's only natural," she said,
this time laughing maybe a little too hard which could easily be
attributed to the weed she was smoking. "Look, the bottom line is
that you two have plans to go to college, and Kessler doesn't. If
you two could somehow convince that kid to at least apply to some
schools, I'd forever be in your debt." And it was at that moment
that Kessler began making his way down the stairs. Before he made it
down, his Mom gave us a wink and a sexy little smile which made it
hard for me to jump up and greet Kessler. Luckily his Mom called him
into the kitchen where she wanted to have a word with him.

"Can you get up right now?" I asked JakeH after Kessler and his
mother had left the room.

"No, can you?" he replied.

Laughing quietly, "Um, no," I replied, and we both laughed.

"What's so funny?" Kessler demanded to know as he returned to the
dining room where we sat.

"Nothing man, nothing," I said as I tried to picture obese corpses and clown zombies in order to rid myself of my M.I.L.F. induced hard-on.

The point is that this kid spent so much time lying about stupid shit, he had lost so much of his actual life to the lies he had told. If you cornered him in one of them and were able to ask him where he thought his lies had gotten him, and where he was going with them, he'd likely answer, well, um, I don't really know, and the truth was that he really didn't know. He was so deep in his lies he truly had no idea where he was with all of them. He had lost so much of his actual life to the one he had made up in order to make his own life seem better than it actually was, that time was lost to him. This is the mildest version of lost time, mine was little more literal.

_____

Just as guilty as you or the next, I, me, they, we are all criminals, thieves of time. Freeze it, lie it, deny it, steal it, waste it, in one way or another we're all are guilty of taking it for granted by just living it. It makes up 100% of the 2% milk that takes us upwards of twenty seconds to find and read the expiration date which is stamped in purple ink. One of the most permanent of mass produced inks, it's even harder to get off than saying soda on the wrong coast when you should be saying pop. I'd rather not know when, deadline blind more or less, and I must admit in my digression, that this would be yet another lost period of time if it weren't for putting the pen to paper, in this case, key strokes upon the blank word-processing page, and keeping the date from ever slipping this glazed mind of mine if you wouldn't mind.

A series of seriously sordid tales from sketchy details hold quick like a hang nail, and the wherewithal to take notes that have become the savior of these tiny lives that only those fortunate enough to have been there and I were the only witnesses left here to remember. Bare witness in our bare nakedness, these times can never be lost now. The single greatest regret, ignorance's bliss, a fairly common flaw of mine, one which causes me great anxiety and depression has been this time I've lost, time I've thoroughly wasted.

Whilst I was using drugs, chasing girls, or writing, only the needles can really tell you what happened during those times. I don't really remember shit on my own, and I threw those particular needles away many years ago. I have misplaced somewhere around four years, three hundred and sixty-two days. Now, truth be told, it wasn't exactly five years, or 1825 days (+- one to three days for the leap year(s)), but what is true, is that it is roughly three whole days I managed not to lose. That scared me enough to begin taking notes. Not a journal per say, but a manila folder that contains a heap of papers doodled on, outlines, short phrases hastily written so that I could come back and based upon three or so words, write a short story of ten to twenty pages. These are the stories, a cheap reminiscing, it's Low Rent.

_____

Know that this will exploit those that have ever suffered from the plight of addiction if it can. What use are we otherwise? This is a tale of the before, during, and after of a soul, a man, who chose a path of addiction over exertion & reality, and pushed on for fantasy, happening upon many great friends, acquaintances, and the occasional great intimacy, all of which he can't quite remember.

What he does remember is the girl, it all began with a girl.

It was roughly three years, and three rough years it was. Three is a number that I say lands somewhere between being twenty-one and when I could socially function without giving anyone the slightest hint I was once a Meth Junkie, among the many other kinds of junk, other things in needles. Methamphetamines was not originally my drug of choice, rather it was the drug that chose me. Like an adolescent's first real love, I was depending on it to keep me so awkwardly and absolutely confined to my attentiveness to it, that it'd keep me from becoming aware of my own rotten toothed reality. It worked for quite some time. Decay, a vicious cycle that not only solved the pain and beat off the inner confrontation, but fed the compost that I beat off to.

Though systematically optimized with lies to believe that I was commandant of my life, the truth was that I was not in control. The other voice, TommyJ if you will, lost good friends & good times, a coward whose trust took years to rewind. A new face now means they know no such times, free from the broken record Rhymes. Ironically, I'm high and tend to song out my writing because of the equal addiction to music and the like, band member, kicked out of most. Like math class I can't win, solve that one. This high is just that, chase that Dragon, but I'll never win. H is a later story...

It started with a girl that fascinated me with her bipolar beauty. Not annoying or sad fetching, but unique in a way I had never seen before. For the life of me, I could no more dissect this girl from afar, as I could with a scalpel already buried six inches deep in one of her barely functioning kidneys. Man did my back hurt all the damn time!! I would get UTI's, Urinary Tract Infections, almost every other week, and it wasn't due to the girl's sickly, unhygienic, rotten fish smelling pussy, it was my own body fucking with me for pumping the mass amounts of drugs into my veins. To me the girl was a new type of Freak, though still to this day I think she was frightfully reminiscent of the "one of us" crew, a Black and White Circus Freak. I was deathly intrigued by her and I was certain that if I got the chance, I would make her mine. I decided that I would go to great lengths to get close enough to this girl to know what made her tick and possibly what type of deodorant she wore, if any. Not just the "my daddy made my cousin rape me while he and my uncle filmed us all the while we were wearing clown suits with makeup to make us look like we should've been in that 80's movie from Killer Klowns From Outer Space", no I needed More. I had heard all those tear jerking stories before, and the only tears came from the teller while I felt like I was getting jerked around after spending all kinds of money on a dinner and a movie, you know those things cost like $100 for two people these days? The eyes jerking tears while I was made to feel like a Jerk for wanting more after the "date," only to have to endure the "my Daddy did this to me" story, ultimately ending up at home left to, you guessed it, jerk myself. She not only had this story, she also didn't mind telling it. The only upside to her version was that she told it in a mild-mannered demeanor. No tears flowing or sympathy expected which was no surprise from her, but greatly appreciated by me. Though, as her short time boyfriend, I did often find myself alone, horny, & jerking off, all alone. Picturing her brains in some other hot chick's body made me shoot my load half way across the room. It was an exciting enough combo to make even the likes of Isaac Newton jealous with my ability to defy gravity with the speed of my hand

and the weightlessness of my projectile cum. Freud simply would have been jealous. I hadn't known many of her kind, bipolar, addicted to meth. An idiot or psychologist's wet dream, depending on which end of the bus stop you're standing at.

I still own hundreds of oddly beautiful paintings, drawings, mixed up media melodies that I, she, we created while "loving" each other. I had met her in an art class I took while I was going to the University in town during which time she lived in a Volkswagen Vanagon that had skulls spray-painted on the side. She moved the van around a few times a week to avoid having the locals notice her and call the cops on her or have parking enforcement tow the thing while she was out trolling the streets. This arrangement worked well in the spring and summer months when it wasn't too cold, but the fall and winter forced her to take refuge wherever she could find a situation that gave her a sleeping spot with heat. This time was a Time when speed went from the stage of a Beatles concert and the saddlebags of Hells Angels bikes to labs in car trunks making it tenfold in potency from the help of cold meds and household cleansers. Ten times as dirty, ten times as high, and we didn't need it ten times a day. To be honest with you, I shot it five times, no, maybe six times a day. If I was lucky, I slept two times a week on anything but the easy ease. Too bad the damn drug didn't make our love for one another ten times as strong. Depending on how you look at it, it could be meth I'm talking about or it could be the girl. However, it sure as hell made the fucking something to write Penthouse Letters about. At any rate, we didn't last long, and I wouldn't say it was love that kept me and meth together. She left me with an addiction, and a hole in my heart, both figuratively and literally. She changed her cell phone number and moved her van. I couldn't find her and would never see her again. She dumped me, and really, it was all for the better, but at the time it really hurt, worse than a sting from a shot in the muscle.

Aside from my addiction, I was for all intents and purposes, Alone. Funny thing though, those around me often said just the opposite, they said that I had plenty of people around that cared about me. Though as soon as they could, they would leave with their backs forever turned to me. I knew my plight as soon as I had plunged the shovel in and dug out the first bit of the grave. When the plunger fell to zero, the wash running circles around the blood, flowing down the endless assembly of veins inside me, I knew life was over for a while and time would be lost to this silly pleasure. It was a pleasure at first, but soon it became an inconvenience. Taboo in the world around me, people started to notice, and people started to bitch, and people started to really annoy me in general. It's as if anything I enjoyed was too good, and should be taken away from me. I thought it was bullshit that the only people that were ok with it were people who had either been junkies themselves, had dabbled in it, or had a girlfriend that had done it. Their concerns lay with me getting noticed by the other folks that they believed would have freaked out if they had found out the truth about me. I agreed that they probably would go caustic on me, but I disagreed that I would get noticed. I was the most functional junkie I had ever met in my life: I had good grades in school; I held a job and did well at it; my family had no idea; and my friends for the most part had no idea. But for some reason, I always seemed to be climbing out of some shit storm, it was chutes and ladders my friend. I hated being alone, waking up, not able to recall anything but my absolutely fucked up hellish dreams. Thankfully, I seem to have lost the bad times, only remembering what's convenient, the less shitty times. The Meth made me a recluse, and I had become so socially inept that I feared having to go out in public, so it only makes sense to have been enrolled in classes at the University and also have a job working for a catering company, both of which consisted of a lot of human interaction, genius huh? The temporary holes in my head caused me to stammer, sentences were hard to formulate, and I lost half of my vocabulary which wasn't all that extensive to begin with.

The functie, functional junkie, truly started to become quite the dysfunctie, and it finally came to a point where I was so socially inept that when I wasn't at work, I was hiding so deeply inside my bedroom, spending most of my time on the internet and playing video games, that I could barley find my way out on weekday mornings to make my way to work. I was a ham-fisted fool, so afraid of the world I abstained from taking a part and playing my role as much and as little as the world itself would allow. When I looked into the mirror and no longer saw TommyJ, so entirely alienated from everything and everyone that I wasn't even familiar to myself anymore, I made a decision to turn around and not look back into that mirror until I was certain I knew who, or better yet, what to expect. In order to reintroduce myself, I needed to reinvent myself, renew, revitalize, re-harmonize my entirety, and this would take great leaps of faith by me and my ability to salvage what I had nearly destroyed. Could I ever trust myself again?

To insure a lesser likelihood of failure I was quite meticulous in planning my escape plan. I decided that the only way I could truly achieve sobriety was to eliminate several enabling factors within my life. Thus I decided that within a single week I would take seven major steps to forever change my life for the better: 1) I changed my cell phone number; 2) erased all the phone numbers I had stored in my phone except for family and a few close friends that had never used any hard drugs; 3) broke up with my girlfriend at the time, MishK; 4) moved out of the apartment I had been renting by myself, and into a house with three friends; 5) quit doing both Meth and Coke; 6) quit selling Coke and pharmaceuticals; & 7) I even applied for and was hired as a sort of grunt at a Catering company. Surprisingly, I experienced very little trepidation when it came to completing these tasks simply because I believed that they were necessary to my survival. However, by taking on all these changes at once, I ran the systemic risk of creating such a total shock to the system that was TommyJ that I ran the risk of sending out an invitation to my own self-destruction. Unfortunately, this twist of irony wasn't realized until the days and weeks that followed, and by then it was obviously too late to soften the blow to my psyche and soul. TommyJ was belly-up toxic, completely vulnerable to the direction in which the moon was pulling his delicate emotions from moments to seconds. His tears filled the gutter of every street he traveled down for weeks to follow, but he trudged on. The sores in my mouth, on my face, in the heart, in my chest, and the heart in my mind ultimately healed without any major cataclysms.

From the hermit without a presence, to completely nationalizing myself, I was hastily freed with a brutality that proved its worth for my salvation. From boy to man, lost to found, floating to grounded, I could breathe once again in front of the camera, and this time, there was film on the reel. Memories and time, like a rebirth, began again. Imagine a timeline that is chronologically coherent for nearly its entirety, then suddenly there is a smudge in the line, and soon after that smudge the line disappears entirely, and then just as suddenly as it had vanished, it reappears on the other end like nothing had ever disturbed it. You try and make assumptions based on a scale of how much of the timeline is lost to the smudging, but you're cut short by the comeback.

This was my timeline, the timeline that's reappearance I was trying to fake as realistically as possible. Time restarted with great memories of a fully restored TommyJ. Some of these first memories that I can look back on seem trivial, yet back then they gave me great hope because it appeared as if I hadn't lost too much of myself to the side-effects of years of abusing toxins. I resembled what I had been before, my wit and cleverness was restored as my proof.

One of my very first memories after being reborn was a dirty trick that I had decided to play on my friends that lived in the building next door to me, the one in which my dealer ReggieJ 'lived' in. In fact it was the day I was moving out of the apartment building I had been living in during the Lost Times, and it was the very week I had taken the seven major steps to save my life. My friend DanR had an apartment on the bottom floor of this building, and his bedroom window faced out into the alley that lay between our buildings, the very alley that was guarded by the gnarly electric fence I had mentioned earlier. Luckily for me, I could easily gain access to the alley, therefore DanR's bedroom window. While I finished moving the last of my shit out of my place DanR was having people over to smoke pot, play video games, and other such stoner activities. There must have been about a dozen or so folks there, both guys and gals. Once I was in the alley I put on one of those scary black ski masks, the kind with two holes for the eyes and a third hole for the mouth. I also made sure to dress in black jeans and a long sleeved black shirt to cover the tattoos on my arms so that I wouldn't be recognized. There was a dumpster on wheels in the alley that I rolled under DanR's bedroom window which was a good six feet off the ground. I climbed onto the dumpster, and lucky for me the window was still slightly cracked, just as I had left it the night before.

I began my preparations for my little practical joke when I was over at DanR's place the previous night to the "break-in." When he announced that he was having people over the next day, I came up with the idea to "burgle" him as I sat on his couch watching a documentary on Andy Warhol's Factory. After the movie I said "I gotta piss," so I walked down the hall towards the bathroom, but I made a pit stop at DanR's room. This was when I opened the window to the alley ever so slightly.

After I pried the screen off and opened the window, I carefully inched my way into the room. Putting one leg and arm in first, I made sure not to knock anything off the desk which sat up against the wall just below the window. Once I was completely in, I pulled out my switchblade which had a blade about an inch longer than the width of the palm. The bedroom door was closed, so I turned the handle and slowly opened it a crack in order to hear exactly what was going on in the living room where everyone was congregating. At first I thought no one was there, but I suddenly heard a large group of people yell "OOOOOOOOOH!" From what I could tell there was at least ten people in the living room as planned. They began several independent conversations after whatever it was they were watching had hit a climactic point, which culminated in a group quacking, "Oh my God, did you see him hit that?" one girl asked. At the same time, another girl, from another part of the room said, "I can't believe someone can be that fucking stupid," and I knew this was the perfect time to execute my simple, yet freakishly genius plan. With knife in hand, wearing my stereotypical burglar suit, I nonchalantly opened the bedroom door and casually walked into the living room.

"OH MY GOD!" several people screamed in unison at the sight of the masked intruder.

"Holy shit man! What the fuck" DanR screamed as he fell backwards over the couch. Following DanR's lead, several of the people in the room cowered into the kitchen which was at the far side of the room from me while yelling, well, pleading really, "What the fuck?!?!"

When I saw everyone I took a more aggressive stance as if prior to walking into the room, I was oblivious to the fact that the room was occupied. I had to do everything in my power not to start laughing wildly, and as planned, I simply said, "Oh sorry, I think I've got the wrong apartment. Is this," pausing to look at a small piece of paper I produced from my front pocket, "8C by chance?" I distorted my voice slightly enough not to give away my true identity, and not so much so that it would seem like a farce.

"No asshole, this is 2B. 8C is down the fucking hall, Jesus Christ man," one of DanR's guests said, and I couldn't quite tell who it was because he was hiding in the back of the kitchen behind a number of other guests.

With an undisguised voice I said, "Oh, sorry about that DanR," as I slowly retreated to the bedroom I came from. Once I was back there, I took the mask off and listened for their responses.

"What the fuck DanR?!? How the hell does he know your fucking name?" one girl screamed at him.

"Yeah, what the fuck? Where did that fucker come from?" another screeched.

Each of them chimed in with various rhetorical question, and there were a lot of what the fuck's. Meanwhile, I was in DanR's bedroom covering my mouth to keep them from hearing me laugh uncontrollably. Once I had more or less regained my composure, I nonchalantly reentered the living room, and with a big shit-eating grin upon my face I inquired, "What's all the commotion about? I thought I heard screaming."

This of course was followed by a lot of boo's, cackling, and loud laughter. "You asshole, I thought that was you!" DanR lied as he rushed at me.

"Whatever, you had no idea that was me!" I somehow muttered with the little oxygen I had once DanR had me in a headlock. He then began to vehemently rub my head with his knuckles. He also had me bent over so I was talking to our knees. "You should have seen the look on your face!" I said as I continued to berate him. This was followed by even louder laughter that was belted out by the entire cast of victims.

"I had an idea, I just wasn't %100 sure it was you, so I didn't say anything," DanR pleaded as he dropped his grip, releasing me from the headlock. By then, everyone was finally breathing sighs of relief. "I have to give it to you though, that was pretty fucking genius man. So how the hell'd you get in?" DanR asked me.

I explained to DanR and his guests how I went about planning and carrying out the prank, "I actually bought the ski mask a few weeks ago for just such an occasion, and I have to say, it really has paid for itself, all $5 worth," I roared with laughter. In my own little sadistic way, I was proving to myself, and the world, that I was no longer impotent, that I was indeed alive again. However crude and dangerous it was, the little prank I played on DanR and his guests worked wonders for my self-esteem.

I must admit that every once in a while I'll slip up and lose long periods of time, and there are months, even years, that are all heaped into a few short memories. These few sad memories my mind has barely been able to grasp a hold of is all that I have left to account for the time in which I paid drug dealers thousands of dollars so that I could inflict the kind of pain and loss that only meth and heroin can give you. I'd nod out, wake up a while later, and look out my window thinking that the sun was rising when it was actually setting, completely at a loss as to where I was in time. I often asked myself, is there something I'm forgetting? Have I left something undone? Is there someone I know out there, somewhere, looking at their wrist watch disgustingly, eventually shaking their head and leaving our meeting spot? It's almost pathetic that I have to carry a little notepad with me everywhere I go to jot down notes, dates, dinner plans, etcetera, just so I can remember them. Nevertheless, I think everyone, especially writers, should carry around a pen and paper because we are all capable of conjuring up something profound every now and then. If we don't choose to jot down these thoughts, then they could easily be lost to time, possibly depriving the masses of something beautiful, eye opening, or just plain entertaining. Enter the notepad, which can keep your epiphanies safe from the wear and tear of time. What good are our insights if they're quickly forgotten and never fully reflected upon?

"Ok ok, I gotta say, I may fall asleep if you keep getting all existential on me. I wanna know who TommyJ is. I know it's kind of a cliché to meet someone and then go into childhood stories with em, but come on, let's hear it," Caribou said.

"Alright then, you want it from the beginning then?" I earnestly stated.

Through a soft smile she quietly replied, "Yeah," shifting her eyes to the floor that barely had a grasp on her feet. Just above a whisper she continued, "From day one, go on."

---

7. Incorrigible Kid

Where, oh where does my little speck in the time of times begin?
Where does it seem to always begin? A nice little American Dream
type family shattered by child molestation, beatings, divorce, and
all the other boo fucking hoo poor me bullshit? I do not need or
deserve your empathy, for my childhood wasn't picture perfect, and
there are a lot of people out there who have had it a lot worse, but
I won't deny having a few of my own fuct up moments either. I was an
annoying little fuck-hole that was destined from the moment I slid
out of my mother to become a shit stain on the sheets of society.
Being the young rapscallion that I was, I constantly infringed upon
the rules imposed by the authority I challenged at home, in daycare,
at school, everywhere and anywhere at any and all times. My
childhood was just the beginning of the exceedingly illicit acts
that would span the first twenty some years of my life.

Portland, Oregon, 1982, I popped out of my tiny little five foot
nothing Mother, that to this day, barely weighs a hundred pounds. We
had a nice little house on the northeast side of town where mom's
brother, sister, and parents also lived. The very first memories
that I recall come from this place, from when I was about two years
old, a time when I was an extra snotty little brat of the terrible-
two's variety. If I were a Mormon couple's first kid, even they
would think twice about having any more little blessings, and
"abortion" would somehow slip into their pristine vocabularies.
Fucking kid's right? The first house my folks owned that we lived in
wasn't all that big. It had a master bedroom for the parental units,
one room for Dad's office, and one for my brother. When I came
along, my crib was initially parked in my parent's room, but after a
year or so they moved me into my brother's room which was adjacent
to theirs. Apparently, I would rock back and forth so violently in
bed at night that it would wake everyone up. Dad's always had a
short fuse, and I guess I must have really bugged the hell out of
him because he finally decided, against Mom's wishes, to put my
crib, me in it, in the basement. That way I could be as loud as I
wanted all the time, and not bother him, or anyone else for that
matter. You could psychoanalyze this situation all you want. You can
say that I was disconnected from my family at an early age, and this
may be one reason for my later transgressions, but it could have
been much worse, at least I had parents. I did, however, grow up
more defiant than most kids, and who knows, this may have been the
cause for my awful behavior as a kid. However, I believe I was
predestined to it, and no amount of abuse or neglect would have
changed that.

"Anyway, boo whoo whoo poor me right?" I said jokingly. "I gotta
pause so I can cry…" I whimpered with a smile.

"Oh shut the fuck up and get on with your damn story, Jesus!"
Caribou blurted out scornfully.

In that particular basement is where I recall my very first few memories. It was a small, half finished basement with concrete walls and concrete floors, which made it pretty cold year round. My first real memory was actually a nightmare I had while sleeping in my crib. I dreamt I was in my crib, standing up holding onto the railing. A hand, and gradually a whole arm, came up through the bottom of the crib, stretching through my blankets. It looked like latex the way it stretched through the blankets, and it suddenly became apparent that this hand was trying to grab me. It scared the living shit out of me, and for all I know, it was my Dad or one of his sadistic friends playing some kind of sick practical joke on me. Well congratulations assholes, it worked. At any rate, my first memory was actually something my imagination most likely conjured up, yet it is something I truly wanted to believe happened. I remained in the basement for another year or two, and the whole time, lights on or off, that basement remained eternally creepy to me. To this very day, I still have a thing about basements.

After I was about a year and a half old I could walk and get myself into all kinds of trouble. Mom told me that at my second family Christmas I managed to snag my Dad's glass of Scotch which I downed while hiding under my grandma's dining room table. I became drunk and apparently, it was a real novelty for all of the adults, and being drunk themselves, they never thought to take me to the emergency room. I swear, every goddamn Christmas until the day I die, even though I very well could have died, they will bring up that stupid story and have a good laugh at my expense. My second memory was also in that basement. Being the real curious shit-getter that I was, I jumped ship, my crib, and wondered around checking everything out. I moseyed on in to the laundry room and I remember looking around and finding a big white bottle. I inspected it for a moment before I got the top off. Oh look, it's liquid, and to a person whose only functions include walking, eating, sleeping and shitting, it looked like a nice little drink. Well it wasn't, not at all, in fact it was a half gallon of bleach, and I drank almost all of it. That's about all I remember. What I don't recall is Mom freaking out when she found me, and I also don't remember being in the hospital where the doctors stuck me with an I.V. and pumped my stomach. I'm sure they found a few highballs in there as well. A few months later we moved out west to the burbs, so those ended up being my only two memories from that home.

At the novel age of just six, the neighborhood parents called me Terrible TommyJ, but what they didn't know was how terrible I'd really become just seven years down the line. I used to piss my old man off to the point where he'd give me a real good beating every once in a while. As well as the regular beatings, I was getting paddled in the ass with spatulas, getting soap shoved in my mouth, and all the other kinds of shit parents do to bad kids.

"Boo-fucking-whoo, again Caribou," I began to sincerely plead, but paused to laugh drunkenly at the little rhyme, "I'm not looking for sympathy here, I'm just setting up the story."

"I know TommyJ, I know," Caribou replied with tears beginning to form in her eyes.

_____

One of my closest friends growing up in grade school was a
neighborhood kid by the name of BenF. I think the fact that he was a
black foster kid in an otherwise all white home fucked with his head
something fierce. He never really spoke much about it, and whenever
I asked him he just made jokes like, "Gee, I never noticed," or
"What the... I'm black?" But I could tell that it really bugged him
that he was given away, and to a white family at that. His sense of
identity was all out of whack during a time when he, and everyone
else our age, was just learning who he really was as a person, and
so like me, he "acted out:" stealing, breaking stuff at home, and
vandalizing other people's property, and other such criminal
mischievousness. He was a great partner in crime because we
understood each other. We both wanted to be free from constraints,
especially the ones we found at home and at school. We found
something particularly freeing about breaking rules and the rush we
got from it.

My memory is fairly fuzzy, but from what I recall, I used to go to a
local supermarket and steal a backpack full of cigarettes, candy,
and a ton of other stuff with BenF. One time, while procuring our
normal take from the supermarket, we decided to steal a box of
condoms which we later sold to kids at school on the playground
during recess. Soon after BenF and I had started this little
enterprise I lost my wallet, which some guy found a few days later
in the street. Inside, the man found only two items with any
pertinent information on it. One was a little card with my name on
it as the owner of the wallet, and the other was my father's
business card. He put two and two together, and mailed my wallet to
my dad's office. There just happened to be one of the condoms in my
wallet which begged the question, what in the hell is an eleven
year-old boy doing with a condom? The truth was that I wasn't doing
a damn thing with it, I was still a virgin.

My dad called and told me how the wallet had been mailed to him and
said we needed to have a talk that weekend about what was in it. As
soon as he had said this to me, my heart dropped into my bladder. I
knew it had to do with the condom, and it was then, for some reason,
that I knew it was taboo. Thus I became both ashamed and fearful of
any reprisals from my old man for the little trinket living in my
money bag. When my father and I met up the next weekend, he had to
do everything in his power to keep himself from laughing in my
eleven year-old face. "So here's your wallet. Money's there,
business cards are there, your YMCA card is there, and last but not
least, your flavored condom is there, strawberry I believe. You want
to tell me what my eleven year-old son is doing with this in his
wallet?" he requested to know as he held up my strawberry friend.

"Gee Dad, I uh... I guess it's just wishful thinking," I said, trying
to break the ice with a guilty smile.

"Now you'd use this with a girl right?" my father asked, probing for
a straight answer.

"Awww Dad, of course I would," I said as I watched the relief wash
over his face.

"Well at least you're using protection, I'll give you that," he
said, finally laughing. And with a slap on the back that was the end

of that awkward conversation. But I'll be damned if he doesn't like to tell this story every few years for a good laugh.

The last time I saw BenF we were both about eighteen, many years after the condom incident. It had also been many years since I had seen him. I boarded a city bus downtown one summer day, and found BenF sitting by himself in the back.

I sat next to him and asked, "How the hell are you man? It's been like what, three, maybe four years?" with wholehearted smiles.

"Pssh, you know… pretty good I guess," he smiled, showing me the tiny balloons of heroin in his mouth, and of which, I made a small purchase.

I've always been a pretty small guy, and I was tiny as a child so I was an easy target for bullies, and I would get into fights all the time. I had become pretty hardened from the beatings my brother and father gave me, so I could scrap better than most of my peers. One kid in particular, we'll call him DickS, liked to antagonize the hell out of me, and I would try to avoid him because at the time he was three grades my senior and about a foot taller. He pushed me down one day and proceeded to kick me while I was on the ground, and that was when I had decided enough was enough. I knew I wouldn't get a fair fight with him, so I thought up what seemed, at the time, to be a great idea to keep him off my back. I went home after school that day and looked around for some sort of container small enough to fit into my pocket, but big enough to carry the specific payload I had in mind. I looked in the shower because I knew there would likely be the perfect kind of sealed container there. I found a little sample shampoo bottle, emptied it out, and filled it to the rim with my urine. I hid it in my room until the next day, the day of retribution.

I got to school the next day and immediately ran into DickS, and he began shoving me around, calling me a shrimp. I said to him "Oh, you just wait until recess," and I ran out of there before it escalated into a full on brawl which would've meant me in the nurses office, him in the principal's, and me out of my get-back plan. A few hours later during our lunch recess, but rather than DickS coming for me, I was on the hunt for him. I tracked him down to a field where he was playing in a scrap football game. I stood on the sidelines where I waited and watched for my opportunity to strike. Towards the end of recess the game ended and DickS began walking right toward me. He was by himself and there wasn't anyone else within the splash zone. Believing it was the perfect time to execute my plan, I yanked the bottle of piss out of my pocket, took the lid off, waited for him to get within throwing distance, and splash! I covered the kid's face with piss, and promptly ran like hell. A hundred yards away from where the assault had happened, I looked back to see DickS throwing up all over the place, including himself. I laughed uncontrollably until a few minutes later when the bell rang to indicate that recess was over.

While sitting in class I heard the school secretary come over the intercom and say, "TommyJ, please report to the Principal's office immediately, TommyJ." DickS had ratted me out, deservingly so I suppose, but a rat he was. My parents had to come get me because I was suspended from school for an entire week, yet once again, DickS got his as soon as I returned to school the following week. My very first day back, I had organized my own glee club that was to perform the standard Birthday song, however this one was for an imaginary person. Upon my cue, twenty or so people began singing happy birthday in the hallway while everyone was passing to their classes. That was when my brother, two of his friends, and I beat the hell out of DickS. Because of the large, loud ensemble, his screams could not be heard, and any view of the vicious beating was also blocked by my impromptu choir. The group, consisting primarily of victims of DickS' grade school tyranny, eagerly volunteered to join in the singing.

This kind of mischief seemed to follow me around all the way up to High School, where it continued until I graduated. I was suspended over six times in both my seventh and eighth grade years, until I was finally expelled for selling pot on school grounds during the spring term of my eighth grade year. This incident really marked the beginning of many torrid years of drug use for me. And I say use, not abuse, because I never understood how one can abuse drugs? It's not like I constantly beat up a bag of pot, or left a bottle of pills buckled up in my car with the windows rolled up on a hot summer day. No, I consumed them for their psychotropic qualities. With all the confidence in the world, I vehemently deny ever abusing drugs. If anything, they abused me!

At the age of twelve I could often be found with my head lost deep within a book, but unlike my peers that were reading books by the likes of Tolkien, I was reading anything and everything I could get my hands on that had to do with true accounts of Serial Killers and their crimes, but my timing couldn't have been shittier. In 1995 the information age was in its infancy, so when it came to literature on serial killers or mass murders (aside from genocide and other war related mass killings), the most I could seem to find were a few books like <u>Helter Skelter</u>, and some magazine and newspaper articles. Though it is possible there was more out there than I was able to search out, they sure made it hard as hell to find. Although we did see the advent of the TV show, America's Most Wanted, the detailed accounts of such gruesome crimes only existed in police reports and other records which a thirteen year old kid had no idea how to get. What I wanted was scarce, which seems to be the story of my life, but in all truth, I liked it that way. I mean, if it was plentiful, I don't think I would have craved it nearly as much as I would if it were right in front of me for taking on a regular basis. I believe the same could be said for most people regarding most anything the world has to offer. My fascination with serial killers was primarily with their breed of insanity, and the image Hollywood had instilled in my brain: mysterious, intelligent, pre-teen psychos that were made by Mommy Dearest to wear their older sister's bra, panties, and summer dresses.

Around this time I had been researching everything from Catholicism to Eastern Metaphysics, and I had even written up a short book with my Step-Brother on a sort of religion of our own creation. The reason I say sort of is because there was no creation myth involved, there really wasn't anything being worshipped, there were no deities, and frankly, now that I put it down to paper, it really doesn't reflect what the definition of religion is at all. I guess it could be called a doctrine, as it laid out a set of beliefs which centered itself around the mystique of secret societies such as the

Freemasons, The Illuminati, and the Skull & Bones; as well as the belief in extra-terrestrial life and the conspiracy of the U.S. Government to cover up any evidence of the existence of anything thought to be from out of this world. As a result of our relentless research on such topics, my brother and I remained fixated on all the new possibilities the world had to offer us, and we have remained reasonably open minded in general ever since.

Middle school was a period of time marred by the angst-ridden tribulations I gingerly defecated upon my parents' chests, Momz in particular. By this time she had remarried, but I had become so accustomed to doing whatever I wanted, I rarely ever listened to her, or her new husband. Dad and his new wife lived about thirty miles south of the city, and I saw them about once every two weeks, so poor mom caught the brunt of my bullshit since I had to live with her. She was always getting called by my school to come pick me up for getting in trouble. I quickly learned that being suspended from school wasn't such a bad thing, so I started doing things to get into trouble. One of my favorites was to wear a skirt to school so they'd suspend me. This happened two or three times before the Principal finally got wise and expelled me. I was working odd jobs for my Step dad at his office for something to do while I was out of school, and obviously, for the cash. I also used to steal my mom's books and sell them to book stores, she hated me for it. She and I would get in these huge arguments which usually ended up with me leaving for weeks on end, or her kicking me out.

"TommyJ, I can't deal with you anymore. Get the fuck out of my house, and don't come back!" So I lived here and there for about two years.

The first time I was kicked out, I didn't come home for almost two weeks. I had stayed over at an older girl's house, which turned out to be quite the experience for me. The house was a White Trash, one level hell hole. They must have had fifteen cats in the place, and the ground was literally covered in cat shit. It stunk so fucking bad I would practically gag the whole time I was there. The only room not covered in shit, was the girls room I was staying in. It wasn't just me and the one girl staying there every night for two weeks, there were two other girls. The best looking girl of the group was TrishaW, and man oh man was she hot. Too bad she was just as equally fucked up in the head. One thing I've learned over the years is that the crazier a girl is, the better lay she is. Ms. TrishaW took my virginity in that shithole, on the floor of the cleaner bedroom of course, and it was over in a few short minutes. Two days later I had her friend, SamanthaW's shirt off in that same room and while I was playing with her tits she was complained about her boyfriend. Later on that night she called him and told him what I had done with her. Thanks Bitch. I managed to avoid the boyfriend for the next few weeks, but when I finally ran into him, he had already come out of the closet, and not only that, he also admitted to having a crush on me. I was flattered. The best part was that he had such a big crush on me that he said he could care less about me fooling around with his now ex-girlfriend.

"Say, you thirsty? I know I could use another beer," I asked Caribou.

"Sure. But you're not done yet are you?" she inquired.

"Done?" I laughed "Baby, I've only just begun," I said as I walked to the kitchen and grabbed four beers out of the fridge in anticipation. I returned to my seat next to Caribou, handed her two of the beers, cracked one of mine open, took a big gulp, and continued on with my story...

––––––––––––––––

At thirteen, I spent many of my spring and summer nights sneaking out of my parents place with my friends JakeH and MikeC, and we'd meet up half way between each other's neighborhoods at a strip mall called Valley. This was just a year or two before we spent our weekends stealing our parent's cars after they went to sleep, and drive all around the city getting into all kinds of debauchery. Before we graduated to grand theft auto, however, we settled for mass criminal mischief, theft, and burglary. We'd troll Valley getting into all kinds of mischief from kicking off sprinkler heads which caused huge geysers to shoot twenty feet into the air, to turning over all the trash cans leaving garbage strewn all over the parking lot. Yet our real passion lay with roof tops. We loved getting on top of as many buildings as we possibly could, and it was a nightly challenge to see how many new buildings we could scale. The old stand—by, however, was the bowling alley in Valley. That's where we would always meet up and start our nights off with a little weed, liquor, or both. Many years later, when we had all gone off to college and were back for summer break, we all agreed to meet on the bowling alley roof one night. Once the last of us had arrived on the roof of the bowling alley, we scaled the twenty foot wall which led to the adjoining rooftops of all the other businesses in the strip mall. Our favorite to sit atop was the miniature-golf place which afforded us a three-hundred-and-sixty degree view of the entire parking lot. We were there for no more than five minutes when a hatch flung open just a few feet from where we sat. Each business had a ladder inside a back room which led to an access shaft, and this particular hatch belonged to the mini-golf place.

"OOOOH SHIT!" I said frantically in hushed voice. I scrambled to my feet which prompted my two cohorts to do the same. We had no time but to look towards the hatch and face the guy. The mini-golf business had just moved in a few weeks prior, so we didn't know the guy like we did most of the merchants in the mall. It didn't take long for him to open the hatch all the way and pop his head out. He looked to be in his early thirties, with messy hair, and a stench of booze so thick, we could smell it from where we stood over ten feet away. I imagined he had the breath to match, and I was right.

"Hey there, thought I heard some peoples up here," he said in a slurred voice as he made his way up the last few steps of the ladder and onto the roof. He was holding a bottle of what looked like whiskey. "Care if I join you," he asked as he pointed to where we had been sitting on a small ledge overlooking the parking lot.

The three of us all looked at each other, each letting out a little laugh and a shrug of our shoulders, "um, no, be my guest," MikeC said gesturing towards the ledge as well.

"Yeah, pull up a seat, take a load off. We're just up here to smoke and drink, um, safely," I said as I laughed.

MikeC kicked me and said "Duuuude!" in a hushed, but pissy tone.

"It's cool man," I said to MikeC, "right man? You're cool right?"

"Oh yeah, I don't give a shit what you kids are up to, as long as you're not breaking shit, or planning on robbing anyone, and by the looks of you's four," he said which made us three laugh, "oh, I means three of you," he said laughing. "Yeah, no tools just booze and pot. You's is harmless," he continued as he sat down between JakeH and I.

"So, you're working pretty late huh?" I asked before taking a swig from a flask I had brought with me, meanwhile, MikeC lit up a joint next to me.

"Yeah man, well not really. I've been living in the back room since I moved the course ins," he said laughing, taking a few swigs from his bottle before continuing. "Yeah, I figure, why the hell pay two rents, one here and one for an apartment, when I could just pay one. Thought about moving the course into my apartment, but I don't think it'll fits."

The three of us boys all gave a fake little laugh for his stupid joke, and MikeC passed me the joint which I gladly took a hit from.

"Heys, uh, you think maybe I could smoke on that too?" the drunk mini-golf man solicited, almost falling off his seat.

"Whoa," I said as I caught him by his arm, keeping him from falling off the perch.

"You really think you need a hit man?" JakeH asked, finally chiming in.

"Ah, the quiet one speaks," mini-golf man said pointing in JakeH's general direction. "Yeah man, I'm cool," he continued, burping at the end of his sentence.

"Alright, whatever," JakeH said as I passed the joint to the mini-golf guy.

"So, what's your name? I'm TommyJ," I said extending my hand to him once he had passed the joint to JakeH.

"GeorgeR, pleased to make your acquaint…" the put-put guy replied, but he was cut short because he successfully fell off the ledge this time, landing on his side with a muffled thud.

JakeH, MikeC, and I made a point to visit our new friend GeorgeR at his shop when we happened to be walking through Valley. As time went

56

by, GeorgeR opened up to us more and more. It turns out that when he graduated college, he was given a trust fund with a few hundred grand which he managed to piss away on partying, and he used what little funds were left to open the miniature golf course. There was never anyone there, I think because no one wanted to bring their kids to a place where the only staff member working was perpetually drunk. Needless to say, the place was going broke, and GeorgeR knew it. He had become such a wastoid that his wife up and left him, taking their two kids with her. Burnout. From what I gathered out of his drunken mumblings, he had knocked her around during an argument, which was the final straw. The guy was a total wreck, and headed to rock bottom in a liquor fueled jet. I had no sympathy for the guy though, I mean, he was just given a huge stipend which he had pissed away. He had the chance to have a family, but he pissed that away as well and now he lived in the back of his failing business. He was the definition of a loser. I'd feel bad for him if his shitty life wasn't the result of his own poor decisions, but they were. The more we got to know the guy, the less we liked him.

One particularly hot summer day MikeC and I dropped in to the mini-golf course to say hi to GeorgeR. Really, we just wanted to get out of the heat and into some A/C which we knew GeorgeR always had on since he was living there. When we came in, GeorgeR was nowhere in sight and neither were any customers.

After playing a few holes and still no sign of the proprietor, I decided it was safe to yell out GeorgeR's name, but there was no response. MikeC suggested we take a peak in the back, so I left MikeC to watch the front while I walked to the back where the office was, which doubled as his bedroom. When I got there, I nearly lost consciousness from laughter when I saw GeorgeR laying face down on the office floor, clutching his nearly finished fifth of liquor with a huge puddle that had formed around his mid section. The bottle stood upright, so there's no way it could have been spilt liquor, so therefore, there was really only one thing left that it could have been.

"Hey MikeC, get your ass back here and check this out," I yelled to him from the back room.

"But what about the front man?" MikeC inquired as he pointed to the front.

"Lock the front door," I replied, which he quickly did before running to the back to see what I was laughing at.

Seeing GeorgeR in all his glory, MikeC laughed as quietly as possible, covering his mouth so he wouldn't wake the mini-golf sleeping beauty as he asked, "Holy shit, did he piss himself?!?"

"I believe so my dear sir, I believe so," I answered in my best British accent, which only made MikeC laugh harder. Enamored

"Wait, shhh," I told MikeC, putting my finger to my lips. "We don't wanna wake him," I said trying to sound scornful, however there was no way the scene would permit me to convey any sort of serious tone which only made us giggle more.

After leaving the room to get ourselves under control, MikeC and I returned to the office door. Laughing at a much quieter, more contained level, MikeC replied, "Oh yeah, and why's that?"

"Because," I began to answer, but was cut short when GeorgeR's body seemed to come to life, "shit!"

MikeC looked at me somewhat puzzled, "Because," followed by a big, smart-assed grin, "shit?"

"No," I laughed, pointing to GeorgeR, but just as suddenly as he became animated, he fell still once again, however this time, he was down for the count.

"Pheeeew," I said, wiping my forehead as if I were overacting in some shitty kids show. "Well Mr. MikeC, what I was gonna say, was that we should…" I cut myself short wondering if GeorgeR was just faking being asleep now. "Shit…"

"Shit? Again? Seriously, what the fuck?" MikeC asked, cutting me off in an overacted, perturbed way which made us both laugh.

"No asshole, come here," motioning for him to follow me out into the hallway. "So here's the plan, I'm gonna sit right up here and watch ole GeorgeR as he sleeps off that fifth of whiskey. Meanwhile, you're gonna go back up front, make sure no one's around, and then you're gonna empty the till. Got it?" I whispered, placing my hand on his shoulder half way through the plan. "Oh, and look for the no sale button. That'll open up the register without making a loud beeping sound," I continued, "Got it?"

"Genius! I'm on it," he answered with both thumbs up. "When we're good to go, I'll queue you with a pssst, ok?"

"Sounds good, now get your ass in gear," I said, slapping MikeC's ass.

"Fag!" he replied as he ran down the stairs headed for the till.

When I got back in the office, GeorgeR hadn't moved another muscle, but he had begun to snore. Within a minute I heard the "pssst", and bid pathetic old GeorgeR ado. MikeC and I made a b-line for my house since I knew that no one would be home for at least a few hours. We ran down to the den where MikeC emptied his pockets. It was $337 day altogether, and altogether not bad.

I decided it was best to just avoid Valley for the next few weeks until the whole thing blew over. When I finally did make it back around, it wasn't a big shocker to discover a for lease sign in the window where GeorgeR's business used to be. MikeC and I couldn't help but feel a little responsible for the company's demise, however, the more we thought about it, the more we realized that it wouldn't have mattered if we had robbed him or not. The guy was simply doomed to fail at any endeavor he pursued in life.

_____

"So it sounds like you spent most of your free time, your down, bored time, getting into some kind of trouble huh? Sounds a lot like me when I was your age," Caribou stated as she wiped something from her eye.

"Getting tired on me already?" I asked, but I knew she wasn't. Really, I just wanted to tease her, to try and get a rise out of her. "Hold on though," I interjected with a raised tone before she could reply, "I must demand that you cease and desist from answering that question because I already know what you're gonna say, and how you're gonna say it." Smiling, I paused to see if she would comply.

I was successful at producing both a giggle and curiosity, "Oh yeah? Ok hotshot, I'm all ears. What would my answer be huh?" she inquired.

"Well first of all, I already know you're not tired, at least I'm guessing so because it's somewhat early and you have yet to yawn. Am I right?"

"Yeah, go on," her curiosity failed to wane.

"And if I hadn't interrupted you, and just asked if you were tired and let you answer, you're answer would've been some kind of adamant denial in a higher pitched tone," I smiled just before I mocked her in my best Caribou imitation, "Nooooo, I'm not tired!"

"I don't sound like that!" she whined.

"I could have guessed that response as well," I laughed. "But my point is that for some reason, anytime you accuse someone of fading off, falling asleep, or even accusing them of being asleep, say, when you're watching a movie together or something of that nature, for some reason, most people will deny being asleep or falling in that direction in the whiniest tone, even if they're guilty. Know what I'm talking about?" I asked Caribou.

"That's so funny! You're so right!" she agreed with my analysis.

"Weird huh? Well, we'll have to test it out later on each other as the night progresses. Though come to think of it, it might be better tested on someone who doesn't know about this conversation, someone who isn't expecting it."

"I agree, but I'm still gonna try and fuck with you," she joked with me.

"Anyhow, I got totally off track. So where was I..." I pondered as I looked at the top of the wall behind Caribou as if my previous words to her had been written there. "Well, thinking back on this time when I got into all kinds of mischief with JakeH and MikeC, I recall a brief, but very eye opening relationship I had with another kid from MikeC and JakeH's neighborhood," I said to Caribou who was already getting comfortable for more of my storytelling. "A kid named GabeC."

"Your age?" she asked.

"Poor kid didn't know his age, and the fucked up part was that he was raised by his biological mother who he lived with when I knew him. I guess she never bothered to remember his birth date. Story of his life..."

---

8. GabeC's Story

I walked into the 7-11 that sat between my neighborhood and JakeH and MikeC's neighborhood and saw my friend BarryN, the clerk, talking to a kid that looked to be about my age.

"Heya BarryN," I said as I walked around the counter towards where the kid stood.

"TommyJ, hey, this here's GabeC, he just moved in across the street, from a, where'd you say you're from?" BarryN asked the kid.

"I didn't, we just moved here from Lansing, Michigan. My mom and I that is, and out dog, Max," the kid said as he extended his hand which I shook.

I had never really known anyone that lived along the main boulevard between me and my buddy's neighborhoods. It was like a class sandwich since my neighborhood, as well as JakeH and MikeC's, was a middle class hood, and the boulevard housing represented a lower class of tenants in low rent apartments and the occasional house that avoided the rezoning when they widened the boulevard by two lanes in the 70's. The sandwich gave me a unique perspective on the people of the boulevard, and meeting GabeC had opened my eyes to its presence and the class system in America in general for the first time.

It was one of those moments in childhood when something revolutionary happens that transforms the world into a place that's a little less perfect than your naivety had led you to believe. As a kid, I saw grey, whilst the adults around me only seemed to see black, white, and red, but no grays whatsoever. Grays were reserved for us kids who saw no lines, no borders, and crossing or stepping upon them wouldn't break our mama's back.

Our friendship was immediate, and it also immediately transcended class, or lack thereof, something GabeC was deathly afraid of since he was so cruelly teased about it by his classmates back in Lansing. Because of this, he became instantly trusting of JakeH, MikeC, and I who only saw another skateboarder like us, never mind his dark skin which was whole other issue in itself for GabeC. He and I had a special bond because we lived with our single moms, women who had some serious 'issues.' I thought my mom's neurosis and light Obsessive Compulsive Disorder was bad, but it paled in comparison next to GabeC's mom's problems.

GabeC's mom, Ms. TatianaC, was born in Romania to unwed teenage parents that didn't want a baby. She was born in 1968, two years after the Totalitarian Dictator of Romania, Nicolae Ceauşescu, had instituted what was known as Ceauşescu's Decree 770, making abortion illegal. By making abortion illegal, his plan was to create a baby boom generation that would grow up to create the biggest proletariat workforce Romania had ever seen. This subsequently backfired, and many of the unwanted babies that resulted were given up for adoption, and many ultimately turned to a life of crime, like a large portion of any lower class often does.

TatianaC was one of these unwanted babies, and she was adopted by a Ukrainian couple, along with many other children, when she was ten. The couple wasted no time at all in smuggling her, and all the other children they had adopted, out of Romania where they were sold as sex slaves to a brothel in Prague. By the age of twelve she was forced to turn tricks, and by fourteen she was pregnant.

TatianaC was one of a very few, very fortunate women that was not only able to escape the world she has been forced into, she was able to do so just two years after arriving at the brothel. It wasn't easy, however, and she wouldn't have been able to escape at all if it wasn't for the help of another foreign couple. The irony was lost on the uneducated young woman, and though she was wary about trusting foreign couples after her first experience, she figured, life can't get any worse, so what the hell, let's see what they can do for me. An American couple had clandestinely approached her with their plan by posing as an ultra-erotic couple with various fetishes, seeking a young woman to simply watch their 'routine.' The couple claimed to be part of a group that touted itself to be the first ever anti-sex-slave trade advocacy group that had become aware of the brothel TatianaC was forced to live at, and the brothel's practices regarding human trafficking.

In a daring raid, the American couple, along with a dozen members from their group, busted into the brothel disguised as the local equivalent of the Communist Gestapo, and freed GabeC's mother along with several other orphans that were 'adopted' by the Madame of the brothel. With the cooperation of the U.S. government, the anti-human trafficking group, the official name it later became to be known by, was able to get TatianaC an all inclusive 'Free-Me-From-A-Commie-Red-State-Grant' that gave her money for school and boarding, as well as a U.S. student/work visa. Since he was born stateside, GabeC was granted U.S. citizenship.

TatianaC was brought to Lansing, Michigan where she was adopted by a young couple from Chicago that owned a medium sized new and used bookstore. GabeC was born a healthy, good-looking little baby boy just a few weeks after TatianaC had arrived in Lansing. During her time in Lansing, she was able to get caught up with her schooling, and was able to graduate high school just a year later than she would have had she gone to school when she was supposed to. She was granted permanent political asylum once the Romanian government toppled in 1989, a place she would never return to.

Not too long after graduating high school, the stress of reality, of the prospect of having to move on with her life and be responsible for supporting herself, and her baby got the better of her. She had a nervous breakdown and was thus hospitalized in the local hospital's mental therapy wing. It was then that it was determined that she suffered from a mild form of schizophrenia, but it wasn't detrimental enough from keeping her from being released from the mental ward.

When she turned eighteen, she was told that she needed to move on with her life, but after her breakdown, her surrogate parents decided to allow her as much time as she needed to figure out her direction in life. It didn't take long before she decided to move to Portland, Oregon for no apparent reason whatsoever, but my guess was that a voice told her.

Once settled in Portland, her mental state worsened and she developed agoraphobia, never to leave her apartment, not even for the mail. I'm not sure what it was exactly that made her snap, but she began taking out her hatred of the world and herself on her son. GabeC would show up to go skating with black-eyes, bite marks, and sometimes even cigarette burns. The first time I saw them, GabeC was so embarrassed he was wearing a turtleneck shirt with a scarf around his neck as well, but it was a seventy degree day out. After MikeC and I had confronted him about it, he became less and less worried about concealing it from us, and on one hot day while we were skateboarding, he took his shirt off to reveal hundreds of knuckle sized bruises, and more than ten cigarette sized burns. We weren't the only ones that noticed either, teachers and social workers took notice as well, but it seemed they never did anything to save the poor kid from his mother, and he continued to live with her despite her almost daily beatings of her son.

TatianaC's abuse wasn't limited to just the physical abuse, she was also quite the cruel witch when it came to belittling her son by telling him "he was really a little girl," and "no girl would ever want him because his penis was too small." One day after GabeC got home from skating with JakeH and I, he asked his mom who his father was, and she replied, "I was raped by a dirty nigger. That's your dad, a dirty nigger Englishman." This of course was followed by a beating with a belt.

Though his mother never left her apartment, she maintained a tight leash on her son, and in an attempt to give her some kind of companionship, a ploy to divert her abuse, GabeC brought home a stray dog that he found wondering around the dumpsters at the 7-11 by his apartment. Surprisingly, she took a liking to the dog, and at first, it was a match made in heaven. She loved the dog so much that she named it Gabe II. GabeC also fell in love with his new, loyal best friend who gave him comfort, when his mother gave him anything but.

As time went on, the beatings increased in severity and frequency, and sometimes it was too much for the kid to take. When he'd see the shock in our eyes at the sight of his new bruises and burns, he would break down and cry, finally releasing all the pent up anger and sadness buried into him by his mother.

A few days before the end of the school year, GabeC came home to find Gabe II dead, cut into pieces that were strewn about Gabe I's bed. At the foot of the bed rest its head, and inside the throat-hole was a note that read:

"ONE GABE TO GO...

♫ OH

♫ OH

♫ OOOOOOH

♫ IT'S MAGIC

♫ YOU KNOOOOOON...

KNOW!

WHAT DO YOU THINK YOU KNOW?"

Scared for his life, GabeC contemplated what to do. At first he was so scared, he ran, the whole mile and a half from his house to mine to tell me the story of Gabe II's demise, which was barely discernable through his erratic breathing, and heavy sobbing. My heart had never ached for someone like that before, and it was all I could do just to keep from crying myself. I held my buddy and told him he could stay with me as long as he liked, and he did, all of one night.

When I awoke in the morning, I found a note thanking me for "everything," and "that he would never forget me." I wasn't exactly sure if it meant he was going to hurt his mother or himself, but I knew I was scared for him. It was the second to last day of school, and he was nowhere to be found that day, and his note would be the last I ever saw or heard from him. GabeC had told MikeC and me that if he made it through his seventh grade year, that is, if his mother didn't kill him, he'd likely be leaving Portland for good. Where, he didn't tell us, which he said was for his safety as well as our own.

TatianaC put a missing dog notice on her front door, but she failed to report her son missing for six weeks. She became the prime suspect in his disappearance, and we all feared the worst. Fortunately, after serving a search warrant on GabeC and TatianaC's apartment, the police found no signs of foul play, and came to the conclusion that TatianaC's agoraphobia was her alibi. It appeared as though the kid had finally just had enough and left.

Years later on Facebook I received a friend request, and message from my old friend GabeC. It had been over fourteen years since we had last spoken. Apparently, after leaving my house in the middle of the night, GabeC immediately contacted his surrogate grandparents back in Michigan who flew out and essentially kidnapped their grandson in order to save his life. They were able to provide him a nice safe home where he grew up to be a pretty normal, happy guy.

The last I heard from him he was living in L.A. where he manages a rooftop nightclub, and sometimes, there are happy endings.

"My god TommyJ, that is so fucked up. People can be so cruel. I just can't believe that boy wasn't taken away by the state or city or some shit!" Caribou exclaimed in pure anger.

"I know, but trust me, my friends and I tried to get him help. It was like no one would listen to MikeC, JakeH, or I just because we were kids. It was completely retarded. Thank god he was saved by his grandparents though, because who knows what may have happened to him had they not…"

---

9. Tween to Teen Dream

When I lived on the street I was what you probably expect a runaway
to look and act like. Aptly titled a Gutter Punk, I was the
scummiest, most fly circled, punk-ass kind of kid. Although I looked
near dead, it was the people of the burbs who were the damned in my
eyes. It wasn't just their reciprocal lives, it was the medicine
cabinets they had at home that were filled with anti-depressants,
sleeping pills, uppers, downers, and the like, and the looks on
their faces as I passed by. Their driveway stares of bewilderment
that left them looking dull and soulless with traces of gray from
the blood rushing somewhere to hide. I absolutely lived for those
looks of cubicle stress-box cases. When I slept on a park bench on a
cold night, their misery was my warmth. The suburbs, as I saw it at
the time, were where the zombies lived.

A light bulb that burned brightly in my early years, a source for
smiles and happy energy, was extinguished by my adolescent anguish,
yet still I carried the bulb around with me while I was more or less
homeless. One morning I was forced awake by the passing of a 6 a.m.
freight train, and the light began to burn again with great
intensity. Finally, it was on track towards full wattage, and it
made me begin to question, was I more normal, more suburban than I
thought or pretended to be? Would I ultimately occupy one of these
ticky-tacky boxes? Would I mope about like a good little zombie
until I blew my brains out one day? Was I on track? Despite the fact
that day to day existential crises plagued me in so many ways that I
think it concurrently mapped itself out in some kind of porous
cipher on my face, POP, OOZE!; no, I was still TommyJ, Thom,
ThomasJ. That gave me everything I needed to be labeled different.
Not for the label, but because it was absolutely true and I wasn't
about to let people see me as camouflage at the local Chuck E.
Cheese. The judgment would be passed upon me one way or another, so
I figured it might as well create an outcome more to my liking.

I made the best of what the world had to offer me, and when it
wasn't exactly offered, I took it. I flew from the city nightmares
to the suburban nightmares, bum camps to hippie camps, and I dreamt
it all better the whole way down. I may have had company, but my
journey was ultimately taken all alone. Did they notice I wasn't
really there? No, and I guess it was to my advantage they thought I
was cool for being so disjointed, so out of this worldly, world.
Wholesomely deprived, yet enthusiastically comforting from a strange
distance was what I've been told, what was so attractive about me
during this time period. I was a cunning little cunt. I came in like
a cloud that hinted at rain, but I never let the wet down. Rather, I
carried the static electricity and filled your carpets with
occasional discomfort. If you dragged your feet around me, you, your
cat, your door knob, you all would have paid the price.

In the burbs I attended an alternative High School, though attended
is probably too concrete a word to describe the time I was enrolled
at C.E. Mason. My junior year I was called into the Vice-Principal's
office to discuss my attendance and some options they'd come up with
for the completion of my high school career. The deal was that I was
straight A student, one of only six for the junior class, yet I had
the worst attendance record in the history of the school.

How did I not only get by with better than passing grades let alone
A's you ask? Well it wasn't easy. It took my entire freshman year

and half of my sophomore year to create an almost foolproof system for accomplishing this. First I'd attend every day of each of my classes for the first week. During this first week I would spend a day or two planning out how and when I would be able to skip class, when all the homework was due, and what that entailed. I was quite the flirt, the social butterfly, so it was no problem for me to warm up to the teacher's assistant. I'd give them my pager number which they were supposed to page in the event of a pop quiz which I would try and rush over to school to complete before the bell rang. Lastly, instead of finals or tests at the end of each term, C.E. Mason had term projects (it was an alternative school after all), topics which were chosen by the students and approved by our teachers during the first week of the term. They were due during the last week of the term in which we presented the projects, so I had to attend all of my classes that week as well.

It may sound like this school wasn't all that challenging, but it was just as arduous and unpreparing for the real world as the next public school, however, in this school, you had to apply to attend. The school had an acceptance process which required the student to write an essay describing why they felt they belonged at this particular school, and what skills and/or talents they had that were relevant to the curriculum taught at the school. After accepting an application package, each candidate, along with their parents, were scheduled for an interview with the principal.

It appeared as though I had come full circle, from the first meeting with my parents and the principal welcoming me to C.E. Mason, to the meeting in which they were so embarrassed by what I had actually accomplished in my time at their school, that they opted not to include my parents in the meeting. Rather than open arms, I was sitting across the desk from a beet red-faced man, arms folded. He was ready to push my ass out the door without giving a shit about what might come of me as long as I didn't bring down their little experiment which was ultimately a way to separate the free thinking creative kids from the herd, so that the herd could thrive in their herd like ways, and not be disturbed by the ideas of the free thinkers like myself.

My Principal made it very clear, I was not going to embarrass him or his school, so he gave me only two options knowing damn well I would take the one I did: 1) they would expel me and I would have to repeat my Junior year at another area high school, at which time I would expose the school for the sham it was; or 2) I would enter a partnership program in which I would no longer attend the alternative high school, rather, I would take courses at the local community college in which my college credits would be acceptable as advanced high school credits. I would not only graduate with a normal high school diploma from C.E. Mason, but I would do so a half year early. It was a no brainer, no reason to dig my own grave, plus I would enter my freshman year of college with a term's worth of college credits already under my belt. With a big, smart-assed grin upon my face, I shook my Principal's hand and left the school grounds victorious. My parents, who had no real idea what I was up to, were told by the Principal, upon our agreement, that I had accomplished some kind of unheard of advancement within the public school system and they thought it would be best for me to attend college in which they, the public school system, was more than happy to pay for.

_____

Laughing to myself as I paused to take a drink from my beer, a story came to mind from that time period, "Oh man, I just thought of the funniest story from that time," I said, chuckling even more.

"Oh yeah, must be pretty funny, I have yet to see you this flushed," Caribou said as she was forced to laugh from the contagiousness of my own.

"Oh, it is…" smirk.

Back in the 80's and 90's, Drug Abuse Resistance Education (D.A.R.E.) was a way more prolific organization than it is today. D.A.R.E. was all over the nation and you'd see advertisements for it everywhere including billboards, trains, and the D.A.R.E. cop cars which were confiscated during drug related busts. Nowadays, people wear the D.A.R.E. shirts as a joke. Personally, I was supposed to be in the Smoke Free Class of 2000, yet today, I smoke over a pack a day, go figure. I'm not sure if there are even D.A.R.E. cops anymore, but there sure were plenty of them when I was growing up.

Everyone in Beaverton, a place we called the Tron because a lot of folks get stuck there and never get out, plus it's a really lame place (the world of Tron, not the movie, the movie and its sequel are awesome), knew one D.A.R.E. cop in particular, Officer DanB. Everyone knew him because not only was he a really nice guy, he also drove a D.A.R.E. Corvette. I met him in Elementary School during a D.A.R.E. assembly, but it would be in High School that I met his son, TonyB. We were never really close friends, but we both hung out with the same group of friends. One week during our senior year, TonyB's parents went on a cruise, leaving behind their three kids, including TonyB, to take care of themselves. Being the oldest, it was TonyB's responsibility to take care of the house and his two sisters. His folks left on a Friday, and the very next night TonyB planned on having a small get-together. It didn't take long for the word to spread and by ten that night his house was full of drunken teenagers. While the mayhem ensued, preoccupying TonyB, I grabbed the only pair of keys that were hanging up in his kitchen with a Chevy key in it, walked through the house gathering a small group of my closest friends, and headed for the garage. As I suspected, the key worked, and we were in Officer DanB's D.A.R.E. Corvette.

"Tits," I exclaimed after turning the key and unlocking the doors.

"What the fuck TommyJ?!? You're not planning on driving this thing are you? That'd be way too fucked up, even for you," MikeC squealed from behind me.

"Relax, no ones gonna be driving this baby," I said with a broad smile, "just get in and I'll show you what we're really here for." With that, I pushed the lever that made the front seat tilt forward so MikeC and the two random girls he and I had grabbed could climb in back. On the other side, our friend SuzieQ got in the front passenger seat which left the driver's seat for me. "So, I've brought you kids here today to experience a spiritual event. Though it may be considered sacrilege in some, ok, most circles, our little circle here'll forever remember this moment as a very spiritually uplifting event. MikeC, pipe please," I declared as the laughter began to almost deafen me. "Now hush hush ladies, we don't wanna alert TonyB to the devious little happenings of our private little party now do we?"

As he handed me the pipe, MikeC replied, "Here you go."

"Tits," I exclaimed once again which made all three girls giggle, "and a little bit of weeeeeeed…" I said as I pulled out a bag that was caught on something in my coat pocket. It finally got loose and came flying out, "Oh shit!" I screeched and everyone laughed.

I looked around for where the bag had gone, but it was SuzieQ that had retrieved it from the floor on her side. "Here, I think some of it may have fallen out," turning on the overhead light.

"Shit, I don't see any. Oh well, if Officer DanB finds any it's gonna be TonyB's head," I said which made everyone laugh even harder. I'd take a better look later that night, but I was 99% sure that none of the buds were missing from the bag. We proceeded to smoke three fat bowls of the most premium Blueberry Weed I could get my hands on that winter. We would go down in infamy for this brazen defilement of a D.A.R.E. vehicle, especially the most notorious of the D.A.R.E. cruisers in the entire metro fleet. TonyB, on the other hand, didn't find it very amusing when he found out a few days later, and to say I got an ear full is an understatement.

————————————

What does a high school student, in my particular situation, do with all the extra time on their hands? Where could I go where the police wouldn't pick me up for truancy during the 90% of school time I was skipping? I always seemed really tired for some reason, so I spent a good amount of my time sleeping. Sometimes ten, twelve, eleventy-seven hours, sleeping forever it seemed. I was convinced for the longest time it meant I was growing, but I was wrong, I've been the same height since seventh grade.

When I finally did venture out of bed, I would try and get my homework, what little I had, finished well before the final bell I so infrequently heard ring. I was also just discovering the world of music, specifically musical instruments, and to be even more specific than that, guitar. I spent hours listening to records as I played my guitar to them. I was self taught and not too shabby by the time I entered college, though I swore I would never be that douche bag covering hard rock songs on an acoustic guitar around a camp fire in college and I never did become that guy. No Joey-tar for me, no thanks, I left that rep up to the more reputable Joeys.

Once all my homework and household chores were finished, I would grab my smokes, pager, keys, and bus pass and head out into town every few days a week. "Into town" meant downtown in the city where I would troll the record stores or cafes where I'd meet people and pick up as much culture as I could along the way. I was a Socialist sponge trying to soak up as much of the world around me as I could before drawing conclusions and passing the judgment that seems so easy to pass so quickly the older you get. Most of the time, however, "in town" meant towards the downtown of the suburb city in which my school was located at the center of, and it was in fact on Center Street.

During the first week of each school term I would try and be at
school in the morning and get on the morning attendance record so
that it may be hard for my administrators to dispute my absence down
the road. After first period I would sneak through the halls, out a
back service entrance, and jump the cyclone fence which imprisoned
us students. I made my way through a heavily wooded area behind the
school's fields and back into civilization a half mile away on a
road which led down to the bus mall in which I had an eternal pass
to. That is, my Mom bought me a monthly pass because there was no
school bus that went anywhere near my mom's house. One such morning
I had made my way through the back field, and being an early January
morning, the dew from the long grass against the fence that the
mowers were unable to reach, had soaked the lower part of my jeans
as I treaded through it to reach my freedom. As I jumped over the
fence as I had a thousand times before, I was careless and
unsuspecting of the affects of my wet jeans. As I swung my leg over
the top of the fence, the weight from the water threw my pant leg
into the grasp of the pointy, twisted tops of the cyclone fence. I
was stuck atop the fence, and I risked ripping my pants wholly off
if I let my grip go. "Fuck me…" I whimpered with a laugh, hoping
that our campus security guard or some upper-classman wouldn't come
along and find little TommyJ stuck there, but alas, I was saved.
From the woods came a very tall, yet slim, stuttering, grungy
looking fellow that at first could be mistaken for an aggressor, but
one moment of his stumbling words and nonthreatening body language
gave away his innocent vulnerability, and it quickly became obvious
that he was painfully aware of and embarrassed by it.

"Na na na need a hahahand?" the gentle giant said, murmuring as he
stumbled slightly as he tripped on a small root that was protruding
from the ground near my projected landing site.

I hesitated because, thanks to my brother's incessant teasing and
berating, I was so accustomed to greeting such tragedies with a
middle finger, so badly wanting to mock the poor stranger with a
stuttering response of my own, I quickly realized I was in no
position to be making fun of anyone. "Oh, yes please! Man, thank you
sooooo much, you don't know how much you're really helping me out
here," smiling from an awkwardly slung position, I was surprised
when he laughed.

"Sa sa sorry but you look so fu fu funny up there," he stuttered as
he reached his grimy hands up to hoist me over the final lap of the
fence I caught wind of what he had been harboring from a shower for
some time, and it would be much later that day that I was finally
able to rid my nostrils of the awful sting. He set me on my feet,
and I straightened my pants and shirt out before extending my hand
to shake his.

"Thanks again man, I'm TommyJ. And you are?"

"Shakes, they ca ca call me Shu Shu Shu Shakes," as he shook my hand
with an extraordinary jostle that made it clear where the nickname
came from. His stutter seemed to have traveled and translated itself
into an unsteadiness of his hands. "Follow me," he said as he began
walking down one of the many paths that led from the fence into the
abyss of the forest.

"Sure," I said, thinking, *why the hell not, I had nothing better to
do*.

"You'll get to meet my ba ba buddy KellyH, so you sku sku skipping school?" my new, Shaky friend asked.

"Yup, I fucking hate being confined to that place," I said proudly of the escape I had literally just made by the skin of my ass.

"I did too," replied the shaking giant. Great, you mean to tell me I could be just like you one day? I thought to myself. So, all those after-school specials on TV weren't bullshit huh? I laughed a quietly enough so that my giant savior couldn't hear me as I followed him deeper into the ever-darker, and ever-creepier growing woods. "Just a little bit fu fu fu fu farther here," pointing down the path we were on. I had never really ventured this far into the forest. Typically, I took one of the paths that ran nearest the fence which all lead towards the main boulevard. "Ha ha here," he said as we cleared a corner on the path. We entered an area where the forest floor was completely covered in a dense moss except for the path where someone had taken the time to meticulously dig out the moss. About thirty yards or so in front of us was a clearing where the sun was able to shine upon the moss floor and this was apparently where Shakes had been leading me. Upon a log sat a thirty something year-old, long haired, hippie looking fellow wearing a tie-dyed shirt. He was sewing up a small hole in the side of one of the two tents which was set up in the clearing ahead.

"KellyH!" Shakes yelled.

"Fuck! You scared the shit outta me!" he wailed as he quickly turned towards us, grasping at his heart.

"We have a a a guest, this here's TommyJ, a Truant." Shakes said.

"Tru-what you say?" KellyH had obviously never heard the term before. I thought Shakes was going to be the dumber of the two, but after not knowing what truant meant, KellyH took the cake when he announced that he was growing Pot in a field near their camp site after only knowing me for less than ten minutes. Who's to say I wouldn't come and steal their plants when they were away or sleeping? Needless to say, KellyH was not the brightest bulb in the duo, and it really pissed off Shakes something fierce when he told me about their pot operation. Once he had calmed down I began to ask simple questions, gradually working my way to asking how they ended up becoming bums. Shakes blamed his homelessness on his rampant drug use as a teen that eventually caused his hands to consistently shake uncontrollably. The irony was that ever since he was about thirteen, Shakes' dream was to become a bartender, and he actually enrolled in the bartending Academy where he flunked out simply because he couldn't keep from shaking and spilling drinks every time he went to pour one. With no other real skills, Shakes assumed a life of scraping by on food stamps and panhandling with KellyH. KellyH on the other hand was more of a closed book, and it always kind of gave me the creeps the way he never wanted to discuss his background.

I spent the next few months hanging out with the bums behind my school, and we did everything from eating acid to swimming in rivers together. The most memorable day I had with these two gents was when we, and about six of my other friends, bought a ton of LSD in the city, and ate it before we all went to see the band Gwar perform. For a fifteen year-old boy, that was quite literally a Trip.

One day when the school year was drawing to a close, I decided to attend my first period class, and skip the rest of the day, so I headed through the woods to visit the guys. When I arrived to their camp site I found that their tents, fire pit, and even the pot plants had all vanished. Stapled to a tree nearby was a notice from the county sheriff declaring the place an illegal campsite as well as a crime scene, warning against further trespassing on the private property I was illegally standing on, and upon reading the notice, I high-tailed it out of there fearing arrest.

I never heard from Shakes or KellyH again. Word on the street was that they were arrested for growing the pot and illegally camping in the woods behind my school, and once they got out and were awaiting trial, they skipped town in order to avoid further jail time. It wasn't too long after their disappearance that I became a runaway myself.

———————————————

While I was on the lamb I truly coveted the freedom I had by taking advantage of all the benefits of having no morally grounded elder voice in my ear at every turn. Common sense may have said it was wrong, but my gut feeling, fed by this freedom, seldom agreed. Ever since I was a small child I had been fascinated by trains. When I was about nine years old my father lived near a train yard where my brother and I would go and play on the freight trains that were parked on the tracks. I was completely taken aback by the eeriness of the empty train yard. By the time I was fourteen my best buddy JakeH and I became intimately involved with graffiti, blossoming into two of the most prolific graffiti writers in town. I would venture to say that we had painted well over five hundred trains apiece, and I'm not just talking about simple little tags, I'm talking about bigger, more intricate pieces of work. JakeH actually had me beat by at least two hundred more trains than I had painted. After spending a great deal of time down at the tracks it was no surprise that the thought of hopping trains for a lift had crossed my mind on many occasions. In fact, I had wanted to jump on a freight train and be like a hobo ever since I was a little kid. Most kids wanted to be pilots, fireman, or cops and I wanted to be a Hobo.

Once I was free from my parents, school, and all the other things that held me to the burbs, I decided that it was time to take a trip. I packed up a small bag which included a few shirts; pants; a package of six brand new pairs of socks; a few cans of beans, pears, and mixed fruit; a can opener; two knives, one switchblade, and one Swiss Army pocketknife; a can of mace; two pocket sized notepads and one standard, eight and a half by eleven inch notepad; a pencil sharpener; and plenty of pens and pencils. At this age I was really into travel literature and I had just finished Jack Kerouac's On The Road, so I was sure to bring the materials to document my own adventures.

I began my journey at one of the main train yards in the city, a place where many of my friends had jumped on trains at before. I had heard there was a website where you could enter the serial number off of the side of a freight train and this would help determine where it was, where it had been, and more importantly, where it was going. I decided to go the old school route and just try and guess. Besides the time my folks took my brother and I to Disneyland, which I can barely even remember, I had never really been to California, let alone on my own. This has taught me that if I ever have kids, I'm sure as hell going to wait until they're old enough to remember such a trip before I spend a small fortune at Disneyland like they did. The plan was to stop in San Francisco where I'd spend an undetermined amount of time, after all, I had no one telling me to be anywhere at any time. I could come and go as I pleased, so I chose not to limit myself to any kind of itinerary other than a the flight path I had already decided upon: first to S.F., then to L.A., San Diego next, and finally I'd walk or hitchhike across the border into Mexico, and just keep going until I felt like doing something different.

It was midsummer, which was the perfect time to escape from Portland, so I could travel lightly and not worry about dying of hypothermia or exposure. In early July, I went down to the train yard one evening without the slightest idea of how I was going to make my train hopping dreams come true. I sat on a hill and watched the trains move in and out of the train yard for a good hour and a half before I felt like I had gained a basic knowledge of how the yard worked. The three sets of rails closest to me were the tracks that the trains passed by on without stopping. The next two pairs beyond that were used for what's called humping trains. Humping is where the engineers fashion the lines of freight cars using a humper which is a small engine that stays in the yard to connect, or hump, the different cars together to be taken away, thus the term humping. The next six sets of tracks on the far side were used to park the various cars before they were humped and deported. After watching the humping for a while I figured out that they used one specific track to place humped cars that would soon be travelling south, and south was it, south was the way. Once the humper started to make the next line on the southbound track I waited until it had gone to the far end of the yard to grab a few more cars before I ran down the hill and jumped through the open doorway of one of the southbound cars. When I landed on the floor of the car a cloud of dirt and sawdust flew up in the air and swirled around in the beams of sun light that were beaming through the trees that sat atop the hill I was just on. The car was empty except for some scraps of wood and metal straps that once held bundles of wood and crates together. I retreated to the far end of the car so that I couldn't easily be seen by anyone who peered into the car. I sat for maybe twenty minutes before the train started to move, and I realized that I was actually pretty scared. Just as the train started to gain a good amount of speed, I saw a couple of guys running next to my car trying to jump in. I decided that if I had to share my car with a couple of transients I had never met before, then I'd better get on their good side right away, so I ran over and held my hand out the door.

"Need a lift?" I yelled over the booming train.

"Sure," the Indian, Native American, said throwing his backpack into the car as he grabbed my hand. "I'll help my buddy," he said once he was in the car. His friend, who was also a Native American, had already thrown his bag into the car as his buddy leaned out the side and helped him in. One was about six foot nine while his buddy was only about five feet tall. They both moved to the opposite end of the car from where I sat.

"So, where you guys headed?" I made the initial small talk.

"California. L.A." the larger one said as he tried to make himself more comfortable by pulling most of his clothes out of his duffle bag and laying them under himself for cushioning on the hard steel floor.

"Oh yeah? What's in L.A.?" I inquired.

"The big sun," the smaller one joined the conversation. We rode the rest of the way without speaking and it kind of freaked me out. I didn't try to sleep or even take my eyes off of them for one second, not really knowing what to expect from them, after all, one has to wonder how these guys got to where they were.

When we finally did stop, I asked, "Hey guys, any idea where we're at?"

"I think we're in Eugene. You hungry kid?" the big one asked me as he and his buddy got to their feet.

"Yeah, kind of, why?" I inquired hesitantly.

"There's a soup kitchen not too far from here where we can get some grub, interested?" the big one asked.

"Sure, why not?" I replied. I was pretty damn hungry by this time, and I was broke when I left Portland so I hadn't had anything really substantial to eat for at least a day and a half.

"Ok, follow us kid," the larger one said as he gestured for me to follow them out of the car and down the tracks. The fact that I didn't know exactly where we were and I didn't even know these guys names, I must admit, I was a little nervous. While we were still in the car, I had made sure to slip my switchblade into my front pocket, and the can of mace into the other, which at least gave me a little piece of mind. We walked down the tracks away from the engine in order to avoid detection by any rail workers that might have been around. The smaller guy pointed to the fence that ran parallel to the tracks as far as the eye could see. Anywhere in the U.S., walking on train tracks is considered trespassing whether it be private property, or in most cases, federal property. When I was about sixteen I learned this the hard way when a few of my friends and I all got tickets from a city cop for walking down some tracks in the burbs. "There's a hole in the fence up here a few hundred yards. Then it's about a twenty minute walk to the church from there," the small one continued.

"So gentlemen, what should I call ya?" I needed names to put to the faces, and make sure they knew mine as well just in case they had anything devious in mind. I wanted to try and make it more personal between us with the hopes of sparking second thoughts of robbing me if they had any to begin with.

"Rusty Can Feathers and this here is Running Mouse," the larger one said as he patted Running Mouse on the back, "but we just call him Mouse and you can call me Rusty. So, what's your name kid?" Rusty slowed his pace so I could walk side by side with the two of them.

"The name's TommyJ, pleasure to meet you guys. So what's this church all about? Do we have to do a prayer or anything like that? I ask because I'm not religious at all."

Mouse and Rusty both smiled broadly before Mouse said, "Yeah, they want you to pray before they feed you, but since we're Indians and we say we ain't Christian, they usually just let us stay outta the place until prayer's done and it's time to eat. Since it's your first time going, I think you should go to the prayer part. It's definitely worth the experience. Plus it looks better if at least one of us in the group isn't a heathen in their eyes," the two of them laughed which in turn made me chuckle hesitantly, not knowing if they were full of shit or not.

"Well, since this is really my first time doing this, I guess I should follow y'alls advice since I'm assuming y'all have ridden a few trains in your day right?" I asked, trying to find out as much about these two as I could.

"Yeah, we've been around," Mouse replied.

"There are some things you should know about jumpin trains if you don't already. First, no matter how much of a badass you think you may be, never travel alone. You're either extremely brave kid, or extremely stupid," Rusty began to instruct me.

"A little of both I think," I interrupted, which made us all laugh.

"Secondly, beware of the F.T.R.A.," Rusty continued, "That's the Freight Train Riders of America. They were formed as a kind of brotherhood of train hoppers, but in recent years they've progressed into more of a violent gang. If you're not FTRA and you're on their train, be prepared to be beaten and robbed. They make examples out of anyone and everyone they can. Now, they don't wear, like, specific colors or bandanas so it's nearly impossible to tell if someone is in the FTRA, but for your sake, especially since you're a little guy, just assume everyone you don't know on the tracks is one of them. They've also been known to have killed some fools. Thirdly, if you're headed to, or through L.A., know that there's been word going round that there's some sort of rich white guy gang that's been going to the train yards at night with dogs, chains, knives, guns, and all kinds of fucked up shit," he said as he shook his head up and down and then from side to side. "And the graffiti they leave behind indicates that they think they're some sort of vigilante crew cleaning up the city, ridding L.A. and the surrounding area of the less than desirable folks. That's us, the homeless, the transients. They're mostly just trying to scare people off, and according to my cousin who I saw last week, they're good at what they do."

"Shit man, I had no fucking idea about all that shit," I said, sounding genuinely shocked and surprised.

"That's not all. There's some Motherfucker killing train hoppers in Oregon and Washington and he's been doing weird shit with their bodies. The police are saying it's the work of one guy, and it's been going on for like three years now. I understand the guy has stacked up quite the body count over the years, fucking sicko bastard," Mouse added to Rusty's words of wisdom.

"Yeah, so now you see why it's not smart to travel alone. You always need eyes and ears available to watch your back, and you have to sleep at some point, that's why one sleeps while the other stays watch. That's also why so many of us have our own mutts, because they're the best eyes, ears, and nose you could have with you. They're really the best traveling partner in my opinion," Rusty shoved Mouse almost flat on his ass, making them both laugh. This is when I could first tell that they were either drunk or high on something. They laughed a little too long as they walked with a noticeable swagger that couldn't be attributed to the rocks on the railway because we were now walking down a paved bike path. "Almost there," Rusty pointed a little up the path toward a street, where civilization started to form in the way of houses and a cityscape in the distance. I felt a little safer the more I talked to Rusty Can Feathers and Running Mouse as I concluded that they were relatively harmless.

Once we had made it to the road, Rusty pointed to the right where we rounded a corner. Down a few blocks on the left I could see a bell tower with a crucifix pointing to the sky. Following the tower down with my eyes, I could see the church was on the corner of the block nearest us. I followed close behind Rusty and Mouse as we walked past the main entrance, and entered what looked like a recreation hall which was at the far end of the block. We were greeted by a mix of smells that ranged from beef soup, to Old Spice, and an ever-present musky smell that drifted in and out of my olfactory range.

The longer I was in the hall, the more the smells seemed to mutate from a musky sort of rotten smell, to stinky feet, to plain old bad body odor. Naturally, I tried to focus on the smell of the soup, and though it ultimately proved futile, it really didn't bother any of us all that much. It's wasn't like we were going to sit down, snap our fingers, and say, Hey waiter, can we do something about that atrocious smell? The rec-room had about seven rows of picnic tables set up to accommodate the hundred or so of us bums. Nearly all the seats were taken but first we had to register with the church by waiting in a long line that we had to wait over a half hour in until we finally got to the front. This is where we met Father O'Leary who had us all sign our names on a nightly log.

"Father, how are you today?" I asked politely.

"It's a beautiful day to be a friend of God," he replied gingerly.

"So my two friends here are not actually Catholic. They're still true to the spiritual teachings of the Shamans from their tribe," I blasphemously lied to the Father, a light fibbing really. However, I couldn't help but feel a little guilty thanks to my Catholic upbringing.

Before Father O'Leary could reply, Rusty walked up beside me and said, "Yeah, so we'll be outside while you're having your sermon. You pray to your God, and we'll pray to Big Bear. Will this be alright with you Father?" Rusty posed, and though I hadn't known him long, it wasn't hard to see the genuine, solemn pleading in his face.

"Oh, well that's quite alright I suppose, but can I ask that after the sermon is over and you've finished eating, if it would be possible to talk with you and your tribesman about our Lord Jesus Christ and his teachings?" Father probed my new friend.

"What do you think Mouse?" Rusty turned to Mouse who was standing a few feet behind us.

After thinking about it for a few seconds, he replied, "Ok, sure, why not?" he said shrugging his shoulder.

"Great, then I expect to see the two of you right after dinner," Father O'Leary said before walking over to the stage at the far end of the room where there was a podium with a microphone was set up. "Hello everyone, welcome to St. Thomas More…" Father said as the microphone lit up loudly before him, signaling the beginning of his dinnertime sermon. The Indians took this as their queue to leave through the same double doors that we had entered through while I sat at a table with a group of bums whose average age was at least twenty—five years greater than mine. The sermon lasted about a half hour, in which I spent the time reflecting upon what Rusty had told me about hopping trains. I have to say, the knowledge I gained from those two Indians made me feel a whole hell of a lot more prepared for the tracks than I was before, yet the reality of it all seemed to freak me out more than I had been to begin with.

"…Amen," Father O'Leary said, gazing upon his decrepit flock as he finished his sermon.

Everyone followed the Father in unison, "Amen," and then we all rose from our knees and filed into line at the serving table on the east side of the room. Lost in my own thoughts, I almost forgot about the Indians. After grabbing a plate of food, I went out the back door to look for my new friends, and though I wasn't able to find them right away, I soon found them by following their laughter. They had set up some milk crates to sit on by the dumpsters in the far corner in the back of the church. When I reached them, they were each drinking a forty ounce bottle of malt liquor. Once they were within earshot I yelled, "Hey guys, sermon's over. What happened to praying to Big Bear?"

Rusty slurred out, "No, no, naaaah, we're still praying to the Big Bear, see," he held up his bottle so that I could read the label he was pointing to, and I felt like an idiot for not picking up on it to begin with. They were drinking forties of Big Bear Malt Liquor they must've picked up before they jumped on the train.

"Oh shit, you guys are hilarious! Well finish up and come get some grub while it's hot," I turned around still laughing as I shook my head all the way back into the church where I was greeted by Father O'Leary who was standing just inside the door.

"So, will your friends be joining us? I'm quite interested in hearing about this Big Bear. I'm assuming it's some kind of metaphor for Mother Nature or spiritual guide. After all, I've never seen you three here before, so I must assume you're just passing through," Father said, looking and sounding quite enthused.

I responded succinctly, "You're thinking it's like a creation myth, right?" trying to match his enthusiasm in order not to give away the fact that Big Bear was actually the devil's fire water.

"Yes my son, exactly. I'm quite intrigued because I spent many years with several indigenous tribes in the Amazon and other parts of South America as a missionary," he said while pointing down to indicate the south, "but never with our local natives here in the states which I've always regretted."

"Wow! The Amazon huh?" I was quickly losing interest in the conversation since I could hear my stomach growl for what was going to be anything but a five-star dinner, but a meal's a meal, especially when you're traveling hoboowise. "That must have been quite the adventure, I can only imagine. Well, if you'll excuse me sir, I'm starving," I said as I began to make my way over to the end of the line. However, I was abruptly thwarted from doing so when Father O'Leary quickened his pace in order to step into my path in front of me.

"Boy, you sure have good manners for a... Sorry, you have to excuse me, what I mean to say is, well, it's not often I am the recipient of such politeness. For what it's worth, you should be proud of yourself son... It's not too often we get a nice Catholic boy like you around here, good manners and all," and as much as I tried to misplace the pedophile priest stereotype from my mind, Father O'Leary's smiling lips and dripping starkness made it hard to shake such images from my mind. "What did you say your name was again?" he asked.

"ThomasJ, sir, like the Saint. Can we continue this when we've finished supper?" Unfortunately, it wasn't the kind of hint Father O'Leary was hoping for.

"Oh sure, I'm sorry to hold you up. Go get your plate and we'll continue this shortly," he said apologetically. I nodded before walking over to the end of the line where the Indians were standing. The bastards had beaten me to the punch.

"So how's ole Big Bear doing anyways," cynically bearing a beasts intent.

"Oh, he's doing," burping and giggling, Mouse answered with an equally cynical smile. "Tasty, the Bear's tasty."

Nearly laughing his way out of line, I propped Rusty up, keeping him from falling out of the free meal, "Keep your shit together man!"

"Yeah he says hi by the way," Rusty mumbled as he swung his back pack in front of him. He unzipped the main compartment and revealed that it held six more forties of Big Bear which were wrapped in a few items of clothing so as not to alert the clergy of their Big Bear Bullshit. "Got one with your name on it for when we split this joint," pointing at my still grumbling belly.

"Fuck yeah…" I hollered, finding immediate embarrassment in the Catholic hall. "I'm surely a lucky man to have met you gents," I whispered this time, "that's for sure. Well hey look, Father O'Leary is really adamant about catching you guys after supper and trying to convert you or some shit, so we'll have to split as soon as we can, or else you guys can kiss the next train goodbye."

"K, you help us get outta here and we'll feed you beer. Deal?" Mouse posed, slurring his plea in broken English. What a lightweight I thought.

"Deal," I said, continuing to whisper. We got our food a few moments later which we scarfed down as fast as humanly possible. I looked around, but could no longer locate Father O'Leary. I kept my eye out for him when all of the sudden, I felt a hand on my shoulder.

Expecting it to be Father O'Leary, I turned around to find some random bum mumbling something about surfing on Cheetos down slopes of chocolate ice-cream bars.

"Shoo fly shoo," I barked as I waved my hand at the pestering bug he was.

"ThomasJ?" I heard from behind me, and there was no mistaking Father O'Leary's voice.

"Yes sir, we were just about to use the restroom and then we'll be right back to discuss Big Bear with you. Where exactly are the restrooms?" I inquired, scanning the room for a sign.

"Right this way, it's just down the hall here," all three of us got up and followed him. The surfing bum began to follow us as well, but I successfully shooed him away once again. "I'll be right out here waiting for you," Father O'Leary stated.

"Fuck," Mouse blurted out. "I mean uh… sorry Father, I just remembered it's my uh. Um," he trailed off.

Rusty quickly came to his rescue, "It's his Mother, my aunt's, Birthday and he forgot to call her right Mouse?" It was pretty damn obvious he was making it up, but what the hell right? "Yeah, I forgot to remind you Mouse, sorry, my bad."

"Guys," I said as I walked through the bathroom door first. Inside were two particularly shabby looking gents smoking from a crack pipe in one of the door less stalls. I walked past them to the windows at the far wall, and as I opened one I said to them "I won't tell if you won't." They shook their heads up and down so violently I thought they'd come unhinged. "Good then. Rusty, would you do the honors? We have to make sure you can fit first," I said gesturing for him to squeeze his huge frame through the tiny window.

"You want me to fit through there. HA! Ain't gonna happen," he shook his head laughing.

"Well, either you give it a try, or you go back out there and risk having to talk to O'Leary which'll likely last hours. Hours man, hours of Catholic, religious bullshit. Do you really want to spend your night talking about God and lying about Big Bear? You choose," I said, but before I could finish he had already thrust one leg through the window frame. Shortly after, he had both legs out, and soon after that he was on the ground outside. He was followed by Mouse, and I was quickly behind. The Indians helped me out the window and I hit the pavement running. We ran down the path back to the train yard laughing our asses off partially due to Father O'Leary and the look on his face that we imagined he might have when he discovered that we had escaped his Roman Catholic grip, and laughing because of the pain we felt from running while impregnated with one of the foulest of meals any of us had consumed in a very long time. When we reached our boxcar I fell down groaning as I held my stomach, Rusty leaned up against the train car still laughing hysterically, and Mouse was throwing up about twenty feet back down the tracks.

"So much for a free meal huh Mouse?" I said, making him laugh even harder. In the distance, Mouse raised his arm in the air and flipped us off while he continued to ralph up his holy sacrament. Once we had regained our composure, we crawled into our car and stumbled to our respective corners. After stuffing myself at dinner and having a jog for desert, I passed out relatively soon thereafter while the Indians drank the night away. At one point I woke up to Rusty passed out, and Mouse who was talking to himself, "If you affix your eyes into a sort of audio squint and remain dead silent, you can almost hear the man's liver shriveling up like a prune," Mouse kicked Rusty gently as he said this, which Rusty replied by grunting back at him before slumping over onto his side. I laughed under my breath as I rolled my eyes before laying my head back down on my bag.

The next thing I knew it was light out again and the train was moving. Both of the Indians were still sound asleep on their end of the car. The sun was already in the sky, but it was still desert cold out. I had shivered myself awake, so I pulled a hooded sweatshirt out of my bag to put on. When I pulled it over my head I noticed signs of life coming from Rusty.

"Morning kid," Rusty grumbled as he sat up and yawned, "aaaaawwwwwwe, what time is it?"

"No idea, but if I had to guess, then I'd say it's about seven," I said as I caught the contagious yawn from Rusty. "Awwwwwwya, heya, if you wouldn't mind, I'll take you up on that beer now," hoping for a small, Big Bear miracle.

"For breakfast? You're crazy white boy!!" Rusty said as he leaned over and grabbed his bag which sat in between him and Mouse. "Here," he pulled one out and held it up.

I walked over and grabbed it from him as if any second he could change his mind and renege on his offer. "Thanks man, I really appreciate it. Can't beat a liquid breakfast," I said as I twisted the cap off and took a few chugs from the fresh forty. "MMMMMMMMMMMMM," I moaned, exaggerating my satisfaction. We rode all day making two stops for a total of three hours in layovers. According to the Rusty, the third stop was San Francisco.

"Well kid, this is where we catch our next ride into the wind. You take care of yourself, and be fucking safe," Rusty said to me. "We can't stress it enough man, get a traveling buddy next time, and if you can, try to at least get one for this journey. A friend, a girl, a hooker, a dog, it don't matter, just something with eyes and ears to watch your back." Rusty walked over to my side of the train and extended his hand. I shook it, and he pulled me with such force that I flew up off my feet, and he gave me a Big Bear hug.

"Ugh, well... Write me if you can," I squealed, barely able to get the sentence out as Rusty Can Feathers squeezed out what little air my lungs could hold. We had exchanged mailing addresses about an hour earlier to see where we'd both end up down the road, or in this case, down the tracks.

"I'll definitely write to you. You do the same, but make sure to wait a few weeks before you send anything," Rusty said as he let me down to the floor of the car. "Big Bear," he bumped his fist to his heart as he finished his goodbye.

"Big Bear," I repeated as I too bumped my fist against my chest, "and Mouse," I said as I shook his hand.

"Be safe kid and take care. Perhaps we'll see you on our way back up," he replied with half a smile, half because he looked sadder more than anything and half because he had so very few teeth. And just like that they were gone, and the train was on its way once again. I didn't necessarily feel sad they were gone, but I certainly felt that there was something missing from the car and the trip. The further I went down the tracks, the more I questioned myself. Did I make them up to feel safe? Were they just an extension of who I wished to be when I was a kid? I quickly diffused my doubts by pulling out the piece of paper that Rusty Cans had written his mailing address on, and seeing that it wasn't my handwriting, I was relieved. A few moments passed and I thought to myself, but what if I took on the whole other personality entirely and just wrote this myself, but in different hand writing anticipating this self-imposed interrogation? What if the other me was trying to trick this me into thinking the Indians really did exist? Man I need to stop doing drugs! I decided that I needed to let the paranoia go, it just wasn't productive. So what if I was the Indians? We, I, whoever it was, we seemed to have a great time together. I decided to take a nap.

After a few hours had passed, the sun had fallen low enough to shine into the car and land on my face so I awoke to the southern California heat turned up to full blast. Being in that boxcar was like being in an oven. I got up, stretched, and walked to the other end of the boxcar where the Indians had sat, away from the setting sun. I stayed up long enough to see the sun fully set and for one quick stop where we dropped off a few cars from the line. Once we were back on our way I took the opportunity to catch more Z's, and fell back asleep almost immediately.

I awoke to someone shuffling in the gravel outside of the train just a few cars down the line. We were stopped.

"Motherfu… AWWW!" a man was yelling in pain as sounds of pounding, thrashing, and violence filled the night air. I could tell by the sounds that followed that the fighting was moving quickly in many directions as if one or two guys were trying to get away from another larger group, until they were right outside my car. I decided I needed to see for myself exactly what was going on so I got down on my belly, and crawled toward the sliding door on the side of my car that just happened to be slightly cracked open.

I could see two men wearing black pants and black t-shirts with baseball bats beating on a transient looking guy. The bum was already down on the ground and by this point, no longer trying to defend himself. It appeared as though he had lost consciousness, yet they continued to beat him despite this.

"Holy fuck," I whispered as quietly as possible, apparently not quiet enough. One of the attackers stopped whacking the bum and looked up in my general direction. The unmistakable metallic smell of blood had filled the air that blew through my car, and for some, this can be hard to stomach. Though I wouldn't go so far as to say that this was something I was absolutely accustomed to, I can say that blood, guts, and gore no longer holds the same shock value with me that it once did. I had witnessed some bad scenes, from knife wounds to crushed skulls, to quarts & quarts of blood. If anything, it was sad to me, but never shocking. The guy I thought had heard me stood there breathing heavily for a moment before he finally spoke to his cohort, "Enough, I think we got another one over here," he pointed his bat at the boxcar next to the one I was in. I calmly crawled back to the corner and listened to them walk past. I took the opportunity to open my bag as quietly as possible and pull out my mace, and as I listened, I heard both of them jump into the neighboring car. While they were occupied scouring the car next to mine, I slid through the crack in the door of my car. I could hear what sounded like running water coming from the other side of the car, and I knew that where there are rivers, there are cities. I hopped in between the cars and walked over to a chain-link fence. Right next to me laid the bum, bloody, swelling, and whimpering what were likely his last few words. He had a small knife sticking out of his chest. This made me think back to what Rusty had told me about the vigilante gangs of yuppie white racists that supposedly roamed the Los Angeles train yards looking for degenerates and non-whites to beat and sometimes even kill. Though I had no escape plan, I was certain that I wasn't going to hang around and try to prove, nor debunk, Rusty's urban myth. As soon as I reached the fence I knew exactly where I was because of the river I was looking at. The L.A. River has a pretty distinctive riverbed made entirely of concrete which runs the length of the city. I jumped over the fence and slid down the slope hoping I wouldn't be detected by the men in black. They may be vigilantes, but I wasn't any fucking Robin Hood, and call me selfish, but I preferred staying alive. When I made it to the bottom of the canal I could hear the two guys back on the hill, and just as I started to walk parallel to the river I could hear the distinct rattle of the cyclone fence.

"Oh fuck look!" one of them yelled. I could hear them begin to climb the fence and I knew they had spotted me. I ran as fast as I could, jumping the river which was no more than six feet wide, making a B-line for the fence on the other side. Being small and only carrying a lightweight backpack, I knew I had the advantage of speed over the guys behind me, plus I had a good hundred yard head start by the time they had made it over the fence. I had cleared the next fence faster than a greyhound on meth chasing a rabbit with a t-bone steak tied to it. I had a good lead on the guys when I heard one of them yell "FUCK! …MAN, FUCK IT!" At first I thought this may have been a trick, so I didn't stop running for at least ten minutes. Finally, I was so out of breath that I collapsed upon a little patch of grass that lay between the street and the sidewalk, narrowly missing a fresh smelling pile of dog shit.

Thank God, I thought to myself between breaths, I eluded both of those, huff, two pieces of shit, ugh, bum killers, and a pile of dog shit. Thank all that is holy and lucky in this world! Because I was so unfit, which I was painfully unaware of, I was seeing stars. I lay on my back with my bag under my feet to make the blood flow back to my head.

"Hey kid, you alright? You got a dollar?" standing over me was a shirtless crack head scratching his neck as he bent over me one second, while retreating a half step back the next. He repeated this two-step dance every few seconds or so, likely the result of drug and alcohol abuse.

"Where's the rave at huh?" I inquired as I stood up, wiping the dirt and blades of grass off my backside.

"Huh? Just, you got a dollar sir? I carry your bag for you, say three blocks?" he reached out the hand that wasn't scratching the skin from his neck.

"I got it, here, fuck off!" I handed him a dollar. He nodded before he fled down the sidewalk the way I came from. I kept walking in the opposite direction I had been running in, trying to distance myself as much as possible from the tracks and the river. I eventually came upon Atlantic Boulevard, a main road, and without a map, I had to trust my instincts, so I turned right and walked down the boulevard for ten minutes until I hit East Compton Boulevard. Great, I thought, a small white kid in Compton just a few years after the Rodney King Riots, a punk ass, bum looking white kid at that. If I wasn't a target of robbery, which I shouldn't have been in the shabby, thread barren clothes I was wearing, I was definitely a target for roving groups of violent gang-banger wannabe types, particularly teenagers and even some preteens. Awesome. I figured if I headed towards the beach that the real estate would get more expensive, and the neighborhoods would likely get whiter and a little safer. Unfortunately for me, I was all turned around so I ended up walking deeper into the ghetto. However, in retrospect, it didn't matter which way I went, I was fuct from the get go. The only safe way I could have possibly walked was right along the river, all the way to the ocean, and after seeing the beating on the tracks, I thought it was safe to assume that everyone in L.A. at that moment was the enemy.

"Heya way, where you think you're goin?" I heard behind me. I knew by the sound of the guy's voice that I must have been in a Hispanic hood.

"Not sure. Just got off a freight train, and had to escape some psycho white boys beatin bums outta boxcars. How bout you, where you think you're going? What kinda question is that anyway? Do I look like I'm headed in the wrong direction? Do you happen to know where I'm headed right now?" I turned around half way through my pissy sounding response to see three gangsters as they erupted in laughter.

"You for real kid?" asked the same cholo that spoke before.

I stopped walking backwards so they could see that I wasn't scared of them in the least when I answered, "I'm a fucking Coño loco! Got it?" I spit out with an evil little grin which made them all laugh even harder.

"Ok, Ok," the biggest one said as he flinched his head up as if to indicate away from where we were. "Where the fuck you headed?" sounding a lot less ominous.

"Honestly? No fucking clue, I was headed West. I figured there'd be whiter, more Coño loco friendly neighborhoods out that way," laughing by myself this time, trailing off into awkwardness.

"It's pretty fucking late to be walking round here man. You should come with us," the bigger one continued. "I'm SosimoC, but call me Guns, this is Coker," he pointed at the shortest one in the group, "and this here is Ranks," slapping his buddy's back.

"Latin Kings huh?" able to read the telltale signs that each banger possessed.

"Something like that. Yo, we're headed west, seriously, why don't you just kick it with us?" Guns posed. "Come on way, you're comin with us. We'll take you to our place, it's kinda like a…" he said with a smart looking grin as he paused to determine the proper description. "… a clubhouse, but you gotta do something for us," he looked at Ranks and they laughed together with Coker joining in shortly thereafter. "You'll see what I'm talking about when we get there," he patted my back and pushed me lightly down the way I was headed.

"I'll see huh? Well it better not be something pussy like a keg-stand or sing karaoke or some gay shit," and even though I had found myself walking with three Mexican gangsters in Compton at two in the morning, I tried not to sound scared. No big deal right? I thought to myself as I imagined who would come to my funeral, what if they never find my body, and I'm just considered missing forever and ever and they never give me a funeral believing that it would be a sign of giving up on my search. Down a few blocks, a right turn, then a left, four blocks further down, then another right, or was that a left I should be taking on my way back. I was losing my way back to East Compton Boulevard by way of pure fear. Another roscoe and I'm fuct, I thought.

"Here we are way," Coker said. Way, why do they keep fucking saying that? I thought to myself, must be some kind of Spanish thing. Coker opened the gate to a white picket fence in front of a house that looked abandoned. Most of the windows on the ground floor were boarded up, except for one on the porch they used to gain access to the place. Something told me that no one was paying rent here.

I'm Super fuct, I assured myself, these guys could do whatever they wanted to me and no one would ever know. I walked into the house praying for something miraculous to happen to secure my salvation. It didn't however.

"Fucking shit, it is hot as fuck in here!" I whined, wiping the sweat from my forehead. It was a particularly hot day for L.A., and it was near boiling inside their clubhouse.

"No shit man," Ranks said, "here, come up this way," and we walked up the staircase that greeted in the foyer. When we reached the top we walked down the hall to a bedroom that held a couple of sectional couches, a long folding table with chairs around it, and a bunch of milk cartons stacked up with a giant flat screen TV standing on them. There were two fine looking girls sitting on one of the couches watching cartoons. When I looked at the TV to see what they were watching I noticed it was being powered by an extension cord that was running out a window which I walked over to, and followed the cord to a telephone pole where it looked like someone had tapped into the city grid illegally by connecting the cord to the transformer way up the pole. How the fuck did someone figure that shit out, I wondered. Better yet, how'd they survive the installation?

"Turn that shit off and get our guest here a drink, fucking lazy putas!" Guns said as he slapped one of the girls on the back of the head.

"Jesus!, I'm getting up you fucking Punta biatch!" the girl who Guns slapped wailed as she got up and walked over to an ice chest that was sitting in the corner of the room. I found it hard to keep my eyes off of her since she was so unequivocally, absolutely gorgeous. She had huge tits, a nice slender figure, and a pretty face. Not bad, I thought to myself, and thanks for wearing the bikini. She must have been anticipating my visit I thought, before realizing I was gawking at the poor girl.

"You like huh?" Coker clenched the back of my neck hard enough for me to scrunch my shoulders up as he nodded at the girl, who was by now pulling out as many beer bottles as she could hold. "Well that shit's mine. You can look, but no touchin ése," he laughed, "her names JuanitaB."

She walked over and said "Here, grab one," with about eight beers pressed up against her tits.

"I'll get em," Coker said as he walked over and grabbed four of the beers. Sitting on a couch, Ranks found the remote, and was flipping through the channels.

"So little man, if you want to kick it with us, you gotta let Guns give you a tattoo with this here," Ranks laughed as he put his feet up on the table and nudged something on the edge of it with his foot. I couldn't quite see what it was because it was across the room, and from where I was standing, his head was in the way of my view. I half expected to see a prison style gun made with a motor from a portable cassette player and a guitar string as the needle, so I was surprised when I saw that they had an actual tattoo gun on the table. I figured, what the hell, I'll have quite a story to tell if I were to in fact get a tattoo from these guys, no matter how ghetto it turns out to be.

"Alright then, why the hell not," I walked over and picked up the gun to get a good look at it. "So, that why they call you Guns?" He looked at me and shook his head no and everyone in the room but me laughed. It was the kind of laughing that made me think they had something awful planned for me, instantly shattering what little confidence I had in them. I figured it was either let them tattoo me, or likely get my ass kicked to the street at night, by myself, in the middle of South Central L.A. Not a good place to be if you're me, a small white kid.

"Whatchya want kid, you got any ideas?" Guns asked me as he started to prepare a section of the table by laying out a blue medical-type paper, "cause I got plenty of ideas if you don't."

"Fuck, I have no idea man…" I said, I better think of something quick, I thought, or I could end up with something really shitty.

"How about an arm band or some shit? You know this is only the second tattoo I've ever done right?" Guns said laughing, the girls giggled too.

"Fuck you, seriously?" I howled, "I mean, wait just a second, I think I got it! You ever seen a lip tattoo before?" I asked as I pulled my lower lip down.

Making a chirping sound by sucking his teeth, Coker barked from the back of the room, "You're fucking crazy kid!" He had walked back to the cooler before he added "Another beer kid?" holding one up.

I slammed the rest of the one I had before I answered in the affirmative, "Sure man," which I quickly followed with a throaty burp. I mused over the fact that I was getting another tattoo by a Mexican gangster, great! As Guns got ready, I made sure to down as many beers as I could before I let the needle touch my lip. I sat quietly as I justified my decision to myself, this way they'll think I'm crazy tough or some shit, you know, kind of like retard strength, and again, the amazing story I'll go home with... The elation I felt was abruptly followed by the realization that, wait, this is going to hurt like hell! You idiot, what did you sign yourself up for?!?

"Get your ass over here kid," Guns pointed to the couch, "get outta his way bitches," he waved at the girls who were sitting where he wanted me at while we did the tattoo. "Alright then, I want you to lay this way with your head over the armrest here," he pointed at the end of the couch where he had set up his tattooing station. I came over and lay down just like he told me to and waited for him to get everything ready. In no time at all he began tattooing me. I had my lip pulled down so the skin was stretched and tight. My face vibrated and tears fell out of the corners of my eyes.

"You crying bitch?" Ranks asked from the other couch. Guns stopped so I could answer him.

"No asshole," I argued, "it's like popping a zit on your lip man, it just makes your eyes tear up no matter what," and as I said this with a half cocked mouth like a retard drooling black ink down the front of my shirt because my lip had gone numb. This caused the whole room to erupt in laughter, "yeah laugh it up, I don't see any of you with the balls enough to get your lip tattooed. Assholes!" I quipped as I began drooling more, causing everyone to laugh even harder. It took Guns a good two minutes to regain his composure enough to continue the tattoo. Just a few short minutes later we were finished.

"Yeah, well this'll put more than just hair on your chest man, it'll put oak in your cock," my tattooist laughed. "All done ése," he wiped the excess ink from my lip.

"Damn, that was quick," I mumbled, trying not to drool anymore.

"Yeah, here take a look," Coker handed me a little mirror, and judging by the white streaks staring back at me, the thing had definitely seen some blow in its day. Also staring back at me was the word "Whiskey" backwards on my lip, and I laughed my ass off at the sight of it.

"Perfect," I said with lips swollen and a funny little smile.

"You're one crazy ass kid ése!" Coker slapped me on the back. For the rest of the night all the way until the next morning when the sun came up, I partied in the clubhouse drinking beers and snorting coke until we had all passed out scattered throughout the house. I found a closet where I could shut out the California sun which is surprisingly brutal that early in the morning, especially to someone in my state. By the time I woke up it was about five in the afternoon, and everyone else was already up watching TV, drinking beers, snorting blow, and causing a ruckus.

"Fucking shit, do you guys ever quit?" I said as I stumbled into the TV room where I had received my Whiskey lip the night before. I was absolutely exhausted and the only reason I was up was because they were being so damn loud. It sounded like there was a marathon coming through the house.

"Hey he's up!" Coker hollered.

"Bout fucking time," I heard from the couch as I caught a beer that was thrown to me.

As I opened it up, I cried, "Jesus fucking Tits!" and I poured the whole beer down my throat.

"Damn kid! Hey Joker, toss him another beer," Ranks said.

"Yeah, I'll have a few with y'all, but then I gotta be on my way," I said as I caught another beer. "I gotta meet up with my sister in Pasadena," I sipped on the second beer, feeling slightly bloated from the first. "Someone got a phone I can use?" I asked as I pulled the notepad from my bag that held my sister's phone number.

"Here," the cuter of the two girls held out her cell phone, "you can use mine." She was.

Despite being told not to, I couldn't help but flirt a little, it's simply in my nature, and at the time, it seemed pretty harmless anyway. "Oh thanks, I appreciate it. Say, I don't think I ever caught your name?" I extended my hand as I looked deep into her eyes with a big smile on my face knowing damn well I heard her name the night before.

"JuanitaB," she smiled back as she shook my hand. I let her go and moved out into the hall where I'd be able to hear my sister a little better on the phone.

I feared she wouldn't answer a call from a number she didn't recognize, but I was in luck, "Hello?" In addition, I hadn't told her or anyone in my family for that matter that I'd be coming to L.A.

"Hey sis, it's TommyJ," I jokingly said in an excitedly high pitched, chipmunk-like cartoon voice.

"TommyJ!" she laughed as she tried imitating my toon voice, "You're calling me from an L.A. number, you down here?" she inquired, straightening her voice out upon the realization. I went on to tell her the whole story about jumping the trains, Big Bear, and my Whiskey tattoo. I made a point to let her know I probably shouldn't be on this particular phone too long, so she gave me an address of where she lived and told me she'd be there in a few hours when she got off work. I wrote the address down, got some general directions from her, and told her to expect me around then.

"Love you sis, pray the Ghetto Gods deliver me safely," I begged. My goodbyes were once again in the chipmunk voice, followed by her laughter, and finally the dial tone.

I walked back to the TV room and handed JuanitaB her phone, "Thanks Love," smiling as I looked intently into her eyes for a second time. It was pointless, just a little fun really. "Any of you fuckers got a car and wanna give me a ride to," I flipped to the page in my notepad where I'd written down my sister's address and read, "Marigold Street in Pasadena?"

"No way ése, you're on your own," walking over to me with a pissed off look on his face, Guns continued, "in fact, you can just get the fuck outta here," he pushed me towards the door almost hard enough to lay me out on my ass. The same feeling of being Fuct that I had when I first got to the house had returned. He pushed me again, this time sending me on my ass through the doorway spilling my beer on the ground. "Oh shit! I'm sorry man, I was just fuckin wit you," he abruptly apologized, and as I slowly regained my composure, he laughed at the genuine fear splashed all across my face.

"You asshole," JuanitaB threw her nearly empty beer can at Guns which barely missed his head, "give the boy a fucking ride, Punta!" She continued as she walked over and began punching Guns in the arm.

He dragged her over to the couch and threw her down, "You want me to give him a ride huh?" he said just before jumping on her.

Between kisses she muttered, "Yeah…gi… give the kid a ride," and they continued to make out.

"Alright, alright… I'll give the little man a ride," Guns laughed as he rose from the couch. "Shit, you alright gringo?" he walked over to the cooler grabbing a few beers, tossing me one. "We'll head out after this one." He went on to discuss something with JuanitaB and Ranks in Spanish which I speak very little, and understand even less. I still wasn't entirely comfortable with these guys, and for all I knew, they could've been planning to drive me somewhere remote where they intended to use me for target practice.

After we finished our beers I grabbed my bag and followed Guns downstairs. "You're gonna shit yourself when you see this car little gringo," he told me as we walked out the back of the house into an alley that ran through the middle of the block in between the backyards of the houses. The house they were living in, squatting in really, had a garage that was only accessible via the alley. "Wait out there," Guns demanded, pointing to the alley as he and Ranks entered the garage through a side door. I followed his orders and walked into the alley. As the garage door slowly opened, Guns Started the car, revving up the engine which, by the sound of it, was a carbureted Chevy big block. At idle I could hear that it had a good sized cam meant for racing, so I knew the thing must've had all kinds of other aftermarket parts. Sitting in front of me was a beautiful bright orange, 1969 Chevy Chevelle. It sat on big flat street slicks in the back and smaller tires in the front. This raked it up in the back making it quite the mean looking beast.

"Oh hell yeah!" I yelled over the rev of the engine, which Guns was pushing to at least six thousand RPM's. Exhilaration doesn't even begin to describe the feeling that made the hairs stand up on my neck and arms. I crawled into the back seat of the pretty lady, safely assuming Ranks had shotgun.

"You ready for this boy?!?" Guns yelled as he revved the engine up as loud as he could. Before I could answer, he was peeling out sending clouds of smoke behind us as we fished tailed down the alley ever so slowly until the tires caught and we went flying down the block. The torque was so great that I felt as though I was riding in the trunk. Ranks flipped on the stereo, blasting Spanish rap that bounced off my back from the thumping bass sending shivers up and down my spine. The only lame part about the Guns Express was that it cut our travel time in half, and we were in Pasadena before I knew it.

"Here you go," Gun said as he pulled the car up to the curb, "that's your sis' according to the address you got," he pointed at a house across the street.

"Awww, that sucks, I wish I could've ridden around in this little more. Tsss, oh well…" I chirped as Ranks got out. I pushed the seat forward and followed him out, "So uh, thanks for letting me crash, and for the Whiskey lip, and the ride. You guys are alright," and that was the last I ever saw or heard from them again. I could care less really, I'm just glad to have escaped with my life and my wallet. As I walked up to the house, Guns peeled out in the Chevelle behind me taking off down the street. This was followed by yelling from a few of the neighbors that happened to be in their front yards doing yard work or what not, demanding they,

"Slow down for Christ's sake!" I knocked on the front door of my sister's house, and while I waited for an answer I looked over a few yards down where I caught a glare from one of the neighbors that had yelled at Guns and Ranks. I smiled, waved and finished it off with two thumbs up close to my smile like a true asshole. I turned to the door as I heard someone coming down a set of stairs inside yelling "I got it!" The door opened and standing there was a girl about my height but a little thinner, around the same age, with beautiful, natural red hair, fare skin, and a few light freckles. She was absolutely gorgeous, though I am partial to Gingers.

"Hey there, I'm Thomas, and you must be my sister's roommate? She never told me your name," we shook hands.

"MaryJ," she said as she smiled, "CarrieB's in the shower," she said as she continued to melt me. I stunk pretty bad, so a shower was exactly what I needed, definitely not the most ideal time for me to be meeting Ms. Convivial MaryJ. "Here, come on in," she said as she moved into the front hallway clearing the way for me to enter.

"Thanks," I took a few steps in, swinging my backpack off of my shoulder so that it landed on the ground in front of me. "Nice place you got here, it's just the two of you right?" I asked as she led me into the living room.

"Yup, just the two of us," she smiled at me from behind the couch that sat between us. "Here, make yourself comfortable, can I get you a drink? Water, beer, wine, you name it, we got it."

"Yeah, a beer'd be great. Thanks love," I charmed on.

After disappearing into the kitchen for only a few seconds, she returned with two beers in hand, "One for you, and one for me," all smiles. She began to walk towards the other side of the room, which I assumed she did so she could show me something. "Why don't you have a seat, or wait, better yet," she stopped dead in her tracks and turned her whole body around without moving her neck, "maybe a tour is in order?"

"Sure, let's see whatchya got here," I arose from the couch I never quite sat down on.

"We'll start with our lovely kitchen," she began in her best tour guide voice as I followed her through an old, Moorish style arch, the kind that is curved up with an upwards point in the center. All the entryways in the house, except the doorways, seemed to have the same arch.

"I love this style," I pointed straight up at the arch I was under as I walked into the kitchen.

"I do too!" she said from her kitchen which had a 1950's appeal to it. The first few things to strike me were the old range and matching refrigerator, as well as the curved countertops, and 50's era decor. I looked around for a few seconds before MaryJ directed me into a hall opposite the way we had entered the kitchen. She turned around as she walked backwards, "Let me draw your attention to our holy windows," sounding quite enthused. At first I thought she meant holy as in they had holes in them, however, the windows she was referring to were stained glass scenes from the bible, and it was almost as if we were entering a church. They didn't appear to actually have the outside on the other side of them. They looked like they had been retrofitted into the wall by having indentations cut out so that the windows lay flush with the drywall to its sides. Lights had been placed behind each window to give the effect that sunlight was in fact shining through. However, the sun had set over L.A. at least an hour prior to my arrival, so it was quite obvious the light was artificial. "Isn't this awesome?!? The owner of the house, our landlord and good friend, saved these from a Catholic Church that was being torn down a few years back on the east coast. I think it was Boston, but I'm not a %100 sure. It was during the pedophile priests' scandal when all those people came forward accusing all those priests of molesting them when they were just kids." She walked over to the wall and flipped a light switch, turning off the lights behind the stained glass windows so that I could look upon them in a different light.

"Wow, this is a really killer idea," I exclaimed as I examined the windows. "Not a bad idea at all. So tell me about your landlord?" I asked as she slowly followed me down the hall from window to window.

"Oh GeorgeP, he's great. He's a transplant from the Midwest, a farm boy turned city slicker working for a financial firm downtown. Rich," she said enunciating the word rich in order to make it apparent that he was quite well off. She showed me where the bathroom was, took me down to the basement where they had a pool table, and finally ended the tour with her bedroom. And in typical female fashion she apologized for her "really messy" room which was, by any guy's standards, immaculately clean. Ending the tour in her room huh? Possibly a sign of things to come. I thought. I had an overwhelming urge to throw her down onto her bed and jump on her, but I knew if I was just a little more patient, good things would come. Anyways, CarrieB was finished with her shower and was just opening the bathroom door. "TommyJ's here!" MaryJ yelled just in case my sister wasn't decent.

I spent the next week mostly hanging around the house when the girls were at work, venturing out on little journeys every now and then to get supplies for the rest of my journey which I planned to continue within a week's time. At night I partied with the girls and their friends. I suppose we were celebrating my visit, or just using it as an excuse to get wasted and go wild. I finished my stay at their house by fucking MaryJ, and leaving in the middle of that same night while both her and my sister were asleep, avoiding the goodbyes which I dreaded almost as much as moving. In less than an hour I was back on a southbound train, Mexico or Bust.

---

10. Running on Empty

The train I was on made its last stop in San Diego. I walked
directly across the border into Tijuana with a non-existent plan. I
came with little less than the design to be accepted, another piece
in their community, another piece of shit. I saw the disabling,
backwoods, third-world, with no real plans of pulling any do-gooder
Harvey Milk maneuver, no pulling of the community together type-a-
shit, because lord knows I can't help from putting my cock out there
on the line for the betterment of numero uno, and numero uno alone.
The only real goal was to get into the drug trade with the idea that
after I had worked my way up the Cartel Ladder, so to speak, I'd
eventually gain access to all the free drugs I could handle. I will
refer to the various Cartels simply as the singular "Cartel," so as
not to divulge which particular border dwelling Cartel I'm referring
to for various, self-evident reasons, but mostly because I value my
life. I got out there, and within minutes I was in the Game of
games. It literally took me minutes to meet all the right people,
and begin making all the wrong choices. Aside from the border boys
who were selling trinkets (garbage really), and what seemed to be an
endless supply of Chiclets, my first encounter with the locals was
at my choosing, at the shadiest place I could find, squalid from ear
to ear. It wasn't the seediest place I could find, but I was trying
to find allies, not get kidnapped or killed. I didn't speak a lick
of Spanish other than Por favor, Gracias, & no abla espanõl, so I
needed to find English speaking locals if I was going to find my
way. I walked up to the bar and ordered a cerveza, which is another
word I suppose I knew. I sat at the end of the bar which was a wise
choice after discovering that the bartender spoke English. We got to
talking and I asked him all about the neighborhood the bar was in,
as well as the city of Tijuana. He could tell I wasn't just another
American kid looking for a Brothel or cheap drugs, and I made it
apparent that I had more serious, long term intentions in mind. He
explained how the city worked from the Cartels to the local, corrupt
government.

After a while he asked if I'd stick around and I waited while he
called someone he said could help me out in my endeavors. I agreed,
and drank another cerveza, this time, one that was on the house.
About a half hour later a local looking thug walked through the
door, up to the bar, and started speaking with the bartender. They
spoke for a minute in Spanish before the bartender pointed at me.
The thug thanked the bartender, walked over, and took the stool next
to me. The bartender came over soon after and gave him the same kind
of beer that I was drinking.

"So I hear you might be looking for work?" the thug asked in perfect
English.

"I am, TommyJ's the name," I shook his hand, waiting a second for
him to tell me his, which he didn't. I continued "Soooo, I'm new in
town, planning on staying for a few months, so I suppose I'll need
some cash. You got any work? Any kind of work, I'm game," I said as
I took a drink from my beer.

"Is that right Gringo?" he let out a small laugh.

"Yup," I smiled.

"Ok, we'll see what you got. I'll give you ten minutes to bring me
someone's wallet. Not your own of course, and it's gotta have cash

in it. Starting," he looked at his watch, "Now!" he roared as he
slammed his hand on the bar and began laughing as I arose from my
perch and exited the bar. Jesus, this guy's not fucking around, I
thought to myself. As I ran out of the bar I continued thinking,
this has to be the most interesting job interview I've ever had, but
I had to clear my mind and think fast about where I was going to get
a wallet, or else I would miss out on what I believed to be the
opportunity of a life time. Think TommyJ, think!

I ran down the cobblestone road in front of the bar looking every
which way for an opportunity to present itself. I couldn't stray far
from the saloon, so I decided to circle the block. I had made it
three quarters of the way around when I stopped on the corner.
Walking by me were guys in construction gear, so I followed the
trail of them down two blocks to the site of a new building that
looked about half way complete. It was lunch time and all the
workers were pouring out into the local restaurants and bars leaving
the site nearly vacant. I stood there for a moment and waited until
it appeared as though there were no one else around, and I ran into
the site, quickly locating the Foreman's shop, which I entered and
began searching through. It took me no time at all to find a safe
disguised as a filing cabinet. Thank my lucky stars, the damn thing
was not only unlocked, it was slightly ajar. Inside were stacks of
what looked like important documents that I pulled out onto the
floor below. Underneath the papers was a steel box that was also
unlocked. Inside I found a stack of cash. I grabbed the Mexican
money, which looked like play money to me, placed all the papers
back the way I had found them, and snuck out the back of the
construction site. I checked my cell phone and I had less than two
minutes left to return to the bar with a wallet which I was still
missing.

I ran down the street frantically looking for a men's apparel store.
I was in luck, less than three blocks from the bar was a small,
cowboy store. I ran inside and quickly found a wallet which I
purchased by throwing down more than enough money on the counter
for. I bolted from the store stuffing some of the money into the
billfold portion of the wallet, and the rest into my pocket. I ran
into the bar thinking I had made it on time.

"You're late!" the thug said as I took the stool next to him. "Did
you get one?"
he asked me.

While trying to catch my breath, I managed to grumble, "Oh yeah, and
I'm not late either, look here," I breathed heavily as I pointed to
the bar clock which had its minute hand just clicking over to the
ten minute mark "see!"

"Ok, ok, I guess you made it. Now let's see if you even got
anything," he turned to me and waved his hand to move things along.

"Here," I handed him the wallet which was stuffed with Pesos, "I
wouldn't say it was someone else's per say, but it is a wallet," I
laughed as I waved the bartender over. I ordered a beer with some of
the money I had just stolen.

"I must say kid, I'm impressed," he bellowed, pulling the money out
and counting it. He made two neat stacks, one of which he slid over
to me, "here's your cut. Now you have to tell me, how in the hell

did you pull this off?" Both he and the bartender looked at me intently as they followed the story I told them.

"No fucking way, I'm calling bullshit," the bartender said as he dried glasses with a towel that looked like it had recently been the substitute for a lack of toilet paper in the bathrooms.

"No fucking way you're drying those glasses with that towel. Remind me to only drink from the bottle when I'm here," I said, and the Thug and I laughed at the bartender who just sneered at us. "It's true, I really did it just the way I told you, why do you think the wallet's still got the price tag on it? And why would the thing be empty except for the money huh? Plus I paid you for my first beer with American dollars, don't you think I would have used Pesos if I had them like I do now?" I finished my beer and threw some of my new found wealth onto the bar.

_____

For the next few months I worked for the Thug I'd met in the bar, whose name wasn't in fact Thug at all, it was PedroC. My work primarily consisted of exploiting tourists by either getting them drunk or drugging them with roofies, and taking their money, jewelry, and any other valuables they had once they had passed out, but we refrained from taking anything from anyone in the community. In fact, we actually gave back in small ways. If we caught wind of struggling merchants, we would extend a hand by giving no interest loans, or we simply gave them money expecting no repayment. This way we'd have the community on our side should we find ourselves in trouble.

PedroC worked for a local Cartel, and his job was to earn cash by creating smaller groups of "workers." For the first few months my group consisted of me and a local kid, JavierF, who was a few years older than me. Later, we added JoseR, another local about JavierF's age. We were expected to bring in a certain amount of money each week in a purse that I delivered to PedroC at the same bar where we originally met. As well as performing our tried and true scams, our duties also included creating new ones. I conjured up my favorite scam one night after work while I was drinking a bottle of tequila. When I reached the end of the bottle, my cohorts were pressing me to ingest the worm that taunted me from the bottom of the bottle. After a moment of slight meditation to calm my nerves and stomach, I tilted the bottle up, and gave the bottom a good slap, which dislodged Mr. Worm from the bottom of the bottle. Down the hatch he went, gulp. One drunk little worm into one drunk, giant maggot.

"Cannannimblalalism." I squawked loudly, but barely coherent as I laughed, falling from my stool to the filthiest bar floor I have ever stepped foot upon.

"Jackass!" JoseR said laughingly as he grabbed my arm to help me up. I sat back down and JoseR and I brushed off the peanut shells and other gross shit that had stuck to me. I did the drunk wobble, leaning this way and that for the next twenty minutes or so, threatening to make another plunge to the floor. Luckily I was able to precariously balance myself with enough finesse to remain seated, and as I sat there, I pondered the worm. I thought about how it was usually the tourists, not me, which I would see eating the worm in the bar, and somehow I correlated all of this with a kind of robbery by using what was already there in Mexico, in Tijuana.

"I've got it!" I yelled excitedly as I raised my arm into the air and pointed to the ceiling which threw my balance completely off, causing me to fall once again to the floor.

"Holy Jesús," this time it was JavierF helping me to my feet, "you gonna be ok you crazy ass gringo?"

"Yes, in fact, have I got the job for us?!?" I sat back down for just a second. "Wait," I got up, "let's go back here and talk." I pointed to the back corner of the room, "and grab JoseR."

My compadres sat across from me with contemptuous looks which was filtered by their drunken humor. Though as violent as we were in our everyday operations, somehow the three of us were happy drunks, go figure. "So ear it iz…" I exaggerated my elocution, gradually becoming clearer, and clearly serious in my tone as my grift ripened. In my drunken state I explained to them as best as I could exactly what our new scam was. It was the scam of all scams as far as all the other scams were concerned, and in theory, it was the most beautiful idea I had yet for us. We planned then and there to carry out the trial run of my con the very next day.

_____

The sun was up well before we arose from our sweat covered pillows, sweat that covered everything really, all consuming at all times like having a perpetual fever. As I made it down the hall to the bathroom, I slapped two of the five doors I passed, JavierF's & JoseR's, they stayed in the same cheap hotel as I did, a hotel we all came to fall in love with, though we could do without the "in-betweens" as we called them, the things living in the walls: rats, roaches, and bugs of all sorts. What we really feared was the fever we risked getting from the rats that bit us in our sleep from time to time. These days the only thing I fear at night is my cat Eva attacking my feet rather than some rat whose name I don't even know. Once we had showered and dressed, the three of us converged upon the café on the corner across from our hotel, dutifully following our daily routine. We each ordered without consulting the menu. We remained absolutely quiet while we were either reading a newspaper or staring off into another dimension. Long ago we had all agreed not to get into any in-depth conversations until we had taken at least two sips from our morning espressos. Today's café compadre silence lasted three minutes, forty-six seconds, and three sips of espresso.

"We all have the same understanding of what we're doing today correct?" I started.

"Si," they both replied.

"First we must get our supplies, that is, our uniforms. Any ideas of where we can procure such items?" I inquired.

JoseR took a long sip from his espresso before replying, "I know a guy a little east of here. I'll pay em a visit after our meeting here."

"And I know the perfect place for you to find your marks," JavierF said pointing at me. "We should see how the market down on Santa

Maria is," sipping from his espresso with his head tilted, peering over the top rim of his glasses at us.

Everything fell into place beautifully that first day, and despite my doubts, we were able to acquire everything we needed to pull off our newest grift. It was also brought to our attention that the marketplace had recently seen a rise in American visitors ripe for the picking. After getting all of our supplies, figuring out the best location for our grift, and running through a few rehearsals, we were finally ready to execute our plan.

The day we decided on was an especially humid day, so I made sure to wear light clothes. After meeting up at the café, I parted ways with the guys and headed towards the market on Santa Maria Street. I began my part in the grift by trolling around the market, stopping at every few booths to eaves drop on conversations of each American group I came upon, until I found one that was looking for something the market couldn't offer, specifically: drugs, pharmaceuticals, Cuban cigars, or really, any other sort of black market item you could imagine. Luckily, Americans are the largest consumers of drugs in the world, so it took no time at all to find my first victims. The group consisted of a boyfriend and girlfriend, and their male companion, all in their twenties.

"I couldn't help but overhear that you were looking for some good pot, and that you weren't able to find anything but… how'd you put it, dried up crap?" I stepped into the groups little circle as I interrupted their debate of where they should go to find the kind buds.

"Oh yeah? You know where to get good weed around here?" the friend of the couple asked.

"I've been living here on a student exchange program for three months now, and I've found a connection with shit that rivals some of the best weed found in the States," I lied through my teeth. "I can hook you up if you'd like."

"Hell yeah! I told you we'd find someone!" the friend nearly yelled with excitement as he lightly punched the boyfriend on the arm.

"Awesome, I'm AliceW, and you are?" extending her hand to me.

"JimmyJ," I said as my alias shook AliceW's hand, then her boyfriend's, and finally their friend's.

"MattH," the boyfriend replied.

"MarlyP," the friend.

"K, follow me," I said as I began walking through the middle of the market towards the center of the city with the three Yanks in toe. "Yeah, the guy lives just a few blocks down. We'll ring his buzzer and then we'll all go up to his place and if it's cool with you guys, we can chill there for a little bit. He really hates it when people only come in for a minute because he doesn't want his neighbors getting suspicious of him," walking just in front of them I turned my head every few steps as I spoke to them.

"Oh yeah that's totally fine. Do you think it's cool if we smoke a bowl up there?" MattH requested.

"Of course, in fact, it's highly encouraged, no pun intended," I said trying to lighten the mood and gain their trust with my cheesiness. They all laughed as they followed me deeper into the trap. "Just a little bit further now," I said as we continued walking, and by this point we were more than eight blocks from the busy marketplace. "It's actually quicker if we cut through here," I pointed to an alley that was about twenty feet ahead of us. Holding my breath, I turned into the alley hoping that I wouldn't get any resistance from them regarding my dark alley suggestion, of which I got none. Half way down the alley there were a couple of dumpsters against the wall to our left, and just before we passed them JavierF and JoseR appeared from behind the last one. They were both wearing la Policia uniforms, each brandishing large night sticks.

"Alto!" JavierF shouted, which meant stop in Spanish. The Americans and I stopped in our tracks and raised our hands above our heads.

"¿Tu habla espanol?" JoseR gestured for us to move back towards the wall next to us.

"My Spanish really sucks, how bout y'all, how's yours?" I asked the group.

"Ours too," AliceW answered for all three.

"No problem," JoseR said in a thick accent. "You are trespassing here on crime scene, so everyone against wall with legs and arms out," his voice grew louder and fiercer as he spoke. We all lined up facing the wall as JoseR began by searching AliceW.

"This is bullshit, we haven't done anything," I said turning my head back as I watched JoseR search through AliceW's purse.

"You're free to go. You go now, just you," JoseR said to AliceW, throwing her purse down the alley the way we came from.

"What the fuck, what about my friends," she demanded from the policia.

"You want jail? You get the fuck out of here now!" JavierF took a few steps toward her swinging his billy-club in the air.

"AliceW, just go down the street a few blocks and wait for us there, we'll figure this out, and be there in no time" her boyfriend pleaded with her.

"Fine," she cried before running down the alley out of sight.

"Now, off clothes," JavierF said partly lifting MattH's shirt with his club.

"What?" MattH asked.

"Get your fucking clothes off now!" JavierF's club hit MattH in the leg with a thud, sending him to the ground writhing in pain.

"Fine, fine, just don't hit us. What the fuck do you want?" I plead with them.

"You get clothes off, give us all your money," JoseR said. Once we had all of our clothes off except our underwear, the Policia proceeded to go through every pocket, taking all of the money, and anything else they were interested in.

"No jail, right guys?" MarlyP said quickly receiving a club to the small of his back which sent him to the ground whimpering.

"You shut it!" JoseR shouted as he clubbed him once more in the back. The whole incident took less than two minutes, and before we knew it, the Policia had disappeared down the opposite end of the alley and out of sight.

"What the fuck just happened?" I cried as I gathered my clothes from the ground.

"Guys!" AliceW came running down the alley.

"I thought I told you to wait down the street?" MattH scolded her.

"They took all my fuckin money, what the fuck?!?" she exclaimed.

"Mine too," I looked like I was checking my pockets which were actually empty in order not to give me away as a cohort in the theft, "a lot better than jail. Jail here is fucked!"

"Yeah, they got all my cash too," MattH wailed, "what the fuck what are we gonna do?"

"I don't know about you, but I'm going back to my place and forget about the two thousand pesos I just lost. I'm so sorry this shit happened guys. Though, I have to tell ya, this kinda thing isn't a rare occurrence." I apologized, "This is the fourth time this has happened to me, and usually I don't carry that much cash around, but I was planning on getting myself some weed today so... Fuck! Well… uh, good luck to you, or I guess I should be saying better luck to you. See ya around," I began walking down the alley hoping for a clean break.

"Wait…" AliceW said from behind me, I thought they might start asking more questions and I'd be there forever, rather, she ran up and said, "Safer travels my friend," she said as she hugged me firmly.

I hugged her back, "You too, all of you," and I was on my way. I walked a total of nine blocks from the alley, stopping every few blocks to smoke a cigarette and make sure I wasn't being followed by the Americans I had just been robbed with. What would have normally taken me ten or fifteen minutes took me nearly an hour to walk to. When I arrived at the place that my crew and I had designated as our post-scam meeting place, my two Policia friends were waiting for me with big grins on their faces.

"You are a fucking Gringo Genius! I love you so right now! We get married and have family ok?" JavierF was ecstatic to see me, immediately embracing me.

"He's right man, this is our best yet. This idea of yours is gonna make us millionaires!" JoseR joined our hug.

"To the Bar!!" I yelled breaking off from the embrace, jumping up and down waving my arms for them to follow me. On our way to the bar we split the trove we had just made off with which totaled around $250 each. Just two steps into the bar under our hotel we exclaimed our intent to buy the bar a round which caused a roar of cheers from the local drunks and new faces alike, instantly making us local heroes.

The "Tourist Meets Policia Grift," as it came to be known, worked so beautifully that it remained the number one money maker for us, and our most used con for many months after its inception. PedroC was more than thrilled with the amount of money we were bringing him, so much so, that he took me aside one day and an earnestly said, "Mr. TommyJ, you keep this up, and I'll have to see what I can do bout introducin you to my bosses, see what they think boutcha," pausing to grin from ear to ear. "Whatya say huh?" he slapped me on the back and let out a laugh "huh?"

"Hell yeah! I mean if it means climbing some kind of ladder, and makin me more money, then hell yeah! When you thinkin I could meet these blokes?" I inquired.

"I dunno, maybe a few weeks. You just keep it up with this new con of yours and we'll see," slapping me on the back, breaking off our embrace. "Speaking of this new con, one of these days I'll have to sit you down and pick your brain about the mechanics of it. I hear it's genius in simplicity, or was it the other way around, simplicity in genius?" Pausing to rub his chin and stare off as if formulating his own brilliant scheme. "Any which way, I'm completely intrigued by what I've heard about the great, what did you call it, Policia Grift?"

"Yeah, that's it," JoseR chimed in from across the bar.

As time went on, I met a few Lieutenants, the guys two steps below the Cartel head. They seemed to like my moxie and they made a point of letting me know it too. I was getting promises of bigger and better jobs and responsibilities in the very near future. According to PedroC, I was working my way up in the ranks of the Cartel faster than any Gringo ever had, even faster than PedroC had, the once proclaimed Cartel Prodigy. Meanwhile, like all good things, the money making Policia Con I had created wasn't going to go on forever, and frankly we had already pulled it off way more than we had originally planned, risking our safety and the security of the Cartel. Consequently, the adrenalin pumping through our veins when we pulled the con had become like a sip of water, it just didn't pack the same punch as it used to. It was time for time to change, and for my story to move on. Accordingly, all thanks to a young American Mother and her seven year-old son, it did just that. I discovered the Mother first, hovering behind the outer booths which bordered the marketplace, the same marketplace where I met my first victims, and quickly spotted the kid and a way to strike up a conversation. Like any other victim, I tried to hang within her general vicinity hoping she would make it easy for the grift to start by simply coming to me to ask for my help in procuring some dope, pills, or what have you. She didn't, so just like any other victim I approached her by making small talk about her kid, gradually leading our conversation to the fact that I had major connections in Tijuana, and I could get her whatever she wanted, and what do you know, she wanted some OxyContin. I told her I knew a guy who had some right then, but I'd have to make a phone call to make sure that we could still meet up. I had learned enough Spanish to tell JoseR on the phone that I had a new Vic, and which alley to meet us at which he agreed to after explaining to the Vic that we had to meet the guy a few blocks away, her and her son followed me the four short blocks to the alley.

Once there, I could see a large group of people gathering at the end of the alley to watch about four or five actual Cops detaining two guys. I knew there was no way it could be anyone other than my two Compadres, but I decided there wasn't any risk in walking by the scene because I figured the cops had nothing on me. When I got closer I recognized one of the people in the front of a crowd that had gathered outside of the alley as one of our victims from the week prior, and they were pointing in my direction yelling something in Spanish to the cops. I wasn't going to stick around to figure out what they were yelling, so I turned around and began to sprint back the way I came. the last thing I remember was running around the corner and seeing a billy-club come full swing from around the corner which apparently hit me square in the forehead and laid me out on the pavement.

I awoke in a cell where I spent two weeks with six other guys that didn't speak a lick of English before I was finally allowed to make a phone call. It was a no brainer, I had have to call PedroC, my only real connection in Tijuana that could do anything for me.

"Allo?" he answered.

"PedroC, it's TommyJ."

"TommyJ, I was hoping to hear from you. I've already got a guy working on your case, and you should be able to meet with him in the next few days. Just hang tight and we'll get you out of there. I'm sure this goes without saying, but make sure to keep your mouth shut like we talked about, alright Gringo?" he advised me.

I nodded through the phone and hung up. He was right, my cell was opened just a few short days later and I was led to a room hear the entrance of the prison. In the room was a light skinned Mexican that I assumed was my attorney, though, he was dressed like he was heading to a soccer match. Great, I thought, PedroC got me the cheapest lawyer he could find.

"Have a seat son. My name is Freedom, your Freedom. Say it with me, your Freedom," the man said in a serious tone. Reluctantly, I said it with him. I'm fuct, I thought, this dipshit's never getting me out of here. He sounded more like he should be teaching grade school, not working in law. Then again, this was Mexican law we were talking about.

"PedroC sent you? Seriously?!?" I whined.

"Yes son, I'm the one who's going to get you out of here. Now first things first,
what have you told them?"

"Let's see," I began thinking back to that fateful day. "After they
knocked me out and I woke up in here, they wasted no time in hauling
me into a room almost as stingy as my cell, and began their little
interrogation. I don't think they believed me when I said I didn't
speak Spanish because they kept yelling at me for what seemed like
hours before they brought in an interpreter, an English speaking
Cop. I told him that I ran because there was a local crazy lady I
recognized from the neighborhood screaming at the cops at the scene
in Spanish and pointing at me and I've heard all about the shitty
prisons here and I just didn't want to end up in one. I told them
that I hadn't broken any laws since I've been here and I was just
scared, that was all. Yeah, but they didn't believe me and they kept
asking me all kinds of questions about the scam and different
Cartels, which of course, I have no knowledge of," I put my palm
next to my eye to hide the wink I sent Senor Freedom.

"Good, you keep that story straight, and we'll be just fine. PedroC
will be at your trial on Tuesday and he'll take care of everything
as long as you keep it zipped. Capeesh?" my attorney assured me.

"Gotcha," I stood up and shook Freedom's hand. "Tuesday then...when
is Tuesday exactly, that is, what day is it today, I've lost track?"
scratching my crotch.

"Sunday son, this is Sunday," knocking on the door to alert the
guard of his departure. I remained seated and thanked the forces
that be for the little blessings that seemed to have kept me afloat
all my life.

Tuesday rolled around and by then, I smelled like something fiercely
resembling that of a whale carcass that had become bloated from
weeks at sea, and had since washed up on the beach to slowly cook in
the extreme heat of the Mexican sun. Smoked TommyJ was a somewhat
comforting smell to myself, but not so much to my celly's. A few
days before I was to depart to my trial, the guard who spoke
English, Romano, came to my cell to instruct me on the various
procedures involved with Tuesday's events. Before he left, one of my
celly's told Romano in Spanish to translate something for him.
According to Romano, he told me that, "I was a piece of shit Gringo,
that I smelled worse than anything he had ever smelled in his life,
that I needed to stay as far away from him as possible, and I'd
better sleep on the floor under the bottom bunk, or else he was
going to beat and rape me." Romano found this hilarious, and began
laughing hysterically after telling me what he had said. I asked him
if the guy was either part of any Cartel or if he was in la Eme, the
Mexican Mafia. Between laughs, Romano managed to answer no to both
questions, and continued to laugh his ass off all the way down the
corridor as he exited the cellblock. As soon as I couldn't hear his
laughter anymore, I turned to the cell mate that Romano had
translated for and rushed at him so fast he didn't have a chance to
react. I began to punch and kick him as fast as I could, and once he
had fallen to the floor I grabbed him by his hair, dragged him over
to the bars, and began slamming his head into them until his eyes
were so far back in his skull, he was staring at his soul. I
employed the help of my other cell-mates to help me drag him over to

the wall farthest the bunks and prop him up so that he appeared to be sleeping with his back against the wall.

That night as I lay on the lower bunk, I became curious what it would be like to lay under the bottom bunk on the floor, so I crawled off my own bunk and laid down on the cold concrete floor. Though somewhat uncomfortable, it was cooler than sleeping on my own bunk, and I thought about how funny it was that if I had just adhered to my cellmate's demand to lay on the floor, I would have been asleep a lot earlier that night. No longer worried about being attacked in my sleep as I had been every night prior, I was the one who became feared, so it took me mere minutes until I was sleeping like a baby.

As Tuesday approached, I began believing more and more that I was going to walk out of that prison a free man that very day, and not only that, I would also have a better reputation in the outside world then when I had left it. The Cartel was sure to recognize the loyalty and toughness I displayed during the whole incident.

The day after I gave my roommate the beating, the guards came to throw our paper bag lunches to us as they did every day, and they noticed that the Celly I had beat up was covered in blood, as was the ground near the bars. A little later a group of six guards came into the cell, four to block us from running out, and two to drag our bloody cellmate out. I was surprised when Tuesday rolled around and there still hadn't been an inquiry into the assault. Luck, it would seem, was finally coming back my way.

Just before the proceedings began, PedroC and my Freedom had a few private words just outside the courtroom doors. I didn't know it at the time, but PedroC had private words with many folks in the court that day. My trial was quicker than going to court for a speeding ticket, and there was only about two minutes worth of dialogue between my attorney, excuse me, my Freedom, and the Judge. In that short of time they were able to discuss the charges against me, and how I was pleading, which was not guilty, after which time the Bailiff came and escorted me over to the Judge's bench.

"Gracias," the Judge stood and extended his hand to me which I gladly shook.

"You're free kid, so gracefully thank the Judge, and walk out of here with Your Freedom, got it?" My Freedom told me, speaking as clearly as possible.

"Gotcha," I followed his instructions adding a large smile and bow for the Judge, who in turn bowed with a smile, and before I knew it, I was outside breathing air that was, refreshingly, a lot less putrid than the stagnant air that hung like death within the prison I had just left, hopefully for good. I took a few deep breaths, accompanied by a few sighs of relief, like I had been drowning and these were my first gasps of air after too many minutes of complete despair. As I stood with My Freedom outside, PedroC approached.

Shaking my Freedom's hand, "Thanks, you'll hear from us again when we need you," handing him an envelope stuffed full of cash that PedroC had slipped me just moments before. "Hopefully later than sooner," I laughed.

"Adios," he nodded, shaking my hand. That was the last I saw of him, but I have forever had My Freedom from that day forward.

"Adios," I was all smiles that Tuesday.

"We go make Party!!" PedroC jokingly broke his English as he slapped me on the back.

I jumped up and down in utter excitement "PedroC…"

"Yeah boy?"

"…I have to piss," I squealed as we both laughed feverishly.

When I got back to my hotel, PedroC told me to grab my most important belongings, and meet him at the bar below. I had a big hockey gear bag that I had been dragging my shit around in since I got to Mexico, and I filled it up with just about everything that would fit in it. When I got to the bar PedroC had two shots of Patrón waiting for me, and after downing both, I ordered a beer.

"We're moving you up and out kid. Tonight I'm taking you to the Compound, where you'll see some familiar faces. JoseJ, JesusI, IstenzaK, just to name a few…" PedroC said, catching me totally off guard with the news.

"Lieutenants huh, this some kind of base? Cartel Headquarters?" I laughed.

"Yeah, pretty much. Aside from the Lieutenants, which you've already met most of, you're gonna meet some guys that are not only the Cartel heads," I was instructed, "but also sit big with a certain Prison run gang that rules southern California. The Compound is a little bit of a drive, so we'll head outta here pretty soon."

"Well don't worry bout me, I know to keep my mouth shut unless spoken to," I said, genuinely enthused.

"That's just the beginning…" he continued, going over the Cartel's specific traditions and rituals which were quite akin to that of a college fraternity from the states. However, I paid close attention as it would likely prove to be valuable information in maintaining my newfound position as a loyalist to the Cartel. One such ritual was to take place my very first night at the Compound, apparently, one that I was expected to take part in, and once the Cartel extends its hand to you, you don't refuse it, that is, unless you plan on waking up without a head.

As we approached the Compound, PedroC told me to take a look around to get an idea of all the money and power the Cartel had. Fittingly known by the locals as the "Great Wall of Mexico," the twelve foot white washed walls that enclosed the Compound stretched to the hills as far as the eye could see. The outer gate had two towers on each side of the road with two separate guard stations at both the bass and the top of each tower. As we pulled up to the gate, we were approached by five guards, each carrying assault rifles which they had fixed on our heads with laser sights I could on the others. There were some words in Spanish exchanged between PedroC, the driver, and one of the guards, none of which I could understand.

"This is where we get out," PedroC said, gesturing for me to exit the taxi, which promptly turned around and sped off down the road we had just come in on. I felt as if I was leaping off the freedom cliff, my own man, writing my own story, yet I couldn't help the one reluctant right leg that, rather than it's leaping lefty brother, tried to stay as a permanent fixture upon the cliff because the butterflies circling my stomach had brought up the fact that there's always a chilly breeze during the freedom fall. Gotta get your feet wet if you wanna swim, I thought. "They're bringing up a car for us," PedroC told me as three of the guards led us through the first gate which had opened just enough to let us walk through. Less than a moment later a white Mercedes drove up to the outside of the second gate where it turned around in a small, cul-de-sac like circle. Once the first gate had closed, the second one began to open, stopping so there was just enough room for us to walk through as the previous gate had done. We got in the car which was driven by a guard who spoke with PedroC the whole journey up to the Compound's main building, a large house. As we drove in the darkness, we tripped motion-censored lights which gave away the location of several out-buildings that lay throughout what must have been well over a thousand acres of land enclosed within the Great Wall.

We reached the mansion where we were greeted by a group of six Butler looking gentlemen that grabbed our bags from the trunk, and lead us into the house which had a foyer that rivaled that of some of the greatest hotels of the world. The architecture was both borrowed from the tried and true influences of the past, as well as a tasteful contemporary feel to it, with archways and railings that ran on modern curves leading your eye always up. At the highest point was a stained glass ceiling that I imagined must have been even more beautiful during the daytime when the light shown through it. I promised myself that, if permitted to, one of the first things I would do the following day was walk out the front entrance when I went for a stroll on the grounds. I still wasn't completely privy to the Compound rules or exactly what my role was at any time. Further into the house we were each taken by our assigned Butlers up separate staircases, waving to each other as we parted.

My room, I later found out, was one of the smaller rooms, but it was so amazingly ginormous that I felt like royalty. The bedroom itself was larger than any house I had ever lived in, and it was filled with a number of great commodities, such as: a giant flat screen TV complete with an X-Box and DVD player, all of which was hooked up to a premium surround sound system; remote control blinds; remote control A/C and fans; a bar with a remote controlled, virtual bartender you could program to make specific drinks; and to top it off, a bed that must have been two California Kings fused together on a wooden canopy frame with silk drapes hanging from above that sloped down the sides of the bed. Amazing doesn't even begin to describe this room.

I was jolted from admiring the room by a knock on the door and a strong, clearly British voice on the other side identifying himself as my personal concierge for the night. "…you are requested in the Rectory sir."

The what, I thought, as far as I knew then, a Rectory had something to do with religion. Religion? What the fuck was he talking about? Was there a church on the property? Were there old Catacombs tunneling under the house from the old days? Better yet, why isn't there a whiskey neat in my hand, my mind wandered off the same cliff I had plunged from earlier, and I would have been lost in the void if it weren't for the Mexican sun pushing thirst upon me like wrinkles on a raisin.

"Dear sir, please fetch me a whiskey neat, whatever you may have teetering on the top shelf, and let them know I will be down in just a moment," I said making the best snoberish voice I could which made me laugh, however it quickly lost its flavor to the blank stare I could feel my Concierge striking me down with.

"It's quite hard to find without my guidance sir, may I suggest that I first lead you there and fetch you a whiskey after you have made it to the Rectory?" he replied speaking loudly so I could hear him through the door.

"Well…" I began to object.

"I insist sir," he commanded, and I began to feel more like a prisoner than a guest.

With my nostril hooked on the moon, "very well then," I opened the door and gestured for my mansion sitter to lead the way. He nodded before showing me the way, and I followed him for what must have been a half a mile through halls, corridors, and breezeways before we finally arrived at the house staff's lavatory.

"Oh, you meant lavatory, I heard you wrong," I laughed, but why would I meet them in the shitter?

"Just follow me sir…" and into the empty server's bathroom we went, which smelled surprisingly quite rancid for such a luxurious home.

"Mmmkkkk…. Sooooo, why are we here?" I asked three steps in. My question was met with silence as the Concierge walked to the far wall, turned to me, and smiled.

"Here sir," he said, almost rolling his eyes out of his skull. He pulled down on the lever that releases the paper from the paper towel dispenser in a rhythmic pattern of six or seven pulls, and suddenly, the stall behind him began to slide in a circular motion revealing a spiral staircase. He nodded towards the stairs, and I began the accent.

"Your whiskey will be awaiting you sir, I'll see you on the other side," he said as he repeated the same pattern of pulls on the paper towel dispenser's lever, and the wall moved back into its deceptive position. When I reached the top of the stairs I found myself in a large hall where an awe-inspiring ceiling with beautiful frescos painted over the entire thing loomed over fifty feet above me. Much like a large attic, there seemed to be a lingering scent of old people, specifically Chanel Number Five & Old Spice, cigars, and thankfully, not of insulation and dust. We walked to the end of the hall where a set of double-doors labeled "Rectory" opened for us from the inside. Sure enough, the one empty spot at the enormous table in the center of the room held a bottle of whiskey with my name literally written where the label had been ripped off. Could this be for real, I asked myself. I figured out how the Rectory got its name when I looked up at the vaulted ceiling and saw the fifteen

foot tall effigy of Santa Muerte, the Saint of Death, hanging
directly above me. How blasphemously beautiful, I thought as I gazed
into the Saint's black eyes, eyes that were as dark as I imagined
her holy soul to be. The Lady of Shadows before me was placed in the
Rectory to intimidate all who are in her presence, and her creator
did so by giving her long, dark flowing robes, and a forward lean.
It was as if she was coming for me with the scythe she held fast in
her hand, and the menacing smile she still seemed to make despite
having no skin. She already knew the world she symbolically held as
a globe in her other hand was hers, and like any good servant, I
didn't dare make eye contact. A venerated, holy witch, worshipped by
millions of no-good-doers, and spat upon by men of a cloth that
safely make their rulings against her thousands of miles away.

What transpired was a wicked silence that seemed to sit with me and
listen to the strange ritual that ensued. It was the traditional
ritual for newcomers PedroC had told me about, what he called "an
induction of new-blood." I was symbolically beaten and ridiculed
through acts carried out on a sacrificial snake that slithered
freely upon the large table everyone was sitting at. The snake was
kept on the table by boards that had been nailed to the edge of each
side, creating a topless box. Each was allowed a bare fisted punch,
swipe, chop, or whatever they chose to inflict upon the poor
serpent, and as it spit venom, some spit back.

———————————————

The next thing I knew I was waking up in what appeared to be some
sort of dungeon like cell, greeted by the sun that was peeking
through a set of bars inside a small windowsill above me. I had a
vicious hangover that was nothing like the typical whiskey induced
shitfest I was used to. No, I thought painfully, there's something
different about the melody of pain pounding out its simple tune in
my head. There's definitely something unusual about the rattle of
the chains clasped around my neck, I ruminated. It took me the
better part of the morning to admit to myself that the pangs of pain
I felt weren't all that bad, and the truth was that it was much less
dour than usual. I had simply overstated the severity in my initial
thoughts for the day because it had been a very long time since I
had been hung over. I suspected that I was slipped some sort of
sedative during the ritual the night before, possibly in the bottle
of whiskey I drank, the one that had my name on it, making sure no
one mistook it for their own.

The last thing I remembered was staring at the snake's carcass after
his life came to a violent end in front of me. As I rose to my feet
to get out of the scorching sunlight that was burning a hole through
my soul, I felt another searing pain in the small of my back. When I
reached back there to investigate, I found a large, raised scab
protruding from an area covering nearly the size of my hand. What
the fuck is that, I thought, feels like some kind of burn.

I found the cell door slightly ajar and made my way out into the
adjoining hallway. Even though I felt brutalized, pissed-off, and
confused, I was happy to find the scent of bacon and eggs beckoning
me from somewhere in the house. As I began searching out breakfast,
my smile quickly flipped to a frown with the prospect of having to
walk a half mile or more through the maze of the Compound to find
breakfast. After wandering the halls for nearly fifteen minutes, I
finally had cold toast and barely warm eggs sliding down my throat,
but I was thankful none the less.

After breakfast, I made my way to my room with the assistance of a butler. Back in the luxurious room I didn't even get to sleep in, I immediately jumped in the shower before getting dressed and ready for the day. The drug I had been slipped in the Rectory was still quite prominent in my system, so I lay down to rest for a moment, but quickly found myself passed out once again. While deeply sunk in the trenches of R.E.M., an influx of sweaty twitching came from sporadic nightmares that I thankfully had a butler to awaken me from. After shaking me awake he informed me that I was being summoned to the southwest gardens. With anything but haste, I stumbled my way outside to my caller, a man whom I had met the night before, Lt. Guevara. The Lieutenant was sitting on a bench in a garden surrounded by box hedges.

"Senõr, have a seat," gesturing to the empty space on the bench to his left. "We talk, ok?" he demanded with a smile.

Sitting down ever-so-gently I replied, "Ok Senõr, wuz up?" I said in a strained voice, sighing heavily from the pain in my back.

"You have fun last night?" more smiles.

"From what I remember…" I sighed again, "it was mostly disturbing, Senõr, and it feels like a gator swung around and hit me in the head with its tail. First thing this morning, I realized…" adjusting in my seat, my smile quickly adjusting to a cringe, "that is, I discovered I was drugged during the ceremony last night, roofied or something. I had no idea how I got there or how it happened, but I awoke in a cell with a huge sore on my back." This drew a look of confusion from my compadre so I clarified further, "a burn on my back, like I was branded or something."

The Lieutenant's eyes slightly lit up in recognition, "Oh si, si Senõr, you're marked in," sitting up slightly and turning to point his ass towards me so he could lower his pants to show me a branding of his own. It looked identical to the one on my ass, and it was on the same spot on his back as well. "You're one of us, and now it's your turn to, what you yanks say, pull your weight, prove your worth," he said looking at me through colored enthusiasm, behind deadpan browns. The Lieutenant went on to explain some of the Cartel's history and some of their ethics, values, and traditions through tales filled with metaphors. It was like listening to an American Indian tell tales at a camp fire, not those of a drug kingpin. I tried my best not to fall asleep while I rested my chin upon a fist that attached a knee to my elbow, however I was shamefully unsuccessful. It didn't take long before I slid off my fist and smacked my head against Lt. Guevara's shoulder.

"Oh! Oh! I'm so sorry! I'm just so wrecked from last night. All that booze and involuntary drug intake," which was met by Lieutenant Chuckles snorting between laughs that were so profoundly obnoxious they could have shot a nose through a gallon of milk.

"No, that good, that just mean we did our job too well. You should feel lucky though, sometimes newcomers have to take part in another kind of ritual altogether, one where you have to give traitor or enemy of the Cartel a Glasgow Smile," he said in broken English, and with more laughs at my expense. Expense, I pondered, I hope my ass doesn't become infected and then I have to go to some shitty Mexican hospital where they cut out a large chunk of flesh because they don't know how to properly deal with infections from burns. But hey,

at least I didn't have to cut some poor guys face up. I had
successfully scared myself awake for the rest of our conversation,
which was a good thing, because I was barely aware of his transition
from lecture to instruction. One second he was finishing a story
about the Chupacabra and its association with the hot dryness that
blankets the plateaus in the region, and the next he was telling me
specific dates and times I would be working in tunnels that the
Cartel had recently excavated. He went on to give me the specific
locations of where the tunnels began in Mexico, and where they ended
in the U.S. I immediately developed a rough plan that I was sure to
forget within the time it would take to find a pen and paper. Seeing
the funny look on my face after announcing the longitude and
latitude of one such tunnel, the hilarious Lieutenant Guevara
reached into his shoulder bag and not only produced more laughs, but
a small notebook as well.

As he went on to reveal my future operations within the Cartel, I
flipped through the notebook which had been meticulously
personalized to cover my day to day activities for the next year.
The reality of the importance of my contribution to the Cartel had
become frighteningly clear, so I felt it prudent to interrupt my
fearless leader so that I could go "drain the main vein," and
"splash some hopefully clear water upon my fuzzy face," I said as I
summoned my Butler for a Piggy-Back ride.

"Butler!" I gestured for him to come over and turn around, jumping
on his surprised back. The Lieutenant cackled as Mr. Butler began to
run aimlessly in every direction with me gingerly mounted upon his
back. With an aching, almost concuss head, and balls that were being
crushed and nearly torn with every jerk and bounce, I stuck a stiff
finger into the right jugular of my butler-beast. "¡Andale bitch!" I
shouted as I pointed towards the main house, this time drawing
laughs from a group of Cartel heads that were walking nearly a
quarter mile away on the vast front lawn.

After my bareback adventure to the restroom, I returned to the
gardens and found that the bench was vacant. I walked up and sat
down anyways and found an embroidered handkerchief protruding from
one of the hedges with "Lt. OFCG" sown into the center in golden
threads. "Lieutenant something, something, something, Guevara I
presume," I said to myself, chuckling. I sat there for another hour
examining the notebook, and peering off into the garden wondering
what happened to the Lieutenant. Though, I spent most of my
remaining time in the garden wondering if such pleasantries would
continue to follow one who spent most of his time chasing so many
unpleasantries. I tapped my lips repeatedly as I pondered TommyJ,
the Mule.

––––––––––––––––

A week after my arrival I was packing what little I had brought to
the Compound with me in anticipation of my departure. I received
numerous gifts from almost all of my bosses, most of which was cash,
as well as some very beautiful Mexican antiques and jewelry. After
my butler retrieved my luggage, I followed him down the stairs to
the main foyer where Lt. Guevara and a few others we're waiting to
say goodbye and send me on my way. A few handshakes later, I was
back on the road headed north. The trip back always seems a lot
quicker than the way there, and in no time at all, I was back to my
border town where I got my start in the Cartel's drug trade hustle.
I suppose that made me a soldier because the Cartels were all at
war. The only difference between that of this war and say WWII, is

that this war has very few alliances, and there are actually more people dying each day.

The streets were packed for El Día de los Muertos, the festival of The Day of The Dead. Before I got back to my apartment, I stopped along the boulevard near my place at a few street merchant carts where I picked up a skull mask and some other festival trinkets. When I got in my place and turned on the light, another light bulb went on above my head. I decided it was the perfect time to rob the corner market down the street that I'd been eyeing for months. Today was perfect because I could wear my mask when I robbed the place, and I wouldn't have to take it off until I was clear from any danger. What's the clerk going to say to the cop, that I was wearing a Day of the Dead mask? I thought to myself, Good luck finding me, the streets were filled with guys my same size wearing the same kind of masks. It was so perfect that I wasted no time in marching down the street and robbing the store blind. With a few extra hundred bucks in my pocket, I celebrated my promotion within the Cartel at three separate clubs that very night.

For the next few months I was a drug mule. I had access to a series of tunnels that stretched from a town just inside the Mexican border, under the border, and into San Diego. Most of the openings came up in the crawl spaces of homes that were either owned or controlled by my Cartel. I was the perfect mule because I was young, white, and fit which meant I could carry greater quantities of dope and for great distances than most of the other mules. The tunnels were fairly narrow, but they all had electricity with running lights throughout, so I had no problem navigating them for eight to ten hours, six days a week.

In two months time I made $65,000 running under the border, but the lack of human interaction and the strange effects the tunnels can have on a person drove me to abruptly quit. I knew I couldn't just go to my Lieutenant and say "Hey, I've had enough, I'd like out," because I knew "out" most likely meant out in a body bag. My last day consisted of making a run north to pick up payment from a client. When I arrived at the end of the tunnel, in one of the safe houses in San Diego, with the earnings I had made as a Mule and the other various jobs I had done for the Cartel taped to my legs and abdomen, I told the three soldiers I was greeted by when I arrived that I was hungry, and I was going into town to get something to eat before I headed back south through the tunnel. Once I was far enough from the house I hailed a cab and rode to the airport where I bought a one way ticket back home to Portland.

"That's it?" Caribou asked, looking astonished.

"What do you mean?" I inquired.

"Well, shit, I thought there'd be some big climactic end to your time in Mexico," she said with her hands out, expecting more of the story to be handed to her.

I laughed, "Well, not all the stories have movie quality endings. This is real shit that I went through, and there's no point in embellishing any of it. Well, not too much." I said laughing again. "I think it's spectacular in its own way. I mean for Christ's sake, how I even survived Mexico is beyond me," I shook my head.

"It is spectacular, but I wanna know more about your time as a Mule," she begged.

"It was what it was, a job and that's it. Though I saw my share of drugs, money, guns, and human trafficking, all in all, it was pretty boring stuff really. I mean, I don't know what else to say. It's a time and a job I'd rather forget about," I replied. Having nothing more to say on the subject, I continued where I had left off…

After finally arriving back home from what my friends and family thought was an extended train hopping trip, I found a place to stay with my good friend JakeH and his Dad, DaveH. I was still on the outs with my mom so she still wasn't allowing me to move back in with her, and I refused to live on the streets anymore. To be honest, draping a tarp between two pine trees deep within the confines of an old growth forest sounded like another adventure I would have likely enjoyed, however, JakeH was the one who put the offer to stay with him on the table, and he refused to allow me to stay on the streets or in a forest somewhere. The fact that I was willing to do chores, as well as pay a small amount of rent every month, made my presence more of a blessing than a burden in both his and his Dad's eyes. As long as I carried my weight, his dad was more than convivial with me. He often rolled joints for the three of us to smoke, let us party, and even led us into some pretty crazy shit from time to time.

While I was living there, we threw some pretty epic parties, especially for being only sixteen to eighteen years-old. There were two huge parties in particular that JakeH, our friend MikeC, and I put together that were particularly insane. The first big one was when we were fourteen years old. We had invited nearly a hundred kids over, most of which brought at least one friend with them. We had a DJ spinning records, two kegs, all kinds of booze, and lots of drugs. I had prepared for the week by purchasing fifty sugar cubes dosed with LSD to sell to party-goers. I couldn't help but indulge in the cubes as well, and I ended up having a blast. Everyone went berserk when they arrived, flying out of the house, running in streets in every direction.

The cops just said, "Alright party's over," and they left just as quickly as our highs. Thankfully, they didn't ticket us or throw anyone in jail.

The last big party we had was the summer after graduating high school when we were eighteen. Like the last party, we had kegs, DJs, and drugs, but this time we had even more people. A kid showed up to the party with fresh mushrooms he said he had picked at a dairy field near the beach, and I decided I just had to have them. They were all wet and mushy so the texture was absolutely appalling, making them almost impossible to swallow. They were so utterly repulsive, that I'm gagging as I write this. MikeC and I decided it would be funny if we got some obscure, smut porn to put on the TVs during the party, so the day before the party, we went to a local porn shop. After thoroughly searching the store, we settled on a film with Germans shitting on each other, and another video that was primarily comprised of scenes of midget women getting railed by average sized men. We also tried to rent porn with autistic people in it, which I can't believe they actually had, or that it's legal, but the clerk said that the one video they had like that was stolen a few weeks earlier.

We waited at the party until the room with the big screen TV was packed full of people, and with a remote, we turned on the shit porn from the back of the room. In stereo, seventy-two inches of German's shitting on and in one another was literally splashed across the screen. Girls began screaming, gagging, and lunging towards all possible exits. It was quite the hilarious scene, and on magic mushrooms, it was twice as hysterical for both MikeC and I. Meanwhile, at the exact same time, I had employed the help of another friend, RickG, to play the midget porn on the smaller TV in the downstairs game room where a good number had also congregated.

The most interesting thing about this party had nothing to do with porn, rather it had to do with a fleece jacket MikeC happened to be wearing that night. To understand why the jacket was so important, I must first divulge some earlier debauchery of ours. By thirteen years old, MikeC, JakeH, and I had been sneaking out of our homes at night once our parents had gone to sleep. Once free, we'd meet up to drink, smoke cigarettes, smoke some pot, drop acid, or both, and steal our parents' cars which we'd drive around throughout the city. Ultimately, we graduated to stealing other people's cars, but mostly we did what is known as Jockey Boxing, an opportunist's robbery. Jockey boxing meant we'd break into cars and steal whatever was inside. The best items we ever lifted were a laptop and a $5,000 projector that we sold to a guy on the internet for $2,500.

A few weeks prior to the party, MikeC and I were out jockey boxing, and on the very first street we visited, we found an unlocked pickup truck. Inside we found a book of CD's and the fleece jacket, both of which we grabbed and quickly departed.

The next day was Monday and while MikeC was in class he overheard some kids talking, "Hey man, did you hear about (so-and-so)'s truck?"

"No man what happened?" the other replied.

"Somebody broke into it and stole his CD's and his fleece jacket. Yeah, but they didn't take his stereo, or the rifle he had stashed behind," the story teller told his classmate a few seats down from MikeC. It just so happened that MikeC knew the kid they were talking about, and not just because of the jump we got on his ride, but because he had third period English with the guy.

Back to the party, MikeC pointed to the kid and said, "See that kid?"

"Yeah I see him," I replied.

"And you remember when we boosted this fleece?" he asked pointing to the one he was wearing.

"Yeah," I replied thinking what the fuck?

"Well, that's that guys who's fleece this is," MikeC informed me before the guy very casually walked over to us. Oh fuck, I thought, the fleece has a large, distinctive cigarette burn in the shoulder, and he's sure to see it. Oh fuck, here he comes! Does he realize it's his? I wondered as the kid walked up to us, his eyes seemed to be locked on. MikeC and our victim started talking, and luckily, he didn't seem to recognize his fleece, or he just chose not to say anything, either way, we were relieved.

After a few months, I felt I was beginning to impose on JakeH and his Dad, and I didn't want to burn any bridges, so I started finding other places to stay at. I remained good friends with JakeH and his dad for years after my stay with them.

_____

DaveH is now in prison for killing a woman when he was blacked-out drunk. It happened about seven years after I had lived with them, and when it happened, it was all over the news. I was at my apartment with a few friends when my phone rang. It was MikeC with no hello, just "Turn on channel eight man…"

"Why, what's up?" eager me.

"Just turn it on! It's crazy man! You haven't heard bout DaveH have you?" he asked me.

"No, but I guess I'm about to find out huh?" I stayed on the line while I hushed my drunken friends down and turned on the channel eight news.

The story was still on, "… Mr. H was allegedly seen bolting from the Sleepy Hollow Retirement Home (butt-ass) naked. He apparently got into his car and drove to his home just a mile and a half away where authorities arrived just hours after the report, and arrested him for the murder of an eighty-four year-old woman who resides at the retirement home. Her name has yet to be released pending notification of her family."

Needless to say, I was shocked, but the fucked up thing was that MikeC and I more or less saw something like this coming since we first met DaveH. Not exactly killing an eighty-four year-old woman, but we always thought he'd do something extremely fucked up at some point in his life.

According to JakeH, his dad had frequented the retirement home where their neighbor of over twenty years had recently moved to. He'd go there to visit with the man as well as walk the old man's dog for him, since he couldn't himself. If this was out of kindness, boredom, or staking the joint out, JakeH didn't know for sure. DaveH had been on the wagon for about two years up until the night of the murder. The cops said he was blacked out drunk and high on crack, and they also told JakeH that his dad didn't remember a thing from that night. Apparently, he had gone to the retirement home around nine in the evening, walked into some old ladies room, and choked her to death. In his drunkenness, he stripped down to his underwear and sat with the corpse of the woman for over an hour. He must have been spooked off by something because he ran off leaving his clothes behind, which included his wallet. He then went directly home and passed out in bed with his wife. The next thing he knew, it was five in the morning, and his wife was waking him up saying there were policemen at the front door.

After his arrest, his family was completely devastated, not to mention the shame they must have felt. Unfortunately, the news channels plastered pictures of their home and names all over the evening news which is what I saw when MikeC called. DaveH was released on bail after copping a plea deal with the District Attorney in which he waived his right to a trial and plead guilty in order to avoid the death penalty. As part of the bargain he was given about three weeks as a free man before he had to report to prison to serve his twenty year sentence.

Two weeks after his release on bail I received yet another disturbing call, this time from JakeH, "Hey TommyJ, I can't come party tonight," shitty news.

"Shit man, why not, I got my girl to bring er friend for ya and everything," I told him, Downer I thought.

"I gotta go to the Idaho/Canadian border to pick up a rental car."

"What the fuck?" Good excuse I thought.

"The cops and the rental car company just called on three way to tell me that my dad had rented a car in my name, and tried to jump the fucking border. The judge didn't take too kindly to his escape attempt, and tacked on an additional four years to his sentence without the possibility of parole or time off for good behavior, giving him a grand total of twenty-four years.

He had really screwed the pooch on this one, and the pooch's cousin, the bull mastiff was screwing him back. He's still just a serial number to this day. I saw a picture of him recently where he seems to be fitting in quite well: he's grown a mullet, gotten teeth knocked out, and from the cross around his neck I assume that he's found God. I guess prison can actually do some good for some who, I suppose, are rehabitable, but mostly, serving time just hardens the soul. Initially he was in maximum security due to the high risk of his escape, but they've since moved him to minimum security where his quarters look more like an apartment than a jail cell. He has shelving and a small table, as well as a miniature, black and white TV that he purchased from a guard the price of an arm and a leg.

"Alright Caribou, I gotta take a little break" I said as I got up, "I gotta piss." A few minutes later I returned to the living room, "So I've kinda been skipping ahead with the story of JakeH's dad going to prison, and the following story skips ahead in time as well, but I wanna stay on the subject of JakeH for now if that's alright?" I posed as I sat down with a new beer.

"Yeah, that's fine. Continue," she agreed.

JakeH had no real Mother or Father, but he did have my folks who gladly volunteered to be surrogates. My step-father, MikeB, took a special liking to him, and they had long conversations about how MikeB served as an Airborne Ranger during the Vietnam War. Without any real parents or any real direction, JakeH felt as though there wasn't much else for him to do but join the Army. He signed up during the second Iraqi conflict with the intent of one day joining some branch of the Special Forces. He served four tours in the Middle East as a unit leader for the Airborne Rangers where he achieved the rank of Staff Sergeant.

Once he had finished the four years he originally committed to when he signed up, he decided against a career in the military, and he was discharged from the Army. He began pursuing various positions performing mercenary type work with several private security groups, but he ended up landing a gig with a division of the government, of which, he wasn't allowed to tell me, or anyone for that matter. His secrecy was his honor and no matter how much I poked and prodded him to try and get even the slightest clue as to what group he was running with, the man never even gave me a single wisp of a hint of a hint. All I knew for sure was that the job required that he move to Washington, D.C., which wasn't a big surprise since it was a government gig. It was actually Falls Church, Virginia where he ended up renting a place, however, before he made it to Falls Church, he had been staying in a motel room for about a week while his apartment was being prepared for his arrival.

During the wait for his apartment he met a tall, blond beauty that packed some brains as well. StaceyW worked for the State Department and lived in a three story condo on the Potomac River in which JakeH moved into just a few days after they had met. JakeH explained to her that he was part of a top secret operation and that he could depart at any given moment, for extended periods of time, year round. A week, a year, who really knew? So it was poor StaceyW who got the raw end of the deal concerning the relationship. She had a heart of steel which made his attraction to her worth the heartache from being separated from her. Though very little got him down, JakeH was always very glum in his tone and demeanor on the days just before he had to leave on assignment abroad. He never could say where he was going or for how long, but we all knew it was some kind of hell that very well could've taken him from us for good. The night after JakeH would call me to go out and have a few drinks one last time before he left again, StaceyW would call as well to tell me that "He left another one of those letters again... His goodbye." The first couple of times I got these calls from her, my heart dropped into my Converse, but after the third, neither her, nor I, was fazed. Though I barely knew her, we shared a love for JakeH which immediately brought us together.

In mid July, 2005, while I was sitting at the desk in my office, about to take a smoke break, I received a call from StaceyW. Through her frantic screaming, I was somehow able to decipher that JakeH was a part of an operation in the foothills of Afghanistan where he was killed by an IED, a road side bomb. I was mute from pure shock for the remainder of the day.

My best friend was returned to me, the United States, my Mother, Father, Step-Father, Step-Mother, and my Brother and his wife, who were granted leave from their Naval base in Japan, we all watched as my best friend's last plane flew in. From the tarmac we watched as he was carried from the tail of the plane, wrapped in the stars and stripes, lying in a box.

Sobbing quietly, "My god, that's horrible, I'm so sorry TommyJ," Caribou said softly between gasps.

"Thanks, it was a pretty awful time. I just felt so bad for StaceyW," I said, choking up a little, "Their plans to become a family, what a shame…" I trailed off. "Well like I said before, I hate dwelling on the sadder stuff, and again, I've been jumping ahead in time with JakeH's story."

"That's ok," she continued whimpering, "I liked his story even though it made me cry. I guess it really," pausing to properly formulate her feelings into expressible terms, "put things into perspective for me, you know, for my life. Makes me appreciate what little I had. JakeH's story just goes to show that it could've been worse, you know?"

"That's exactly why I shared it," I answered, "not just because I was there when it happened, or because it's a crazy story, but because it puts my whole life story into perspective, and really, if you think about it, it ended up giving you some of your own." There was a long silence that followed as we sipped on our beers and reflected on JakeH in an unannounced moment of silence. "So let's back up to when I just moved out of JakeH's place…" I said before moving forward...

After I moved out of JakeH and DaveH's place, while I was couch surfing, my mom got in contact with me and told me I could come back and stay with her as long as I followed her rules. I had become so used to living by my own rules, which were none, that it was hard to switch my blind obedience switch on. It felt awkward, as though it was only because she might look like a bad Mother if she didn't allow her teenage son to come home, so a few days after coming back, I left in the middle of the night. The next place I started staying at was on a bench in the dugout of the baseball field at a private high-school not too far from my mom's house. The teachers at the school were all priests that lived on campus, and it was kind of ironic that I was sleeping there because I used to work in the priests kitchen a couple of times a week before I was homeless. The dugout provided was positioned in such a way that it kept me from being seen easily. The only real way you could see me was if you walked onto the field or to the dugout itself. When I slept there in the winter, I would wake up in the morning to hundreds of worms crawling on the pavement below me so that they could drown in the warmth my body created. I wrote a really sappy Emo song about it, "King of the Worms," and man, was it a pathetic. The lyrics were all about living on the streets, and how I stayed in the dugout off and on for six months.

During those days, I would bus it into downtown and pan-handle change from the business folk walking to and from work. The money I got was usually enough to get me food and smokes for the day, as well as bus fare back and forth to the dugout. Those were shitty days. When I couldn't get enough for bus fare back to my sleeping hole, I had to find somewhere to sleep in or near downtown.

Moreover, if I didn't have money for food then I'd have to get my meals wherever I could. Dumpster diving, for instance, was not beyond me. Sometimes I would find dumpsters for cardboard that were unlocked, and I would stay there for the night. It was actually quite ideal because it had a roof, it was dark, it contained only cardboard so it was fairly clean, and I usually didn't get fucked with since I was so well hidden. I'd also have to hunt down partially smoked cigarettes from ashtrays that often made me sick.

One night, sometime after midnight, I was walking downtown looking for a place to crash. As I walked around a corner, I literally walked right into the middle of a group of Skinheads. They all seemed to be wearing the same exact outfit, a sort of uniform that gave away their political social-retardo beliefs: white t-shirts, blue jeans with the cuffs rolled up exposing steel-toed boots, suspenders, and freshly shaved heads. Neo-Nazis, drunk fucks who were out looking for a fight, and they found one, one that was very one sided, just how they liked it. There were five of them and one of me, a single me that got the living shit kicked out of him. The smallest guy in the group knocked three of my teeth out with two quick punches to the jaw. As I fell to the ground I was immediately slammed by the fists and boots of the other four in the group, and that's the last thing I remember before getting knocked out.

I was awakened a few hours later by pouring rain, lying on cold and wet bricks that made up the sidewalk. Blood was flowing from my mouth to the ground, through the streams around me, and into the gutter a few feet away. It was strangely beautiful, but the throbbing pain that enveloped my entirety kept me from enjoying my pain in motion for too long. I used my legs to push myself to the inside of the sidewalk against a building. I cried like a little girl who just found out she wasn't getting the pony she so desperately wanted for her birthday. It's not like you have a lot of pride when you're homeless, but when the little bit you do have is smashed out of your face… Frankly, all I really wanted was to roll up in a ball and cry. Between a vicious, fever-like sweat fest, aching pains from the beating, and chronic diarrhea of the brain in the form of nightmares, I was somehow able to fall asleep right there against the building.

The city was bustling with people walking and driving by in the morning rush to work as I awoke to a pounding headache. The sting from the brutal beating I had received was exacerbated by the sun's ninety degree rays, and the dirty looks I got from the people walking past me, looks that were accompanied by barely audible gasps. It was a very different day than the brutal, rainy night before. How long have I been out, I wondered, days? Couldn't be, I'd be in the hospital or in the drunk tank if that were true. I looked down at my shirt and saw that it was caked in a thick mat of dried blood. It looked like an elephant had used me as a tampon. The people walking by me made sure to walk as far away from me as they possibly could without walking in the street, either not to disturb me, or to avoid catching whatever horrible diseases they thought I may have had. When I got to my feet and walked down the street, destination unknown, people continued to treat me as if I were a leper. I was just a kid, yet none of these fuckers even thought to stop and ask me, "Hey man, are you ok?" especially in the self-proclaimed progressive city that it was.

I eventually made my way to a nearby park that had a fountain where I was able to wash most of the blood off, some of which had gotten on my jeans so that it looked like I had pissed blood all over the front of myself. Great, just great I thought, my clothes are torn to shit, even my leather jacket had the sleeve nearly ripped off.

On the up side, I was successfully able to bum change fairly quick that day. It was painfully obvious that I had had my ass kicked, not to mention the fact that I was a small, young looking guy, so people must have felt bad for me. Voice cracking, balls dropping, and I didn't even have hair on my face yet. In just a few hours I had made enough money spanging to buy a bagel sandwich, a coke, and a pack of smokes I scored from a vending machine in the back of a pub I snuck into. I sat on the curb out front where I made myself at home between a Chevy Iroc-Z that sat on three flat tires, which I could relate to, and a delivery truck. I finished my meal and lit up a Lucky Strike, it was getting breezy and I needed to put my coat on, but the thing was in shambles. I'm by no means a pack rat, in fact the only items I own today, besides my bed, can fit into my car, but I must admit, I used to have a really hard time parting with the few items of clothing I owned. This was partly because it was so hard for me to find and acquire something I liked and partly because I would become attached, almost literally, to my clothes. So, back in those days, it wasn't uncommon to see me with my sewing kit repairing a pair of jeans, fixing a hole in a sock, or repairing some other piece of clothing. On this particular day I had to use fishing line in lieu of thread in order to repair the sleeve on my leather jacket, normal thread simply wouldn't be strong enough. The thick black leather proved to be quite difficult to penetrate with the over sized needle I had, which was the only needle with a hole in the end large enough for the fishing line. Ultimately, I employed the use of pliers to push the needle through one side, and once it was through, I would flip the jacket over and use the pliers to pull the needle through. I finished sewing my armor up, and placed the tools I had used back in the bag I carried around with me. I pulled out a Lucky, lit it up, and remained perched upon the curb surveying the world. The delivery truck I was sitting next to was for some sort of medical company. On the back door there was a sticker reading "Driver's Wanted" with an 800 number that I wrote down on a pad of paper I had in my bag.

This was when I began taking on the kind of shit jobs that most folks dread, and many refuse to ever do, despite how desperately they may need money. The way I looked at it was: sometimes people find themselves in certain situations, like me and the one I was in, where they become intrigued and attracted to that which they utterly abhor; the same cliché that screen writers engaged in way too much in 80's and 90's action movies and dramadies where the two lovers absolutely hate each other at the beginning of the movie, but their disdain for one another takes an abrupt u-turn in an amazing embrace while they're held up behind a sofa during a shootout with the big bad boss' henchmen. Hate fuck. Think about how many people bitch about their jobs on a daily basis. I'm guessing it's easily more than half of all Americans, most of us, you and I alike.

I was primarily fixated on attaining the oddest of odd jobs I could find around town, though my main goal was stable work since I had none to begin with. A position as a delivery driver was the most desirable, so I was on the prowl for yet another delivery job, and I had to keep in mind and keep it a secret from everyone, for various reasons, that I had three jobs as it was: Loan Officer for a mortgage broker up in Vancouver, Washington; Medical Waste Management Technician, which is a fancy title for a guy who picks up and delivers medical waste in a special kind of biohazard-safe dump

truck; and a Pizza Delivery Driver at a pizza parlor downtown.
Delivering pizzas also happened to be the very first job I was ever
hired for, with many more pizza jobs to follow. Obviously these
three jobs were all part-time. I spent most of my day marketing my
ass off as part of the mortgage job, soliciting the nerves clean off
suburban family dinner plates; a brain dead zombie by night running
around town smoking pot, drinking beer, and uh… oh yeah, delivering
pizzas from time to time; and very part-time, weekends only, I was
in creep-mode, dropping off abortions, amputations, and other bodily
junk at specially designated medical waste centers and research
labs. I saw my fair share of the grossest shit the world had to
offer, and medicinal or clinical waste is by far the nastiest, most
putrid shit deliveries I've ever made in my life. Next in line of
putridity would be the deliveries I would be making the very next
summer for the funeral home, Norbert & Sons.

Among the many duties I preformed while employed there, I primarily
drove the hearse. I absolutely, positively, Loved this job. It was
the only job I've ever had where I would rather have worked then had
the day off. My craving to be driving a dead body around the city,
and the joy in scraping dried blood and other leftovers off of
embalming tables never languished, just being on the clock made the
hairs on my neck stand up. The bodies, blood, and gore of it all
fascinated me. I often saw people as a mass of muscle and tissue and
what they might look like broken and dead. Lips moved and words came
out, yet what I saw was the voice box and tongue working
synchronously to shape the sounds I often tuned out.

"SIR! Can you please move so I can help the next person in line?" I
was lost between the functions of the living human, and the
fascination and mystery of the death and decay I had befriended in
those long, semi-lonely rides.

Though my enthrallment with the malevolence the world had to offer
was essentially brief, it had enough time to lay permanent roots
into my young, developing psyche. I eventually had to put this
unwholesome passion to bed when such considerations as kidnapping,
rape, and murder began plaguing my thoughts. The light was hard to
switch off and the Z's seemed as if they would only exist if they
were hovering over the beds of the innocent, animated faces of
sleeping cartoons, and not over me and my thoughts of sleep. I did
not, however, misplace my love for things like cars, mine in
particular, and living girls while I worked at the funeral home.

Much to the chagrin of my coworkers, I was the Captain of the 1963
Cadillac Hearse that made most of our deliveries. To this day, and
probably until I am dead and gone, that hearse will be my most
beloved car of all time. She was painted the standard hearse black
with chrome trim that accentuated her beautiful curves, fine edges,
and black skirts covering the two rear white-walled tires. Inside
she had a real slick looking black leather interior (not leatherette
like most new cars have these days), power windows, power seats, and
even power locks. I named her Friday and I loved her. I felt so cool
cruising around in her, never mind the corpse in the back that
farted, burped, and made all sorts of other squeaking sounds any
time I hit a bump or took a turn too sharply. It seems that just
before they die, the dead purposely hold in all the gas and other
bodily waste they possibly can, as if they know that I'll be their
final driver and I will be forced to smell their shit. Jerks. Really
I just felt bad for Friday because the corpses would expel a variety
of fluids that, every once in a while, found its way off the
stretcher and onto the poor lady's carpeting.

Ms. Friday the Hearse had been in service for the funeral home for some twenty years, and she was winding down toward her last days of service when I began working for the Norbert's. I begged and pleaded with my boss to allow Friday to remain in service, but he was worried that she'd break down with a client in her bed, so I convinced Mr. Norbert to go ahead and purchase a brand new hearse, a 2003 Cadillac DTS Landau Coach to be exact. It was beautiful in its own right, but it was no Friday, and it would never fully replace her. Unfortunately, my boss's fears of Friday's death with a client un her belly came true, but at least we were on a pick up from the hospital morgue and not in a funeral procession on our way to a burial.

It was a cold and rainy January morning, and just a few minutes after leaving the hospital, while on the freeway, I felt the engine start to sputter. It sounded like had run out of gas, but that couldn't have been, I had filled Friday up the night before, and I still had over three quarters of a tank.

After about a minute or so of sputtering, there was a small explosion inside the engine compartment. It didn't take me very long to figure out that the engine had somehow seized up, and large chunks of pistons, rods, and other parts had shot out of the bottom of the engine, flying from the back of Friday as I coasted to the shoulder. Oh the irony, I thought, Friday was dead. I knew this was the end of the road for Friday, so to speak, because she'd need a whole new engine dropped in, and that would have cost more than she was worth. I immediately called Mr. Norbert and told him what had happened, and he showed up in the new hearse about twenty minutes later.

Once he arrived I could've sworn I heard the new hearse snickering and making snide remarks under its muffled breath. We needed to take everything that was in Friday and load it into the new hearse, which included our new client who was patiently waiting for us. Unfortunately, the dead guy, who died of congestive heart failure due to a hefty diet, had a death weight of just over three hundred & twenty pounds. Mr. Norbert and I looked at each other, looked at our client, and then looked at each other again and had a good long laugh.

"Well then," still laughing, "shall I venture over to the gas station and employ the help of a couple of guys to help us hoist this fat fuck out of Friday?" I said gesturing to a Shell gas station down the road about a quarter mile.

"Sounds like the only option we really have. You know, it's just our luck that we had to have a giant of client this morning," he said, shaking his head with a great big smile before taking a seat on the back of Friday.

I walked to the gas station but there wasn't a single customer. The two workers were Mexican and spoke very little English. I couldn't help but laugh at the over abundance of luck I was having at the time. The two attendants didn't seem to mind that I loitered for damn near ten minutes until a truck containing three burly looking guys in construction gear pulled into the station for a fill-up. After they had made their order and the gas was pumping, I walked up to the driver's window, "How y'all doing today?" I asked with a dodging grin upon my face.

"Ok, can we help you?" one of them replied with a look of curiosity.

"Well, I have a very strange favor to ask you guys. I drive a hearse for a funeral home and it broke down the road there," I said as I pointed to it, "and I have a dead guy in the cab. So my boss showed up with our other hearse to transport the dead guy, but the two of us can't quite move him by ourselves. He's, uh, just too big." The three construction workers peered down the road trying not to laugh as I told them about my predicament.

"What do you think guys? Personally, I don't mind," the driver inquired as he turned to his friends.

Almost in unison, the other two agreed, "Sure, why not."

"Great, I can just jump into the back here if you don't mind?" I requested, pointing to the bed of their truck.

"Sure thing," the driver chuckled as the attendant handed him his credit card receipt. I jumped in the back and we were down the road, parked behind the hearses in a matter of seconds. We all piled out of the truck, and without introductions, Mr. Norbert and I directed the three men to each grab their own section of the ginormous dead guy. We hoisted him up, walked him around the new hearse, and placed him in the rear cab. Once the fat man was secured, we thanked our three helpers amidst a barrel of laughs, and they went on their way with a good tale to tell their construction cohorts. Mr. Norbert and I, on the other hand, had a secret to keep as we had broken several different laws, not to mention what some might consider unethical behavior, regarding the transport and handling of a corpse.

Many years later I bought myself a cherry red 63' Cadillac Deville, and named her Friday in loving memory of my lost hearse. She too seized up and her bottom end blew out while I was driving down the freeway. I suppose I don't have the greatest of luck with Cadillac's…

The next gig I worked was at an ice rink where I worked part-time for a few years. I mostly worked the concession stand, but I also drove the Zamboni. On my off time I played on a senior league hockey team, better known around the rink as the Beer League. Unfortunately, I was no better than a photographer with a tripod the way I balanced myself on my hockey stick as I skate.

Despite my inability to skate very well and my lack of a hockey upbringing, I had two glorious moments at the ice rink that made me a legend. The first took place in a game during my first season in the Beer League. The team I was on consisted mostly of younger guys, some of which played on semi-pro teams and the rest were old timers, pushing sixty in some cases. Our rival team was called the Cops, and for good reason, they were either active duty or retired city police. In one of our final games of the season I was crowding the puck in the corner near the Cop's net. I had one cop on my back so I was kicking the puck around with my skates, and swatting away the cop's stick until all of the sudden one of the older retired cops came from across the ice at full speed and blindsided me into the boards. He did what's called boarding to me, and it's not only a penalty in all levels of league hockey all the way up into the pros, but it's one of the cheapest, most brutal things a player can do to someone on the ice. It's something that you just don't do to anyone, no matter how much you hate them, because you can seriously injure someone. It's not unheard of for someone to break their neck when they've been boarded. I was lucky, I wasn't broken anywhere, but I was out cold for at least thirty seconds before I came to and saw gloves & sticks on the ice all around me.

My team went berserk after the hit, and there was almost a bench clearing brawl that broke out. The only reason the cop that hit me wasn't pummeled was because my team agreed that they'd let me settle it once I was back on my feet and on the ice. Luckily, I received my concussion in the first period because it took me until the third until I was ready to rumble. The ringing in my ear ceased with a little over six minutes remaining on the clock, and the desire to pounce on that fifty-something-year-old-piece-of-cheap-ass-shit-Nickelback-cop kicked in.

I got in the next line that was to go out, and I made my way to the ice right when my man's line made their way onto the ice. Everyone knew exactly what was to happen, most importantly, the cop who'd given me the cheap shot knew what was to transpire. As soon as I stepped onto the ice I dropped my gloves, and charged the old man. Did I mention he had at least six inches of height on me? Well, I used this height deficiency to my advantage, and as soon as I was near my opponent I crouched down, ducking his initial jab and ferociously, I swung my fist with an end-all upper cut that lifted the old man off the ice, and sent him flying into the wall that was at least twelve feet from where he stood. As soon as he hit the wall I skated over, jumped on him, and punched & elbowed him repeatedly until I could clearly see his blood soaked eyes roll so far back in his head that I was nearly satisfied. "Fucking pig," I spit on him. "Who's the punk now bitch," I yelled at him, instantly inciting the benches to clear. A twenty minute brawl ensued that brought not only the whole rink staff onto the ice, but all the spectators and even some on-duty police to finally break it up.

The other deed I became legendary for occurred on my last day of work at the rink, a day I had planned out the details for months before. Like any good concoction, there is always a recipe to follow, and mine called for a cape, so the cape was already in my locker. I was called into my boss's office and given the bad news just before the last ice cut of the night. I was able to convince him to let me have one last ride on the Zamboni as long as I made it quick and clean. However, I did the exact opposite; in fact, my last cut was slow and dirty.

Before the cut, I made my way to my locker in the back of the rink and grabbed the cape, walked down to the ice pit where the Zamboni was parked, stripped down to my socks and shoes, and put on the cape. After opening the double doors to the ice, I quickly backed the Zamboni onto the ice and began my final laps. Though it was late on a Friday, there were quite a few people still in the rink lobby milling around, and at the other end of the rink was a bar that had eight foot tall windows lining the wall facing the ice. The bar, which was connected to a bowling alley as well as the rink, was filled because of a bowling tournament. I really couldn't have planned a better time to have been fired. As I drove the Zamboni, I stood up with one leg on the hood and the other on the seat to keep it from dying (there was a kill switch on the seat that was weight sensitive), and I waved to my fans, the best of which flashed their tits from both the rink and the bar. As soon as I had parked the

Zamboni, at the request of my ex-boss, I was promptly escorted out the back door of the rink by my ex-coworkers.

Over the years I've had a great variety of "normal" jobs: Busboy; Caterer; Juice Bar Server (wheat grass flashback, yuck); Cab Driver; and anything having to do with the operation of a pizza parlor, and that included everything from delivering to managing. Aside from being a Hearse and Zamboni Driver, I had some strange jobs as well. The strange work included being an extra on a TV court show (scripted, all reality TV is these days, there's really nothing real about them); an Assemblyman on a line where I worked a machine that dunked newly pressed gas tanks into a tub of water to see if any bubbles arose which indicated leaks; various gigs with a marketing company, my favorite of which had me handing out cigarettes at bars to people that answered a few survey questions; and a short stint as an Administrative Assistant at an abortion clinic.

I never realized how many of the jobs I had worked over the years had something to do with death in some way or another until now that I see it in print. I've never been afraid of death or dying, no, quite the contrary. Though my fascination with Death was seemingly harmless, I put a stop to my association with the cloaked Anti-Claus of the shadows before someone sniffed me out, and in their haste to be the hero for every occasion, exposed me as having some unhealthy obsession.

Amidst hundreds of stitches, four concussions, three homes but no real home at all, and a few seriously demented jobs, I had somehow become a Man. They say the life you live as a child and as an adolescent defines the man you later become. Yet for the most part, I turned out alright, though there was much more living on the very edge to be done... The need to teeter on that edge was much like the continence I lacked when it came to just about every beautiful woman I encountered, single or not, I was a dog of the lowest form. I possessed an evil afflatus, and with great fervor, I was a shitty little kid, a bully, a trouble maker, simply put, I was an exceptionally bad guy.

"Damn, you've really had quite a few jobs man!" Caribou blurted out drooling beer down her chin, neck, and through the mountainous crest of her cleavage from which our laughter echoed about like the sound of music.

I was barely able to get out "waiting for your turn to speak patiently huh?" which made us both laugh even harder.

Once the laughter subsided, Caribou continued "Sooooo, as I was sayin, you had a lot of jobs in your short life, that's pretty amazing. You're not full of shit are you? I mean that's an awful lot of jobs for someone who's under thirty."

I quickly responded with "Girl I've been working since I was thirteen," I said in a sassy, fem-voice while waving my index finger about, making us laugh yet again. "I started at my Step-dad's office and I worked there until I could legally work elsewhere. I typically held most jobs for a year or less, sometimes even just a few days," and I was telling the truth. "If I had my way, I'd be an English Professor teaching writing at a University in the states, or even abroad. It's crossed my mind...Japan maybe"

"Really, who would've thought," Caribou joked.

"I know. I don't exactly look like the scholarly type do I?" I asked as I stretched my arms out displaying my tattoos.

"Yeah, it must be kinda hard to get certain jobs with all those huh?" Caribou replied, referring to my tattoos.

"Not really, I have them all in places that are easily covered up, all um... let me think... yeah twenty-seven of them," I had to pause to remember exactly how many I had now.

"So tell me, what did you get for your very first tattoo, and what's the story behind it? Show it to me." she inquired, asking the same question asked of me a million times before, however this time was different than all the other times people talked small with me. It was different because most of the time I would simply show them my first tattoo, which is a gaudy tribal tattoo covering most of my left bicep, and tell them I got it in high-school in an attempt to look cool. This time, in the spirit of story-telling, I decided to tell Caribou the complete story behind it. I had disclosed the entire account to just a handful of people before this, and to be honest, the following story behind my first & worst is probably the only reason why I haven't had the stupid thing covered up or removed...

---

11. TATTOO

I was looking to buy a couple of pounds of weed, and a younger friend of mine, BryanP, told me about a gangbangin Crip (blue do-rag, tear drop tattoos, pressed khakis, the whole bit) who could hook it up, and on top of that, he was a tattoo artist. When BryanP finally introduced us, he was just as I had pictured him: a big imposing fucker, like a bull-dog, and garnishing the stereotypical garb, tattoos, and the like of a American-Mexican Gangsta. At first he wouldn't talk directly to me, instead, he whispered things into BryanP's ear who in turn would relay the messages to me. It was like being in an old gangster movie, and I was just some local shopkeeper coming to him for a favor.

In due course, he spoke up and addressed me personally, "So BryanP here tells me you're aight."

"Yeah," I answered short but sweet.

"He tells me the two of you go back five or so years that him and you have been doing business together in some way or another for most of the five."

"That's right," I smirked as I raised my eyebrows for a few seconds.

"So you want to do a little business with me huh? So I gotta ask, what's my time worth to you then, huh kid?" he solicited.

"About fifteen pounds and $20,000," I replied.

I guess I was worth his time because the very next day we did our first deal. Over the next month and a half we had three more transactions, each running smoother than the previous, and we became more and more comfortable with one another as time went by. Once I was content with our weed dealings, I decided to take him up on his offer for him to give me a tattoo. I thought I was cool shit getting a tat from this dude because I wasn't quite old enough to legally get one in a shop, and so no one else that I knew that was my age had any either.

My first tattoo covered nearly all of my upper-arm, and it was done all in one sitting, five grueling hours of pain, but it was well worth it at the time. As it turned out, I was the fourth person he had ever worked on, and being that he hadn't quite mastered the gun yet, he dug the needle into my arm a lot deeper than it was necessary to get the ink to stick. The guy was by no means a teddy bear, but he sure as hell was an accommodating motherfucker. He made sure to take breaks every hour or so to smoke a cigarette, drink a few beers, and smoke a little pot in order to calm my nerves. It's a good thing too because I ended up with a really shitty tribal tattoo, and had I been wholly sober, I would have flipped my lid at my poor decision, and his poor hand at the craft...

"Yeah, I know what you're thinking Caribou, but come on, give me a break, it was the 90's after all," I said as Caribou lifted up my sleeve and laughed at my horrible tribal tattoo.

When I went pay the Crip for the tattoo, I pulled out a big wad of cash, and I handed him just a small chunk of the wad.

"Hold on real quick before you leave, I got somethin you might be interested in…" he said to me before I could get away from the high nightmare I was in. So as I sat back down the dingy garage where I was just given my very first tattoo, the coño went inside the house to grab something, something I accurately guessed to be a something he was going to try and sell me. A minute or so later he came back with a small plastic box in his hands.

"You're gonna like this my man!" he said to me as he cleared the tattoo gun, ink, and all the other supplies off the little table he was using while tattooing me, after which he placed the box on the table.

"Now, you sell the weed right?" he inquired as he began some kind of sales pitch.

"Yeah," I replied reluctantly.

"Well then you're definitely gonna need this," he said as he opened the box to reveal a handgun.

"$150 man, check this nine out. Watch the trigger though, she's got a full belly," he said as he pushed the thing in my face.

"No way I'm touching that shit man!" I could tell by the abundance of gunpowder scent that the thing had been fired recently, so I turned him down, thanked him for the tattoo, and left amidst the whining of a gangsta, wailing, "come on," over and over again. I wasn't ever quite sure what stunk worse, the gun or his desperation.

"After the tattoo I was able to find a new, better weed supplier, and I never saw or heard from the Crip again," I said.

Caribou looked like she had something she really wanted to say, so without delay I asked "You wanna say something?"

"I do, I do," she hopped up and down in her seat giddily.

"Well, go on then," I demanded.

"Ok, so this is my first tattoo," she turned in her seat and lifted the back of her shirt to reveal a badly done rose in the center of the small of her back.

"Nice! A flowery tramp-stamp huh?" I chuckled at her deformity.

"Yeah, yeah, I know, it's a tramp-stamp, ha-ha. Anyhow, my story is not too far off from yours, though I remember only a few hazy moments. It was about six years ago when I was all methed out and I had gone over to my dealer's house to pick up a bag. When I got there, there was a guy giving away free tattoos because he had just bought his first tattoo gun and he needed practice, so I got the rose. I plan on getting it covered up, one of these days…" she said, sounding slightly embarrassed as she trailed off, staring at the floor.

"Yeah, well, anyone with more than a few tattoos has at least one or two they hate. Hey! Guess what?" I asked her, suddenly very excited.

"What? Did you just remember something?" Caribou asked.

"Yeah, I have another great story! This time it's about when I was addicted to Meth, about this time I went over to my dealer's house," I said, but before I went on, I wanted to make sure Caribou was even interested in listening to it, "that cool if I tell another one, or did you want to tell a story this time?" I asked.

"No, no, go right ahead. I'm completely intrigued by your past. The more your history I hear about, the more I want to hear more of your stories. So please, go on," she begged.

"Ok, cool. Here goes then…" I said, beginning yet another story from my not too distant past.

---

12. Chemical Shells

Have you ever shot a pistol indoors? The ringing lasts for at least three days, and it burns like the sun in your eyes. Between the ringing, and depending on what you did with those bullets, you'll likely be hard pressed to get much sleep for those three days. Personally, I slept very little.

_____

I went to the place to get a bag of speed, and if I was lucky, I'd be getting my hands on a ten cent pistol as well. I liked the heroin because it helped ease me down from my four to seven day meth high. It's true, I was a junkie. Usually, he would make deliveries to me at my place, but he was sick with a cold, and I had the super flu from the dope, so I made the paranoid journey out of my house to pick up my cure. When I arrived at his place, I knocked at the front tdoor and stood there for a moment while I waited for someone to answer.

"Who's there?" someone shouted from inside the apartment.

"TommyJ," I said thinking, hurry up man, don't you have a peep hole? I coughed for the sake of coughing as he indeed peeped me through a hole, not from the door, but from an adjacent wall.

"Hey man, come on in," I was greeted as the door opened and I came in, shaking and pale. I quickly made my way into the apartment with my arms wrapped around myself to try and keep warm. Sick, we coughed in unison. He was TimD, and he was looking like quite the mess himself. In a bathrobe, rings around his eyes, wiping at his runny nose, he spoke with a subtle wheezing sound that seemed to come from both his nose and his throat. However, he paled in comparison to his home, the place was a total shit-hole. There must have been two years worth of newspaper scattered over so much of the place, I couldn't even see the floor. The only way I knew there was carpet was because the way the floor felt soft under my shoes. If I had to guess what color it was, my bet was that it resembled something like that of an alliance between dirty grays and drab browns likely produced by dried blood and dope from the thousand highs that had occurred there, sucking the dirt from our junkie shoes. Flies could be seen to my left near an archway leading into the kitchen, while some of them were stuck, trying to fight their way off of the fly paper that was hanging directly above an overflowing garbage can.

A further look into the kitchen revealed many more strips of fly paper hanging from various spots on the ceiling with food and trash all over the counters and even the floor. The smell was so overwhelming I ceased to breathe through my nose for the entirety of my visit.

To my right, about three feet from a TV, sat two younger girls. They were maybe sixteen or seventeen, and they looked so alike with their slim physiques and naturally blond hair that I assumed they must have been sisters. They were wearing fur coats, high heels, and nothing else which was quite aesthetically pleasing, though I did my best to keep my looks surreptitious since I felt like somewhat of a creep for staring. Chimo. The girls held onto each other tightly and their peculiar eyes told me that they were high as kites. They were both twiddling their fingers around, contorting their arms, and moving in the discomfort that is the tell-tale sign of a meth head.

128

On TV they watched as a crocodile stalked a water buffalo in river on the Discovery channel.

Sitting on a couch against the far wall on the right was a man and a woman, and judging by the rings on their fingers and their closeness to each other, I assumed they must have been married, but not necessarily to each other. Then again you never can tell when it comes to junkies, they just don't have the same body language as most people. Trying to read a Junkie is like to trying to make sense or Burroughs' dreams.

"Follow me huh?" TimD said as he led me down a hall into a bedroom that was slightly cleaner than the rest of his place. Though the room had clothes strewn all about, the odor that beleaguered the rest of the place was much less prominent in this room. "What you need son?" he didn't ask how I was, or introduce me to the other people in the apartment, and don't get me wrong, I didn't necessarily want to meet them, but it's the principal of the gesture that was worth considering. But who was I kidding, did I really expect faces of meth TimD to have manners? All I really wanted, what I was there for, was to get well. He had my medicine and I was his patient.

"What you holdin, cause I'd like a twenty of each if you got it?" I replied, hopeful he was moving his usual cache.

"You're in luck my boy," he said as I thought, yeah, most of the time. "I just picked up both dis morning." Luck has nothing to do with this dirty business. He opened his closet door to an apothecary of ten or so shelves fully stocked with various street and prescription drugs. He dug through a bag of goodies sitting on one of the shelves, pulled out two small bags, and handed them to me. I took a close look at each bag and knew that even if it wasn't fair in size, I still would've accepted them because I was so utterly sick at the time.

"Looks good to me," I said as I handed him $100, a bill full of haste. I took a look behind me down the hall, "Care if I fix in your bathroom?" I implored politely, bowing my head.

"Not a problem, just lock da door," TimD instructed as he made the motion of turning the lock with his hand, "and don't die in there either! We got enough of a mess round here as it is. I'll be out in the livin room." He strutted off with a creepy little smile.

"I know it's a junkie-ass thing to say, but don't worry about me, I know what I'm doing," I said with a slight smirk that made its way to my mouth, as well as a funny little twitch at my side as I turned and staggered awkwardly down the hall. As I gingerly made my way toward the bathroom I thought, oh the pisser, my saint, the room that was seven times a day my savior. It's where I gave release, where I gained my peace, and my piece was about to be all mine. Once inside, I took a deep breath, genius TommyJ I said to myself in the empty bathroom, smells like an ass with a case of rotten owner in here. I pulled out my traveling junk kit and began to prepare a fix. Seconds to minutes, minutes to more minutes, got to hurry up! Slam!

I lay on the floor of the bathroom for what seemed like an hour, yet really, it was more like ten minutes. No thoughts in the world, except the acceptance of a blank mind, and the impending clean up of my blood from the floor, cabinets, and counter that was required of me before I left. The rig, still sitting uncapped in my upturned hand, tears rolling out from the corners of my eyes, I neglected everything. I even forgot to blink.

Whilst drooling brown bubbles in dreams far away from the dirty linoleum I had become one with, I heard a huge crashing sound come from the living room, a sound I recognized as the front door being kicked in. I jumped to my knees from my slumped position, and in the process, I stuck myself in the leg with the needle I had just used. After pulling it out, I sat the rig on the counter and listened as the girls in the living room screamed bloody murder, as well as people scrambling to their feet, rushing down the hall past the bathroom.

At the same time I heard windows breaking and someone yell "GO! GO! GO! FUCK!" Soon after came two loud cracking sounds, what I quickly discerned as the firing of a gun. Fuck, it's a shotgun I thought, wait a second, I never heard anyone say Police, so this must be a robbery that's going terribly wrong.

Paranoia, being the best friend I never wanted, never let me leave my house without my thirty-eight caliber Ruger, and this day was no different. Just a little thing, it was easily concealed, and it would do the job if I needed it too. I pulled it out, cocked it, and sang it a quiet song about being my hero from the nearest lobes in my head. "What the fuck? How the hell am I supposed to get out of this bathroom?" I quietly demanded of my pistol after finishing my tune, and almost as if I awaited its reply, we silently stared at each other in the mirror.

From tense to intense and back again, worry was life's little wart, and I had no intention of finding out just how far those bumps could spread. As I sweat out every last drop of the drugs I had just shot in myself, the adrenalin quickly replaced the artificial high with a more natural one, and it felt as though it was trying to bust through my chest and make a run for it.

As I tried taking deep breaths to calm myself, I was interrupted as I told my heart how much of a pussy it was by a deep voice bellowing my dealer's name. It was obvious that the voice was that of the man robbing the place, and it sounded as though he was acting alone, a Solo Invader. I heard him move down the hall, past the bathroom, and into the bedroom. Looking intently into my reflection's eyes, I took a deep breath before swinging the bathroom door open just in time to see a large, long gray haired man standing in the doorway of the bedroom with his back to me, and I could just make out a sawed-off shotgun in his hands. I raised my pistol, aimed at the center of his back, and Crack Crack went my Ruger. Two flashes in the dark and two broken eardrums later, I found myself running out the front door, down the block, and into my car.

Instinctively, I headed home, Wait, bad idea I thought, I'd better go to a bar instead I decided. I had put two in him, but I didn't have time to see where they had landed, God I hope he ain't dead.

Within minutes I had made it to a hole-in-the-wall bar about six blocks from where I was living at the time. I was too sober and I needed a drink, yet the last thing on my mind was dipping into one of the two bags I had in my pocket. As far as I was concerned, you can either break the law and the law will break you, or you can break the law, and make damn sure the law can't find you. I was pretty good at running down that latter path, but I would later find out that they have cameras on that path too... I proceeded to put back two full pitchers of beer to myself in just under an hour and a half, and the weight of what I had just been through seemed to float off my back like an angel giving me a second chance. I hurriedly executed my last beer as humanely as possible, threw my money down on the bar, and exited rear stage.

Being intoxicated from various sources, it took me a few minutes to remember where I had parked my car, yet I knew right away that it was time to head home. Wandering down the block, I finally found my car and climbed in. Ok, I'm drunk, I admitted to myself, and the fact that I couldn't find my car after leaving it less than two hours before is a good sign I probably shouldn't be driving. So, I continued talking to myself, it's probably best to get rid of this gun before I go very far. I looked in my rearview and saw only one guy meandering around the corner behind me, and I decided it was best to wait for him to leave before I made any moves. He stayed, and stayed. Fuck it! I'll ditch it on my way home, I said as I started my car and proceeded to drive home.

On the drive I kept thinking about the robbery, or whatever it was that I had just been through. While it was happening I truly believed I was either going to die in the bathroom of the shittiest apartment I'd ever seen in my life, or I was going to die in the living room of the shittiest apartment I'd ever seen in my life. All the sudden my car jumped a little as I heard a loud thumping from underneath me, and I knew immediately that I had run over something while lost in my reflections. I pulled the car over, stopped the engine, and got out to find a small gray cat in the middle of the road. The poor thing produced the most awful screeching sound while it seemed as though it was trying to run away. From what I could tell, I had run over its front section, crushing its neck, skull, and front legs. I pulled out my pistol for the second and last time that night, pointed the barrel at the kitty's head, and pulled the trigger. With a deep breath, the realization of the day's events had finally hit me in its entirety. I was sad for the kitty, and only curious about the man I had shot.

I didn't want to hang around too long after firing off the round, so I made to leave. I got down on my knees and apologized to the kitty's carcass as I reached over him to toss the pistol into a storm drain near the closest curb. Can this day just end? Please? I plead with the world, and it did. I was home and in bed within minutes.

Two days later I got a call from the girl, NickiT, the junkie that had introduced me to the dealer TimD. She was in school to be a nurse, and much like me, no one had a clue she was slamming drugs at the time. That was, unless you saw the tales only her arms could tell. She was a pretty blonde, blue-eyed, independent girl about my age. For a junkie, she was really something. Eventually, she got clean, got her college degree, and is now working as a Registered Nurse at a local hospital making quite the comfortable living.

"TommyJ?" NickiT's cell phone breaking up.

"Yeah I'm here," I answered, thinking here it comes.

"Did you hear about the dealer?"

"What happened?" I played dumb.

"Some maniac stormed his apartment and shot the place up! I guess he was just some crazy, just fucking crazy. From what I understand, he didn't even steal anything," she told me the news.

"Crazy," I jokingly mocked her.

"Yeah, I got a call from CindyK, a girlfriend of mine that was there, and she told me all about it. The guy kicked the front door in and everyone scattered out windows and ran away. Everyone that was in the apartment was fine, but CindyK said some guy was in the bathroom and she didn't know what had happened to him. The next day she came back around and asked the neighbors what had happened, and they told her they saw the crazy guy walk up from the parking lot with a shotgun and kick in the door, so they called the cops. When the cops got there, no one was there except the crazy guy, and he had been shot twice," she explained.

Bull's-eye I thought, "Fuck, that's crazy!" I said again.

"The cops found TimD's stash, his scale, all that crap," she said.

No highs gonna get us for a while, "Well, where's the dealer?" I asked.

"No one knows, and that's as much info as I got."

"Well where the fuck are we going to re-up from now on?!?" Junk Junk JUNK!

"No worry about that, I've got a guy in my neck of the woods," she said as I thought Phew. "Just let me know when you need some and I can arrange it for you, k?" That's my girl.

"Alright, well thanks for the heads up. You know I'll be in touch, later love," and I hung up my cell.

The real worrying began right then. I was the mystery man, but the real mystery was where the dealer was at, and if and when he gets caught by the fuzz, would he squeal my name? No one actually saw me pull the trigger, and no one even knew I had a gun, so it could have been any one of the other people there.

––––––––––––––––––––

Three days after the incident, and the day after NickiT's call, I got another unexpected ring on my cell. This time, it was from a number that wasn't saved to my phone. This always made me a little weary.

"Hello," I answered in a weary tone.

"TommyJ?" TimD's voice.

132

"Yeah, where you at?" I requested.

"Just got out on bail." Why the fuck is he calling me?

"What'd they charge you with?" Digging.

"Possession and intent to distribute narcotics, but hey look, I'm calling to let you know that I'm back in business! I'm staying at my ex-girlfriends, KellyW's, your remember where she lives right? You need to re-up or anything?" he pried. This smells like a trap through and through, I thought.

"No man, I'm OK. As a matter of fact, I quit, so please, don't call me anymore," I hastily spit into the phone before hanging up.

I immediately called NickiT to warn her about TimD, and she happily heeded my advice. I never told her I was the trigger man that crazy night, or the details of what went down. I figured the fewer people that knew what I did, the better. I told no one.

I thought I was in the clear when the cops didn't contact me about the incident, at least not right away. It took them years to catch up to me...

Caribou wasn't going anywhere at this point. I had her in the palm of my hand, so I just continued on...

"More?" I posed to her.

"More! Definitely more please!" she exclaimed in over exaggerated jubilance.

---

13. Tossing Dough

After not speaking to each other for over a year, my mom and I
reconciled our problems and she invited me to move back into her
place which I did for about six months. During this time I sold
drugs, got more tattoos, and got into even more trouble. I needed to
get out of the suburbs, and I knew that the only way I was going to
do so was if I got a real job, and an apartment of my own. That's
where my happiness lay, at least that's what I thought at the time.
By seventeen I thought I was out of my mom's and the suburbs for
good, but alas, I did a few more stints at her place over the years,
stretches like prison terms.

In the meantime, I got by on numerous pizza parlor jobs. My first
pizza job was at a joint downtown called Rocco's, which is still
there today. I worked the night shift on weekdays after school, as
well as every other weekend from five at night until around two-
thirty in the morning. I thought I was the coolest asshole on the
block when I worked there, and all the coolest cats around seemed to
come through the place: musicians, artists, skaters, punks, the
fashionable, the Young Turks, pretty much anyone I thought was
important to the local urban culture at the time.

We didn't make much more than minimum wage, plus tips, which we
split up at the end of the night. The greedy boy in me decided that
I deserved more, so I became the king of the register's cash out
key. What I mean by this was that I had a small amount of tens,
fives, one dollar bills, as well as some change that I had placed
under the cash register, hidden from the customer's view, and when
someone made an order I would pretend to ring them up, but actually
I was just using the register as a calculator so I knew what change
to give them from under the register. Then I'd hit the cash out key
which would open the register. I would make it look like I was
getting their change from the register when actually I was taking it
from my "register" below. I would end up pulling in about a $100 a
night which was cool with my manager as long as I brought a bag of
weed to work with me every time I worked with him.

Other than my part time skim off the top, I spent most of my time
doing deliveries in my 72' Chevy Chevelle. She had a straight body,
orange paint job, and black racing stripes, she was a real beauty. I
spent most of the money on that I made while working at the pizzeria
on her, and she was well worth it. I built the motor, boring it out
to a powerful 383 Stroker. The front end would get about three
inches off the ground when I took off from a dead stop. Mini-
wheelie.

I met a lot of great people while I was working at Rocco's. One
chick in particular was the quintessence of a total trip, MaryJoe. I
could tell she was the product of free-love, hippie-dumb parents who
conceived her in the late sixties. MaryJoe was high on smack all the
time, and she was always nodding off at work, but she made up for it
with her hilarious antics. She taught me to take the soft drink cups
and fill them up with beer so it looked like we were just drinking
pop. MaryJoe and I would get drunk nearly every night we worked
together. Her boyfriend, MarkA, was a burnt-out rocker type that I
had a little deal with where I sold him weed, which he paid for in
cash, as well as free concert tickets to any and every show I wanted
to see at his work. He was the Events Crew Chief at the biggest
venue in town, and he got two free tickets to all events as part of
an incentives package they gave him after he had worked there for a
year. The only time I took him up on his offer for free tickets I

went and saw a really stupid radio band that's not even worth mentioning. A band worth mentioning happened to be the biggest delivery I ever had to make, and they were performing at the venue MarkA worked for. It was the all girl group TLC, and they had ordered over thirty large pizzas that filled every seat in my Chevelle to the ceiling. It was a chilly fall day, so my windows fogged up so badly I had to stick my head out the driver side window just to see where I was going. When I drove up to the back of the venue I pulled up to a security check point where I was instructed to park next to three tour buses fifty yards from the gate. Once there, another security guard met me, asked for the bill, and started to count the cash she had in her pocket. Meanwhile, a few other guards began to take the pizzas to the buses. I was thinking I might get to meet the "band", like I really cared, but it would've been a funny story, but they never even got off their bus. On top of that, the guard handed me exact change with NO FUCKING TIP, Cunts.

While working at Rocco's, aside from chasing girls around, I spent a lot of my time writing graffiti. My most prolific graffiti writing days were from 1998 to around the year I graduated from high school in 2000. I got up a ton during those few years, in layman's terms, I wrote my graffiti name, which for my sake we'll just say it was Tomio, quite extensively throughout the city. I literally wrote my graffiti name in thousands of places across town. A co-worker at the pizza parlor, JJ, wrote graffiti as well, and we both worked the night shift quite often together. This meant we got off work together at around three in the morning every night of the week we worked. Rocco's was perfectly located in the center of downtown Portland, and consequently, as soon as we got off work, we'd immediately take to tossing up tags and burners (larger lettering with usually one color as the fill, a second as the outline, a third as the 3-D, and a fourth color was used for an outer-outline) as we walked around a desolate downtown. Before we got off work each night, we'd spend our entire shift planning our attack on the town. We often met up with one or two other writers who would come along with us on our nightly quests for domination of the city's walls.

Our nights usually went like this: JJ and I would plan out our path through town with specific buildings on our route that we had already staked out; if we were meeting up with our other buddies we'd have them just wait out front of the parlor for us to get off and then we'd start our walk; then at each building we'd take turns painting by sending two of us to scale a building or wall via a fire escape, or other such ladder while one or two of us walked around the block keeping an eye out for security, building management, or cops; and if we saw one, or sensed some kind of impending trouble, we either whistled, or started singing loudly like a drunk crazy person to alert whoever was up top to take cover. It worked flawlessly, and not even once did we get caught on one of our rooftop runs. All in all, I ended up having over forty separate roofs, ledges, and fire escapes quite literally to my name.

From rooftops to fire hydrants to ceilings in bathrooms, Tomio was everywhere, and the town took notice. So much so that the Mayor at the time, Vera Katz, actually identified me, JJ, and two of our friends as being on the top of her top ten most wanted graffiti writers list. I was number three and JJ had made it all the way to number one. The main reason we were so successful at getting noticed was because we had hit up such a ridiculous number of rooftops in the downtown area that we had ended up painting numerous buildings owned by the same, few real estate moguls who had some pull at city

hall. My guess is that they were pressuring a response from the
Mayor's office regarding the rise in graffiti around the city,
specifically their buildings, and they got their wish. Not only did
she name JJ as her prime target, she also created a new division of
the police department which she aptly named the Anti-Graffiti Task
Force, a unit that had its own budget of nearly a quarter million
dollars.

JJ made the arrogant mistake of trying to strike back at the Mayor
by writing "Fuck Katz," signed "JJ," and other such anti-incumbent
rhetoric all over town just before she was to seek her third term as
Mayor in the upcoming elections that year, 1999.

It didn't take long for the Mayor to take notice, and quickly devise
a plan to rid herself, and the city, of JJ and his crude propaganda
once and for all. During Mayor Katz's first two terms she sought to
rebuild Old Town/Chinatown in downtown Portland into a more
economically viable section of the city. She planned to do this by
first cleaning it up and changing it from the decrepit, crime
ridden, gloomy industrial area that it had been for the last hundred
plus years, and make it more attractive to new business and condo
developers. Her success was swift, quickly rezoning the area,
attracting business and real estate investors, and transforming the
area into her vision. The area is now known as the Pearl District,
and it truly is considered the pearl of the city. It's one of the
more expensive places to live in town or lease office or commercial
space.

The first piece to the transformation was an apartment complex that
went up where a condemned building stood for many years. Once the
apartment building was finished and over half of the units had been
rented, the Mayor planned to hold a press conference in the
courtyard of the complex to make a speech about how her vision was
finally coming to fruition. As she wrapped her speech up, she
woefully apologized for the rising graffiti problem the city was
facing, but assured the people that at least a few of the writers
from her top ten list would no longer pose a threat.

Apparently, a month long investigation into those people from her
list was coming to a close that very day. It just so happened that
JJ and another graffiti buddy had recently moved into the very
apartment complex the Mayor was making her speech at, setting
himself up for the perfect bust for the Mayor and her new Anti-
Graffiti Task Force. The Mayor couldn't have written the story of
JJ's demise any better herself.

During the final moments of the speech, police from the new Task
Force served a warrant on JJ's apartment where he and a few friends
were sleeping at the time. All three were arrested on various
charges related to graffiti and property damage, and they recovered
tons of damning evidence: books of drawings, photo albums full of
pictures of painted walls and trains, and hundreds of pens & cans of
spray paint. Needless to say, they were fuct. Luckily, however, JJ
was seventeen at the time, so he could only be tried as a minor, so
he got off quite light, considering.

After pledging her unwavering pursuit to apprehend every last person
from her list, and pleading with the people of her city that the
success of the anti-graffiti campaign depended on every citizen's
cooperation, she finished her speech by naming me, Tomio, as the
new, number one most wanted graffiti writer. She topped it off with
a chilling personal guarantee, "Tomio, I assure you, we're coming

for you, and you will be next!!" I wasn't kidding myself, I knew that sooner or later she would.

The next day the Mayor was on the front page of our local newspaper and they had quoted her speech regarding her personal quest to see me arrested. Next to the article was the new top ten most wanted graffiti writers list with me at number one. I always thought that was funny because the media and the local government was helping expose graffiti writers to the public a lot more efficiently than any of us writers ever could have hoped to do on our own.

It just so happened, however, that I was graduating from high school that very week, and just a few short weeks thereafter, I moved out of the city to go to college. I was never arrested, and I never heard anything about the name Tomio ever again. I assume the Mayor believed she was successful in scaring me off with her threats, and in part, she was right.

Another cat I knew from the pizza joint was one of the bums that came around at closing time looking for a free slice. Most of the bums that came around assumed that we just threw out the pizza we couldn't sell each night, however, what really happened to the leftovers was quite different. We'd box them up and put them in the walk-in refrigerator until the next day when someone from a local homeless shelter would come by to pick it all up. We never gave freebies to bums, instead, we handed them a broom or a mop and put them to work. That way we were feeding the needy, getting our work done for us, and getting out of there a lot faster.

"So I forget the name of the particular bum the following story is about, so we'll call him RudyQ if that works for you?" I posed to Caribou.

She laughed before replying, "Uh, ok, I guess. RudyQ it is then," she said before snorted out another laugh.

RudyQ was coming around once or twice a week and helping me close shop in order to get some free food in him before climbing into a stairwell somewhere for the night. He was a nice guy, late twenties, but like most street dwellers, there was something off about him, something I couldn't quite put my finger on, but that something was readily apparent. Though not a bad twitch, it was a twitch just the same. He became somewhat of a staple in my nightly schedule, so I could usually count on him to show up right around closing time, but after about five months he stopped showing up altogether. Other hobos came and went, and I realized how pleasant RudyQ was compared to all the other ones. He typically didn't smell bad, and he was actually quite the pleasant conversationalist. I kind of missed the bum.

One night, about half way through my shift, I got a call from a buddy of mine, TeddyD. He and about a dozen other kids were taking one of their parents' boats out to a place called Government Island to go camping for the night. I was getting off work at two in the morning, so I would have to meet them at the docks in the wee hours of the morning to be ferried in late to the party. Closing time came just a few hours after I got the call, and that's when RudyQ came strolling in.

"TommyJ, there's my man!" slapping my hand five.

"How ya been? Where ya been?" I asked. With slicked back hair, new clothes, and a new pair of black rimmed glasses he was looking very dapper. He was glowing so damn much I assumed he was either really high, or really Really high.

"Shit man, you look really good, I almost didn't recognize you," I said as I thought, bums never cease to amaze me.

"Yeah I was walking in the rain down in the park blocks one night, mmmm," he said, looking up to retrieve a thought, "about three months ago, and this lady came up from behind me to share my umbrella that I'd found earlier in the day." Smile beginning to emerge. "This lady was no supermodel by any means, but she wasn't a skank either. Lucky for me I was able to take a shower and clean myself up at the shelter earlier that day, so you know, I guess she was more inclined to continue walking with me. We got to talking and it became quite obvious that the lady had no idea I frequently slept on the park benches we were walking by. She told me I was cute and she wanted me to go with her for coffee. I was like, shit yeah, a hot cup of coffee on a cold ass night like that with some broad, why the hell not right? So we walked down a few blocks to a café, and once we were there we ordered some coffee, and I explained to her that my wallet had been stolen earlier in the day along with my cell phone and house keys." Chuckles… "So this lady and I talked for like an hour or so right, and then she asked if I wanted to check out her condo which was just a few blocks towards the river in a high-rise," he said as he nodded his head with a big ole shit eating grin on his face.

"Na uh?" I said utterly stunned.

"Yup, so we got up to her place, which is on the 19th floor of a newer building, and man, I'm telling ya, it's got the most amazing view. Yeah, so I ended up staying with her for a few nights, and of course, she was asking all about who I was, you know, where I lived, where I worked, and all that kinda shit. So of course, I lied. I guess she saw right through it, but she let me think she bought my story. She let me stay with her and never pressed the issue of staying over, or even seeing my place," he said, making the bunny ear quotes with his hands. "One weekend, a couple weeks back, she took me to the mall and got me a suit and some other clothes like this shit I'm wearing now. Monday morning rolled around and she had a job interview lined up for me. I haven't had a real job in something like, three years, fuck man, I got the job. I was workin the mail room at the newspaper down there on Broadway," he went on, amazed himself.

"Man that's fucking great, good for you. You liking it?" I inquired.

"I was liking it, that is, until I got fired. I managed to save up enough dough to move into an apartment on the eastside with someone I met on the internet. But now that I'm jobless again and that lady left me, I'm once again, homeless," lowering his head.

"Wow man, you changed your whole life around, and in an instant, it fucking collapsed on you. That sucks!" I empathized. Rags to minimum wage riches, and back to rags I thought.

"Yeah, go figure," RudyQ laughed. "Shit'll turn around again soon, I can feel it," he smiled. "But hey look, the reason I came down here was because I wanted to thank you for all the times you gave me work and talked to me like I was a human being. That shit really meant a lot to me, so I wanted to thank you," he smiled broadly, holding out a small, cellophane baggy with something small and white inside. "Here, it's a couple of hits of acid."

"Thanks a lot RudyQ, I love acid. Say, what're you up to tonight?" I asked him as I put the bag in my pocket.

"I have no idea, I was really hoping we could grill on this shit together and walk around town," he explained, but I had a better idea.

"I'm headed down to the river where my friends are going to come pick me up in a boat. We're goin to camp on Government Island, you wanna come?" I asked him.

"Yeah man, sounds like fun!"

After finishing closing up shop, RudyQ and I jumped in my car and drove to the docks where I was told I'd be picked up by the boat. Half way there, I gave my friend with the boat a call so that we'd all arrive at the dock at about the same time. Hung up phone, dropped the acid, and floored the accelerator. Humming down the road, listening to the whispering whistle of the highway air impregnate the cabin of our automobile, the engine's hum gradually became a roaring growl, and the thought of what kind of beast might be under the hood led me to far, and we missed our exit. I must be high, I thought, "I must be," I went on, this time thinking out loud.

"Kicking in huh?" my bum bro inquired, I froze like the icicle I saw myself as, and never answered his question. Instead, I pretended to be completely consumed by the task of parking the car. As well, waiting on the arrival of the boat took nearly all of my attention.

It was a beautiful summer night, clear skies, and about seventy degrees out. Perfect, I thought as we floated from my car onto the dock, this is meant to be a great night that begins Now. With each passing minute the stars shined brighter as my eyes adjusted from the uniform city lights to the darkness of the riverbanks. Before we had entirely melted into the night sky, and just before the hum of the crickets had completely entranced us, our river chariot arrived with great fanfare, shaking us from our LSD slipping. My buddy, MikeyD, waved for us to board the boat as he secured a rope to a cleat on the dock.

"MikeDeeee! How are you my man?!?" I shouted, throwing myself unexpectedly aghast with the echo that the river's banks provided. "This is my friend RudyQ," quieter this time, yet leering at the embankment nearest me as if daring it to try it's little trick on me again.

"Hey, MikeD, nice to meetcha. Climb on board and we'll head," MikeD pointed inside the boat.

As RudyQ and I walked down the dock toward the boat we were noticeably more cautious with each step we took, as if the unsure ground below us could give to wetness at any second. "Terra firma," I mumbled.

"What's that TommyJ?" MikeD asked me as I drew within earshot.

"I said uh… How's the island huh?" I stumbled, both figuratively and literally.

"Watch your step," MikeD said laughing. "The fun's just begun...Man your eyes are huge! Yours too RudyQ!" Busted.

We jumped into the boat, RudyQ and MikeyD shook their hellos and we drifted out to sea once MikeD had untied us from the dock. With the pull of the cord the outboard motor revved up, and we were on our way. By the time the boat arrived just offshore of the island, RudyQ and I were feeling the full effect of our acid. Trippin, trippin hard.

I introduced RudyQ as a buddy of mine and no one ever suspected otherwise. Little did they know, but I had not only brought a bum to camp with me, he and I were also on acid. Eventually someone noticed that I not only kept talking to myself, but I was often staring off into the darkness, finally coming to the realization that I was high as a kite.

Most of us partied until four or five in the morning, but RudyQ had tired himself out early, so he disappeared from the party pretty early. Later that night I found him curled up, straddling a log near the center of the island, and judging by the large wet spot on the crotch of his pants, he had pissed himself. Many photos and laughs later, we left the bum to sleep with his new evergreen girlfriend. Unlike mine, his high was able to avoid detection entirely.

As I watched the sun slowly rise, I also watched as some of the fellas geared up to go wakeboarding. I walked over to them and volunteered to go first, as I had never tried wakeboarding before. The water must have been thirty degrees, and as soon as I jumped in I felt my nuts crawling back inside me. I tried four times, unsuccessfully, to get up on the water as the boat dragged me all over the river. Afterwards, once everyone was up and all our gear was packed in the boat, we headed back into town. RudyQ had me drop him off downtown, and I never saw or heard from him again.

To this day, not a single soul that went camping with us that night ever knew RudyQ was a bum on acid.

After hours upon hours of laying out the better parts of my sordid past for a whore I called Caribou, the time we had fought so vehemently against had finally caught up to us. We conceded to a sun that had thus risen well above the horizon, a sun that was relentlessly reminding us of the day that had crept up on us by shining it's rays through the single pain windows on the east side of my living room.

"Damn, it's like noon already huh?" I inquired as we heard noises coming from my roommates' rooms. Before Caribou could answer, one of them shuffled from their bedroom to the bathroom above us on the second floor.

"Yeah I guess so," we both laughed as she looked up towards the sounds of the rising roommates.

"Well shit," I yawned, "I have so much more to tell you, maybe even the better parts of this story, my life," I said disappointingly.

"Really? You're telling me you have stories that can top the ones you've already told me?" Caribou demanded to know as she rose to her feet, stretched her arms out, and yawned.

Just then, as I walked into the hall towards the kitchen, I had a great idea come to mind, "Check it out, how about you give me your address, and I'll write you. I'll put a story or two in each one. How does that sound?" searching for a pen and paper from a drawer in the kitchen. Success, I returned to the living room to Caribou sprawled out on the couch. "Here, write your address down for me," I handed the pen and paper to her.

She sat up and grabbed it, "Ok, but they better live up to these claims of yours," she demanded as she wrote her address down and handed it to me.

"Alright then, and you know you have to write me stories too, ok?" I folded the paper and stuck it in my back pocket. "Give me at least a week ok?" I gave her a hug "Good night Bou."

"Goodnight TommyJ," there was a hesitation on her part, as if she wanted to kiss me. Being the last thing in the world that I wanted at the time, I quickly retreated to my bedroom, alone. There was no way in hell I was going to make that mistake, though I wish I could say the same for my roommate. Apparently, later that week, I found out that JohnnyB had stayed up late talking with Caribou just as I had done, however rather than just walking away, he ended up with his dick in her (quivering, dry heaving, etc.). It wasn't really a big surprise though, based on the girls he had been with in the past, he had some pretty low standards.

Six months had passed and I had forgotten all about Caribou. I was moving into a new house and I stumbled upon the piece of paper she had written her address on.

Three nights later, after I was all moved in, I decided what the hell, what could it hurt? So I wrote down a story and put it in an envelope addressed for Vegas, to Caribou. I figured that if she didn't live in the same spot, she likely was having her mail forwarded to her new address.

Six months had passed and much to her surprise, my first letter finally arrived. Caribou was already late for a lunch 'date,' but to

her, nothing else mattered when it came to my letters: she put
everything on hold just to read my next story.

When I went to write the first letter I decided it would be best to
begin where I had left off: at the house I was living in where
Caribou came and stayed, where I began sharing my sordid tales with
her…

Dear Caribou:

**Nearly six months have passed and surely, you've likely figured me
to be a flake, but alas, here I am pen in hand with stories as
promised. I won't immediately give away my current situation because
it will be explained in the following letters… So without delay,
let's go swimming!**

---

14. South of Powell

For the last year and a half, I've lived in a two story, turn of the
century, Victorian home near the Willamette River, just south of
Powell Boulevard on the lower east side of Portland. I'm assuming
that Brooklyn, the oldest neighborhood in the city, got its name
from one of the first settlers to the hood in the mid 1800's, likely
a New Yorker. This is the house I was living in when I met you Ms.
Caribou, and as you know, I was living with a few guys that I also
worked with, and one of their girlfriends. We all played in various
bands at the time: a few with each other, and a few with other
folks. In total, there were six bands practicing at our house every
night of the week. All six bands shared the basement, a space that
was transformed into a Speakeasy by night. We had built the bar out
of old wood crates that we covered with black linens that we had
stolen from the catering joint we all worked for. Though it was
janky as all hell, the bar was actually pretty sturdy. We sold beers
for a buck, joints for two, and mixed drinks for three. It was a
real happening place in the summer months, with parties almost every
night. A band always seemed to be playing, and I always seemed to
have a different girl in my bed every few days. The constant
debauchery ran rampant like a pandemic on the six o'clock news.

Like most small, tight-knit communities, ours came with a local
drunk, CharlieB. It wasn't long after we had moved into the hood
that he had taken notice of the new kids on the block. It also
didn't take long before he took a liking to us, dropping by quite
often to see what we were up to. Moreover, just before I left for
work every weekday morning, I had the pleasure of saying "good
morning" to CharlieB who'd be on my porch drinking his first tallboy of the day. Like clockwork, he'd be sitting on the porch at the
same exact time every morning because, as he explained whilst trying
to convince me that he wasn't an alcoholic, the mini-mart at the end
of my street didn't start selling beer until eight o'clock, and
"there was no way in hell he was gonna walk all the way home before
drinking (his) beer." According to CharlieB, those three additional
blocks to his house were the longest blocks in the city, and when I
asked him how, exactly, he knew this, he answered "Because, I had
the city come out and measure them," and I tried not to laugh as I
peered through his lie. This went on for almost a year before he
fell asleep in a recliner on the porch while smoking a cigarette
that caught the chair on fire. When I came outside to leave for
work, CharlieB was sitting on a smoldering puff, snoring obliviously
while I pondered what to do, let him burn, or wake him up? Though
initially in a panic, I quickly realized that more than anything, I
was pissed at the damn bum, and these morning visits of his needed
to stop.

I decided to have a little fun with CharlieB, while at the same time
getting back at him for nearly burning down my house, so I grabbed
the garden hose, turned it on, and sprayed the hell out of him. He
shot so far up in the air I thought he was going over the railing, a
fifteen foot fall that could have easily broken the old man's back,
hip, and/or legs. I've never seen a bum move so fast, that is, a bum
that wasn't also a crackhead. After I put the flames out I told
CharlieB that he was banned from our property until further notice.
That was the first time we had to kick him out.

The drunkard CharlieB mostly hung out at the local bar, The Clam's
Claw, but when he wasn't there, you could find him harassing people
for change, or at his Mom's house that he had yet to move away from.
The word on the street was that CharlieB had been in and out of
prison for his entire life. This was confirmed when I learned that

his last stint, and I heard this straight from the horse's mouth, was just over ten years for armed robbery. At forty-eight years of age, CharlieB was homeless and his Mama had had enough of his bullshit, so she refused to let him stay in her house. Instead, she allowed him to sleep in the backyard as long as he routinely performed basic chores for her. This invitation prompted him, with his carpentry skills, to build an adult sized tree fort which he lived in until his dying days. The man was perpetually tanned because he not only lived outdoors, he almost always worked odd jobs outside as well because no one trusted him enough to let him into their homes. More than anything, they feared for their liquor cabinet's safety.

In the wee hours of a mid-February morning, as I stood at the kitchen sink getting a glass of water, I saw CharlieB taking a big stinky bum shit in our backyard garden. What the fuck man, I yelled in my head, at least he could've shit on the lawn or something, but not in our vegetable garden, Jesus H. Christ! "CharlieB, what the FUCK?!?" I whaled so loudly that he could hear me through the closed window. He rose, caught my eyes, and shuffled off, stumbling here and there as he tried pulling up his pants. I couldn't help but laugh as he tripped over himself as he attempted to escape my line of sight, as if it would all be forgotten if he could just get away. Really CharlieB, you really think this is something I'll soon forget? After discussing it with the roommates, it was unanimously decided to, once again, ban CharlieB from the house as well as the yard, especially the garden, indefinitely. The boys of Pershing Street, the boys he lived vicariously through, the boys were going on without him, and he was heart-broken.

Thereafter, whenever we visited the Clam's Claw and CharlieB was there, he would quietly exit through the back door in shame. The first time it occurred I got talking to the bartender who had been in the neighborhood for a number of years. She informed me that I wasn't the first victim of CharlieB's backyard attack, and I wasn't the least surprised. In fact, the bartender went on for a pitcher's worth of time with stories about the constant mayhem CharlieB had inflicted upon the Brooklyn neighborhood over the past forty years in which he and his mother had called the hood home. Most folks had little to no sympathy for CharlieB, but we all felt bad for his mama. Though she was seventy plus years old, she was a regular at the bar, and it just so happened she was in the Clam's Claw while I heard the bartender's tales. I hadn't noticed her until MarthaW was just finishing her last CharlieB tale, and luckily for me, she was at the other end of the bar which led me to believe she hadn't heard a word of my conversation with the bartender.

The next time we allowed CharlieB within spitting distance of the house was five or six months after we had banned him when we threw a party for the 4th of July, and the only reason he was allowed in was because there was plenty of people to keep an eye on him for us. The party ended up being an end-all blow out that featured six kegs, and a few hundred partygoers.

Drunk as hell, and despite the thermostat reading in the high nineties, CharlieB showed up to the party wearing a heavy track suit that he had surely scored recently from a local dumpster. There were, after all, quite a few Russian mobsters that lived in and around Brooklyn. When I first saw him at the party he was in our front lawn surrounded by a group of kids hassling him about this and that, "CharlieB, CharlieB, CharlieB… What are we gonna do with ya huh?" one of them asked rhetorically.

"Well, in the spirit of the festivities, I suppose we can let you hang out…" I said as I handed him a beer.

Staggering up our lawn and onto our porch he replied as he grabbed the cold beer, "Awww, thanks TommyJ, happy fourth!" He was absolutely shitfaced, and in retrospect, I probably shouldn't have let him drink more beer, but what the hell, I thought, he's a grown man after all. Within twenty minutes he had another crowd gathered around him. This time, however, they listened as he told ridiculously daft stories about travelling to the moon by train and kicking Buzz Aldrin's "Pussy-Ass" up and down a giant crater he so aptly named "Buzz Aldrin's Ass Was Here & CharlieB's Fist Was Too." This had everyone, including my roommates and me, laughing out tears. In and out of the emergency room, he was in and out of stitches. Poor CharlieB thought he was laughing with us, but the fisting reference had gone so far over his defectively, slow minded dome, that it only made our group cackle further and further. Part of me would have liked to believe that he was just putting us on, but he sure had convinced that he was a complete dunce. If so, bravo CharlieB, you had me fooled. It was sad really, like comedians and cocaine, he was a duo parading around like a one man show. "I don't believe in hypothetical situations," he said to one girl after she had what-if'd him, "I believe in TV." And with that, my head threatened to explode through my ass, so I finally convinced myself to move on from CharlieB's presence before I had to change the underwear I wasn't wearing.

I had ventured back into the basement to grab another couple of drinks and tend to the bar so I'd have a better view of the band that was playing. Twenty five minutes or so later, after the band had finished their disappointingly short set, I decided it was probably a good idea to go back and check on CharlieB. He was rapidly growing more and more belligerent as usual, so I made a pact with my roommate AaronL to keep an extra eye on him, and make sure he didn't get into any trouble. When I made it back to the front yard CharlieB had his shirt off in an effort to impress some young ladies. The reality was that his saggy man-boobs proved to be both entertaining and creepy. Before I could reach the old bum, he had already began talking to two new partygoers, and when I say talking, I really mean spinning around in slow circles, telling some story about a car wreck he was in where the car spun around when it was hit by a dump truck with wings. When he finally ceased his graceful pirouettes, he fell to the lawn and threw up all over himself. When he finally caught his breath he looked up and saw that I was standing over him, laughing hysterically. "Looks like you…" laughing progressively harder, "drooled a bit there," and I could barely muster the words.

"Oh fuck off TommyJ!" he yelled at me as he stood up. "You think you're so cool because you don't have any droolies or pukies on your shirts. So yeah, yeah, fuck you!" he reached his arm out toward me and extended his middle finger. This put his drunken weight so off kilter it caused him to sway violently from side to side. Eventually he lost his balance entirely which sent him crashing back to the ground. Laying face down on the lawn, he proceeded to puke even more which drew yet another crowd, and we were all doing everything and anything within our power not to fall over laughing. The fun didn't stop there, oh no, CharlieB's inhuman amount of vomiting caused a chain reaction of vomiters in my front lawn. After catching his breath once again, CharlieB managed to prop himself up on his hands and knees, but you could tell it would take him quite a while to make it all the way back onto his feet.

As people began to disperse to the innards of the house and away from the Puke-A-Thon, I noticed something strange on CharlieB's arm. At first I thought it was a piece of puke that was stuck on him, but when I got closer I realized it was some kind of growth. Judging by the amount of sun his skin got on a daily basis, I surmised that dear old CharlieB had a malignant tumor almost literally on his hands. In a pure moment of genius, I devised a plan that would both help CharlieB, and be quite entertaining to those who braved baring witness.

"My God man, how long have you had that thing?" I asked as I pointed to his arm. The look upon my face of awe stricken disgust must have jolted him slightly sober because his response was given in a much more subdued tone.

"Oh, I guess maybe…uh… uh a year and a half now, maybe two years."

"Man that's bad," AaronL said from over my shoulder.

"Why, why do you ask?" he replied pausing every so often to spit up the remaining chunks of shit in his mouth.

"The Tumor Man!" I screamed in his face, "You know that thing's gotta be cancer right?" I was infuriatingly sad for and at him by this point.

"I suppose so" he answered, "I just… Uh… I just don't have insurance you know?" and though this was true, if something is truly threatening your life, you'd think the last thing you'd give a shit about is having insurance, but this was how CharlieB's brain, or lack thereof, worked. It was debatable who had worse wiring, CharlieB or any Volkswagen from that time.

"Well you know man, we're gonna have to cut it off, and I mean like right now. Whatya say huh?" I begged him, trying not to sound too ecstatic about the prospect of cutting him open. "In all honesty I've successfully…" bullshitted old farts like you into any and every con I've ever tried my hand at, that is, "…done little surgeries like this before, and I tell ya what: those men are alive today and thanking me for it." The conniving smirk in my head was far bigger than any I could possibly hope to produce with my lips, jaw, and teeth. With this record breaking smile I thought to myself, I would like to thank my Mom and the Academy for this award.

"Wha," CharlieB and AaronL both began to question me in unison, but before they could even reach the "t," I continued on with taking control of the situation. Control over the man's fate really.

"So here's what's gonna happen: you're gonna stay right here with AaronL while I go get my tools. AaronL," I gestured for my roommate to come stand by CharlieB. "Make sure he don't go nowhere," I exclaimed as I ran to the house and ascended the stairs to my bedroom. After shuffling through a few drawers in my desk, I had successfully procured two number two pencils, a "G" guitar string, and an old ratty, but clean, t-shirt. By the time I made it back downstairs, word had travelled around the party that there was going to be a surgery performed on the front lawn by yours truly. "Ok,

CharlieB, I'm gonna need you to sit in this chair," behind him, I
unfolded a lawn chair that I had grabbed off the porch on my way
down, "and I'm gonna need you to stick out your arm for me," I held
my own arm out straight behind me as an example.

"Oh… Uh… I don't know TommyJ," CharlieB mumbled. This was
immediately met by the heckling of the crowd en masse, a crowd that
had grown to almost sixty people. "Oh alright," he finally gave in
and sat his drunk-ass down in the chair.

"Ok now," I began twisting each end of guitar string around the two
pencils. "AaronL, I will need you to hold this pencil, and when I
count to three, you pull it toward you as fast and hard as you can."
I wrapped the middle of the guitar string around the base of the
tumor that sat near the elbow on CharlieB's arm. "Ok, ok, ok…
CharlieB, you ready?" I asked him in all seriousness.

"Born ready," CharlieB was now trying to look tough for the crowd,
more specifically the ladies, which numbered near a hundred by the
time his surgery was taking place.

"Ok, on three then," my eyes met AaronL's and we both smiled. "One,"
our smiles grew bigger with the count. "Two," that is until we both
shed our smiles on "three," and we yanked so hard on that guitar
string that it snapped, making a slight twang that seemed to hover
over the crowd as everyone gasped into a collective silence,
disappearing once everyone had grimaced in response. The tumor was
thus severed and sent flying across the yard to the jeers of a
hundred plus drunks, but unlike a bride's bouquet, no one went
diving for the tumor. However, everyone there did their share of
clapping and cheering, and one guy even grabbed the tumor and raised
it in the air in triumph as if he had just accomplished some great
feat himself. Gross, I can't believe he touched it.

Meanwhile, the blood came pouring out from the silver dollar sized
hole in CharlieB's arm, so I grabbed the t-shirt I had brought from
my bedroom, wrapped it around his arm, and tied it off in hopes of
stopping the flow of blood. Over the course of the night,
unbeknownst to me, the blood never actually coagulated, and it
continued to bleed for the next three days. I believe this was
caused by a combinati0on of three things: 1) the constant high level
of alcohol in his system; 2) the size of the wound; and 3) a side
effect of having the specific cancer he was inflicted with. If he
had the tumor for almost two years like he claimed, then in my mind
it was likely that at the time of the surgery he would already have
had the cancer throughout his body and not just where the tumor was
on his arm.

On the third day of bleeding his mom finally took him to the
emergency room at the hospital where they gave him sixteen stitches
to finally stop the bleeding. While they were at it they conducted
numerous tests, including a biopsy, to see if the tumor was
malignant or not, and if there might have been cancerous cells in
other parts of his body as well.

———————————————

About a week and a half after the party, as I got ready for work, I
smelled burning hair, and let me make it clear, I hate that fucking
smell! It's right up there with the smell of burning human flesh,

yuck! And don't ask me how I know what the smell of burning flesh smells like; that's a whole other book in its self.

When I was all ready to depart I grabbed my keys and walked out the front door. As I locked the deadbolt I looked over to my right and there sitting in out recliner on the covered porch was CharlieB. He was passed out with a giant can of Camo beer (yuck, cheap yuck) in his lap, and his other arm was slung over the side of the chair with a lit cigarette that had once again set the chair ablaze. Holy shit, I thought, this can't be happening. This has got to be the worst déjà vu I've ever experienced.

It turned out that the burning hair smell I had sniffed out while getting ready for work was actually the smoldering innards of the old smelly chair that none of the roommates sat in because stinky old CharlieB had treated it like a second home, not to mention it was charred to hell from his first attempt at burning down our house. The chair wasn't showing flames because it was just smoldering in the center, so I wasn't so much concerned with the house catching on fire, as I was with waking CharlieB up with a shockingly cold blast from the hose as I had done before. I got just as much satisfaction blasting CharlieB with the hose as I did kicking him off our property, and this time he was banned for life. When the water hit him he went flying from the chair onto his hands and knees, groaning loudly from the shock.

After the chair was out I went back to the side of the house and turned the water off. When I returned CharlieB was polishing off his beer, "Hey old man, that's it, I've had it! My roommates have had it! We've all had enough of your shit! You've gotta go old man," I yelled at the top of my lungs, shaking my head, and shaking my finger in his face.

Just then, AaronL came out, "What the hell happened here?" and the scene quickly came into focus. "Oh man, again?!?"

"I fucked up… Jesus! I'm a moron! I'm so sorry guys!" CharlieB appeared to be truly genuine for once in his life, but it was too late, far too late.

"Sorry man, but you gotta go, and never come back. In fact, don't even try talking to me. If you see me coming, turn around and walk the other way. If I come into the Clam's Claw and you're there, you finish your beer as quickly as possible and you get the fuck outta there or else I'll make you myself. Now git you piece of shit! Git!" I pointed down the street while AaronL stood next to me with his arms folded.

"Sorry boys…" he began walking down the sidewalk towards his Mom's, and before he rounded the corner he turned back to face us, "By the way, you guys were right, I do have cancer. They gave me two months to live. It was nice knowing you boys. Take care," the tears were building in the broken man's eyes, and he was doing everything in his power to keep them from streaming down his face which was evident by the choking, knot-in-the-throat kind of way that he sounded as he gave us the news.

"I'm truly sorry to hear that, but it don't change shit," and it didn't, not in my mind anyway. I couldn't give in just because the old man was sick. If I did indeed relent, he'd certainly abuse my leniency and fuck up again, and there were no guarantees that the next time wouldn't be worse than the last. It's no secret I liked my house, and I didn't want to worry about coming home one day to a blazing heap of fags.

"You did the right thing man, I mean, if we let him continue to pull shit like this, next time the whole house could go up," AaronL read my mind.

"Thanks man. It ain't easy, especially after learning that he's dying, but he gets no sympathy from me. He's fucking half a century old, he's gotta know by now that shit like this carries consequences. He's like a fucking child. He's the fucking quintessence of a piece of shit, the goddamn epitome of trash," I shook my head as I rolled the smoking chair down the porch stairs and to the curb by the trash cans which were out for pickup that afternoon.

As more time went by I thought about CharlieB and our last encounter more and more. It takes a lot to piss me off, and even though I had had enough of his idiocy, I threw my eyes at my feet in shame whenever the old man's name came up. I should have been more sympathetic, but I just didn't feel it for him at the time of the second fire. I wasn't the only one either, many in the neighborhood, including his mother, had had it up to their eyeballs with CharlieB, the poor bastard.

_____

I ended up getting a great job on the west side not too long thereafter, and at about the same time, I was offered a place to live in my great-grandmother's house on the hill overlooking downtown. The day I was moving out of the Brooklyn house I ran into CharlieB's mom at the Clam's Claw, and learned that her son was still alive and kicking, though his health was rapidly deteriorating. He was hanging out on her porch most days where people apparently came by and made donations towards his medical bills. The doctors all but told him he was a lost cause, so I'm sure a lot of the donations went not to his medical bills, rather his drinking habit instead.

A few months after running into his mother, CharlieB came up in a conversation with one of my friends, so I decided to stop by his mom's porch with my girlfriend on a nice Sunday afternoon to say hi. We arrived to an unexpectedly empty porch, so I knocked on the front door, but no one answered.

"Maybe he's finally at the hospital, or hospice, wudaya think?" TracyJ, my girlfriend at that time, inquired.

"You're probably right… Hmmm, but what's this?" I walked down to the end of the porch, and posted on the wall just above a reclining chair quite similar to the one CharlieB had set ablaze on my porch was a giant novelty "Get Well Soon" card with a bunch of signatures on it, and the date "7/24/08" was written all over it as well.

"Huh, check this out Babe," I motioned for her to join me under the card.

She walked up next to me and began reading the different entries people had inscribed upon it. "What do you think the importance of July 24th is?" she asked me.

"Well, I'm guessing from the wording most of these people's used, that it's the date he passed away. They must've gotten the card when he was still alive, and when they all went to sign it, he had died," I pointed at a few of the inscriptions.

"I bet you're right," TracyJ agreed.

"Well come on, let's go to the Clam's Claw and see if they know what's up," I grabbed her by the waist and led her back to my car. As I opened TracyJ's door for her I speculated that "there's gotta be at least one bloke down there that knows the plight of old CharlieB, or at least where he's at."

"Agreed," and five block later we had parked outside the bar. We walked in and there were a few locals chatting up the bartender, MarthaW. She was about CharlieB's age and had actually lived in the neighborhood since she was a kid. She knew CharlieB all too well, probably more than she really wanted to. Everyone said "hi," which TracyJ and I returned with big welcoming smiles.

"What'll it be kid?" MarthaW smiled at me after looking at TracyJ and back at me, shooting a little wink of approval regarding, I assume, how easy TracyJ was on the eyes. Most agreed that their first impression of her, aside from the obvious aesthetics, was based on her warm smile and, for lack of a better term, shocking demeanor. Covered nearly head to toe in tattoos, accompanied by lip, nose, and multiple ear piercings, TracyJ looked like quite the badass mamacita you did not want to cross, however, her big smile, bright eyes, and genuine politeness could fool even the most respected shrinks into believing she was an innocent, naïve little lass from the suburbs.

In my best Irish accent I ordered "a pint of PBR for me, and a vodka-cranberry for me love here."

"Hi there, pleased to meet you Ms…" TracyJ smiled as she extended her hand.

"Ms. MarthaW, and the pleasure's all mine, I assure you," she replied as she daintily shook hands with her.

"Oi! Lay off lass, she's mine!" I exclaimed. "All er little pink bits and shiny drippins," I went on in my over exaggerated Irishness.

The accent was an ongoing joke we had at the bar that was started when a customer came in one day faking an Irish accent. It appeared as though he was trying to get the attention of the girls in the bar, and this accent was somehow supposed to impress them or something, but who knows really. At any rate, he failed miserably at accomplishing whatever it was he had come for as it seems one of the cocktail waitresses working that night was actually from the city of Cork, Ireland, and she instantly recognized his accent as a fake. She called him out in front of everyone at the bar, sending him running out the bar with his tail tucked between his legs.

When MarthaW came back with our drinks I inquired, "So, what's the deal with CharlieB? Where's he at these days?"

"Hmmm, you haven't heard have ya?" and my heart began to sink like the titanic. Well CharlieB passed back in July. Here…" she said as she walked to the other end of the bar to grab some kind of flyer that was sitting on the bar. She handed it to me and continued, "this here's the info for his service which is coming up next weekend. He had no money, so it took them quite some time to raise enough to get him a tombstone, as well as a plot in the cemetery."

I looked over CharlieB's funeral program before replying, "Oh wow, he got a plot at that cemetery over on 21st and Morrison huh? That's awesome!" I paused, trying to remember if I had anything planned for that day. "Yeah, I'll be there, I mean, why not right? You're going right?" I asked MarthaW.

"Oh, I suppose," she answered. "Despite all the grief that buzzard caused everyone, he was still a person you know? Still a part of our lives…" and she was absolutely right.

Since I've only included one story in this letter, I thought it might be lacking a little, so I'm adding something I've been pondering all day today: a list of things I want to do before I die. This is what I came up with so far: 1) I want to go to Mexico during the Day of The Dead Celebration. If I remember correctly, there's a certain city or village where the festivities originated or are centered or something like that. That's where I want to go; 2) fly a plane and jump out of it. I wouldn't let it crash, I'd have another pilot there to take over for me. Don't ask me why it's important that I fly the plane, it just is. Call it a boyhood dream, and we all know how wacky those can be; 3) I suppose I should have some kind of will drawn up, though I don't own shit, so what's the point really? And when I do finally die, there's two things I want to happen: 1) make sure my tombstone reads "For a Good Time, Dig Here ↓" and 2) I'd want to become a Zombie and create my own gang of zombies. I'd turn a bunch of kids with a few bites, and then I'd make them dress up as clowns so that they're super creepy. Then, my brains permitting, I'd create a list of people I hate that also have Coulrophobia, and hunt them down with my gang of kiddy clown zombies.

Well Ms. Caribou, that's it for my first letter to you, and I sure hope it finds you. At the very least, write me back so I know you got this, and so I know I have the right address for you. If you're feeling up to it, please return the favor and share another one of your stories. Until then, take care!

XOXO

TommyJ

154

Before I received a return letter, about two weeks after the first letter, I decided to write the next installment of what was shaping up to be TommyJ's Memoirs. I wrote it all out, put it in an envelope, and did everything but mail it. I held back from sending it off with the hope of receiving a return letter from Caribou within the next few days, and I told myself that was the absolute longest I was going to wait.

Four days had passed and nothing had come from Caribou, so I decided to go ahead and mail the second letter off.

Dear Caribou,

I am writing this before receiving a return letter from you. That is if you even wrote one at all, assuming of course you received my letter. For now, I'll just assume these letters will find you somehow. If your letter is in the mail then just disregard my rambling. At any rate, I certainly hope to hear from you soon.

So without further ado, let's get this shit on the road.

Since the first story is quite short, I have not just one, but multiple stories in store for you in this edition. Each letter I write from here on will be greater in length.

Enjoy-

---

15. TATTOO II

Five and a half years after my first tattoo, I was Downtown getting my twenty-somethenth tattoo at a nice little apartment I rented with my buddy NickC, A.K.A. Knife Fight Nick, a guy who's story you'll hear in a little bit… This time around I was getting a picture of a model dressed up as that fairytale princess who was best known for her seven dwarves. In the picture she's looking back at you, winking as she lifts up her skirt so you can see her garter belt, red panties, and a little bit of her ass. I was strung out every waking hour during that lifetime; I, me, & my old junkie buddy, Salinas, the man responsible for the naughty fairytale pinup tat on my arm. Salinas had been living on my couch for about six months in exchange for free tats for NickC and I. Fucking sweeeeet deal as I saw it.

Beer after beer, crystal after crystal, our minds were the headlines of the next day's newspaper: some kind of crime vying for the spotlight. As we slowly got more fucked out of our minds, Salinas and I did a very thorough tweaker clean up of the kitchen in order to stave off the risk of infection.

In the meantime, NickC cooked up some dope at the end of the counter.

"So, we ready?" I asked Salinas as I positioned myself on a bar stool in the best place possible for the tattoo to be done as comfortable as possible.

Salinas sat next to me and replied, "Yup," as he readied himself. He looked at me with a really glazed over look in his eyes, and an alarming shakiness to his hands as he said "Man I can't do this right now. I can't even see what the fuck I'm doing here. I'm just too fucked up man, this is a bad idea," shaking his head.

"Well hmmm…" scratching my chin, "You think I could tattoo myself then?" I requested, almost reluctantly. Just as I asked him this, the syringe that NickC had left uncapped and hanging off the side of the counter got knocked off by Salinas and landed sticking straight out of my hand. The damn thing went all the way through the back of my hand and the tip was sticking out of my palm. NickC started laughing hysterically so I asked, "What's so funny?" I was so fucked up out of my mind that I hadn't even felt the thing penetrate my hand.

NickC kept laughing as Salinas exclaimed, "Look at your fucking hand man!" Salinas pointed to my hand. I looked down and saw that it was going straight through my hand, and all I could muster in my state was a tiny yelp, like someone had stepped on my tail. I pulled the rig out of my hand as quickly as possible, and threw it across the room.

"Fuck you guys!" I laughed. I ended up tattooing my leg with a tiny book with a ghost of a tooth on it. Meth rots your teeth…

This moment will forever be ingrained in my head, my knee, and my holy hand. I can't deny that, while I lived a junkie's life, I had some really fucking glorious moments from time to time.

---

16. Kitties

I named her Brody, she was a little black kitten. My girlfriend gave her to me for my Birthday because I had said I was lonely at the apartment I had recently moved into. At least I thought I was lonely, but the truth was that at the time, I was emotionally imbalanced from all the different drugs I had been shooting up. My girlfriend didn't have a clue about my dope habit until we were about six weeks into our relationship, and once she did, she decided it was best that I hide it from her. That way, it was out of sight and therefore out of mind for her. She acted like everything was normal, as if I wasn't an addict. It was a little weird to say the least. She was MishK, my M, who I also called kitty. I loved her, she loved me, and we were good to each other. Well, for the most part, our relationship was pretty rocky during the first few months.

Frankly, I was a shitty boyfriend. I seduced her after only knowing her for only a short time and it was quite obvious that she resented me for it. I think she was mad at herself for letting her guard down, and she took it out on me because I brought out her vulnerabilities. Though, even before we had hooked up, before she resented me, she was always rather brusque with me. I think she was attracted to me from the first time we met, but she didn't want to admit it to herself, so in some kind of misguided defense mechanism of hers, she was quite prissy towards me.

Not too long after we first met, M turned nineteen years old, and on the night of her birthday, she had rented a limo for her and her friends to run around town in. Around ten o'clock that night a black, newer model, Lincoln Town-Car-looking stretch limo pulled up to the curb directly in front of my apartment building's front door. NickC and I just happened to be outside smoking when the limo arrived filled with her and her visibly intoxicated entourage. NickC, who originally introduced me to M, came outside with me, and after NickC and M had a brief conversation, she invited him into the limo. However, she claimed there wasn't enough room for me, even though I could plainly see there was space for at least two more people, and quickly shut the door, but not before giving me a cynical little grin. Just before I could walk away M's window rolled down, and she went on to tell me that they were headed to a party. She rolled her eyes and sighed heavily before   I could follow the limo if I wanted to. Before I could answer she shut the door, and the limo began to drive off leaving me in the gutter.

What the hell, what a bitch! I thought, but less than a minute after they left I received a text from NickC with the address to the party. I bolted into my place, explained the situation to my two buddies who were there, and the three of us headed to the party.

A twenty minute drive later we arrived at the party which was in full swing. There were about eighty to a hundred kids around my age, but I was somehow able to find M rather quickly. She seemed standoffish at first which wasn't a big surprise, but as the night progressed, and she got a little drunker, she seemed to warm up to me. What I didn't know at the time was that she actually had a little crush on me.

After the party shutdown due to a brawl that broke out over a spilt drink, we all went back to my place to continue on with our own party. By we, I mean NickC, the two friends I had brought with me, me of course, M, and all the people she had brought with her in the

158

limo. When things began to wind down, around six in the morning, I went to my room and passed out.

When I woke up in the morning, to my astonishment, there was M sleeping on my floor. She just happened to be wakening up as well.

"You know it's much more comfortable up here with me," I explained with a broad grin.

"Yeah, um, I'm fine down here. Thanks though," she replied in her most callous tone.

"Suit yourself," Well, at least I tried.

We laid there for another ten minutes before she got up and left the room. A few minutes later I followed her out and found her sitting on the couch in the living room which was a complete mess.

"Looks like y'all had some fun last night," I said cynically, but with a hint of playfulness.

"Yeah, I guess so," she replied as she surveyed the ship wreck that was my apartment. I went into the kitchen and after some digging, I started a pot of coffee. When it was done I poured myself a cup and offered her one. After cream and sugar we sat on the couch together and drank our coffee as we watched TV. I managed to get her to laugh her ass off with a few ridiculously random conversations I started. It didn't take long for us to realize that everyone else had gotten up and left the apartment already. We were home alone.

Within another half hour I had her pants off and I was in her. I looked at her and thought she was the most gorgeous little red headed lady I had ever seen. Mmmmm ginger. We had talked and talked until I had talked her clothes off. We fucked for over an hour from the living room to my bedroom and back to the living room. She said she wasn't taking birth control, so I blew my load on her leg, which she didn't take too kindly to, but hey, where was I supposed to put it, on my couch, or on the floor? She was lucky I was polite enough to not only do that, but get her a towel so she could clean herself off as well. I think that's the exact moment when she began resenting me.

"Well, I've got to go. I've got a lot of errands to run today," she said as she put her last shoe on, now fully dressed.

"I'll walk you to your car?" I said with the hope of making a new buddy at the very least.

"Sure," and I finished dressing. As I walked her to her car I convinced her to sit on the curb and have a smoke with me. We continued talking and I steered the conversation towards her and who she was because I really didn't know all that much about her, plus it was safe to assume that she'd like talking about herself because most people do,, especially women. That way, she felt comfortable talking to me, and I was able to show that I was not only interested in her, but also that I was willing to listen. It seemed as though all of her closest friends were extraverts, talkative types, so this was a nice change for her. This conversation was really a turning point for me because up until this point, I was quite the extravert myself, and I rarely ever took the time to just sit and listen to someone. Talking with M on the curb that afternoon taught me not only that I could listen, but also that I was good at it and I liked doing it. From that day on people actually began coming to me with their problems, and I've often found that the best thing I can do for these people is just listen to them. One of the most important lessons I would later learn from M is that women like you to listen to their problems, not try and fix them. I learned that one the hard way. Men, on the other hand, usually call with a problem which they expect me to provide a solution to.

I sat on the curb and listened to M for well over an hour, and in her sudden haste to depart, I was unable to get her phone number. NickC and I didn't see or hear from her for more than three months thereafter. The deal was that she had a boyfriend at the time, something she failed to mention to me that day on the curb.

When I saw her next, she had come over to my apartment with a friend on the pretext of hanging out with NickC, but to my surprise she had actually come for one reason, and one reason alone, to see me. She asked me for a cigarette, so once again, we sat on our curb and conversed through the night and through a case of beer. She spent the night with me, and that marked the beginning of our relationship.

Though we hadn't actually had the talk confirming the title, M already had it in her head that I was her boyfriend. During that first week together as a 'couple,' unbeknownst to me, M had come over to my apartment one night to hang out with NickC and their friend HaileyG. NickC had arrived home after I had, and saw that my bedroom light was on from under my closed door assuming that I was there. M asked NickC where I was, and he told her I was in my room, so she came in without knocking and to everyone's surprise, she found me sleeping in bed with my on-again, off-again Lover, DanielleA. I awoke to M gasping as she clasped her hands over her mouth, so I immediately jumped out of bed, threw some clothes on, and ran after her onto the street. Though I had just slept with DanielleA, I convinced M that there was nothing between her and I other than the occasional casual sex, and that we were just friends. I didn't mean to hurt her feelings, but frankly, I didn't know that M felt so strongly about me and our relationship because she had yet to tell me so. However, the fact was that DanielleA and I were in bed together, butt-ass naked, so really, try and talk your way out of that one. M seemed like she wanted to believe me by giving me a second chance, but then the DoryV incident transpired a couple of weeks later which made things even worse between us.

DoryV was an acquaintance of mine. She was very pretty, but according to our mutual friends she was also very prude. At least that's what I thought until one strange night when I was sound asleep in my bed with M. I was on the side of the bed closest to the door, and M was between me and the wall. All of the sudden I awoke to the realization that there was another girl in bed beside me that wasn't M.

"DoryV, what are ya doin here?" I asked, as I nearly shit the bed.

"Oh good you're awake! I am so fucking high! I put two pills of ecstasy up my ass and I am so fucking horny," she exclaimed as she grabbed my cock.

"Who the fuck are you?" M asked in a very sleepy but agitated tone. Meanwhile, in my half awakened state, I was foolishly thinking there might have been a threesome about to happen.

"Oh shit!" DoryV screamed directly in my ear, apparently unaware that I was not alone. "I'm sorry, I'm so sorry. Oh my God…" she slurred on, utterly shitfaced and embarrassed.

DoryV got out of bed amazingly fast for how wasted she sounded, and she slipped away from my flat just as quickly as she had appeared. I suppose the embarrassment was too much for DoryV because it was the last time I ever saw or even heard from her again. M should have broken up with me right then and there and saved us both a lot of future heartache, but I believe she relished the abuse, at least in the beginning.

Our relationship wasn't all bad, and I can comfortably state that we had more ups than downs. The way I see it, is that the point of a relationship, whether it be an intimate one like ours (you the reader and me the writer as well as M the girlfriend and me the shitty boyfriend), or even a friendship, is to make each other happy, or at least provide some kind of mutual benefit. Therefore, when the happiness is gone, that is to say, when one or both of us are unhappy with the other for more than half the time, then what's the point of continuing the relationship? I recall one particularly crazy-fun experience we shared about a year into our relationship that occurred at the unlikeliest of places, a second-hand clothing store called Value Cottage. They were having a half-off everything sale that day which we had been planning to go to for the last few weeks. What we hadn't planned on, however, was the wild lust of a young couple's new love to take part over while shopping of all things.

After perusing the store in our respective sections and grabbing a few clothes to try on, we met back up mid store and headed for the dressing rooms. We each entered our own room and began trying on clothes, all the while talking to each other about what we had picked out. At one point, M had put on a dress she thought was really sexy and asked me to come out and tell her how it looked on her. I came out and found it hard to keep my chin from hitting the floor. I threw my arms around her and began kissing her as I rubbed her ass. Before I knew it, we were in her dressing room ripping each other's clothes off. I grabbed a breast with one hand, and gripped her nipple with my teeth ever so lightly, though just tight enough so that any effort to pull away would have invited an even sweeter pain. I eventually worked my way down onto my knees, threw one of her legs over my shoulder, and dove into her. My humming created a vibration that travelled from deep inside her, through her entire body, and I could see it wash over her face in rhythmic pulses. She poured out high pitched grunts and groans in a sort of primitive beat which I fluttered my tongue and worked my lips to. If it weren't for me propping her up, she surely would have been on her hands and knees. As she sank deeper into the stall, I sunk my tongue deeper into her. Her enjoyment was more than obvious by the droves of cum that came running down my neck. Grabbing my hair, she screamed "Fuck me!" in my ear, but there was no immediate risk of

getting caught as we were still the only people in the dressing
rooms. She put her hands on the wall and I took her from behind as
we stood on the clothes she had been trying on. I was so worked up
that it took just a few short minutes for me to cum. M picked up a
dress she wasn't going to buy and wiped the cum from the both of us.
We expertly escaped the dressing room undetected, made our
purchases, and scurried out of there before anyone was the wiser.
The funny thing was that sex never really played a big role in our
relationship, but I didn't mind, and neither did she, especially
when we had the occasional wild experience like the one we had that
day at the Value Cottage.

Possibly the worst moment in our relationship occurred in February
of that next year when I returned home from a trip to Chicago. Why
go to Chicago when the temperature reaches below zero you ask? The
answer is simple, business. No one in their right mind would travel
there for pleasure during anything but the summer. The weather there
seems to be pissed off pretty much year round, but it seems to be a
lot less angry in the summer months, though even then it can reach
into the hundreds.

Portland wasn't faring too great itself that winter, and the day
before I was to fly back into town, there was a huge, and I mean
ginormous, ice-storm that shit all over the city leaving a blanket
of ice that was nearly six inches thick. The stuff was on the roads,
rooftops, trees, power lines, you name it, ice was destroying it.
And to top it all off, I didn't bring nearly enough ice
(methamphetamines) of my own, and I ran out a day before I was to
fly back. The flight was impossible for me, but I managed not to let
the withdrawals get the better of me. Due to the storm my plane was
the last flight that the FAA allowed to land at the Portland
International Airport for the next three days so I felt quite lucky,
at least for the moment.

When I got to the baggage claim and saw that there were barely any
cars outside picking people up, I assumed the roads were going to be
pretty bad. That was an understatement. I rode in a cab for nearly
an hour and a half at a maximum speed of twenty miles per hour which
we only achieved once on a straight away on the freeway. A feeble
attempt had been made to de-ice the roads with rock salt and gravel,
but the damn ice was just too thick, so they abandoned the salt
trucks and plows. Chains had very little effect on the ice, but as
long as we drove in grooves made by previous drivers, we seemed to
be ok. I was actually quite impressed with the cabbies ability to
drive in such circumstances considering he came from a desert
country that barely even had any ice makers, let alone icy weather.
On our way down the freeway, we must have passed a dozen jack-knifed
semis, a half-dozen accidents abandoned by the drivers, and miles
and miles of city that had no power. The only lights keeping the
city awake were the hundreds of emergency vehicles flashing their
red and blue emergency lights. It seemed as if there was a cop or an
ambulance every hundred yards or so on and off the freeway.

For the entire ride I only recall seeing one other brave taxi driver
attempting to negotiate the roads, but that was it, I failed to spot
a single other car anywhere on the road. For a cab ride that
normally would have taken a total of minutes and cost about $40, I
rode for an additional hour and paid an additional $150. Bummer.
Unfortunately I was unable to go straight home. First I had to go to
M's place and get my keys so I could get into my apartment where my
sweet medicine awaited. I had lent my car to M while I was gone, and

she was supposed to have picked me up from the airport, but I told her that it was impossible for her to drive there. I called her just a few minutes before I arrived at her place, and told her to meet me outside with my keys. I hadn't seen her in over a week, so she was upset that I wasn't coming to stay the night with her. What she didn't understand was that I was strung out and I needed a fix, and on top of that I was being very short with her over the phone which only exacerbated the situation. She simply thought I was being cruel to her, and I knew if I explained any of it to her, she still wouldn't fully understand, so I just let it be.

When the cab pulled up to her apartment she was standing on the sidewalk shivering and crying. Not an over-the-top wallowing, or even a quiet, soft cry, but somewhere in the middle. I saw genuine pain in her eyes, a pain that said I just don't get you, why are you doing this to me? It was a look that I will never forget, and always regret. I took my keys from her without so much as a kiss or a hello because I was so furious, so irritated by that point, that I could have killed someone. I was mad at her for not coming to terms with my addiction, for shutting it out and not confronting it, and I was mad that it had to bite her in the ass like this. The ice-storm, having to come all the way out to M's place which was a good two miles past my place from the airport, the super long cab ride itself, and M's painful look had burnt the end of my fuse. I was ready to be home, get high, and crawl into a ball and die. Though it didn't outwardly appear so to me at the time, in retrospect, I believe that night was really the beginning of the end for us.

We carried on for a good four more months after my trip to Chicago, and everything seemed to quickly return to normal between us. Half way into those four months, M became pregnant. We had a short discussion about it, and we both decided that an abortion was in our best interests. I paid half and offered to drive her to the clinic, but she insisted on having her sister take her.

It was hard on both of us, but for obvious reasons it was especially hard on her. I think she resented me for getting her pregnant, and it was really the straw that broke the camel's back. After that, it seemed like she was looking for any excuse to get in a fight with me.

In the beginning of that summer, M came over to surprise me with beers and lunch and when she arrived she found me sitting in the living room talking to a girl. The girl was in fact a guest of NickC, but just before M arrived, NickC had stepped out to go to the corner market to pick up a pack of smokes. I tried to explain this to M, but she didn't believe me. She threw the beers and sandwich at me and ran out of the apartment. I tried to run after her, but she wouldn't stop to listen. So like any stupidly distraught boyfriend does, I grabbed the beer and left in my car. I drove around my neighborhood chugging beers, listening to music, and thinking about M.

Aside from the two prior stories, I also thought about how M had never really caught me cheating, even though I had done so on many occasions. How ironic that in this instance, the one time I really wasn't cheating, she actually thought I was. Go figure. Each time I finished a beer I made sure to drive past a dumpster which stood in the street around the block from my house so I could throw my empties in it. Once I had finished the entire case of beer and thrown them in the dumpster I headed home. I stumbled into my room and passed out halfway on my bed and halfway on my floor fully clothed shoes and all.

When I stumbled out of bed the next morning, I barely made it to the kitchen sink in time to fill it up with puke.

"Nice," a sarcastic voice said from behind me, "you also got some shit on the porch waiting for you." I turned to see NickC walking away towards his room.

"What shit?!?" I slurred after him, but he didn't respond. After wiping the puke from my chin and grabbing a glass of water, I headed for the porch. There, all lined up on the railing were twenty four empty beer cans with a note taped to one of them:

Dear Drunk Driver,

Please refrain from throwing your beer cans in our dumpster or we will be forced to report you for drunk driving, as well as littering.

Thank you,

Concerned Contractor

How funny, I thought, well that's the end of that dump site. I turned around to find yet another note awaiting me. This time it was an envelope with my name on it taped to the door. I opened the envelope and found a strip of photo booth pictures and nothing more. In each picture was M, by herself, and she was holding up a piece of paper. In the first picture the paper said "I'm", the second one said "**Leaving**", the third paper said "**You**", and in the fourth picture she was gone, leaving just the empty booth. I was almost pissed at her in a way, I mean did she really need to go and get all creative and be so damn *cute* about our break-up? Rather than the plain old "I just got dumped by my girlfriend dumps, I felt like I had been burned quite harshly, and worst of all she did it in such a way that made her look like some kind of hands down, no doubt about it, take-all winner. That is, of course, assuming that there's even such a thing as a winner of a break-up. My tears tasted bitter, and my beer buzz had abruptly fizzled off into the sunset much like my girlfriend had.

It really tore me up when she left me because I truly believed we could have accomplished so much more than we had together. *If only I hadn't been such a fuck up,* I told myself repeatedly, determined to never again make the same mistakes that drove M away. The truth was that I hated the idea of being the one that caused all the grief and heartache for M and I both, an idea that plagued me even more than the pain I felt from actually missing the girl. When M and I parted, Brody became my only love. This wasn't the last I saw of MishK, however, years later we became friends, getting together for coffee or whiskey's so we could catch up on one another's lives post us exclusively.

It seems like it's been years since I've seen Brody make an outdoor appearance. As she strolls into the front lawn at my house, she begins to chomp at the taller blades of grass. The sun is beginning to dip behind our house, barely casting my head's shadow behind me as I watch Brody roll around in the flower bed lining the front of the house. Ten degrees cooler, I sit in the shade of our rhododendrons on a tall patch of grass with my kitty close by watching neighbor after neighbor stroll by with their hounds as they trot by on their leashes. She's slowly making her way to the opposite end of the yard as if I'm the embarrassing father and she's the reluctant daughter, unable to look cool if she stands next to me as she sees the enemy pass mere yards from where her perfect winter coat is shedding pounds of down quality softness across our yard.

By the time M left me, Brody was no longer the tiny black kitten she was when M first brought her over. She had grown into an entire cat with her own little personality and all sorts of quarks to go along with it. My favorite thing about her was that she liked to sit on my shoulder which I found rather endearing. Her soft beautiful exterior is only matched by the rough, pissy demeanor in which she displays towards every other animal, and humans are no exception. She could be the sweetest friend, cuddliest lover, and in the same hour make me feel like I was going to be signing divorce papers as she bitched at me in long droning meows. They were meows of discontent: no food, nor water, no hugs, or going outside could calm this attitude of hers. Perhaps she left us in search of that which would calm this ill temper of hers, a possible cure to what appeared to be some kind pain. From the first day I had her, Brody was equally sweet, as she was snippy. My kitty, it seemed, was either bi-polar, or some kind of feline pathological liar.

For the first year of our relationship as pet and owner, Brody and I lived in a flat on the fourth floor of an old hotel in downtown Portland. Seven hundred square feet of hard wood floors to run around on, but I felt bad that she didn't have a yard to frolic in, no mice to mangle, and no freedom outside my apartment walls. Luckily for her, we moved to the house in the Brooklyn neighborhood while she was still a kitten. There were two other cats there that belonged to a roommate that only lived there for half of our first year there. Poor Brody and the other two cats had to endure multiple bands practicing at the house almost every day of the week, and I always wondered if that had deafened her at least a little. I was working a minimum wage job so I was unable to afford her spaying, and at the time I wasn't aware of the various animal shelters and veterinarians that offered low cost, and sometimes free, spaying and neutering deals. Thus, little Brody quickly made quite a few boyfriends in Brooklyn, especially when she went into heat. She would crouch real low to the ground in front, and raise her little ass in the air, and her little back legs would walk in place while she meowed long and loud. The boy's came-a-runnin, and she became pregnant within weeks of her first heat.

A few months of a chubby, whinny, constantly hungry kitty turned into a punk ass brat that was barking in my ear in the middle of the night. Waking up next to her, I realized my head was in a puddle of what have must have been her broken water. Yuck. I carefully picked her up and placed her in the large box I had lined with towels for the birthing. Despite what I had read about kitten birth, I really didn't know what to expect. It was three in the morning on a Tuesday night, and aside from Brody, I was all alone. I caught every Kitten as they came out, and being Brody's first litter, she was quite

confused by what was happening to her and too freaked out for her
natural motherly instincts to kick in. Therefore, I had to take on
her motherly duties by wiping away the placentas, tying off the
umbilical cords with dental floss, and severing the cords with
sewing scissors. Brody gave birth to five gorgeous, healthy kittens.

That single experience changed my perception of life and death
forever, and I will never be the same. I was somewhat aware that the
event was going to be extremely significant, yet somehow when it
happened, I was utterly unprepared for how it was going to affect
me… My perspective, appreciation, and all around love for life took
a complete U-Turn that is still in effect to this very day.

I kept one of the kittens, the last of the litter to be born, which
was the only one that looked like Brody's Siamese boyfriend. I
assumed Brody had been knocked up by at least two males, which is
possible for cats, and the kitten I kept, Eva Braun, was the product
of this strange anomaly.

_____

While writing this letter, Brody went missing. After two weeks of
putting up missing signs, and scouring the neighborhood for any
signs of her, I finally received a call from a neighbor that had
seen my posters.

"Hello, is this TommyJ?" she asked with an uneasiness in her voice,
and somehow I knew what was coming next.

"Yes, this is TommyJ," heart stopping to begin sinking into my
belly.

"I believe I may know where your cat is," dead. The biggest knot I
had ever felt was forming in my throat as she muttered the words
into my ear.

Apparently there was a black cat that had been hit by a car on the
main road by my house, Cully Boulevard, and she had either crawled
under or was placed under some rhododendrons along the sidewalk
making it hard for passers-by to see her. The caller had found out
that there was a cat there because every time she walked her dogs by
the spot, they would go sniffing at her carcass, and she thought
nothing of it until she took the time to look deeper into the bushes
and that's when she discovered the dead cat. She had seen my Missing
Cat signs and thought that I would like to know rather than not know
what had happened to her rather than wonder what had happened to my
Brody for the rest of my life. While talking to her on my cell phone
she directed down a few blocks from my place where her husband was
waiting on the corner to show exactly where the cat was. Sure
enough, it was Brody. She had been dead for quite a while, most
likely the full two weeks she had been missing. I couldn't bring
myself to pick her up off the road until a few days later when I had
the help from a bottle of whiskey. I never thought I would be so
torn up over a pet, but the truth of the matter was that I was
crushed. Utterly devastated. I cried so loud when I got home the
dogs next door howled in response.

_____

17. Knife Fight Nick

I want to write this now before I lose this sinking feeling. I got it last night when I was there, the place where I gave NickC the name Knife Fight Nick. The grounds of the hospital are a vast hill side dominated by a number of enormous buildings, a beautiful view to have when you're dying. I went there last night to take a pizza up to my M and her friends who were waiting in the maternity ward for their friend to give birth to her first baby. Three days in labor, water broken and dilated, and suddenly there was baby Giovanni. The last time I was at that miserable place I was also with M, but rather than a birth, we had come to visit NickC. That sinking feeling would have come back to me ten-fold if it wasn't for the fact that I was drunk and high. Not the smartest thing to do before entering a hospital, the maternity ward at that, but I would have done anything to avoid the nervousness of that sterile place. To me it's one of the itchiest itches you just can't scratch, and the biggest itch was Knife Fight Nick's stay there.

_____

It started at a pub called Scooters 13th Street, a block off West Burnside. I met a few friends there for drinks, and NickC was supposed to show up at anytime. A few hours went by, and I was becoming pretty drunk. My phone rang and it was a number that I didn't recognize, but I answered my phone anyways.

"TommyJ, man I got jumped. They took my money, my dope, and my phone!" whimpering. I knew immediately it was NickC and that he was in pain.

"What the fuck! Where are you? Who was it?" I inquired a little panicked.

"I'm waiting for them outside of Kelly's," he replied, fool heartedly trying to regain his pride.

"What are you going to do? How many of them are there?"

"This guy knew I was selling dope at the Greek, and out of nowhere he just sucker-punched me the fuck knocked out. Fuck man, he took all my shit: my pot, my wallet, even my phone. When I came to, some other guy was there helping me up, and he pointed out the guy out who had jumped me. The guy who helped me up described my assaulter to me, and I knew immediately it was that douche bag Damien."

"Damian, who the fuck names their kid Damian? Well I guess he's livin up the evilness associated with his name huh? No irony there," I said in an attempt to guide NickC's thoughts elsewhere.

"Yeah, uh, whatever… Are you even fucking listening to me?!? Jesus… Anyways, I saw the fucker as he was leaving the bar with a bunch of his buddies, so I followed them out. They're just next door now, you know, over there at Kelly's. I'm gonna wait for em to come out… I'm gonna stab this motherfucker!"

168

"Are you fucking crazy!!! It ain't worth it man, it just ain't worth it!" I yelled at my friend so loud that everyone at Scooters went quiet and stared at me. "Sorry everyone, it's a little bit of an emergency, but I apologize."

"Huh? Who the fuck are… Doesn't matter, I gotta go," he replied.

"Hang tight man, I'm not that far away. Just don't do anything until I get there ok? Just wait for me," listening. "You there?" Fuck me, he hung-up.

I related the story as fast as I could to everyone I was with at the bar before rushing off on my skateboard. NickC was nine blocks away straight down Washington Street. I skated as fast as I could, but I was too late. I arrived outside Kelly's and found a huge crowd gathered outside blocking the intersection at 4th and Washington. As I made my way towards the center of the crowd I heard people talking about a fight and someone being stabbed. The people ahead of me were parting like the Red Sea for a guy who was trying to make his way out.

"He stabbed me!" a guy kept repeating in broken screams, and when I passed him I could see that he was bleeding from wounds that appeared to be all over his body.

I can't believe it, the crazy bastard actually did it. Now where is that kid? I made my way to the center of the crowd where the fight was, and it was just as I had guessed, three guys were beating the living shit out of NickC. I got there just in time to see four bouncers from the Greek as they stopped the other three guys from killing NickC, after which they dragged him into their club.

Seconds later a drove of cop cars and ambulances pulled up and the three guys who were beating on him ran off along with most of the crowd. I couldn't stick around because I had dope on me, and I sure as hell didn't want to get caught up in the drama or have to talk to the cops who had came sporting helmets and shields.

The air was thick with testosterone, and the crowd was extraordinarily hyped up from the liquor and the fight, so the prospect of being consumed by tear-gas, and riding in a paddy wagon was beginning to look more and more likely. I hung around just long enough to see NickC being loaded in an ambulance before I skated back to Scooters. I walked in and sat back down at our booth I had hastily departed from just thirty minutes earlier looking as pale as the day my Irish ass was born.

"What's wrong? Where's NickC? Did he get in a fight?" DanielleA threw this particular guess out there because NickC was well known for his drunken violence, but she could sense that something was actually wrong. "You don't look so good TommyJ. Oh my god, is he ok?" she gasped as her eyes dilated and her hands covered her mouth.

"He's headed to the hospital," beating neither on or around any bush.

"How bad is it?"

"Stitches, lots of stitches," and I found my beer still intact on the table, in fact, it was still cold. "Can I get three shots of Jamieson please?" hailing the tenderness of the bartender.

"What an asshole! So, what'd he do this time huh?"

"From what I can tell," my own eyes lit up, "he stabbed some poor bastard, and then the guy's friends, well, I'm assuming they were his friends, kicked the shit out of NickC. I'll be honest with you guys, it looked really, and I mean really bad," my shots arrived and I downed two of them before anyone could even blink. "My guess is that he's gonna be in the hospital for at least a few weeks, you know, the way he was lookin."

"Jesus... Do you know which hospital he's at?"

"I didn't stick around to find out. There were cops everywhere, and there were so many drunk Joeys out on the street that it looked as though a riot was gonna break out at any moment," down the tube went my last shot. "So I hightailed it outta there before I could find out exactly where they took him."

I drank for another hour at Scooters before leaving on a solo mission to meet up with M, MishK. I waited until I saw her in person to tell her about NickC's fight, who was, by this point, a very close friend to both M and I. She took it hard, and crying, she had the same questions for me as my group of friends at the bar had. Amidst her interrogation of me, my cell rang out from my jeans pocket.

"Is this TommyJ?" a professional voice asked.

"Speaking," I answered as M intently stared at me.

"This is NurseE calling from Oregon Health Sciences University," here we go I thought. "NicholasC has asked that we contact you in order to let you know that he has been admitted into our Intensive Care Unit after an altercation he was in earlier tonight."

"How is he," relieved to know where he was, but wary of what the nurse might say next.

He has a few abrasions on his face, two black eyes, and a great deal of swelling, but he is stable and he's being seen by an ophthalmologist as we speak. That is all the information I have at this time," and the sound of papers being rifled through could clearly be heard on her end. Ophthalmologist, that can't be good. There must be something she's not telling me. Doctors and nurses are trained not to divulge heart wrenching news over the phone because they fear that the patient's loved one might drive erratically on their way to the hospital. "He's requesting that you come to see him this morning at your earliest convenience. Shall I tell him you're…"

"I'm on my way," I interrupted.

I grabbed M, and we were at the hospital in a flash. When we arrived, it was around two in the morning, and the only other people in the main lobby were a small group of kids around my age. It was obvious that each group were friends of each party that was involved in the fight. We waited for almost an hour to see NickC, and all the while the group across the lobby continued to glare at M and I. The tension was thicker than the stagnant, sterile hospital air. I hate the smell, chemical cleaners, human waste, death, and decay, all the lovelies your nose hates to swallow. Plus it brings back all kinds of bad memories.

The other group was called back to visit their holy friend first. Apparently, the guy was a mess: eighteen holes sown up with over a hundred stitches. The same nurse that had called them back reappeared moments later to whisk us away through a labyrinth of halls, elevators, and various departments.

"You and I talked on the phone right?" I had recognized her voice so I decided to make small talk with her as we were led down a long hall to a large elevator, the kind long enough to fit a bed or stretcher in.

Again, M asked the nurse how he was doing, and she replied "stable," yet again.

What kind of answer is that? I mean what the fuck? That could mean all kinds of things. Does it mean he's lost a leg, but not dying? Is his face is smashed in beyond recognition? The elevator took us down about five levels to the Intensive Care Unit where NickC was convalescing. We were then led into another waiting room, and told by the nurse to take a seat for just a moment while she made certain he was ready for a visit. Rumor had it that he was being quite difficult with his attending nurses, so they were a bit behind with him. Almost 4 a.m. and it's a work night, Why couldn't he have gotten beat up on the weekend, I selfishly questioned the world at large with a frown.

"You two are here to see NickC?" a different nurse inquired as he stuck his head through an open doorway.

"Yeah," we stood up, "that's us."

"Right this way." As we walked with the nurse he explained that NickC was lucky not to have lost an eye, which was in fact slightly damaged as a result of the fight. The nurse went on to explain that NickC had a bad concussion, and his cheek bone was broken. It seemed as though it took forever for us to get to his room as we walked through two large doors, and down yet another corridor lined with rooms occupied by recovering patients. All the other rooms had their lights out except for the room we were being led to. Inside NickC was conscious, but the dope was pretty doped up.

A painful laugh passed through his split lips, "Glad you could make it to my party. Come in, come in," and he couldn't help but smile, which stretched his lips causing a stitch to pop out, and a small stream of blood to begin leaking down his chin. Dummy.

I don't think I would have been laughing if my face looked the way his did, but the MD had given him some drugs that seemed to be doing the trick, probably all too well. He had two black eyes, one of which was swollen shut, and his head was the size of a watermelon. At the sight of a broken NickC, MishK shattered like a tiny porcelain doll, crying into my shoulder as she hid from his monstrously mangled face.

"Perhaps it's a good idea if you wait to cry until we're not in the room. I don't think that he's seen a mirror yet," I whispered in her ear.

I took a few steps into the room, leaving M in the hall. "Hey buddy, looking good. The nurse says you'll be alright, just gotta hang out here for a few days," but in reality, he was going to be in there for almost two weeks while he recovered from the wounds and subsequent surgeries to his face in order to repair his fractured cheekbone.

"You see that bitch right there?" he pointed at the nurse preparing a shot of some type in the corner of the room.

"I see a nurse," she could obviously hear him.

"Yeah that bitch," he kept pointing. "That bitch stuck a goddamn tube up my dick, can you believe that shit?!? That hurt more than getting the fucking knocked outta me shit…um, I mean, the shit knocked outta me," and we couldn't help but laugh at NickC's incoherency as well as the poor nurse who shot us a heavily stifling glare. However, she couldn't help but smile herself, a grin that she tried to hide by turning her back towards us.

"Your little friend here has been giving us nothing but trouble. We had to give him medicine to make him sober up in order to give him proper painkillers. His blood-alcohol level was over three times the legal limit to drive when he came in, though neither drug has seemed to calm him down one bit." The nurse then asked us to leave because she needed to perform some procedures on him that required privacy. When I rejoined M in the hallway, she grabbed me and started crying even harder. It was difficult for both of us to see our friend in that awful state, and I nearly shed a tear myself as I consoled my girlfriend.

Two weeks later NickC got a ride home from his mother. I was out hustling at the time he arrived, but when I got home I went straight to his room. He was all doped up on painkillers as he watched TV in his room. His face was all black and blue still, and it was almost as swollen as it was when I first saw him in the hospital.

Quietly, I asked "How ya doin man?" as if any loud noises could easily have broken his eardrums.

"I'll be alright for a few days, but then I gotta go back and have more surgeries done to my face. Fuckers said they're going to make a pin sized hole in my cheek, stick a hook in it, and pull my cheek bone back into place because it was smashed into my skull," he explained as he attempted a cynical smile.

"Jesus tits man," I laughed. "I guess that means we should get high then huh?" Though I didn't really have to ask, I knew he wanted to, whether I had asked him or not. Even though he was all doped up on morphine in the hospital, I knew that he missed the sweet calm that only morphine's big sister, heroin, could provide. A spoon, clean water, and the skag, then all I needed to do was hold the lighter underneath the spoon so it got just hot enough to melt the chiva into the water. I stirred it around with the plunger from the syringe, and then I dropped a little cotton ball in which I stuck the rig into in order to suck just the dope up, and not all the other crap the Mexicans cut their dope with. The rig was fixed. He was never any good at shooting himself which I always thought was funny because his mom is a phlebotomist, so I always had to do it for him. I found a vein, and pushed the needle in. I sucked his blood into the needle to make sure I was in fact in a vein, and then I pushed the plunger down, releasing the chiva upon him. He lay back as he enjoyed the rush while I fixed myself. So nice, so nice it was.

"You know who you are now?" little eyes now, pins.

"Who?"

"You're Knife Fight Nick," I Knight Thee my friend.

A little while later I moved into the apartment building on 14th and Clay which was just across the street from the one I lived in with Knife Fight Nick. This is where I was living in the story I told you earlier, Dead Wind. It was during this time that he had another little incident that would confirm his title as the Indisputable Knife Fight Nick.

One night when I was just about to leave my house to meet up with JohnnyB, a friend of mine that lived in the apartment building next to mine and would later live with me in the house in the Brooklyn Neighborhood, my buzzer rang. I knew it couldn't be JohnnyB because I had just spoken with him on the phone, and we were supposed to be meeting outside the back door to my building in five minutes, but the buzzer indicated that someone was ringing me from the built in phone at the front door. My building was five stories of brick, used as a hotel for over eighty years before it was converted into apartments in the nineteen-eighties. It was U shaped with the front door in the crotch, better known as the courtyard. I was on the fourth floor in the dead center of the crotch, and my balcony looked down upon the courtyard as well as the cityscape of downtown Portland. I ran out onto the balcony assuming that the person ringing me was concealed by the building's front doorway which was directly underneath me.

"On my way down," I yelled without looking to see if they had backed out of the doorway for me to see who it was.

I ran down the four flights of stairs that were on the front side of the building, and when I got to the bottom floor I saw a fresh streak of blood oozing down the elevator door. There was no one within earshot, and the elevator was right there on the bottom floor. Ok, what the fucking Creepy right? The elevator was a turn of the century, four person ride that had swinging doors on each floor, and behind it was a sliding iron gate which made the whole scene even creepier. I ran out the back door where my friend JonnyB had agreed to meet me.

"JonnyB, you've gotta come see this," and he could tell it was well worth checking out based solely on the urgency in my voice.

We walked back into my building, and I showed him the blood which, by this point, had slid four feet down the door, dripping onto the ground.

"What the fuck?" JohnnyB Sherlocked as he noticed a trail of blood going towards the back stairwell. We followed cautiously, with quick feet as the trail led to the third floor where it looked like the person had fallen down, and laid there for a moment leaving a small pool of blood on the carpet before they got up and continued to climb the stairs to the fourth floor.

"Fuck me," I said as we stared at the smear of blood on my apartment door, then as we looked at each other I thought: what the fuck is this, some kind of joke? Are you fucking with me JohnnyB?

"He cut me," a faint voice could be heard from down the hall.

"The Motherfucker cut me," a full scream this time, and JonnyB and I bolted down the hall following the voice. The trail of blood seemed to follow the yelling as well, both of which led us to an apartment that was rented by a friend of mine.

"I'm bleeding," cries, laughter, and moans. "I got in another knife fight, but this time I'm the one who got

Without thinking I walked through the open front door and down a short hallway. There in the bathroom was Knife Fight Nick. He was sprawled out in the bathtub with a menstruating vagina of a gash across the entire palm of his hand, and blood was squirting out from an artery that had been severed. Pale, Knife Fight Nick was drunk off his ass as usual and losing blood fast.

AaronU, whose apartment we were in, was digging through a first aid kit. "Fuck TommyJ, he's cut bad," hysterics from Mr. No MD or PHD AaronU.

"Well don't tell him that," I whispered harshly to AaronU in response.

"I'm taking him to the hospital," AaronU informed us.

Don't know no insurance, but fuck it, he's dying I thought.

"Stitch me up," Slurring Knife Fight Nick stood up wearing a bloody sleeve. Without lingering any further we left NickC in the care of his savior, AaronU, and we left with a good tale behind us.

Those are my stories for this letter, and I'd love to chat more, but my hands hurt from typing and I'm tired. I know, I know, boo hoo, poor TommyJ! Anyways, until next time Caribou.

XoXo

TommyJ

A few days after sending the second letter, I received Caribou's
first letter to me. Honestly, I really didn't expect to hear from
her this quickly, or really ever for that matter, so I was a little
taken aback when I did.

TommyJ-

I wanted to start by thanking you for your letter. I was quite
surprised when I found it in my mailbox yesterday, and it put a
smile on my face. I wish I could share a story with you, but I just
don't know what to write, plus my mind is so preoccupied with all
this shit that's going on in my life right now. First of all, I'm
moving to L.A. next week, so I've been scrambling around trying to
get everything in order to get the fuck out of Vegas. As soon as I
know my new address there I'll let you know what it is. I've also
run into a little legal trouble recently, trouble I don't feel
comfortable in sharing quite yet. Sorry, I hope you don't take it
personally, I just don't want anything getting out, and if for some
reason this letter didn't make it to you and I had written about
said legal troubles, then I fear it may end up in the wrong hands
and be used against me somehow. So again, please don't take it
personally. Please, please, please TommyJ, please keep sending me
stories, and I was thinking, maybe it's a good idea if one of these
days you could put all of them together and create some kind of
memoir, a book of your own. Well, like I said, I'm busy as hell, so
I got to run. Hope to hear from you soon.

XOXOXO Back at you!

Caribou

Dearest Caribou,

Sounds like you got just my first letter, and the second one should
have found its way to you just a day or so after you sent me your
letter, so I hope you enjoyed that one as well. Thanks for writing
me back, even though you didn't include a story, but I understand
your situation. I do, however, appreciate you taking the time to
write me back.

Sorry to hear about your troubles, maybe sometime you'll be able to
tell me what your "legal trouble(s)" are all about, but until then I
understand your security/privacy concerns.

At this point, writing these letters has become more therapeutic
than anything. Therefore, whether these letters find you after your
move or not isn't necessarily the most important thing as long as I
can get you the stories at some point. Though it would be nice to
think someone is actually reading these…

At any rate, I hope you are well and maybe one of these days I'll be reading one of your stories, hint, hint. For now, I'll continue to address these letters to your old place, assuming the post office is forwarding your mail to your new, L.A. address. Without further delay, here are some new stories as promised.

_____

18. Squirt Gun

This story begins at the Clam's Claw, the Brooklyn hood bar that
CharlieB, the neighborhood drunk, called home. Like CharlieB, I
frequented the bar that was just a few blocks from my house. The
same faces drank the same drinks year after year there, and new
faces like mine came and went and came back again. Most of the
bartenders that worked there had been there for at least ten years,
but there was a weekend position that was filled through a revolving
door. One such short term employee was a gorgeous little girl that
was about eight years my senior. DaisyD liked to party hard, smoking
pot and drinking to excess, but she didn't seem too wild, at least
not enough to be the topic of bar gossip. It was also no secret that
she had two kids that she was raising as a single mom, and by all
accounts she was a good Mother.

We met while she was working her very first shift, and she impressed
me from the get go. It was like she had been working there for years
the way she carried herself and seemed to find her way around there
with little to no direction from the manager that was training her,
RickO. I had been sitting in the back of the bar with a few of my
roommates playing darts when DaisyD came in to start her shift. She
must have noticed me checking her out because she made a point to
come my way and give me an unmistakable look of interest.

"Hey hun, you doin alright?" even though I knew she could clearly
see that my glass of whiskey and coke was more than three quarters
full even from across the bar thirty feet away.

"Thanks, but I think we're all fine back here," I raised my glass to
her and she replied by giving me a look that let me know that I had
my invitation to pursue her. Just like the next person, I love the
chase, so I did my best to prolong it by not sleeping with the girl
until she couldn't take the wait any longer and more times than not,
the girl would jump me and beg for sex. I lived for that moment.
This, of course, was all back in my prime, in my early twenties.

I began coming into the bar more often, gradually getting to know
DaisyD a little bit better as time went by. I had gained her trust
one night when I helped her kick a guy out of the bar that had
disrespected her and the bar-back that was waitressing that night.

It also turned out that we had some mutual friends that lived in the
hood near the bar, and one day, when I went over to our friend's
house to smoke some pot and jam out on the guitar and drum set they
had set up in their living room, to my surprise, there was DaisyD
sitting on the couch when I arrived. She demanded that I sit next to
her, and we ended up having an amazing conversation that seemed to
go on for hours. I also got to play a few songs on guitar and sing a
little as well.

In other words, I got to show off for her, and I already know what
you're thinking Caribou, cheesy right, really immature? Well,

178

whatever it was going to take to get her to like me more, I was more than willing to give it a shot.

_____

As I had said earlier, the sexual tension was thick between us, and the thicker it got, the more likely it was to explode into a wild abandon-like sexcapade. To be entirely honest with you, I'm a mediocre musician, but to someone who is not really musically inclined, even the mediocre can appear amazingly talented. I left her with the promise of a visit the next day at the Clam's Claw when she was scheduled to work next.

As promised, I came by the bar, "Hey there Daze, what you got goin on after work today?" middle of a summer Saturday that I had big plans for…

"Nothing really, just a few errands, why?" her wide smile appeared to reveal her perfectly straight, white teeth.

I reached across the bar, placed my hand in hers, and looked into her eyes, "I was hoping I could steal you away for a few hours and take you to a secret spot of mine."

"Secret spot huh, sounds like fun! I'll just have to tell the sitter that she'll have to watch the kids for a few more hours, she was looking for the extra hours anyways. I have to be home no later than ten ok?" She looked genuinely ecstatic.

"Awesome! Your off in what, twenty minutes?" looking at my cell phone for the time.

"Yup," she was all smiles.

"Ok, before you get off, I have to run out and grab a few things for our adventure today. I'll be back in twenty minutes alright?"

"A few things huh?" she leered at me before cracking another wide smile.

"Alright then, I'll see you soon," and with that I finished my beer and left the bar. I jumped in my car out front, and drove down to the grocery store where I picked two bottles of champagne, a half gallon of O.J., and a forty ounce of Big Bear malt liquor just in case she wasn't in the mood for mimosas. I also decided it would be a good idea to pick up some condoms just in case she wanted me to wear one, or two, or three, or four… Even though I was highly educated on STDs and other sexual matters, I wasn't the safest when it came to sex back in those days because, and let's be honest here, even the thinnest lamb skin doesn't compare too skin on skin contact. To tell you the truth, I consider myself very lucky not to have contracted any withstanding diseases, let alone a child or two, or three, or four...

I made it back to the bar just as DaisyD was clocking out. Some of the old timers in the Claw must have caught wind of our date because about six or seven of them dispersed throughout the place kept giving me dirty looks.

"You ready Daze?" I asked as I approached the bar.

She was still behind the bar wiping down taps while the next
bartender to come on shift, MarthaW, was behind DaisyD switching out
the cash drawers in the register. "Sure after my shift drink. Now,
what can I getchya?" she asked as she walked back to the cooler that
held chilled pint glasses.

"Oh, just a PBR for me pretty please," and I could hear a few
snickers and sighs from a few of the old timers that sat the bar.

"Alright old timers," I stood up on my bar stool and stepped up onto
the bar. "As you may have heard, DaisyD and I are going on a little
adventure today. Now don't let this break your little hearts, she's
still single, and we are just going out as friends. Ok fellas?" I
walked slowly up and down the bar as I had said this. I finished
with my palms held out, as if I was waiting for an "Ok" from all the
old ball busters. "I said, ok fellas?"

"Ok," from one end, "Yeah, yeah," from another, and a few replied
"sure ok." It seemed as though everyone in the Claw had chimed in.

"Alright then," I said as I stepped down from the bar. Meanwhile,
MarthaW and DaisyD were behind the bar having a good laugh at my
expense. Apparently, as I had made my speech, my fly had inched its
way open, likely from my climb atop the bar.

I really thought I was going to be in for a romantic day, but I
wasn't too sure what I was going to be doing with DaisyD for the
long run. I could barely take care of myself, let alone her two
kids," so it seemed as though we were neither destined for a lengthy
relationship, nor to have many days like this one, and what a day it
would turn out to be. I decided not to tackle the particulars of our
dilemma right away, and just wait and see where day went first.

DaisyD and I finished our drinks as we watched the Blazers beat the
Lakers on the boob tube which I remember because it was a rarity
during that era. We jumped into my car and left the bar. Once we had
started down the road DaisyD put her hand on my knee. "So, where we
headed?" she squeezed the end of my leg at the knee, successfully
tickling me.

I laughed as I said "Hey hey, you'll just have to wait and see."

"Oh come on! Tell me! Pretty please!?!" squeezing my knee harder
this time, forcing me to grab her knee and tickle her back. We both
laughed for a few blocks, but I refused to let her know where I was
taking her.

"Don't you worry, we're less than ten minutes away so you'll find
out soon enough," and I was right, we arrived in just under ten
minutes. I turned the car onto Sparrow Street which ran east and
west, and drove west down a few blocks under a train track trestle
where the road ended. That's where 19th & Sparrow Street intersect,
and this is the corner where I parked the car. Just west past the
intersection you could see the Willamette River, one of only two
rivers in the whole United States that flows north. The other is a
smaller river in North Carolina called the New River. My father
happened to own a vacation home in the Appalachian Mountains near

the New River, and the one and only time I went swimming in it my brother and I were chased out by a water moccasin.

To the south of us, behind the car, was an entrance to a riverfront park where my secret spot lay in wait. "Please tell me you didn't bring me here to kill me did you dear sir?" she politely inquired as she sunk deep into the corner of her seat nearest her car door.

"Of course, that's what the Mimosas are for: to get you drunk and then have my way with you," I explained as nonchalantly as possible while I undid my seat belt, and reached back for the grocery bags.

She put the back of her right hand to her forehead and rolled her eyes back, "Oh please, someone save me!"

I got out of the car, walked around the back side of it, and opened the door for DaisyD. I helped her out of the car before leading her by the hand through the park entrance and onto a path that went down a hill into a small forest that filled the park.

"Where are you taking me huh? This is so pretty!" she said as she looked at her surroundings. Although it was a beautiful summer day and it was nearly eighty degrees out there was a beautiful but eerie fog hovered thinly just below the forest's canopy above us.

"We're almost there, it's just over that ridge over there, across some bedrock, and then we're there," I pointed down the path in front of us about a hundred yards ahead. "You see, I read about this place in a book called Fugitives and Refugees: A Walk in Portland, Oregon, by Chuck Palahniuk, you know the same guy that wrote Fight Club. Apparently he lives here in Portland, and he's part of that Cacophony Society. They're the ones that do that big Santa Rampage every year, you know, when you see hundreds of drunken Santas all over town one day a year?"

"Oh my god, is that what those Santas are all about? Right before Christmas last year I was in a mini-mart picking up beer or something and I heard a car wreck out front. When the clerk and I peered out the window to see what had happened, we saw a minivan followed by a limping cab pull into the mini mart's parking lot. There were like six Santas that crawled out of the cab to inspect the two cars, it was so bizarre. For the rest of the day I saw Santas all over town, and I mean all over town. Come to think of it, I guess it makes sense that you say they were drunk," she laughed periodically as she hurriedly related her story to me.

"Yeah, the Santa Rampage thing and the Society is all covered in that book of his. It's all about places and things to do in Portland. One of the places is a castle that sits on the hill above Portland State University (PSU) that used to be rented out to bands and other types of entertainers when they were traveling through town. I think the Grateful Dead and the Stones might have stayed there, anyways, I used to rent a room in the house right across the street from that castle, crazy huh? You know, speaking of Christmas time, have you ever noticed the Martini glass made out of Christmas lights on the hill there above PSU?" I asked her as we neared the top of the ridge.

"Oh yeah, I know exactly what you're talking about," she slipped a little but I caught her before she took a tumble.

"Well that's two houses down from the castle and the house I stayed in," I told her as we came to the top of the ridge, and to the edge of the river bed. "Well here it is. This is one of the places in Palahniuk's book, it's called Elk Rock Island, and you can only get to it in the summer months when the river is low enough to cross over to it." I said as I pointed to the bedrocks that we were about to be walking across. The island itself sits in the very middle of the river for most of the year, so it remains pretty untouched by humans, sustaining its natural beauty. It's about two to three hundred yards long and just as wide. It's thick with brush and old growth fir trees as well as manmade paths that seem to be well maintained or barely used.

"Gorgeous, I can't wait to check the rest out," she said as she ran ahead of me and began to jump from rock to rock making her way to the island. I lagged behind making sure not to let the bottom fall out of the grocery bags.

"Hey! That way," I yelled at her, waiting for her to turn around so she could see me pointing towards the left edge of the island where she would be able to clearly see the beginning of a path.

"Got it," she yelled back. Once she got there, she began jumping up and down, "Come on, come on! I wanna explore!" She yelled to me as I tried to speed up. Her excited demeanor was enough to convince me that I had picked just the right adventure for us.

"Coming!" and as soon as I made it to the path DaisyD grabbed my hand and led me into the woods.

"Oh my god, look!" DaisyD pointed to the top of the tree line at a large bird's nest.

"Wow, that's a huge nest." I had been to the island two or three other times before, and I had never noticed it until now. Perhaps it's new. Suddenly, a large, full grown bald eagle came flying out of the nest.

"Oh wow," DaisyD said gently, "how pretty," her voice lowered to a whisper.

"Seriously beautiful," I said as I watched the eagle fly out over the river, dive in, and just as quickly as she was in, she was flying out with a salmon in her claws that must have weighed as much as the eagle itself. It was like it was right out of a movie or from the archives of the best of the best shots from National Geographic

"Holy shit that was awesome!" DaisyD said as she clutched my bicep.

"Yeah, you know, I paid him to do that right when we got to the island." I laughed and DaisyD punched me in my arm laughing as well. As we stood there in total awe, we watched as the bald eagle flew up to her nest with lunch for her little ones.

"Follow me," I said as I clutched her hand and led her further down the path into the island's woods. The path looped around the island and along the way there was a bluff just off the path that sat twenty or so feet over the river. This is where we found a spot to sit and make our mimosas. We talked and drank for nearly two hours

while the sun beat down upon us with all its force, reaching over
ninety degrees.

"Hey, you wanna go for a swim?" DaisyD leaned in and asked me.

"Sure, I didn't really bring..." I began to say but was quickly
interrupted.

"We don't need any swimming gear, lets just go with what God gave
us" DaisyD said, both frightening and exciting me with the prospect
of skinny dipping with her, as well as the potential to butt heads
with her possible religious beliefs, and my lack thereof.

"Right," I said following her lead as she began to take off her
clothes. Soon, we were butt naked, standing at the edge of the
cliff.

"You think it's safe to jump in from here?" DaisyD asked. Just then
a boat cruised by a mere hundred yards away, and we were quickly
hailed by the seamen's whoops and hollers.

"Well, there's only one way to find out," not wanting to be eye
candy for much longer, I took a few steps back from the edge of the
cliff before quickly running past DaisyD as I jumped out as far away
from the island as I could get, yelling through the air. When I hit
the water I was welcomed by what seemed like freezing water. When I
resurfaced and I had wiped the water from my eyes, I could hear the
people from the boat screaming and hollering as I just barely caught
sight of DaisyD just as she hit the water a few yards from me.
Thankfully, the boat wasn't completely filled with obnoxious morons,
and they began to depart before DaisyD had even surfaced. I began to
swim over to where I thought I had seen her land, but she must have
had the same idea and swam under water towards the direction that I
landed because she surfaced there, and by then I was where she had
landed. We both laughed as we swam to each other, meeting halfway in
between where we embraced and had our first kiss. It was one of the
finest, most romantic kisses I have ever had, even to this day.

After climbing back up the rocks, dressing, and drinking a few more
mimosas DaisyD said, "So, I have to be getting back soon to relieve
the babysitters," making a little flinch like she had said something
wrong.

"Babysitters huh? One's not enough? Is it a couple, like their
grandparents or something?" I inquired as I put my socks on.

"Yeah, they're a couple," said a reticent DaisyD.

"Since you need a ride home, I'd be more than happy to give you
one," anticipatory TommyJ laughed at his own, stupid joke.

"Well, I hope you wouldn't just leave me on this island! Anyways,
that'd be great. God, you are great! I had so much fun with you
today. I had no idea about this place, and I've lived less than a
mile from here for over three years. This was really fun... I can't
wait until I get you home," sly little smiles on both of our faces.

We were at her place in no time, still wet with our clothes sticking
to us. "Hey why don't you let me throw your clothes in the dryer for

a bit, the kids won't be back for at least an hour. I forgot that the sitters," she chuckled before continuing, "said they'd watch them for a little longer tonight, till eight." I'm so sure she forgot, I think she just said "earlier" so that if the date went horribly, she had an excuse to bail on me, but since it went incredibly well, the truth has come out.

"Sure, you got something for me to wear in the meantime?" as I took off my shirt.

"Yeah... Well, it's laundry day, sooooo, I don't have too much," as she left me in the living room and walked into what I assumed was her bedroom in the back of her apartment. "Oh here, it's perfect," she said as she walked back into the living room holding a pink silk nightie.

"Seriously?" I tried to contain myself from bursting with laughter.

"Of course I'm serious, why, what's wrong with it? I think you'll look absolutely adorable in it," laughing so hard that I almost fell over.

"Alright then, as long as you enjoy it," I said as I took off my pants.

"That's right," she replied as she handed me the nightie, but before I could get it on, DaisyD couldn't control herself, grabbed my arm to stop me from dressing any further, and kissed me. Before I knew it, we were in her room, in bed, but getting her clothes off proved to be harder than usual because she was still wet and her clothes were sticking to her like super glue.

"Oh God fuck me!" we slammed to her bed as I finally got her last piece of clothing off.

"Oh I'm gonna fuck you. I'm gonna make you scream! Gonna make you beg for it and beg for more," I purred in her ear as I slid my hand up her leg. It was so heated, and we had both become so extremely whet with anticipation over the last two months, that her pussy dripped droves of wetness onto my hand and my cock became harder than it had ever been before. I smelled her sweetness as I breathed through my nose while I kissed her.

"Fuck me! Fuck me!" she screamed.

I pulled her hair with one hand sending her hair back, exposing her neck, and I brought my other hand up from her pussy. Dripping with her juices, I placed it around her neck as I choked her ever so gently. With a big smile on my face I replied to her request, "Maybe."

"Oh you asshole, I said fuck me, so this is the part where you fuck me you jerk!" she said as she grabbed my cock. I lost my chance to play with her any further, and she had me in her quicker than I could fight her off.

"OHHHHH GOD! Oh God!" I moved upon her slowly. She grabbed my ass, pushing me to fuck her faster and harder which I obliged vigorously. Soon after, she motioned for me to flip her over so that she was on

top of me, digging her nails into my chest, and bending my dick to
the breaking point. DaisyD screamed my name, God's name, and even
baby Jesus' name over and over again. With one hand on her ass and
the other in a pool of what I initially thought was sweat, I soon
realized I was almost literally swimming in a pool of DaisyD. She
had cum three times and it must have been a half gallon each time.
She only came when I was on top of her, and when she did, I felt a
highly pressurized stream squirting into my pubic bone which turned
me on to an even hotter setting than before.

After her third, I flipped her over and fucked her from behind
pulling her hair back so she could almost see that I had my eyes
rolled back in my head as I neared my climax. I began to grunt
gently, gradually becoming louder and louder. She felt that I was
close to cumming and just as I began to release, she began to cum
for a fourth time, squirting her cum on my balls and even below and
beyond, all the way to the pillows on the back of her bed three feet
away. I was so, so, so impressed as I flipped her back over so she
was facing me when I came on her face. Hotter than hot, I thought,
yet grosser than gross. I lay next her drenched in our sweat and cum
while she lay next to me as we held hands, breathing in the heavy
summer air.

"Water," she whispered as she squeezed my hand and began to make for
the bathroom.

"Please," I muttered, "one glass to throw on me, and one glass to
drink from, k?" I directed her to my further desires.

"Will do," she whispered, barely audible as she walked down the hall
to the kitchen where I could hear her grab two glasses and fill them
up. She walked ever so slowly back to her bedroom which meant full
glasses. Suddenly her steps stopped short of the door and I heard
her gasp. I turned to look just as the freezing cold water from the
glass in her hand came splashing down upon me.

"YEEEEEOOOOOOOOOUUUUUUUWWWWW! That is fucking freezing!" I screamed
as I jumped high enough off the bed to hit my head on the ceiling.

"BWAHAHAHAHAHHAHA!" DaisyD laughed hysterically, but not for long
because I jumped down from the bed and grabbed the other cup from
her hand dumping it all over her with a similar "YEEEOOOOW" to
follow. I grabbed her and slammed her to the bed fucking her for
another twenty minutes or so thereafter. I fucked her so hard this
time that the shit coming out of her mouth could be taught to
retards as a new dialect of their own retarded language. That may
have cum out wrong, I don't mean to say she sounded retarded, but it
was definitely groans, shrieks, and mumbles that a re-re is likely
to make in a fit of excitement. Yippy the short bus is here, yippy,
drrrr, uh-drr, dirrrp dirp, yippy, I love Nickelback! Drrrrrrrrrr
Play Nickelback on the bus! Drrrr Yipp-drrrr-yipp yipp yipppy!
Drrrrrrrrrrr... I continued to think about this retarded voice in my
head as I fucked DaisyD, and after a while it began to sound like a
cross between Governor Schwarzenegger as a child & Bobcat
Goldthwaite slowed down by the consumption of a few eighty milligram
Oxycontins (which is really enough to put down a bear, but not this
retarded Bobcat).

After finishing all over DaisyD's tits this time, and she came yet
again, I laid flat on my back on the floor trying to catch my
breath. She did the same on the bed, but soon came to the floor to

join me where she put her head on my chest and nibbled on my nipple ever so gently.

"Do you want to see something great? I mean absolutely amazing? Three hundred and fifty dollars amazing?" she asked as she bit harder into my nipple.

"Yeah sure what you got?" I said pulling her head back by her hair so she would stop biting me. She got up and walked over to her closet, opened the door, walked in, shuffled her things around for about a minute, and when she came out she was holding a pillow case. She grunted as she heaved it over the bed and I could tell the thing was heavy by the way she was lugging it. By now, I had risen to my feet and slid onto the bed which was absolutely soaked in our cum. It made me wonder how often she bought a new mattress, or like me, just flipped the mattress over.

"So check it out," she said as she opened the pillow case so I could see the contents, and to be honest with you, based off this girls behavior, I half expected a dead animal or possibly even a still born child to appear. I wanted to close my eyes and not be forced to peer into the case, yet curiosity kept them open as I thought the sooner we got this over with, the sooner I could leave. Inside the case was a pile of dildos and vibrators, not too shocking, but I was definitely impressed. The sheer number and variety were enough to make any porn-star blush. Not only were there over forty little friends of hers there, they were all different colors and types: black, blue, pink, orange, battery powered, some that plugged into the wall, glass ones, metal ones, big ones, small ones, and the leader of the pink taco parade was a behemoth of a vibrator she had named Maybelline.

"This, TommyJ, is the Queen of the Castle," she said with her palm out towards me. "Meet Maybelline," she said, extending her hand down to her pussy with her vibra…, uh, I mean, Queen Maybelline.

"Well hello there your highness," I said as I slightly bowed laughing. "What the fuck is that thing? It's got like twenty buttons," I demanded to know just before she handed it to me. I pushed a few of the buttons at the base and it made various humming sounds as the pace of the vibrations and the motion of the tip varied from setting to setting.

"This thing cost me $350, can you believe that?" she said as I handed it back to her. She pushed a few buttons and it came to life. "Bzzzzzz. hummmmm. Biiiiiizzzzz," it sounded like a fountain drink dispenser, then a jack hammer, and of course, like a vibrator.

"Wow! Was it worth it?" I watched as she slipped it into herself. "Oh fuck yeah it was! oooh!" she said as she sounded like she was talking into a fan from how hard the thing was jamming her. I watched her fuck herself with it for a minute until she squirted again, but this time I made sure to be clear of the soaking zone.

"Damn, that thing does a better job than me! I don't think I like Ms. Maybelline," I shook my head as I got to my feet and looked around for my clothes. As I gathered them up and began to put them on, DaisyD continued to play with herself, adjusting the settings every so often which produced a new and unique sound out of her each time. I got my socks and shoes on and I was tying the last knot in my laces right as DaisyD climaxed for the last time. I kept thinking to myself that between the amount of sweat and cum, she was going to be really super thirsty afterwards, so I walked down the hall to her kitchen, found two drinking glasses, and poured us each a glass of water. I reached in her freezer and pulled out an ice tray which was empty. I filled it up with water and returned it to the freezer where I found yet another empty tray. What's with people putting empty ice trays back in the freezer anyways? So I filled up the second empty tray and stacked it on top of his buddy in the freezer before I walked back to the bedroom with our glasses of water.

"Oh God, thank you so much!!" she said in a chalky voice, sounding absolutely parched.

"You're welcome baby," I said after taking a long drink. I put my glass down and sat next DaisyD who was now lying on the bed with her back on a few pillows that were bunched up against the headboard.

"Whatchya got goin on for the rest of the day?" she asked me, still winded from play time with Queen Maybelline.

"Goddamn, she sure gave you one hell of a work out!" I adjusted the pillows behind me. "Well, let's see, today...hmmm. Today, today, today. Well, I have band practice at about seven, but other than that I was hoping that I could get laid a few more times," I smiled broadly.

"Oh yeah? Who's the lucky girl?" she laughed as she spoke.

"Some girl I met at this bar called the Clam's Claw. She started working there recently and I got her phone number so I thought I'd give her a call."

After finishing the water she set her glass down on the night table next to the bed "Is she cuter than me?" she inquired as she swung her legs over the edge of the bed so she was sitting next to me. She leaned down and turned back toward me so I could see her bat her eyelashes over wide blue eyes.

"Oh yeah, she's way hotter than you, and sexier too" I laughed as she socked me in my arm, something that was becoming somewhat of a habit for her.

"Well have fun fucking her because you sure as hell aren't getting any more from me, that's for sure," DaisyD opened the drawer on the nightstand and pulled out a bag of weed and a glass pipe. "Care to smoke?" she held the bag up, and the smell of it, even a few feet away, was overwhelming. It smelled delicious like something fresh from a bakery, sweet, even edible.

"Sure, why not? I have to tell you though, I haven't smoked in like a year or so, and when I do smoke, I'm socially retarded. I become completely inept, so don't expect any meaningful conversations out of me for the rest of the day. Do, however, expect a really good lay," I explained as she loaded the pipe.

"That's ok hun, it'll just be more fun for me to fuck you then." I grabbed her around her waist and tickled her, which would have most certainly sent the pipe flying across the room if I hadn't of thought ahead and grabbed it from her hand as I tickled her with the other. When I stopped tickling her, she breathed heavily as she cowered back against the headboard. I thought she had been subdued, but I found I was mistaken when she suddenly lunged forward at me as she began her counterattack, tickling me into the fetal position.

After a few minutes of back and forth tickling, we finally called a truce and focused our attention back to the weed. Except for our breathing, the apartment filled with silence for nearly twenty minutes as we enjoyed our high until there was a sudden knock at the front door.

"Oh shit, what time is it?" DaisyD jumped up and scrambled around as she looked for something on the floor. "Have you seen my phone? Fuck!" I leaned over to my right where my pants were laid out on the ground, reached into the pocket, and produced my own phone.

"It's six thirty-five, why, who's at the door?" I asked.

"The babysitters, um they're also my neighbors, and uh…" stalling, I knew DaisyD was hiding something now. "They're my parents. Shit, I didn't want you to meet them," scrambling to get her clothes on.

"Why not, most parents love me," I laughed.

"Don't worry, they smoke Pot too, but there's something about them you should… well… they're deaf," she enlightened me as her shoulders slumped and her head bowed to the breaking point. I did my best not to give away what was coming next, but no matter how hard I tried, there was nothing I could do to keep from feeling awkward and paranoid, all of which could be blamed on the weed. If I hadn't smoked any, it wouldn't have been that big of a deal, but it was really hitting me hard. You see, normally I would have been able to deal with such a potentially awkward situation like that with a smile and a convincingly good natured reception, however, thanks to the pot, I was unable to make the slightest expression other than a look of fear when DaisyD told me about her parents situation. I was about to meet her deaf parents and her kids and I was in total retard status. "No big deal, I'll be nice and quiet. I can't sign though," I told her as sweat began to saturate my clothes.

"That's ok, they don't care, and they're really easy going, old hippie types," she told me which made me feel a little bit better. The knocking was getting louder and more frequent, so DaisyD walked over to the front door and let everyone in. Sitting on the couch in the living room I thought oh man, here we go… Fuck, why didn't she just tell me to leave earlier, this sucks. Her folks were portly, stubby little people that were constantly smiling. I think they were just as stoned as I was.

"Mom, Dad, this is TommyJ," DaisyD signed as she spoke. I stood up, made a slight bow as I made sure to make eye contact with each of them, shook their hands with a firm handshake, and signed the one and only thing I knew how to sign: "nice to meet you." DaisyD made it clear to them that this was all I knew and not to expect any more out of me, but they seemed impressed nevertheless. They told DaisyD that they thought it was sweet of me to try.

Even though the initial meeting went smoothly, I still felt super awkward. Great, I thought, if either one of them were to walk into her bedroom right now I'd be a dead man. The bed was soaked and there were dildos everywhere. What a scene that was.

They signed back and forth with one another, as well as DaisyD who translated everything they were saying for me. The kids disappeared into their bedrooms which is exactly what I would have liked to have done at the time. Instead, I just sat there silently, waiting for an opportunity to present itself that would allow for me to duck out of there. I came up with an excuse that I had to go to work and I would have to leave after a few minutes or so, but before I could execute my escape, they interrogated me through DaisyD. She tried to answer most of the questions for me, but they wanted details about my job and family, the standard parental interview. I really just wanted to say, "Truth is folks, I was only planning on fucking your daughter, nothing more, and I think she had the same idea."

"DaisyD, can you tell them that I have to go to work now?" I asked her.

After twenty minutes of this, I was able to convince them I was late for work and that I needed to leave. "Oh sure," and she signed to them, and they signed back. "They say it was a pleasure meeting you, and they hope to see more of you. Not likely. I got up from my seat and walked out the front door with DaisyD close behind me. She came out front and gave me a hug, "When will I see you again?" she asked with her arms still around me.

"Tonight, you're working aren't you?" hugging her back.

"Nine to close," and we released our embrace, but I kept my hands on her waist.

"See you then," I kissed her and then walked to my car. I left feeling as relieved as I had felt the last time I was released from jail. I never went to the bar that night, in fact, I didn't return to that bar until I had heard she was fired for handing out too many free beers to her friends. I avoided her at all costs, to the extent of ignoring her calls. From the get-go, I never really intended to be her boyfriend, or even fuck her more than once, so I didn't feel like I was being a jerk, aside from the little lie about coming to see her at her work the day I fucked her. Any chance she had at seeing me more than once went out the window when her stoned, deaf, hippie parents came into her apartment with the kids.

———————————

Years later I heard that she was pregnant with her third kid, and she was engaged to be wed. Shotgun. This was all through the grapevine, mind you, so who knows how true these rumors really were since I never heard anything else about DaisyD thereafter.

———————————

Well Ms. Caribou, I'd like to jump right into the next story which is about Knife Fight Nick and a certain world renowned rapper, but NickC and I had a rather nasty falling out before the preceding story occurred, and I believe I should explain why, so that you can see the big picture.

19. Knife Fight Nick Now

I had been at a bar on Burnside with my buddy MikeC discussing astrophysics or the G-Spot or something when Knife Fight Nick showed up with his ex-girlfriend, SkyV.

"So… you two back together?" I inquired.

"Fuck no," Knife Fight Nick sneered as we watched her walking back towards us after visiting the powder room.

We drank until we could barely walk and somehow Knife Fight Nick got his drunk-ass kicked out the bar. Right after the bouncer had pushed him outside SkyV ran up to me and stuck her tongue down my throat. We made out for the next fifteen or so minutes until the bartender yelled out "last call." We got a couple of shots, put them back, and as soon as we got out the front door we saw Knife Fight Nick slumped over next to a light post on the sidewalk. I couldn't just leave him there passed out, he was liable to get picked up by the drunk police and thrown in the drunk tank to detox for the night, a place he was all too familiar with, so I grabbed him by the arm and dragged him with us as we walked a couple of blocks down to where my car was parked. We jumped in my car and headed for NickC's mom's place where he was living at the time. On the way there, the two ex's cussed up a storm about God knows what. When we arrived, I stopped the car to let them out,, and they were still fighting. I'm not entirely sure what happened next, as it was behind me, but fists were exchanged.

"Just drive, get me outta here!" SkyV yelled at me after jumping back in the car.

"Alright," gas to the floor, we left Knife Fightin Nick.

SkyV and I ended our night at 9 a.m. the next day when we finally stopped having sex and attempted to sleep. Rabbits.

Around noon there was a knock at my door, it was Knife Fight Nick. He had made it through the outside door into my apartment building which was actually a house split into three units, and he was banging on the double doors to my unit, doors that had a crack between them so that one could see into my place. I was in my room to the right of the front door, and the bathroom was across the hall to the left of the front door and that's where SkyV was. Naked. She had no idea he could see through the door, so she ran across the hall to join me in my room.

"That's my girlfriend you Dick. I saw her, she's naked! Fuck you guys!" he screamed. Heated, he left my house in a hurry.

"What the fuck? You both told me you weren't back together," I grabbed my cat gently by the tail as I had said this and she looked almost as confused as me.

190

"Well… actually we got back together last week," her and I calmed ourselves down, watched some TV, and eventually got back to fucking. This time it took the form of a hate fuck for to her deception. Slap, Tickle, and a Punch-Kick-Choke.

The girl I was seeing at the time, KathrineK, was in Connecticut visiting family for Thanksgiving. When I went to pick her up from the airport a few days later, she had a strange demeanor about her.

"What's up? Something's bugging you?" I finally asked once we were back at her house.

"I got a call from Knife Fight Nick while I was in Connecticut," Uh oh, Motherfucker! She went on to point out all the lies I had told her, and demanded an explanation that I simply didn't have. I had lied to a really great love of mine, and it cost me dearly. The conversation and our relationship ended simultaneously, and the two of us didn't speak for an entire year thereafter. Ultimately, she got over it, and so did Knife Fight Nick. My apologies.

The next time I talked to old Knife Fight Nick was a phone call at 6 a.m. on a Sunday morning. He was still drunk and just getting out of Hooper (the drunk tank in Portland). He had called me up the night before to see if I wanted to go out and drink with him, but I was more than wary, because the last few times we got drinks together he ended up drunk off his ass and I had to virtually baby-sit the stupid son of a bitch. Back then, when he got wasted, he liked to start fights with just about anybody he could antagonize to do so. Strangers, friends, me, trees, windows, pint glasses, you name it, he's fought it at least once. Foolishly, I thought what the hell, he can't be that shitty all the time. Wrong.

We met the Matador again and when I arrived, the place was packed as usual for a Saturday night. I found him in the back of the bar making out with some girl he had probably just met.

"Nick?" Quiet. "Nick!" grabbing his attention this time.

Slur, slurp, sucking face, "What up TommyJ?" wet lips dripping.

"Just got here, we need a pitcher?"

"Yeah, sure, PBR," like he needed anymore, but that wasn't my call, he's a grown man after all.

We put back a few pitchers of beer while Knife Fight Nick laid out our plans for the night. We decided we were going to go to the Kool Keith show at a place called the Chad Dirt, so we headed out there. This was the time when Knife Fight Nick was slinging Coke, and all sorts of other kinds of dope, but mostly Coke. We got to the venue and there was a line at the front door stretching around the block.

"Follow me," and I followed NickC to the front of the line. "What's up man?" he asked the door guy who says hi to him, shakes my hand, and introduces himself. $16 to get in, but not for us, we got in for free.

"How'd you hook that up?" I asked him thinking lucky us.

"He owes me some loot," he replied and I knew he wasn't the only one, but really, who didn't at that point, fuck even I did. We preceded downstairs where Kool Keith was already on stage. Again "Follow me," and I followed.

We headed towards the right side of the stage where we walked up five steps and entered the backstage Green Room. There was a buffet, booze, and there was even a jar of weed all laid out for Kool Keith and his entourage. We had to piss but there weren't any bathrooms nearby, so we pissed under the cushions on one of the couches. Classy. Ten minutes and four beers went by before the show sounded over, and seconds later Kool Keith and his motley crew joined us. Kool Keith A.K.A. Dr. Octagon, Black Elvis, Poppa Large, Dr. Dooom. I was sure they'd ask who we were, but the question never came up. At Keith's request I rolled a blunt and lit it up for him. After passing it to him, I noticed a porn magazine on the table and started flipping through it. "Damn these skanky bitches are all haggard and shit," I said as I scanned the pages.

"Shit man that's my new mag I just put out," and sure enough his picture was on page three, Editor and Chief, and I remembered that he had a thing for porn.

"I'm just playin with you," I laughed. "I knew this was yours," lying through my teeth, however, he must have believed me because he laughed with me and called me a "Punk-ass Robot," which had NickC and I falling over with laughter.

We hung out with Keith and the others for about two hours, before Knife Fight Nick got too wasted and started making a total ass of himself. After the fifth or sixth retarded thing to come out of his mouth had raised the awkward level beyond a tolerable level, one of Keith's bodyguards asked me to get him the fuck out of there. Without delay we left through the empty bar, and spilled out onto the street. I wasn't too surprised when Knife Fight Nick immediately tried starting a fight, and he did just that. The first two guys we saw walking down Burnside were two giant black guys.

"Hey you! Yeah you, ya dumb ~~motherfucker~~ (enter your own expletive here, his was indecipherable, but it sounded like "mother"-something), I'm talking to you," NickC yelled at them.

"Come on NickC, what the fuck are you doing?" I plead with him.

One of the guys shoved Knifer Nick to the ground while the other held me back. It didn't take long before Knife Fight started getting the shit kicked out of him. Done. The guys ran off down 7th Street, leaving Knife Fight Nick barely conscious in the middle of Burnside. He got to his feet, ripped off his shirt and screamed like a banshee. To top it all off he threw his phone about forty feet down the street where it smashed into forty little bits. No phone. I got to him, picked his ass up, walked him over to the sidewalk, and went looking for his phone. I managed to salvage his SIM card for him, but when I turned back to where he was laying up against a building, he was nowhere in sight.

After I found my car I drove around for twenty minutes looking for the dumb fuck, but the search was to no avail, he had simply disappeared. Gone.

The next thing I knew I was waking up in bed to a 6 a.m. phone call, "Hey! Thooooooomassssss? TommyJ?" Really quite drunk still, it was Knife Fight Nick.

"So tell me, what the fuck happened last night?" I asked in a tone that said I already knew there was bad news, and I wasn't the least bit excited to hear it.

"Drunk tank."

"Figured."

"Yeah, it blew."

"Also figured."

"Oh yeah, did you figure on losing me last night as well? Was that part of the plan?"

"Seriously?"

"Dead."

"No way Jose."

"You sure?"

"Positive."

"Because you can tell…"

"Hundred percent."

"Seriously, you can tell…"

"Look," I slowed the roll, "you'd made a total ass out of yourself in front of Dr. Octagon, and got yourself kicked out of the after-party. Then, once we were out on the street, you picked a fight with a guy twice your size, a guy who was just minding his own business and…"

"Seriously?"

"Quite."

Sighing heavily, "Well that'd explain all the bruises." Slumping deep enough into his seat, I could see it through the receiver of the phone.

"Well, where are you now?"

"On the bus headed home," rising in his seat. "Look, I'm… uh… sa, sa," he had used the word he was looking for so few times in his life that he was literally unable to recall how to say it. Though, I imagine the wicked hangover didn't help any either.

"Yeah, yeah, I gotchya. Go get some sleep and call me later today," and I hung up. What a dipshit! I knew he was gonna end up somewhere like that last night. Not his first visit to the drunk tank, and not his last visit either.

I wrote the next little tale a while back which I've copied it to this letter, and I took the liberty of throwing in some additional details as well as some much needed editing. I believe the following will give you a better idea of how crazy my life was when I was slinging blow. I thought this was more than proper since I sold you a bag, and we did some lines together when you were in Portland. Hope you dig it Caribou…

---

20. Blow You Away

My face is on fire, like I just got sprayed with military grade
pepper-mace. Snot and tears pouring out of my face, I can't see, and
I can't stop sneezing. I'm at an art gallery during a large art show
consisting of five artist's work, kegs, DJ's, and a couple hundred
people. It's on the fifth floor of a building on the same downtown
block where NickC got his new name. This was supposed to be a really
fun night, but now I have to run home with my tail tucked between my
legs because I'm an idiot. It burned so badly, I thought I was going
to have to go to the hospital at one point.

I literally had pounds of Blow at home, and always a little in my
pocket. I was a street urchin with a degree in Cocaine, with a
slight Addiction myself. It was all the free coke any one person
could possibly handle. Rot your nose, rot your life.

I liked to carry a little baggie of it that had a straw stuck into
it with a rubber band wrapped around the bag at the base of the pen
to prevent any spillage. Wherever I went I always carried that
baggie in the smaller right pocket of my jeans. I got my blow pretty
close to what you would call pure, and I would cut it myself which
made me a lot more money. I saved the uncut shit for personal use,
and that's what I had in the baggie in my pocket. I grabbed Salinas
and had him follow me out of the show into a stairwell, and up a few
flights. I pulled the bag out of my pocket, stuck the straw in my
nostril, and plugged the other with my thumb. Just as I was about to
take a little snort, BOOM!! PaulyK came running around the corner
and slapped the wall with the palm of his hand which scared the shit
out of me so badly that I took a huge snort instead of the little
bump I had intended to take. In a tenth of a second I had shot a
gram of cocaine up my nose that was just a cunt's hair away from
being pure. Bloody hell this burns! My eyes were watering and my
nose was gushing bloody snot. I tried to hang around the party, but
within ten minutes I knew I couldn't stay, so I began walking the
twenty plus blocks home. I was sick for weeks.

I wasn't living on my own, but I was the only one paying rent at the
place. My two buddies, Salinas and Mac, were staying with me for the
time being. This was the year after Salinas lived with me and Knife
Fight Nick in exchange for free tattoos. At this time I was living
by myself in the building across from that previous apartment, the
old hotel where Knife Fight Nick left the creepy trail of blood and
ended up in my neighbor's bathtub.

Mac, who I had met through Salinas, was a southern-fried buzzard,
but as loyal as a German Sheppard. Originally, they were only
planning on staying for a few months, however, they ended up staying
with me for over six months which proved to be mutually beneficial.
On top of the free tattoos from Salinas, the two of them acted as a
kind of guard for me and my business in exchange for free rent and
free drugs from time to time.

There was anywhere from a few ounces to over ten pounds of coke in
and around my person at any given time. A lot of blow passed over
the very fingertips typing this letter. On top of the snow, I often
had all kinds of different shit I either traded for, or buy on
occasion: smack, meth, ecstasy, pot, to name a few, and all kinds of
pharmaceuticals: Morphine, Vicodin, OxyContin, Xanax, Ritalin,

Valium, Adderall. If you could name it, I either had it, or I could get it.

I was nearly drowning in all of the cash I was quickly accumulating. Within the first three months of playing the game, I had tens of thousands of dollars in shoeboxes and safes spread throughout my apartment in various hidden compartments, cubby holes, and all sorts of other hiding spots. I kept two of the safes with money and blow in them very well hidden, while I left two other safes that were full of rocks out in the open in hopes of deceiving any would be thieves. The idea was that if I got robbed they'd take the dummy safes and split, spending as little time as possible committing the robbery. It was a simple but genius precaution I came upon by accident one day while I was trying to collect a debt. I had gone to a debtor's house to get the $565 I was owed, but no one was home. The guy lived down a dead end and he was known as quite the sissy, so I subscribed to my rage rather than any fear, and without much thought, I kicked in the front door.

The place was a toilet bowl, and I suddenly found myself a victim of my own fear, believing I would never find what I was looking for in such a mess. Lucky for me, I found a small, but ridged briefcase safe sitting in the center of the bed in the master bedroom. I grabbed it and headed home only to find that it was filled with rocks when I finally cracked the thing with a crowbar some hours later. Anyhow, the fake safes were meant strictly as a precaution when no one was home at my apartment. If I was there when they kicked my door in they'd likely have me open them right then and there, saving them an exorbitant amount of time lugging them around and trying to crack them.

I'm not the biggest guy, and way too many people knew about my business, so I carried a pistol with me at all times, and I armed my Guard as well. We never left home carrying too much money or too much dope, but we also never left home without our weapons. Wherever I went I was always accompanied by at least one of my guard.

I sold strictly out of my apartment which had both its benefits, and its pitfalls. On the one hand, it was hard to have girls spend the night because there was no door between my room and the living room where the guys slept. We were also perpetually high, the worst influences on each other. On the other hand, I had armed thugs standing guard 24/7, 365.

There would be plain clothed officers trying to act their way to bureau academy awards (one more stripe on their arm), but being in the game for long enough meant that, much like Superman's x-ray vision, I could see through the 'plain clothes,' right back to their cherished little badges they had tucked away in their desk drawers back at the precinct. They might as well have pinned it to their foreheads, or their well researched 'street wear.' Detectives? More like extras in a 70's B-movie: no talent and no real chance at the big screen. Detected I made a point to screen my major clients because I didn't want to deal with weak minds or weak wills, various undesirables, and most importantly, I didn't want to accidentally get caught up by dealing to any undercover cops. I never had a debt that wasn't paid to me one way or another, and I never got locked up, I could always count on that. What I couldn't avoid was the unpredictable side of the scum bags that were willing to sell my drugs. From time to time even the toughest of them made the kind of mistakes that were expected from a jealous drunk girlfriend.

My business model was simple: I bought coke, cut it, and sold it at a mark up. Capitalism. I sold smaller stuff at the beginning, but it took no time at all for the number of requests to become more than I was able to handle by myself. Unlike Santa Claus, I wasn't able to be in more than one place at a time, delivering little goodies that put smiles on all the kiddies numb little faces. I was only given one choice, so this is when I began employing my own elves to help with sales. At the height of my business I had seven guys selling for me. Each of them was given one to two ounces that I had already weighed into grams and eight-balls.

Two of these dealers in particular are worth mentioning: ThadB and BrandonR. The first to arrive at the North Pole looking for work was ThadB who I had met through an ex-girlfriend of his. ThadB was the kind of guy that talked and talked, and most of the shit coming out of his mouth was bullshit, but I really admired his way with words and the way that he commanded attention during any conversation. The only thing I didn't like about the guy was his ego, one that put Kanye West's to shame. Though he thought he was hot shit, the truth was that he was very productive, so I asked him to find me someone we could trust to help him out with his workload, and that's when he introduced me to BrandonR.

They began asking me to front them an extra ounce on top of the ones they were paying for, which worried me slightly. I had been hearing stories about ThadB's lack of loyalty when it came to drugs, money, and friends, so I feared that they were plotting to rip me off. I decided to show them that I was just too crazy to fuck with, and I wanted there to be no doubt in their minds that they would suffer dearly should they decide to get greedy and try me and my guard who already had issue with ThadB's big mouth, especially Mac. After expressing my fears to my Guard, they immediately began plotting various methods for the disposal of a few corpses should it come to that. ThadB and BrandonR usually came together when they picked up more weight, so I planned a little 'event' to occur during their next visit.

When they arrived I was shirtless, making sure they saw that I was carrying a gun in my waistband. "Come on in fellas, have a seat," I said as I pointed to the two chairs I had set out facing my couch. "So I wanted to have a little talk with you two," I said as I sat on the couch facing them. In front of me on the coffee table were a pair of pliers, hydrogen peroxide, a small bowl, and a few rags.

"Sure, what's up?" ThadB asked.

"Well, I just want to make sure you two know how serious I am about making money, and how much I enjoy spending that money. Do you two have any idea how serious I am?" I asked as I picked up the pliers. I had to do everything within my power not to laugh as they both looked at each other with puzzled looks, followed by complete silence. "Look here," I pointed to my eyes, "and answer me," I demanded.

"Yeah, we know," ThadB responded.

"Good, because we're going places, up to be exact. Business is picking up and being that you are two of my best sellers, I'm depending on you guys to make sure everything runs smoothly," I continued as I opened and closed the pliers. "I want you two to know that I really don't like fronting whole ounces, but for you two, well, I know I can trust you," I said as I put the pliers in my mouth and began yanking on a bad tooth that had been aching for days, but they didn't know this little tidbit of course. Again, I wanted to laugh right in their faces, but the looks on their faces let me know that my message was getting through loud and clear. Plus it's kind of hard to laugh when you've got a mouth full of pliers and enough pain to make a whore squeal.

"I dunna hava ta fine out ya fuck me ana have ta fire ya do. I like ya do doo mut," I mumbled as I successfully freed the tooth from my gums which was followed by a river of blood. I casually set the tooth in the bowl and grabbed a rag to catch the blood. "Sorry," I said, "I dun't wanna have ta fine ou ya're fu'in me and have ta fire ya do, like I zed, I like ya doo mut."

"Jesus," BrandonR finally chimed in, clutching his lower jaw.

"Ya boys get me point?" I asked as my voice became clearer and I pointed the bloody pliers at them.

Loud and clear.

They never gave me any trouble, in fact, their profits rose over %25 over the next week and kept climbing. Unfortunately for BrandonR, he wouldn't get to spend too much of the money he made working for me. A few weeks after our talk, he was found stabbed to death outside of a bar he frequently sold at. They found no drugs or money on him, not even his wallet. It was a simple robbery, poor kid.

––––––––––––––––––

I had three groups that I made very happy during my business venture in blow: the first was my original source, which only lasted a few months because eventually, they couldn't supply me with the amount of product I needed; the second was the source that replaced the first and remained my source until I quit selling, a group we'll refer to as The Southerners; and the third group was all the dope fiends that bought my product. It wasn't long after I started selling cocaine that I needed a source where I could purchase more product, and this is where the second group came into play. The guy I had originally been getting it from was small time, the street hustling kind of small time, so I put the word out that I was in search of a wholesaler. The fiends were always looking for a handout so they all had 'a guy' who they thought could supply me, so it didn't take long to find one. What took the most time was sifting through all the fiends' bullshit in order to find a real supplier. It just so happened that I began buying from a guy in the high rise apartment building directly across the street from my place with Knife Fight Nick. What're the chances right?!?! It was like the Columbian Coca Gods were smiling down upon me, as well as snowing down upon me.

This neighbor of mine was a known gang-banger, a drug dealer, and he had recently done a stint in San Quentin State Prison. He was originally charged with Murder in the first degree, but a great attorney, a butt load of cash, and some corrupt witnesses amounted to an Involuntary Manslaughter conviction, and just three years in the prison before he was let out on Parole. His release was some time before I ever met him, and a few years before his move to Oregon. He loved telling me the story of how he ended up in prison whenever we got drunk together, a story about a murder that was the result of an unpaid debt of ten-measly-thousand dollars. I mean to most people $10k is a lot of money, me included, but to ReggieJ, it was chump change. At least that's how it appeared to be with his constant, flamboyant display of large wads of bank notes which he carried in his pocket at all times. To him, it was the principal of the matter, it was the fact that if he let some sap take him for ten large, what was there to stop his other customers from thinking they could get away with it as well. It wasn't the amount of the debt that really mattered. It's basic management, but I respected his stance. $10k is still $10k, even to someone like Bill Gates. Every once in a while a situation like this popped up and ReggieJ would request a fellow Crip, lackey, or even a customer like me to take care of the collection of such debts for him. He made sure that the collector relayed the message that it wasn't wise of them to try something like this, and they were lucky it wasn't ReggieJ himself coming to collect the debt… and the next time it happened… Well, "lets just say there won't be a next time" was a direct quote from ReggieJ.

There was nothing exceptionally unique about the particular situation that ended with ReggieJ. The client treated the debt like it was an ex-girlfriend that just wouldn't leave him alone. He wouldn't answer his phone when he saw that it was ReggieJ calling, or any other unknown phone number for that matter, and he was going around flaunting the fact that he had no intention of ever paying him. ReggieJ could have easily had one of the lower level members from his gang take care of it for him, but this time, as he would do from time to time, he took the task on personally. This was done for several reasons: 1) he had to remain on his toes at all times because, in his mind, there was always someone out there who thought they could take his position if the opportunity presented itself, therefore, he had to keep a certain level of freshness to his street viciousness, and drug dealing vivacity; 2) it was simply fun for him; but most of all, 3) he would take care of such situations himself in order to keep up his reputation, the façade which portrayed him as a murdering sociopath that would kill through the grapevine for the slightest of infractions. His hands covered in blood left little to question about the man, and once that blood began to coagulate, then he knew it was time for him to step to the plate once again, and get out on the streets. This $10k kid had the heat of the summer coming down on him like a baseball lost in the sun.

"What time is it?" looking at his empty wrist as he remembered that he had taken all of his jewelry off before he had left his house earlier that day.

"A quarter past three," the driver, a Crip from the same gang, answered as he looked at ReggieJ through the rearview mirror. ReggieJ had him driving one of his very whips, a newly acquired 1963 Chevy Impala. At least that's what they thought they were in. It turns out they thought it would be a great idea to eat a bunch of acid, a.k.a. LSD, before they went on their little mission to collect said monies owed to them, so in reality, they were in a four-seater golf cart they had stolen from the garage of an elderly couple in an affluent neighborhood that bordered a golf course near where they were presently parked. They also just so happened to be in front of the $10K kid's house which took them nearly fifteen minutes to realize.

After much silence one of them finally proposed, "Shall we knock?"

"Let's," they climbed out of the Chevy golf cart and proceeded to the front door of the house. As ReggieJ knocked on the door they could hear shuffling inside, sounds that were amplified in their minds.

"The door is telling me to kick it down," and as ReggieJ said this, he gave a lunging kick to the door which flew off its hinges into the front entry way where it made a loud crashing sound as it took out a small antique bench. As if Superman himself had just kicked in the door, all of the inhabitants ran screaming towards the back of the house, likely headed for an exit. What ensued was a blood bath.

"Get on the floor," ReggieJ screamed as he flew into the house after the blurry shadows that were running in front of him. Once he had made it to the living room he stopped on a dime, pulled the trigger, and unloaded the entire clip of his modified AR-15 assault rifle in a sweeping motion through the middle of the house. Following his lead, his partner sprayed the contents of his nine millimeter Uzi randomly throughout the house. In an instant, the loudest tidal wave of chaos imaginable had crashed into a dark silence. For a full three minutes this darkness ensued until there was a faint creaking sound coming from the timber hiding between the walls, splintered by the barrage of bullets. Even fainter was the hiss of pressurized water leaking from a ruptured water pipe, making the sound of the blood that was pouring from a house guest's leg to the floor even less audible.

A few moments in the deep dark silence and both Crips were thus crouched down low to the floor in the foyer. They had never gone any deeper into the house than about ten paces from the front door. From the depths of the dark house came a low groan, not low enough to be a man's, but the painful moan of a woman.

"What was that?!?" With a look on his face much like that of the tabloid made famous picture of Britney Spears with the newly shaved head atop her crazed looking face with her eyes & mouth wide-open, ReggieJ stood frozen facing his friend. Knees bent, arms out at his sides caulked up like he was about to tackle the guy with the football, he waited patiently for a response.

"Do we have the money?" ReggieJ asked as the woman groaned loudly.

"No, but we have solace in the holes in the drywall that they'll have to patch up." Maniacal laughter, "I'd hate to be them, they've got a lot of work ahead of them," babbling on in their LSD ridden dementia. The surviving people hiding in the house must have thought that they were doomed at the hands of two lunatics. The survivors were two, and the Dead were one. The $10 Kid had actually made it a few yards out the door into the backyard when a stray bullet struck him in the back of his head killing him instantly. It was determined later by a world renowned forensic anthropologist that the bullet that killed him had actually ricocheted off of a nail that was sticking out of the wall in the hallway leading to the back door of the house. Not his lucky day.

"Where's the kid?"

"Don't know for sure," the driver replied to ReggieJ who could barely hear him over the woman whose moans were getting louder and louder with each passing moment. The background chaos was noise in their heads and in their eyes now as well. A dog never barked and the phone never rang, not even a cell phone.

"Shall we?" the two Crips swiftly left the house, ReggieJ moving backwards at a slow jog just in front and facing his friend. They jumped into their getaway car, and ReggieJ drove them through the lawns of every house they passed for many, many blocks.

They drove around for twenty minutes before they were surrounded by about a dozen police. They had crashed their car into a roadblock after a spike strip had popped three of their tires. ReggieJ was convinced it was a conspiracy against him and his unborn child by the Mayor who wanted to make sure that neither he nor his son or his son's son could ever be the President of the United States, something he would later convey to the police back at the precinct.

The driver, whose encounter with the airbag struck him as rude, was reassuring everyone that "It's ok, I'm with the owner, so it's ok." He was unable to understand why they wanted to put shiny bracelets on him and ask so many weird questions. It was like a scene out of the second hour of a Stanley Kubrick movie if it had met a David Lynch scene while fighting the affects of taking four Ambien after fifty-nine hours without sleep. Believing the two were on PCP, the cops maced them as a precautionary measure, and they were left to flop around on the ground and wallow in pain for a few moments before three large officers descended upon each of them. Damn shame they had to finish out their Trips in jail, a damn shame indeed.

Despite the fact that we were polar opposites, ReggieJ and I became quick friends. He listened to rap, had braided hair, and dressed the part while I, on the other hand, was a dirty punk rocker sporting a leather jacket and a mohawk. He refused to call me a 'client,' opting instead to refer to me simply as a 'dear friend.' What we did have in common, something he greatly admired about me was my felonious past, a past that bare numerous similarities to his own. Neither of us can vote in any election, or purchase a firearm, but on the upside, we're forever exempt from jury duty.

Three and a half years later he was out of the clink, and in no time at all, he had re-established himself as a man in demand, a Man of significant flamboyance and disregard for his looming incarceration, a man I had quickly ascertained was anything but level headed. Destined to die young. When it came right down it, he was a really nice guy, a side to him that likely stemmed from his drug numb half-wittedness, always flying by the seat of his pants, fueled by his own Gomeresque ambitions.

He owned, among many other cars, five brand spanking new cars of expensive taste: a Mercedes SL Class, a Hummer I, a Range Rover, a BMW 600 series, a Ford Cobra, & his classic which was a 1958 Cadillac Deville, a real beauty with fins, skirts, leather, tint, TV's with DVD players, & many more custom modifications, and all of these cars were paid for in cash and none of them were registered in his name. He rented three apartments, two of which he grew pot and/or sold drugs out of (the one next to my apartment was one of these), and the third apartment was where he had, what he called, his "Back Up Bitch" living at. On top of the rentals, he owned the home he grew up in, a beach house on the Washington state coast where he would escape to at least once a month. He also owned a house in the city where he slept most nights, one that few knew about. Home. I gained this knowledge about his assets and operations in just a few short weeks after meeting him, and it was learned not by the loose lips of any associates or friends of his, but learned from his very own ship sinkers. The Dipshit told me everything, and it sketched me out because it wasn't like I was anything but a client to him, and I know for a fact that I wasn't the only one who knew about the greater half of his life drenched in crime. What I saw as his greatest character flaw proved to be more annoying than anything, and I believe it was ultimately his undoing. He was way too willing to open up about all of his endeavors, both good and bad, to just about anyone who would listen. I could ask him anything and no matter how personal or grossly inappropriate the question was, I could always count on the unequivocal truth. He was drunk and high a lot of the time, and it was then that he was most amicable, when he was feeling at his best that he opened up the most.

I remember one such instance when we were at a bar, both drunk as hell. I sat at the bar watching the Oregon Ducks football game on one of the big screen TVs while ReggieJ played video poker. The poker machines, or as I like to call them video crack, was located in a hallway adjacent to the bathrooms which was fitting really, Shitbags by the shitters. At the machine next to the one ReggieJ was playing on was a young man who looked just old enough to be in the bar. Wrong place at the wrong time.

"Any lucky today's?" a few drops of ReggieJ's spit landed on the man's chin and in his eye making him flinch, he was amazed at how the spittle was able to make the sharp turn to hit his face since the man was facing away from ReggieJ altogether. Like JFK's magic bullet, it was Spittle from the grassy knoll.

"Excuse me?" the man then turned to sneer at ReggieJ as he wiped the spit from his chin.

"I mean your lucks."

"My luck?" he smiled as he removed a pack of cigarettes from his jacket pocket, slid one of them out, put it to his lips, and lit it with a lighter he had simultaneously produced from his other pocket.

"Si, felicidad hombre. L-U-C-K," ReggieJ reiterated with an over roll of his bourbon basted tongue as he leaned towards the man.

"No FRIEND," the man leaned in as well. They shared an uncomfortable silence and a stare that could have quickly gone from bad to worse in a George W. heart beat.

"Can I tell you something?" Interjecting on their staring contest, ReggieJ asked as he reached into the inside jacket pocket under his left breast, extracted a fist full of cash, and he made sure his new friend could see it, but didn't appear as though he was affected by it. ReggieJ then pulled a twenty dollar bill from the roll and slid it into the slot in the machine.

"Does it really matter how I answer, I mean you're gonna tell me any which way aren't ya?"

A fake little laugh before ReggieJ spoke next, "Did you notice who's in the bar tonight?" continuing to play his machine.

"Well that's more of a question…"

"Excuse me?"

"You asked if you could tell me something and instead you asked me a question."

"Sorry smart ass are you'z gonna let me finish what the fuck I was sayin, or are yuz gonna make this difficult? You know, if one of the newbie puntas in my gang ever talked to me like that, they'd get their mouth slapped…" There was a short pause as ReggieJ faced the video screen and played a few more hands. "Anyway, what I was going to ask you was, did you notice who's in the bar tonight?"

"Sorry, what I had meant to say was," the man said after realizing he was at a severe size disadvantage, so it wasn't so much a matter of being out matched as it was the great difference in size that made him feel outnumbered. "Um… Is there someone special or something like a group I was supposed to have noticed?" he said, but all ReggieJ heard was clucking as the shape of the gambling man's lips began looking more and more like that of a duck's bill.

I walked into the bar just as ReggieJ began to reply, fumbling over his words so terribly that he was thrown from the stool he had perched his slight frame on, a very annoyed and embarrassed stool that would have ripped out its own stuffing just to get rid of the bumbling fool resting his bum upon it. I walked over and put my arm around ReggieJ to give people the impression that we were lovers, "Hey sweetie! So we gonna have a few more drinks before we head home?" I hovered over him as I leaned into his space, speaking with a heavy lisp.

"Hold on pinche cabron! I'm telling this culo here what I think about some shit goin down here in the bar, but you can get me another beer ése," he commanded his daddy, completely oblivious to my gayness. I then headed to get a beer and shook my head knowing the poor kid was really in for it, even though I had no idea what they were talking about. Speaking much clearer now, ReggieJ continued the conversation with his new vid-crack-compadre, "So?" expecting an answer which he never got, the man barely made even the slightest of sounds. Instead, he gazed nervously at ReggieJ, then at his machine, and back to ReggieJ, making sure not to stare or create any tension with his baby blues. "Well, since you suddenly seem to have lost your tongue to a cat or something, I'll answer my own question. Yes, I'd say there are some special people here, and I'm surprised you hadn't noticed. Half the people in here are students at the University downtown, mostly white like you. I sell drugs to at least three of the students that are here right now, or at least that's as many as I can count from here. Then you got the Crack Heads that come in and out of the bar about every twenty minutes trying to look like they're supposed to be there as they wait for their dealer. That dealer ain't me, see? I don't sell crack, I'm strictly a Coke and Heroin man. So yeah, you could say there's some special people in the bar tonight. Right?" The open air dialogue was nonsensical really, serving no real purpose other than to pump up ReggieJ's ego, and scare the poor guy he was talking to.

ReggieJ's true intentions, however, were to look for an opening, an invitation, a reason to fuck the guy up with his psychological warfare as well as his psycho fists. What gets me though is why he feels he needs to divulge such incriminating information to a man he planned on squishing under his thumb.

The opening came sooner than anticipated when, from under his breath, the guy said "Fucking crackhead Niggers," not realizing that ReggieJ was half black. He also thought that ReggieJ had used the word 'nigger' as a racist slur, and not as a sort of term of endearment, which was the way that ReggieJ was actually using it. What a dipshit though, ReggieJ was obviously dark skinned. Not white. ReggieJ had no qualms about kicking this guy's face in right then and there as the word had set him off like a fuse on a firecracker.

"I'll show you Nigger!" Wham!! From the bar I could hear a crashing thud coming from the crack room, and I knew exactly what was going down. ReggieJ had picked up his bar stool and leveled it across the guys head knocking him down to the ground where he'd lunged on top of him and proceeded to beat the word "Nigger" right out of the guy's vocabulary. I rushed back just in time to see ReggieJ landing the final blow to the guy's face. Blood sprayed from his nose and oozed from large splits in each of his lips. Unconscious. Then, he calmly picked his jacket up from the stool he had been sitting on and said, "Well, I guess it's time to go now." It wasn't graceful, and the mix of adrenalin and alcohol created a mean swagger in his step. I had to hold him up as we left through the back door of the bar. We attempted a surreptitious retreat, but we were like bulls with machine guns in a china shop.

"Hey asshole, you forgot to pay your tab!" the bartender had run out the back of the bar holding up our receipt. I propped ReggieJ against the wall of the apartment building that was adjoined to the bar and turned to walk over to the bartender.

I pulled out a twenty and handed it to him. He was an old friend of mine from high school, so I told him to "Keep the change."

"Thanks man, but hey look," he moved closer to me, refraining from looking me in the eyes. "Now don't get me wrong, I like you guys, and you yourself are not eighty-sixed. Yeah, you're cool, but your buddy over there can't come back, ever," pointing to ReggieJ who slid down the wall in a heap. "You can't come in here, ever. Don't think I didn't see what happened in the video poker room. I mean, we got cameras all over the fucking bar you know," he spoke louder so that ReggieJ could hear him as well. "The boss'll see that shit too, and he'll put a picture of him up all over the bar saying something like "this guy's 86'd." Anyways, that guy your friend beat up is in real bad shape. Y'all better scram before the cops show up," lickidy-split. I turned around just in time to see ReggieJ getting in a cab on the corner, and I laughed a little as I began to run towards him, but as soon as I had started running I realized this was my golden ticket. What was panning out to be a Friday night of babysitting a grown man was suddenly shaping up to be ok. I even got laid later that night by some random chick I picked up at the bar.

It was nights like this that made me wonder why isn't this guy in prison? There would be many more days like this, certain days that will forever be ingrained in my memory.

Since ReggieJ knew that I had a lot of friends and connections around town, he thought I'd be the perfect candidate to sell his product for him. There was an instant trust there for him, and he started me off by fronting me a half pound. I guess it also didn't hurt that he knew where I lived. Within the first week I had sold every last gram of that half pound, which blew him away.

After that he had no problem fronting to me from there on out. The more time that went by, the more involved I got in his day to day operations. One day, about three months into selling for him, ReggieJ called me up and asked me to come over to his apartment to help him with something that he wouldn't go into detail about over the phone. I told him I'd be over just as soon as I finished taking care of one of my clients, so a half hour later I was walking through his unlocked front door where I found him in the kitchen putting the finishing touches on two margaritas.

"TommyJ! How are you ése?" he asked cheerfully.

"I'm alright," I said as I shook his hand. "So what'd you need help with huh?"

"Come ere, I'll show ya," he said as he walked down the hall towards the back bedroom. "Help me grab this shit, we're gonna do some cutting today!"

"Sure thing boss," I said, becoming excited by the prospect of learning how to properly cut blow. We gathered up a bunch of tools, a couple large sandwich bags full of coke, and headed for the kitchen. He then showed me his personal recipe for cutting coke. First, we took two large bowls, one for each of us, and put a bunch of coke in them, followed by vitamin B12, acetone, and water. Then we mixed it all up like we were making pizza dough. Once there was a nice smooth consistency, we threw the bowls into the microwave so the moisture would evaporate. Once the coke was nice and hard in the bowl, we took to it with a knife and a potato masher until we had mostly powder in the bowl. Finally, we took the bowls into the back bedroom where ReggieJ had a big manual machine press set up. We'd dumped the coke into the flat slate in the middle, turned the bar on the side of the press which moved the top plate down upon the coke, pressing it into a nice big solid brick. Then we cut the brick up into various weights and bagged it. All in all, it was about an hour process, and we'd end up with a few pounds each time. I helped him do this over forty times in the months that followed, and I must say it never got old. It was like we were printing off counterfeit money. What I mean to say, is that I didn't see cocaine when we were cutting it, I just saw dollar signs. Our product was still very high quality since the coke was nearly 80% pure before we cut it, and the profits we gained by cutting it were over 600%. Living the dream.

Through ReggieJ, I met the larger second group I dealt with, The Southerners that I mentioned earlier. They were able to supply us with real weight when our first connection couldn't. Their stuff was much better, 80% pure, something I had mentioned earlier as well. Before ReggieJ would take me to meet the Southerners he sat me down and explained a few things about them. The point he stressed most was that if I knew what was best for me, I'd "keep my fucking mouth shut" because ReggieJ would do most of the talking.

This was a highly organized group that originated in the Californian prisons which is also where they run the gang from. Their headquarters was called Pelican Bay's Shu, a really bad place to be if you're a little white guy like me. ReggieJ wasn't actually a part of their organization, but he was considered a valued associate, which meant I was also a valued associate. On the one hand it was good to know I had real muscle if I needed it, yet on the other hand, I really didn't like these guys knowing who I was. If things went sour, I'd have to disappear from their radar for the rest of my life, but I really never wanted to leave Portland, so I had no intentions of ever trying to rip off the Southerners. They're the type of guys that never forget, so if something did go wrong and they were after me, they may wait ten years to pay me a visit, but that was just it, they'd never let it go. I'd have to go away forever.

I had actually heard about one guy that had quit the organization, but was still collecting drug money in their name. When the organization found out about it, he immediately stopped working under their name, and nothing happened to him or his family so he thought he was in the clear. Three years later, however, he found himself without a head. They never forget, ever.

ReggieJ called me up one day in the summer and asked if I would come with him to pick up a large order of blow from the Southerners which I agreed to do. I met ReggieJ in front of his place where he was already in one of his many cars waiting for me. When I got in I failed to notice the sub-machine gun on my seat and sat right on it. When I reached under my butt and pulled it out, looked at it, then at ReggieJ, and back at the gun which made us both laugh as I placed it under my seat.

"So that's really where you keep that thing?" ReggieJ said as he laughed at me.

"Yeah, you should see what else is up my ass fucker," pointing at it. "Why do you need that thing anyway?" I inquired, becoming a little weary of our trip.

"Oh," he started to reply as he pulled out a small oozy from under his coat which was on a strap over his shoulder, "that one's for you, and this one's for me. We won't need it, but it's always good to come to these things strapped. You know, just in case the cops show up or something," he said with a funny smile on his face, a smile with which I was unable to tell if he was dead serious or not.

Great, I thought as I lit a cigarette, today's the day that I die. "Well thanks for thinking of me," I said as I laughed.

"You're welcome."

"So, where we headed?" I asked.

"South… California," he replied. We drove non-stop for seventeen hours before we arrived in San Diego. We talked very little on the trip other than some basic questions I had for ReggieJ about our little adventure, all of which were met by cryptic answers. I was, however, able to decipher that we were headed to a large pickup somewhere in the greater San Diego metropolis. Pounds in the hundreds was my guess.

After exiting off the Five in San Diego we drove for another twenty minutes heading east away from the city. We arrived at a business park and because it was a Sunday it looked abandoned. Parked near the loading docks of a warehouse was a brand new Cadillac Escalade with four Mexicans in it. When we pulled up to the bay next to them they got out and walked over to our car. Beforehand I had put the gun, which had a strap like the one ReggieJ had, under my coat, and when the Mexicans approached the car, I took the safety off. Something told me that ReggieJ had brought the guns for a reason other than "just in case." Though he was kind of a dumbass, I trusted the man's intuition when it came to such matters.

One of the Southerners came over to ReggieJ's door, and in a heavy Mexican accent said, "We're waiting on the delivery, but they should be here any minute. Just hang in your car, and we'll let you know when to get out, K?" As he walked back towards their ridiculously ginormous SUV I flipped off the safety on my gun.

ReggieJ started laughing before he turned, leaned in, and asked, "Was that the damn safety I just heard?" and his crazy sounding laughter was enough to bring me slightly out of my sneer and snicker state.

"Perhaps, so what?" I posed, still laughing. "Shit man, for all I know, these guys will just smoke us and take all your loot. Even though you say you trust them, and you've done a bunch of business with them in the past don't mean I have to trust em. You know what I mean?" I asked after I stopped laughing and spoke in a more serious tone. Within a few minutes, a 1970's AMC Gremlin rolled to a stop a few hundred feet in front of us. If you ask me, it's a fucking ugly car, but the green lemon rolling towards me brought back a lot of memories. For starters, it was the first type of car my buddy MikeC and I had ever stolen. The particular one we stole wasn't running, but we stole it nonetheless. MikeC got in and steered while I pushed it down the street until we hit a hill where I jumped in. We coasted down behind a movie theatre where we knew the car would be well hidden and for the next week me and my buddies would meet up at the car and just hang out in it. We all felt like honest to goodness bad-asses.

It just so happened that my second experience with a Gremlin occurred pretty close to where ReggieJ and I sat at the moment. I had gone with a group of friends to race cars at nearby Business Park that was almost identical to the one we were currently sitting in. The place was a hotspot for weekend drag racing and the place was packed when we got there. I was riding in a turbo Honda Civic hatchback, a really, really fast little rice-burner, and our first race was against a guy and his girlfriend in a gremlin. Both my friend driving and I were laughing our asses of, but we weren't laughing so hard after the damn thing smoked us by four car lengths at the finish line of the quarter mile run. Sleeper.

Back to the business at hand, the Gremlin rolled up with a single occupant, a Mexican driver, and he didn't speak a lick of English. He got out, shook everyone's hands, and had a quick conversation in Spanish with one of the men from the Escalade while the three other guys from the Escalade went to work on the Gremlin. To my astonishment, they opened numerous false panels all around the Gremlin which they pulled hundreds of pounds of heroin and cocaine out of, and loaded them into the trunk of the Escalade. While two of the men were loading the drugs, another went to work on the Gremlin's dash board, and I never would have believed what was behind it if I hadn't seen it with my own eyes: there was a man behind the dashboard, he was the dashboard really. In order to get him to fit under the dash they had to empty out the space by rerouting the wiring and fabricating a lounge like area for him. When he crawled out of the car he did a bunch of stretches and was given a bottle of water to drink. I couldn't imagine riding in a car with the heat of a Mexican summer's day in those cramped conditions. Frankly, I felt sorry for the little guy.

"Hey, c'mere," the guy who was doing all the talking with ReggieJ said, as he waved ReggieJ and me over to the Escalade which we obliged. "Here," the guy said, handing ReggieJ and I each two grocery bags full of bricks. "Twenty five right, right, you boys have a nice day," and with that, he put his hand up to his forehead and saluted us.

"Right, right, gracias Senõr," and we took the bags to ReggieJ's ride. Like our Southerner friends, ReggieJ had hidden compartments in his ride which we filled with the bricks. We waved goodbye to the Southerners, got back on the highway, and began the long journey home.

It was rare for the Southerners to bring ReggieJ a shipment in Portland, so this was a normal trip for ReggieJ, one that he would make nearly eight times a year. I was fortunate enough to be asked to accompany him on the trip south five more times over the next few years, and even after the fourth trip, I still got an awful nervous pang in my stomach that lasted the entire trip.

Well, well, well Ms. Caribou, I hope you found my stories/letter entertaining and insightful, and please please me: write me back lady!!! Until next.........

XOXO

TommyJ

Dearest Caribou-

I can only guess as to who these letters are making it to since I'm assuming you've moved by now, and I haven't received a second letter from you with your new address. I can only hope that you're having your mail forwarded to your new spot. If this is not Caribou then I hope you are at least enjoying these letters, and if you get a chance, please feel free to return the favor by sharing some stories of your own creation with me (my address is on the letter).

As of right now I am sitting on the roof of my house smoking a joint, watching the sun set. Ahhh, this is the life. Did I mention the cold beer, oh yes, a nice tallboy of PBR is keeping me cool as well. Beer is a frequent sidekick of mine, but rarely do I ever smoke green cigarettes.

As you can tell, this letter was too long to fit it in a standard sized envelope, so I was forced to purchase this bigger one. I expect reimbursement of 86¢. Why items in a postal store always seem to have odd-ended prices for everything, from the obvious stamp, to the box of notepads for $4.73 is beyond me. Anyhow, in the last letter I left off by explaining how I got into the Blow trade. Just after I sent that letter to you another story came to mind about a certain customer of mine, and the hasty plummeting of our professional relationship. This will be the first of many stories in this letter, a story I have unambiguously titled Bad Deal. Enjoy.

---

21. Bad Deal

HankW was a big talker, a small guy with a giant head on his shoulders, a guy that thought he was some kind of refined hustler. Granted the kid sold a lot of blow for me, and I mean a lot of blow for me, HankW was what we referred to as a Nickelback. That is to say, with an urban translation, he was more commonly known as a douche-bag. Somehow, he had three times as many friends and acquaintances as most people, therefore he knew three times as many people that did coke. $ Cha-Ching $ He came off as a really nice, harmless kid, and he even had me fooled…

I fronted small amounts to him here and there because he would square up with me on time, every time, so I became quite comfortable fronting larger and larger amounts to him as time went by, and the last thing on my mind was getting screwed by him. Well surprise, surprise, of course he tried to screw me over. He owed me $320 which was the most he had ever owed me at one time, and I hadn't heard from him on the day I was to collect his front money, or for a while thereafter. I put the word out that I was looking for him, and it didn't take long for information to start rolling in. A little info for a little dope was given to those with the best info, but mostly I'd just pat them on the ass, tell them they did a real nice job, and that would be enough for most of them. It turned out I wasn't the only guy he'd been buying from, and from all the various bits of info I had gathered it appeared as though he had screwed us all over at the same time.

One of these dealers had a friend who also knew HankW, so he got this friend to call HankW and get him to come over to an apartment complex because the battery in his car needed a jump. When he got there, the battery wasn't dead, but somehow the friend was able to bullshit HankW into thinking someone else gave him a jump. He was also somehow able to lure HankW into a vacant apartment where a certain drug-dealer he just happened to owe money to was lying in wait. HankW was quickly tied up, beaten, and tortured so badly he kept passing out every few minutes or so. Eventually, the dealer let HankW go, but not before making sure HankW had more than a few permanent reminders of his debt. This wasn't the first such incident where 'creditors' caught up with HankW, and took their time putting the hurt to him. Minus three digits. Toes. Finger.

I also got word that he had just moved to New Orleans, but unluckily for him, Katrina hit just three days after he got there, and I suspected that this would bring him back to Portland fairly soon.

About a month later I got a call from a guy from my old graffiti crew who now lived in L.A. "Hey what's up man, this is Guillermo," 18th Street Crip calling.

"Heyyyy man, been days since I've heard from you!" months really.

"Yeah man, no doubt, but hey listen, I heard you been lookin for HankW, right?"

"Right," happier to hear from him than I was a few seconds before.

"Well that motherfucker's in Hollywood! I saw the little bitch walking on the North side with some of his nerdy friends. A day or so after I saw him, I ran into Hector, and he told me Tomas from

Portland was looking for this HankW kid, so I give you a call. I didn't get a chance to talk to HankW so I don't know exactly where he's stayin or any of that, but I could definitely put some guys on it for you, try and find out where he's at," he was a loyal old friend.

"Shit man, I'd really appreciate it if you could," I said, feeling like a King.

"Yeah, yeah, I'll get back to you. Stay up," he replied enthusiastically before he hung up the phone. Reaching across lines.

A week went by before I got another call from Guillermo telling me that he had heard HankW was back in Portland, and he even found out where he was going to be on that coming Wednesday night. I was all smiles, payback would be mine. I planned on heading him off that night with my roomie Mac.

It was ten at night when we pulled my car around the corner from a club where HankW was supposed to be. I just got the car turned off, when another car pulled up and parked two cars ahead of me. I can't fucking believe it, HankW's getting out of the car right in front of us, and he's brought some friends, great. Luckily, only one of them was a guy and the other two were girls. We let them go by, and thankfully they didn't notice us because I didn't want him to get the jump on me, or see what car I was driving. We watched them round the corner behind us before we got out and started catching them by briskly running after them. As soon as we turned the corner, we slowed to a fast walk just enough to catch up with them, but quiet enough not be obvious. I got right behind him and said, "Heya HankW, say, how was your trip?" he turned around looking frightfully anxious.

"Oh, TommyJ! Man, I'm sorry, don't hurt me!" but it was useless to beg, I punched him square in the jaw, and down to the concrete he went. Meanwhile, Mac made sure none of his other friends intervened. "I don't got it, I swear man! Please!" he continued to plead. Let's see if he's the bullshitter he appears to be.

"Oh yeah?" Sometimes you win it all, and sometimes you lose so bad you get the shit kicked outta ya. I gave him a swift kick to the jaw which he crawled about on his hands and knees, and it laid him back out.

By this time the girls he was with were screaming, and the guy he was with were saying shit like, "Come on guys, do you really have to do this?" and "Leave him alone will ya?"

"What the fuck do you mean 'do we have to do this?' Of course we do! This Motherfucker owes us money! You want to get your jaw broken too?" Mac yelled at HankW's entourage.

"No man, it's just… fucked up," one of the girls said so quietly I could barely hear her.

"No, you're stupid fucking friend here, HankW," I said his name in a mocking tone, "has fucked up, and now he's paying for it."

By then I had hoisted the kid up by his collar and demanded that he produce my money. He wasn't budging, so I went through all of his pockets and that's when I realized that he was carrying a purse. I took everything he had worth taking, his wallet, cigarettes, cell phone, everything, and threw it in the purse if it weren't already in it. Three or four minutes had passed since Mac and I had first approached the group, and I figured it was time we split before the cops rolled up on us. After all, we were on a major boulevard in a seedier part of town where crime was high, and cops were a common sight.

"Hey, we're out," I gestured to Mac and we started running back to my car. One of the friends decided that they were finally going to get tough, and I saw him running after us once we were over a block away.

I turned around and yelled, "You better turn the fuck around unless you wanna end up in the hospital!" I had to keep the guy from seeing my car either. It was obvious luck was on my side yet again when, sure enough, the kid turned around and ran back to his friends. No balls. Mac and I ran around the corner, got into my car, and got the hell out of there before the fuzz arrived.

When we got back to my place we wasted no time at all finding out what else he had in his purse. It was no surprise that it held his ID, some cash, and a few other typical items, but we felt like we had hit the jackpot when we discovered a plane ticket back to L.A. departing the very next day. Apparently, he was just visiting for a week, but it appeared as though this would be an extended trip. He easily could have had the ticket replaced, but he sure wasn't flying anywhere without his ID. In the end, I was much happier having him grounded than having the money he owed me. Payback was mine.

Fast-forward three years - I'm sitting in a local pub with a couple of friends and a few acquaintances of mine. The two friends invite me to go with them to a hockey game, but they have one friend going to the game that hasn't shown up to the bar quite yet. They would've just had the guy meet us at the game, but he was in the area already, and we had his ticket. Eventually, one of the people in our group points to a guy walking into the bar, and announces that the lost member to our hockey game troop has arrived. Low and behold it's HankW. He says hi to his friends, and sits right across from me. I can't believe it, he doesn't even recognize me as he extends his hand and says "HankW…"

"TommyJ," and we shake hands.

Time-out Ms. Caribou! I thought I'd break down the structure of my normal letters, and just go off on some tangents for a change. In the following chapter I've titled Rampant, you will find pieces of work I discovered laying about my place that are part poetry part prose, what is known as prose poetry. I thought maybe you'd like something a little different, something a little wild for a change…

---

22. Rampant

I'm in third grade watching some of the fifth grade boys fucking the
class gerbil, Waffles, with their number two pencils, q-tips,
paperclips, and a plethora of other foreign objects. One day not
long after, Waffles suddenly died. His Death Certificate read "Cause
= Unknown", but I knew the reason: Waffles had been violated to
death. The poor fucker died from internal bleeding that was the
result of being impaled by those demonic older kids, the bastards ♫
The moment my cat arrived in my arms as a gift and the months it
took me to finally bury her ♫ Late on my rent again ♫ The ice was so
thick when we woke up that we were trapped on the hill where my
house stood for days. I was in heaven in front of the fire with my
best friend's gorgeous girlfriend for days. The coconut on her hair,
on my pillows, coconut smells of guilty pleasures ♫ Sneezing,
orgasms, taking a great shit, and thankful I stopped wetting the
bed, thanks yogurt ♫ Grandma's Choo-Choo Fairytale in the land of
lost little boys always began once upon a time when we were all
runaways and orphan. It was a place where we all ran free in
adolescent social-anarchy with communal sugar showers and
everlasting smiles as brothers-in-arms with no exit strategy ♫

The neighbor finally remembered My Name today: Mud. I might as well
occupy my time as a seamstress of sorts. I'm guilty by way of these
crimson hands, & I have much to keep with so little time...

Q.) Jealous?

A.) Not in the slightest.

Q.) What has been your level of awareness concerning this fault of
yours?

A.) Almost non-existent, minimized to the greatest degree by denial
as design. Acknowledged? Yes. Accepted? No.

Q.) You seem like quite a busy man.

A.) Always.

Q.) Between this & that, and I could go on, how do you find time to
interview yourself?

A.) Easy. That is, I'm easy. Why, what do you purpose?

Q.) Would you like some water? Here, let me pour you a glass.

A.) Oh, no thanks. I don't drink water, fish fuck in it.

Q.) What's the story behind that scar on your face?

A.) A drop top bald spot accelerating to the speed of light. Don't
ask me to drop trout, unless you're buying the beers. Then you'll
see a real bald spot. Next question won't you?

Q.) Are you as thirsty as I am?

A.) Parched. Though I don't believe I will ever trust anyone who speaks through their teeth, unless of course they're a cartoon and considered edible, like Mr. Peanut. I'd let that guy housesit my place anytime. Although, come to think of it, my cat is allergic to peanuts. Maybe I'd just trust him with personal secrets. I guess the cartoonists as well. They can talk through their teeth all they'd like, but that doesn't mean I'm listening.

Q.) Ninja of bed sores, or sore by ninjas?

A.) Hmmm, I'd have to say that I was born to die and dying to be born.

Q.) Besides the obvious connotations, why "Low Rent"?

A.) Well… (he pauses for almost a full minute, fidgeting in his chair, running his hands through his hair, and rubbing the scruff on his chin as if to physically stir up a lost memory that could easily be on the tip of his tongue)… To put it simply, it's a woman's fault. To make sense of it, it's the love child of this generation in the vernacular in which it was bred in. Not quite slang, but a very definite description. Only two words from the mouths of every single one of my peers can be accomplished. She's just as much mine as she is yours. Not mine and mind alone.

Q.) Perhaps you've considered…

A.) (Abruptly interrupting) I have definitely run each and every realistic possibility of the lasting kind of LOVE that's worth the time through my patient mind. Frankly, I don't mind at all, why do you ask?

Q.) What sort of kindness would this killer bee without tit? Now, would you get naked, or would you run from your dullest dreams?

A.) I would scold the Physician that would apologize for treating such a travesty with his own home remedies. Tilt your head to the right, cry frantically, cry my name, call an ambulance, and tell everyone in the room that it's ok to be my friend. Put your finger in me. Put me away, "I should go."

Q.) Where would you go next? Where do you plan to be next?

A.) I would lie about it, and then as soon as you turned around, I would whisper I love you and then fall to the ground. So the answer is invisible. Yes, I would exist invisibly in the next episode, and my lie, well it would grow faster than Pinocchio's nose, and anyone who understands will get the same old wilting rose.

Q.) Are you ok? Are you making a smile, or is a smile making you?

A.) Living the Dream is making my nightmares less and less of a shame each time. I'm not alone in this. I'm the kind of hot pink that makes a grandma look more like a marathon. Run her. Two million turns to find the right words.

Q.) Why are you so obscure with your answers? Dear, are you high right now? And if so, on what, and may I have some?

A.) (The man reaches into my pocket and produces a lighter. He holds it up between and in the middle of our eye level so that as we look into each other's eyes, the lighter remains out of focus. Seconds pass… more seconds pass… He puts his other hand into the inside pocket of my second hand jacket and pulls out a square of tinfoil. He holds the foil up next to the lighter, but this time, we both focus on the foil, inspecting it. It's like a mirror). Are you fond of making guesses?

Q.) I guess I may like what that shit's hiding.

A.) I'm hiding what you'll admire, that's for sure!!

Q.) What do you think the future holds for you?

A.) Well, I guess I could call my Brother in Japan and ask him. It's four in the afternoon tomorrow over there, seventeen hours later. Perhaps he can tell me what the future holds for me.

Q.) I meant, a little farther in the future.

A.) There's a lot of white, some harps playing, and some guy in a plaid suit trying to sell me the car I already own. His name tag reads Belial.

Q.) Dear MC Hammer Pants, please do not show up in my Goodwill, Value Cottage, or Rat-Tailed white trash neighbor kid's dead lawn. For god's sake stay off the lawn. Are you making a comeback, or have you been here for years?

A.) Florida. Been down in Florida.

I have cultivated my hysteria with pleasure and terror.

- Charles Baudelaire

String people up and slap the corners off their teeth until they squeal for the police knowing damn well that the 911 threats are all part of the play. The cord was never plugged into the wall, therefore, if I was asked to leave, or if I was told what to do, I wouldn't have believed or done either. I was on my time and that was always the right way. I was forever wrapped in the Blue Velvet that was an absolutely, 100%, unique mucus squeezed out from our confrontations. It made me toast to my 'so much's' and 'so fuct's.' Cheers! So fucking creeps, so bottoms up and be polite, here's to has-beens. I can make em do whatever I like, I thought. Did he hurt your little face? Do a little babysitting for the prospective candy-snatcher, and the Bitch, Mama loves you? Jealous, yet still Candy Colored Sandman in Roy's Dreams? Zombie virus fuct. Does anyone want to go on a joy ride with us? How about you? Now it's Dark. Let's fuck anything that moves. Enter 80's pop-rock beat and glowing lines

218

shooting like tracers across a highway in rural Iraq: no-scare -
it's sordid and predictable. Kiss me with a punch and leave my lips
red with envy. Dripping jealousy that drifts away in the wind lie
sideways in a love letter with two pages and ninety-nine instances
of the word in one form or another baking in the sun, it's first
read not by the author, but by the other. Frank spoke it, and it
made scribbles smack dab at the end of my stupid hand as I ran with
the pen clasped tightly between pink tights. I have no want to be
the toilet for this family, just give me my royalties and let off.
If you have any sense of time as it relates to rhythm, then you have
had the opportunity to receive all of that which the charmed beating
will afford you. Lack it and you may be bunk-bed ridden to a
soulless drift that will likely pull your plug and never leave you
to rest. I've received my beatings, and through my often concussed
mind, I have still been able to recall all the moments worth
remembering.

_____

The time I've lost should be a lesson to us all. A metaphor for
wasted time, taken for granted time, easily forgotten time that we
are all guilty of haphazardly casting aside, like we got all the
time in the world to actually sit back and appreciate what's
happening right in front of us, to us, and by us. Ultimately, those
split seconds and flown-by decades will be carelessly repeated by
the generations to follow in the same naive fashion we put our
lifetimes to waste unless we do something to assure such atrocities
of the commoner will not be the mark of modern American society.
Doomed to be consumed by flaws flaunted en masse in our faces
everyday by the flicker of the TV light, that we cannot change, but
what flickers through our retinas is surely ours to define for the
remainder of these lives and the future of the lives that carry the
world after us. This requires the ego and image be cast aside for
the sake of the more advanced images, egos, ids, that which is the
consequence of Us and Our Time in this small town, Time that we can
find on a watch, or time that we lose to a good kiss or the moment
we remember being grounded by an epiphany.

_____

23. Beach Bummin

I'm sitting here stuck at work. It's mid-November and getting cold.
I was working away on a file when I hear my cell phone beep,
indicating I had received a text message from GlenP:

"Woke up with Harry Belafonte and a good buzz. Goin to the coast w/
a Sparks, suit, and a board. You bored? Get in the van!" I am bored,
and I wish I could go, but I'm stuck here at my godforsaken work!
I'd give anything to get out of here right now and go surfing. Tough
shit I guess.

The last time I went surfing was also with GlenP, as well as
SierraL, Captain Sensitive, guns, and beers. Captain Sensitive and I
drove over to GlenP's, and the three of us piled into GlenP's early
80's passenger van which had windows all around which was great for
checking out the scenery on our way there. The only downside was
that there were only two seats, the front driver and passenger
seats, and therefore only two seatbelts. You'd think that after
having three of my friends from high school die in a van just like
this one because they weren't wearing their seatbelts I wouldn't
make the same mistake, but I had a death wish back then, plain and
simple. In the back were two surf boards, miscellaneous gear, and
cushions from several different couches to sit on.

Before the three of us headed west, GlenP had to make a call.
"SierraL! Wha, wha, what are you doing?" he asked, pausing to listen
to her. "GET IN THE VAN! We're going to the beach, and you're comin
with us, so put your suit on. We'll be there in ten minutes!" he
yelled into the phone in a goofy voice, and with that he hung up,
started the engine, and declared that we were off to the beach after
a quick stop at SierraL's. Exactly ten minutes later we were out
front of her house, she was running out of her front door, and
jumping into the back of the van.

GlenP said the waves weren't supposed to be all that great, but big
swells or not, we were on our way. GlenP drove the first leg from
the city, and after forty miles or so, GlenP pulled the van over at
a gas station with a farmer's berry stand in the parking lot. We got
a couple baskets of fresh raspberries, which were delicious, and
filled the van with gas. GlenP decided he didn't want to drive
anymore, so I took over for the rest of the drive to the beach. I
went about twenty miles when I spotted something on the side of the
highway. "Hey check it out man," I pointed in the direction of an
older gentleman who had his thumb up. Hitching.

"Pull over, lets pick em up!" SierraL smiled. The rest of us agreed,
so I pulled the van over in front of the hitcher, and waited for him
to catch up. Captain Sensitive opened the sliding door on the side
of the van, and welcomed our new passenger, "Come on in, where you
headed?"

"The name's JimB, thanks for the ride," he replied, either avoiding
the question, or he just didn't hear the question. He had long gray
curls and a long gray beard. Our new friend was quite slender,
wearing a heavy down jacket, dirty jeans with holes all over them,
and little bony knees protruding from the knee holes. He looked like
an anorexic, homeless Santa Claus. He was carrying a fishing pole
and a small plastic bag that I was guessing held his fishing tackle.

"Sooooo, where ya headed to JimB?" I asked, thinking it must be the same direction as us since he's hitching that way.

"Goin fishin at the coast, but anywhere closer in that direction is just fine by me," he said as he sat on a sleeping bag in the far back of the van by the double doors. He hunched his knees up to his chin with one arm resting on the edge of a surf board, and the other holding his fishing pole and plastic bag as if they were in danger of being stripped from him.

"River or ocean?" GlenP wondered.

"Both I hope," JimB adjusted himself in his seat to get into a more comfortable position. He then proceeded to stare out the window quietly for the rest of his ride with us.

The only plan we had for this trip was to get to the beach, and get on some waves, but plans never really work out exactly how they're laid out.

"Where's that market you were talking about that sells gas, corndogs, vintage porn, and guns?" Captain Sensitive asked GlenP.

"About five miles up the road here, and yes, we're definitely stopping there! Corndogs!!" GlenP hollered in his goofy voice. He was obviously in love with the place, he went on and on about some place he stopped at with amazing corndogs and vintage porn magazines when he came back from his last surfing trip.

"Hey Captain Sensitive, what would you think about getting a gun with me? That is, put it in your name cause I'm a felon, plus I've only got like $90 on me. What if we both throw down the loot for it, fifty, fifty?" I nearly begged with him.

"Hell yeah, let's do it," and the Captain's response sent poor JimB into a silent fit. He began clutching tightly at his ankles as he began to rock back and forth with his head tucked between his knees. For him, it must have been like the beginning of a scary movie that was going to end with him in a shallow grave in the woods. We went on to debate where we'd go shooting, and we finally settled on a logging road preferably in a heavily wooded area. Poor JimB.

Within ten minutes we had arrived at the corn 'n porn market. "You coming in JimB?" SierraL asked him as everyone else poured out of the van.

"Uh, no thanks," he hesitantly answered, still clutching his ankles.

"Ah, come on, we'll get you a corndog and some porn."

"No thanks, I'm just gonna stay here," JimB replied as he continued to cower in his corner.

"Suit yourself, but I'm still getting you a corndog." As she shut the sliding door of the van and joined the rest of us who were making our way up the steps to the entrance of the market. When we walked in we were immediately greeted by a rack full of 1960's porn magazines. I, of course, had to flip through a few of them until I started to get a chubby, and decided it would probably be best not to look at anymore T & A before I had to walk around the store looking like I had stolen a banana and shoved it down my pants. After my wood subsided, I walked over to a display case with various handguns that SierraL and GlenP were checking out. Above the display were over a hundred pictures of local hunters proudly displaying the carcass of an elk, deer, or bear. Fresh kill. I found a nice little 9mm pistol and asked the clerk if I could take a closer look at it which he grumpily agreed to. I knew as soon as I put my hand on the grip that it was going home with me.

"Whatchya think Captain? Is this the one?" I asked as I handed it to him.

"Oh yeah, lets get it!" and that we did. One 9mm cheap-shit pistol $125, two boxes of ammo $20, two 1960's Penthouse magazines $6, and two corndogs $4.50. The look on JimB's face when we got back in the van with the pistol, priceless. I'm sure he thought his days were numbered. We climbed back in the van and found our seats while JimB remained in the back, rocking back and forth with his arms still clutched around his legs.

We had driven for about five miles and were at least ten miles from the beach when JimB spoke up, "You, um, yeah, here is good. You can just let me out here, this is just fine." I think old JimB was doing everything in his power not to piss himself in the back of the van after we had talked about shooting pistols on a desolate logging road, and especially after showing him the one we had just purchased. GlenP pulled over at a truck stop where JimB got up out of his crouching position, opened the back door, jumped out, and fled down the highway in a funny little run/walk. We all had a good laugh watching old JimB walk away from the van just as fast as his old legs allowed.

After dropping the old guy off, we continued down the highway towards the beach looking for a good logging road to go shoot our new pistol on, and we found one fairly soon after leaving JimB behind. We drove up the road a couple of miles until we were far enough from the highway where we wouldn't be seen or heard by anyone but ourselves. We had been drinking beers the whole drive so we had plenty of empty cans to shoot at. After spending a hundred rounds, we piled back into the van and headed back towards the beach.

We surfed for hours and drank until we couldn't get any drunker. It was a nice enough night to build a fire on the beach, so we did just that. Once it was late enough so that the only sound we heard were the waves, we passed out.

_____

When we woke up we immediately hit the waves yet again. After a few hours of surfing and lying around the remains of our camp fire, we packed up our gear and headed off the sand to get some breakfast. We found a local restaurant and started the day off with a few rounds of mimosas. After a good meal and many laughs that surely pissed off the locals that were dining there, SierraL left us to join another group of friends from Portland that were staying the night at the beach. We said our goodbyes and after a quick stroll on the beach boardwalk, we were back in the van headed home. GlenP was tired from surfing and digesting, so he asked me to drive yet again.

Just ten minutes down the road from the restaurant the power vanished entirely throughout the van. No electrical, no engine, no go vroom, dead on highway 101. I pulled the giant metal carcass onto the shoulder which proved to be quite a bitch due to the sudden lack of power-steering. GlenP was already asleep in the back, so I woke him up and asked "What the fuck is wrong with your van?!?!?" As I talked to GlenP about what the problem could possibly be, a local beach cop pulled up behind us with her emergency lights spinning round. Shit, we've got open beers in the van. I sure hope she didn't see that we just broke down a minute ago. Luckily, GlenP was thinking the same thing, so he did his best to cover them up with various pieces of clothing from the van.

"Good afternoon Gentlemen, what seems to be the problem?" It was a lady cop, butch with a rad stylized mullet full of long blond curls.

"She just died as I was going down the highway. We think it's something electrical," I sounded a little nervous as I tried not to laugh at the cop's totally awesome hair.

"Well, let's take a look," she said as she walked to the front of the van.

GlenP, the cop, and I popped the hood and tried to look for any obvious problems while Captain Sensitive just sat in the passenger seat where he remained as quiet as a mouse. After some debate, I had GlenP turn the key in the ignition, while the cop and I peered under the hood. Nothing. After a while, the cop walked to the side of the van by the sliding door to take a look around and see why the Captain was being so quiet, to which he replied, "I'm just tired," and that was all he said. As I came around to that side, the cop looked at me with a glare that could pierce an arrow. In her hand, she was holding one of the open, full beers that we had been drinking while driving home.

"Your buddy GlenP says he was asleep, and you were driving," she pointed at me, "so who's beer is this?"

"Well it ain't mine," Captain Sensitive finally decides to start talking. What a fucking idiot, I mean think about it man! Who's beer is it if it's not yours or GlenP's? Um, hello!

"So… GlenP here was asleep, you say it's not yours, so that leaves you," She pointed the beer at me, "but you, were driving correct?"

"Yeah, I was driving, but I swear it's not mine." Captain Sensitive, dumbass, your turn to lie.

"So I'm going to assume that it's yours then," she pointed to the Captain, "because if it was his," she said as she pointed to me, "I'd have to issue him a DUI." Come on man!

"But it's not mine," both Jonny and I countered in unison.

"I guess that means you opened it after you broke down then, right?" she lifted her eyebrows.

"Yeah I opened it after we stopped, I guess I just forgot about it," I said, thanking her with my own eyes.

"Well good then," and she handed the full beer back to me. Wow, what a cool cop! She looked at the Captain and declared, "Boy, you must be the wet blanket of the group huh? You haven't said very much at all the whole time I've been here." GlenP, the cop, and I started laughing at the wet blanket as it shrugged its shoulders. She laughed at Captain Wet Blanket as well. What a Nickelback! GlenP and I both thought, sharing our feelings through a look.

"You guys have AAA?" she inquired as she looked at me and then GlenP.

"Yeah, I do," I replied.

"Really man? Oh, thank you so much man! You're a life saver!" GlenP exclaimed.

"I'll call them for you, and then I'll be off. You boys take care." Just as she was walking to her cruiser, it dawned on me that we had multiple concealed weapons in the van, some of which weren't even registered. Pheeew!

About a half hour after the cop left, a flat bed tow-truck pulled up in front of us. The driver hooked us up and asked who was riding in the front with him. GlenP and I decided Captain Sensitive would do the honors for almost getting me thrown in jail, so that GlenP and I could ride in the van on the back of the truck. GlenP and I slept most of the way to Portland which was a little over a hundred miles, and the rest of the time we drank a half rack of beer we had leftover from the night before. Score.

When we arrived in Portland, I could see through the back window of the tow-truck that the Captain had fallen asleep, and I had to call the Wet Blanket at least six times before his dumbass woke up so he could tell the hapless driver where exactly we were going. It was ten at night and the auto shop that GlenP usually took his van to was closed, so we dropped it on the street in front. We realized we had a lot of valuable items in the van, so we only take what we could carry with the hope that his van survived the night untouched. That meant we had to carry three pistols in our waste bands. Just a few blocks from the auto shop was a bar, the Jolly Inn, where I had played several shows with a few different bands I had played in. It was a Friday night and there was sure to be a rock show which would cost anywhere from $3 to $5 at the door. The boys and I were thirsty, so we decided to pay the cover charge to get in the Jolly. We had a few beers, we watched an awful band 'play', and once we couldn't take anymore, we poured onto the street where a cab had just pulled up for some poor sap that had called it there. No ride for him. We jumped in and told the cabby that I was the caller. To the next bar, fully loaded...

I can't go on any further without letting you in on a little secret, something I may have already mentioned to you, or something that you may have already figured out on your own. Junkie. I have been an addict for many years now, and with the help of my new lover, Jade, I have been able to overcome Heroin. I don't think it's fair to you or myself or even Jade for that matter, to go on writing without confronting this topic.

---

24. My Old Friend Mr. H. Wise

I've decided to split this, H Chapter, into two halves, two
subchapters: the first will consist of various pieces that I either
wrote while I was high, or conceived while I was high, but written
at a later date; while the second half was written while I was
quitting or after I had quit. I must admit, I wrote some of my
craziest, most creative work ever while I was on that stuff, but the
point of sharing this work with you is not to show you the crazy,
rather it's to give you a glimpse, a chance for Caribou to compare
my clear-headed work side by side with my cloudy-headed work. . .

HIGH

What I want to know is what I don't know. I want to know what it's
like to be a rebuilt engine in a car with a new paint job. More than
zero, but less than one. Immune to last chances and last dollars. A
want to be in shock, but without the injury. I want to go out in
style without the therapy. Push me into the garage and take your
time with me, be gentle and don't give up. I'll dance until we're
weightless and all you can feel is me standing on your neck. Magic
without the card up the sleeve, folk without our folks there, just
meaningless jabber this and Quaalude that. Live the dream so we can
go on with this life. Like most of us, in fact all of us, we are
predisposed to give too much away. You are becoming so predictable.
How are you supposed to make time for me, when you not only fail to
take the time to reflect in a mirror, but you fake the part you play
so well. You'll read it, but you still won't grasp it! Like jumping
into a river when you can barely float in the lake, that is, power
minus you equals Godspeed.

Why in god's name did I decide to quit smoking on a Friday? Genius
right? Now Saturday begins to end out the windows of this room.
Streets start to fade into the weight of the night. I've smoked
three, drank one, and once upon a moment ago I was made to recite
this very story. Needless to say, things aren't going as planned.
Like a split personality that took over years ago, it is trying to
relinquish power to that old boy, that haggard shadow of a man-boy -
it ain't goin to be easy. No - it sure ain't rollin, mostly a
violent rockin that forgot to roll altogether. The intake is slowing
to a stop, but really it's just digging its heels into the side of
my head, really accomplished footing - split skull and off it goes -
awful.

I shot the stars right out of the sky, no brains on the horizon
where the sun don't ever rise. Can't sleep, can't fuck, or shoot any
target at all. Life sucks, and no days go on. Why wait for a
daughter when a soul can buy you one? We'll melt on our ice-cream
and make our own snow. Can't plug in or plug out. Nest no eggs, nor
the rooster. There will be no barbequed breast brooding in our
blood. No more dried brown crust, coagulated. Insanity's for those
of us whose rock has found color rolling over us. Makeshift baby-
maker covered by the bloody crust. The time is now, to sleep all
day, and drink a few dreams as I slip away. It fucked my mind out
clean, till the dirt they had on us went peacefully down the drain,
in a wash, and to the seven oceans. Plant a kiss and watch it grow.

I ran into my grandfather in a dream late this afternoon, the whereabouts of which are unknown. I settled into this world of his with a comfortable attitude that made the advanced decay of the vessel we once called Gramps a little easier to bare. His hands felt like cold sticks and stones on my face as we exchanged blows, a traditional greeting with the men in my family meant solely to eclipse all other shows of love, loyalty, or friendship. If you are willing to sail that kind of ship, then you can sink anything. We had the same rash spreading over our arms and we blamed ourselves for inflicting the other with the itchy bitch which quickly turned into a bouquet of flowers blooming from our forearms. I grabbed the old man by the arm and led him down the street to a local haunt of his where I bought the old-timer lunch and a few beers. He sat across the narrow bar from me, where he acted as the bartender since the place was empty, save us, and Gramps served us shot after shot. I wet the bed in the real world, and somewhere in the dream I felt a warm wind blow across my body as if I was sitting naked in the bar. I devoured each and every worm that wiggled its way free from my grandpa's nearly fleshless nobility. An act of war to most anyone else, but quite endearing to a maggot like me and my Gramps. He announced he had been keeping a journal of his times in the underworld which he flashed in front of me, but his little form of torture was not to allow me to read a single word from it. He said I'd have to see for myself when I got to my own hell. I feared, however, if I argued to see it, I would win the sight of blank pages and an eternally butt-hurt Gramps, so I didn't push the issue. I sawed off my shackles with the help of a shoe-shine boy who appeared seemingly out of nowhere. I cast the spell entitled "Girl Scout Turned Inside Out."

Free from sobriety and consciousness, my next move was to seek out the highlights of fury unleashed, but instead I put on eye make-up and sent a thousand word text to Barbie, Ken, and all the entire Garbage Pale Kids troupe. I let my Grandfather know that hope had failed me and left a hole in my converse the size of my grandpa's living self's altruism. We compared our port tattoos which were all portraits of beautiful, exotic pin-up ladies approved by the navy, dancing around the fully blooming flowers on our forearms. I hadn't had much else to say to the old man, but what I did tell him was mostly lies of gluttony, a hundred ship fleets, admiral's quarters, and Bangkok wives. Syphilis had shaped up like a funnel cloud and once fully touched down it completely devastated Grandpa's morale and greatly reduced his Viagra intake. Every broad in the dream town knew of his sick dripping dick thanks to doctor douche bag and his lack of confidentiality. He was Grandpa's age and his only competition for demonic tang in their hell together. Ole Gramps no longer power walked through town in his tiny jogging shorts sporting more than just a pair of runner's legs. It made me sad to see times were changing. A tear or two fell from the corners of my sleeping eyes which melded with the sweat I had poured out in buckets upon my sheets. He pulled his shorts up past his bellybutton, so far up his ass that his half rotten, soft gray wiener hung out the right leg hole of his shorts. He became a favorite at the dog park. I'd rather kick it with clowns on LSD than see Gramps go running in this dream ever again. He always had popsicles in his basement freezer and Lawrence Welk on his TV. The bubbles in the show seemed to float into my room as I awoke having to pee.

I can make quick friends and quit loose ends. Make the best of swimming by learning how to drown. Welcome rain like a child in an air raid. What's a world war bomb without the wings, the war, the mass destruction, alive or not, keep the bullets flying. Did we wake you? Oh well, in that case, get off your ass, clean up, eat something, and get off probation. Buy me a scar from the seniors that tell tales of syphilis and Betty's who all danced well, and gave even better hand jobs. However, you really don't have to spread your legs to be me. Know me as the next time you water the plants. You can't live the dream when you can only see the tornado, and you don't see the fight. Smack! Overwhelming with a greatness that is both beautiful and shocking, I've painted the ugliest prints I would've paid June's paycheck to feel forever. The happy kind of puke that lasts one Heimlich, and impacts the rest of the social performance that's worth a best-supporting actor. How come everything in your pockets are bent up and sweated on? . . . And where did they find that nervous fidget of a touch? The matches won't light and the cigs have no home. They break so brittle, and the filters surpassed us a few hours ago by high blood pressure, swollen veins, and screaming arteries breaking holes in a fleeting heart that shared the rush with a fleet of artists.

Do you sew? What I mean to ask, is have you ever had a sewing project where there are a lot of pins? For instance, following a pattern, hemming a dress or pants, or even making a garment from scratch… Whether you have or not, you can easily imagine that as the project progresses, becoming more complete, those pins lose their purpose and place, cast aside. They usually end up in that little cushion that's specially designed with them in mind, a pin cushion. I am much like that lowly group of pins, though I don't consider them kin or even anywhere near having ever been on the same level as me, arrogance on my part I suppose. I, they, we exist as cushions to such projects, and it exists on the sidelines. I was and always will be a pin cushion. I front as a functioning member, but I am a lucky breed that is able to successfully fool those around me into believing that the truth doesn't apply to me, and I have the world, you included, fooled, because I appear at first glance, impression, congregation … as something creative and unique. Tom-foolery I suppose, yes, here lies a very revealing, self deprecating paragraph. I'm a casualty of my own stupidity, "Ouch! Fuck me," nodded out.

I just fell asleep reading a book with a cigarette in hand and the damn thing burnt a hole through the track shorts I'm wearing. It's pathetic that the only mark or stain on these shorts, rather than sweat, dirt, or road rash blood, is from a cigarette. It's even more pathetic how many of pairs of pants, shirts, and blankets have cigarette burns in them from nodding out while smoking. I'm an arsonist many times over, though the stupid thing is that I don't have renter's insurance.

Since I was a small child I had always slept on my right side, switching to my left in the middle of the night. Nowadays it's a different story, I awake to shooting pains, shooting from my shoulders to my hands. I had collapsed… bad circulation… Running a funeral for my veins and eventually my entire arm, I'm buried in the sand. Laying next to me, my cat Eva is on her back twitching with dreams of chasing mice through the back yard and swatting at flies inside the house that are bouncing off the windows trying to escape. It's sobering.

No more can I pretend to like this, than I can pretend I won't miss it. I already do - I certainly wasn't going to cuddle up to the fact that the bag is empty, well, maybe... ok, you got me, I'm out and I'm Jones' in. Who is Jones anyways? Was he some really depraved person who never got what he wanted? Did he constantly crave things to the extreme? Do the Dew Mr. Jones.

I hadn't quite made a plan, even though quite a bit of it had made me. Got a bat by the back door, and a switch in my pocket. Steel blade. Never had a problem walking, a bit of a slouch, and an inch to one leg gave a smooth, painful strut. Never had to two wheel it in the world before, but know that one of the three wheelchairs I own is cocked to the side, barely staring at me in the middle of the back lawn fighting rust and retardation, yet ready to lay down its hand and fold into scrap. Wars won and lost on so many fun hills per hour, per chair. Its smile is a permanent wound ironically scared to the point of a debilitating degree forced to enjoy it until the next hill, the next buck eighty.

AFTER

It's no Nazca Line, there's no great mystery into how or why I became addicted to Heroin, I was a weak, drunkenly uninhibited moron. I was a one piece puzzle. Chasing escape. Now I happily wear black holes for eyes that stare right through you, but a smile to greet you just the same. My best friend's a cat and I hate dentists. My neighbor spied on me today and that's no delusion, I heard him on the telephone outside my window.

"He's burning holes in the lawn, it's gross," adjusting awkwardly. Alkaloids

---

The bacterium is my invisible little foe, invisible to the naked eye. I had gone three years without a single infection from shooting up, but of course, during my last week of use, I had to go ahead and get an infection in my wrist from the second to last shot I took. I didn't even realize anything was wrong until a week after I had quit. One morning, seemingly out of nowhere, my wrist had swollen up to the size of a softball, and the pain was excruciating. It turns out that the needle I had reused, I never once shared a needle, had bacteria that had grown on it since I had first used it, and it had entered my wrist causing an infection and cellulitis. If I moved my hand, sharp pains would shoot through the tendons in my forearm. I tried lancing the bastard with a razor, but wherever the puss was, if any existed at all, was under too many layers of skin for me to get at. The next morning when the pain became nearly unbearable, I decided to employ the services of my local Emergency Room, and thank god I did. The first thing the doc told me when he saw my arm was that he "sure hopes he can save it." I must admit, I was a little freaked out, but I was so fucking high, nothing could touch me at that point. Turned out I had to have anti-biotics pumped into me via an IV for about an hour, every twelve hours, for three days to knock the damn thing out of my arm. No insurance, big fucking bill.

It's kicking it again, the last eagerly awaited visit. Before sucking down the Afghani death, I murdered burgers deliciously conceived with all the fixings. 100% choice roast beef, ground into a patty, some Sedaris (bro or sis, don't much matter), and tits in my face by a pool in the Hamptons. Pistols, independence, and tolerable tunes in my I-ear, stitch me up I'm bleeding proverbial tears of timeless budgets that I can't afford. Fast forward to dessert where I'll see the fruits of my maybes mostly stiffen up like a cat going dead faster than a maggot turns fly. I don't have all the answers, thoughts, or ideas of my own, and they might as well be a special kind of ESP. Involuntarily separate a chunk of an old tree, fill it with scribbles, and top it off with the shortest hand of any shortage I've ever known. I shake sweaty nightmares in unconscious anxiety as a darling of mine makes it into my dreams in the worst way when she tapped on my bedroom window. Let me in, she shouts through the storm screen. This was in the real world, and her rapping was light but enough to wake me, but in my dream it was a jackhammer slamming at the door of the taxi cab I was in, on my way to who knows where in lower Manhattan.

Rap Knock Slam!

I awoke fully clothed in a lake of sweat with the pillows and blankets cruelly strewn across my room. I was almost afraid to pick it all up and put it on the bed fearing I would find my cat mutilated by my sleepwalking tendencies. Sleepwalking is the term, but sleep is the only accurate part about it. Ever since I was a toddler, until I was about thirteen, every now and then I would violently rock back and forth in bed. On even rarer occasions I would arise from my rocking and run around my house, and even my neighborhood. I would swing my arms about and scream like a madman, punching and kicking trees, bushes, houses, cars, animals, and even the occasional person or two. Rubout. Therefore, it wouldn't have surprised me if I beat my poor kitty to death. Ms. Eva Braun, or possibly even Ms. Jade. In that dream, their blue and green squinters would squabble over scraps of dignity in the foulest sense.

Independence Day Eve, 2007, after being friends with Mr. H. Wise for nearly a year, I decided it was time I try and kick this old friend out of my life for good. I acquired a small stash of the pill Suboxone which is a newer pharmaceutical that had been touted as a miracle drug that was supposed to be twice as effective as methadone, but without the addiction. I had a number of friends who had successfully kicked dope with the help of methadone, but they had inadvertently become addicted to the methadone. Like N.A., when you kick your drug of choice, you simply replace the void it creates with another addiction, often it is alcohol or pills, and for N.A.'ers it's typically God, yuck, no thanks. I tried to go to an N.A. meeting one time, Thanksgiving of the same year, and I vowed never to step foot into one of those pathetic meetings ever again. It was a group of pathetic wastoids who had successfully made it off of their Narco-habit, but they hadn't quite made it out of the trailer park. On top of that, I just don't see how sitting around and sharing the same boring stories from your life can really help.

They would say I'm missing the point, but just because there's a point doesn't mean it holds any real meaning for me, and it doesn't necessarily mean it needs to be taken. For me, the best remedy is out of sight, out of mind.

Sitting around blowing my chatterbox off about our addictions is only going to stir up memories of being blasted into another dimension thus causing undesirable cravings for said dimensions. So I was gunning for an Independence Day kick and luckily, my Father and Step-Mother had gone out of town for two weeks and asked me to housesit for them which was rad because they had a huge, over 3,400 square foot, house in the west hills looking over downtown Portland, just a few blocks from where I had lived in my Great-Grandmother's old house. Unfortunately, even with the hoard of Suboxone I had taken for the last four days, I was still very dope sick.

By day five I couldn't bare it anymore, so I called my dealer at the time, a guy known as Uncle. He said to meet him in twenty minutes at the end of his block on the northwest side of town just a few blocks north of Burnside which was a five to ten minute drive from my Dad's place. I got dressed so quickly, I even neglected to tie my shoes. When I jumped into my car I was shivering and twitching with every movement. I made it to his street in just over five minutes so I called to tell him I was a little bit early. He told me to sit tight and he'd meet me in less than ten minutes, so I decided to circle the block a few times before double-parking on 22nd Street, between Glisan and Hoyt streets. It was a Saturday so traffic was pretty thick with shoppers, and I had to wave quite a few cars around me as I sat with my hazard lights blinking. At one point, just minutes before Uncle came to meet me, a larger, bearded man pulled up behind me in an older Toyota Corolla. He sat behind me honking his horn, so I stuck my arm out the window and waved him around, but rather than go around me like all the other cars before him had, he just sat there and continued to honk at me. Ultimately, I stopped waving him on and just sat there shaking my head thinking, what the fuck is this douche bag doing? A minute passed and all of the sudden, he pulled forward ramming the front end of his car into the back of mine. "What the fuck!" I yelled in my junkie sick mumble. I got out of my car and marched over to his window: I was fed up with being sick, I had reached my limit. As I approached his car I could see a cynical looking smile on the guys face, and I knew it was now my duty to wipe it clean off. I rushed at him as quickly as I could so he wouldn't have a chance to retaliate. When I got to his window I immediately grabbed his seat belt with my left hand, which he still had fastened tight, and pushed it as hard as I could across his neck and right arm pinning him down, and with my right fist I proceeded to smash his face in with a flurry of blows that would have impressed any Golden-Glover. In less than three punches I had succeeded in not only wiping off his smile, I had also knocked him out cold, and the icing on the cake was the full cup of coffee he had been holding had spilled across his lap and was steaming up on a ninety degree day, indicating it was fresh and very, very hot.

As soon as I had let go of the seat belt and surveyed the damage I had inflicted, I started to hear people on the street yelling at me. I turned to see a few separate groups that had formed to witness the assault, and I knew I had to high-tail it out of there if I was going to not only score from Uncle, but stay out of jail for assault and battery, I jumped in my car and peeled out down the street, disappearing into traffic. I rang Uncle on my cell right away, gave him the short version of what had just transpired, and asked him to meet me a few blocks away in the opposite direction of where the pummeling had occurred. In just a few minutes Uncle was in my car and I had accomplished my mission. After I dropped Uncle off on a

nondescript corner, Mr. H Wise and I sped off to my Dad's place
where the needles and spoons awaited our arrival.

Later that day, after getting well, and making my way over to my
Mother's house in the Tron to hide out from a possible encounter
with the Portland cops, I received a call on my Mom's land line, it
was the police. How they had my Mom's number was beyond me, but I
took the call knowing that it was probably unwise to avoid it.

"Hello?"

"Hello, ThomasJ?"

"Speaking, how may I help you?"

"This is Officer (Oink Oink) with the Portland Police," this is the
part where my heart sunk through the soles of my shoes. "I have a
report here from a Mr. GaylordD and a witness to the incident that
you assaulted Mr. GaylordD at about one this afternoon."

"Well, there was an incident, yes, I won't deny that."

"Are you denying the assault happened?" he demanded sarcastically.

"Well, to be honest with you, it was, I believe, in self-defense."

"Go on, after all, I am calling for your statement."

"Well you see, I was double parked waiting for my friend to come out
from his apartment and I had my hazards on. Mr. GaylordD you said
was his name, right?"

"That's right," and I proceeded to tell him what happened with a few
minor details either left out, or changed 'slightly.' "So I came up
to his window, to you know, ask him why he hit me and get his
insurance info. When I got to his window he was taking the lid off
of his steaming cup of coffee and it appeared as if he was about to
chuck the scalding java all over me, so I punched him, you know, in
defense, trying to avoid getting burned, and then I took off fearing
the guy was going to beat me up or hit my car again. I mean, he
looked pretty big."

"Well, hmm…" the cop paused for a second, and I could hear the sound
of shuffling papers. "Well yes, that is pretty consistent with what
the witness said, except Mr. GaylordD said you attacked him,
unprovoked," and before I could interrupt in a whinny, pleading-like
manner, he continued, "but, after hearing your story and looking at
your profile information, and his, I am more inclined to believe
your story. You're both clean as far as your record goes, but Mr.
GaylordD is six foot six, and it says here that you're just, wow,
five foot six. Jeez kid, you sure did a number on Mr. GaylordD," and
he tried to cover his mouth, but I could still hear a muffled
chuckle. "I mean, you beat him up pretty bad. Broken nose,
concussion, two black eyes," I gasped.

"Seriously?"

"Yeah, seriously," another muffled chuckle, "but you know what? I am not going to arrest you, or charge you with anything because, frankly ThomasJ, I believe you, and I'm actually pretty impressed you were able to handle such a big guy. However, I am required to turn in a report to the Assistant District Attorney, and it is up to him if he wants to pursue charges against you. But rest assured, the report will favor your story, and I'm sure after I speak with Mr. GaylordD here in just a few minutes that he will not press charges against you like he originally wanted to."

"Wow, thanks Officer, I really appreciate all your help!" I exclaimed, utterly shocked at the outcome.

"Take care Mr. ThomasJ," and he hung up. I was relieved to have Officer Oink Oink on my case, otherwise, I would have surely been cuffed by the day's end if it had been any other fascist cop. It's been over two years now and I never heard anything more about the incident from anyone involved. Bullet dodged.

I'm sitting at my computer listening to Miss Jade as she wheezes quietly just a few feet from my desk, or is that her vibrator? Either way, I know she wishes I were in bed with her. Part of me wishes I was lying with her, yet here I am, typing away. As even my most visceral, base side slipped away from me and I feared losing my life to a heart attack from being caught and forced out fully culpable, pants down, there was one slide in the show that was able to save me and she did. She is my Jade. After admitting to her that I was a fragile orchid, and at the time, not knowing exactly what I meant by it, made the suicide attempts seem a little less empty. The cleaner the windows, the screens, and the floors became, the less indignant, odious, and cantankerous I became. Color me Jade, lighten me opulently, and leave me in a state of genuine honesty where I should finally pay Abe my dues. These were my negotiated terms of friendship and love with my Jade, though we needn't barter or trivialize our affection for one another by attempting to perfect it.

Jade has been a savior, allowing me to make the right changes in my life, the right everything in my life. She gave me a path lined with health and happiness that she has gracefully led me down, holding my hand the entire way. She couldn't have appeared at a more perfect time: following the release of my monkey, Henry, from the shackles of my back. From the simplest of gestures has come the greatest of pleasures. Home has become a farmhouse, and love has the look I get from this green-eyed girl. Jade has made any and every word worth speaking, any and every day worth living through, and every kiss taste of the greatest benevolence anyone can ever receive. She has taken me in, and become my home. Home is wherever Jade is, Jade is my love, Jade is my home.

Though I often found myself missing my old enemy-friend, Jade made sure the monkey would never, ever, come back. Senõr Henry and I had our ups and downs, but there were some things about him that just can't be replaced, some things that I'll never be able to forget. Before I let him go, he helped me write some of what was written in this chapter, hell he wrote most of it himself...

---

25. Turning the Paige on Felony Flats

After bailing on the University of Oregon, and moving back to
Portland, I got the job at the Ice Rink and found a house near SE
82nd and Burnside, a neighborhood historically known as Montavilla,
but known to us locals as a part of a larger area known as the
Felony Flats. Our house was a two story, turn-of-the-century
Victorian home on the corner across the street from a church. I
occupied the entire second story which contained the master bedroom
because I had found the house for us to rent, so I got first choice
of rooms, though I did pay a little more rent than everyone else.
Not only were my roommate's long time friends of mine, they also
happened to be my co-workers at the ice-rink, and they were both
named Matt. Because I had so many friends named Matt growing up, I
often referred to them by their last names. Matt Bonzai was my
neighbor growing up, and the other Matt, last name Bender, I met
through my brother.

The biggest attraction of the house was the fact that it was just
that, a house and not an apartment. Other perks included the fact
that the three of us would get to live together, and the rent was
really cheap. The reason it was so cheap was because there was a lot
of low-income housing in the neighborhood, and the crime rate was
the highest in the city at the time.

In the middle of a summer afternoon Bonzai was in the bathroom and
he had just finished taking a shower. He had stepped out of the tub
to dry himself with a towel, and through the window he could see a
man trying to get into my car in the driveway. He screamed for me
and when I got to the locked bathroom door he yelled out what was
happening so I ran outside, there was a guy with a Slim-Jim in his
hand running away from my car, so I gave chase. Though I didn't
catch him, the same guy would get arrested early the next morning
after robbing the grocery store down the block, getting in a
shootout with the cops, and finally taking a hostage during a
standoff with the police.

Both Matts and I were in front of our house playing drunken midnight
basketball that very night, just hours after the guy attempted to
steal my car. Midnight basketball games were a common occurrence at
the house, and after the attempted theft, we felt it was especially
a good idea to keep an eye on the street that night. Amidst a heated
game of horse, a city cop car suddenly appeared with all of its
lights off flying by us on our street, the same one the grocery
store was on, 81st. The car pulled over to the side of the road
behind the store, and the cop driving jumped out, and drew his gun
as he stood shielded by his door. Seconds later, two masked men came
running from the side of the grocery store into the street directly
in front of the cop. They were both wearing ski masks, carrying a
gun in one hand, and a pillow case in the other that must have held
the money they had just stolen. The cop didn't even yell "freeze,"
or "stop police," not a word before he fired off his service weapon
twice at the running thieves. The shots appeared to have missed and
we watched as the cop jumped back into his car and drove off giving
chase.

What blew my mind was that the cop just shot at them, unprovoked,
and it was on a residential street, so that meant that at least one
of the bullets had to have gone into one of the houses that sat in
the background. Bender called 911 and told the dispatcher what we
had just seen, and within an hour there was a policeman knocking on
our door. Rook. He took a quick statement from us as a group, and

when we got to the part about his fellow officer shooting at the thieves, our friendly community policeman looked at us sternly, and interrupted by saying, "Sorry, but you have it all wrong. The suspects fired upon the officer." We tried to correct him and say that we all knew what we saw, and what we saw was the cop shooting and missing the thieves, but no matter what we said, he insisted that his fellow officer never shot his weapon.

It was abundantly clear that the cops were trying to perpetrate a cover-up. Seriously, is this really happening? Isn't this only supposed to happen in the movies?!?! And it WAS just like a movie the way the cop pressured us into dropping our claim that the cop shot at the thieves. Before the two Matts could continue to argue with the cop at our door, I spoke over them loud enough to quiet them, "You know what officer? You're right, it was pretty dark and hard to see, so it's quite likely we mistook the cop for a thief," to which the Matts both snickered before I continued, "So I guess you're probably right, it was the suspect that took the shots." By the end of my plea I had raised my arm up to a height on the door jamb so neither Matt, nor the Cop could see each other.

"Great," sarcastic piggy, "you gentlemen, have a good night, and thanks for calling this in," the Pig said smugly as he slowly stepped backwards down our front stoop before he rejoined the other city sponsored goons that were congregating on the corner discussing Krispy dreams. As the copper walked away, the two Matts pawed at me in drunken agitation to get me to turn around so they could see my face when they asked, "Just what the fuck was that all about?"

As soon as the cop was around the corner out of sight, I finally let go of the door jam, shut the door, and turned to face my accusers, "Before you guys freak out on me, let me explain something," It was some kind of cover-up, a conspiracy, though not a complex Hollywood type story, still it was what it was. They knew as well as I what it was, but what my roommates wanted to know was why we should give them what they wanted. For me it was simple: did I really want a target on my back for the rest of my days in Portland? The answer was simple: hell no. No one got hurt, so what would it hurt if I adhered to the cop's demands and retract my statement? No one, at least not in the immediate future.

Meanwhile, the crook had broken into a house and taken the only occupant, an eighty-nine year old man in a wheelchair, breathing from an oxygen tank, as a hostage. After standing off with a S.W.A.T. team all night, the thief eventually gave up the next morning without harming a hair on the old man's head.

Both of the Matts' had brothers that I also happened to be friends with. I knew Bonzai's brother since I was a young boy, and we still talked via email every once in a while since he was living abroad at the time. He had spent most of his post high-school years volunteering his time for various humanitarian aid projects throughout Africa, particularly in war torn countries where poverty was high, and crimes against humanity were some of the worst ever documented, places like: Darfur, Somalia, Rwanda, and Sudan, just to name a few. Bender, on the other hand, had three brothers, all of which I had met playing hockey at the ice rink where I worked. PaigeB, the last of the brothers to meet me, was the eldest, and though he was ten years older than the middle brother, he had truly lived more life than his two brothers combined. He was homeless at the time and his brother Matt asked Bonzai and I if it would be possible for him to move into our basement for the winter which we agreed to. Once this was decided, Bender told us the short version of his brother's amazing life. I was immediately taken aback by the man's story, how he had suffered so greatly in his thirty-five years on earth, and rather than overcome the adversities that faced him, he avoided them altogether, leaving his life behind him to live on the streets, to live the streets.

After hearing of his invitation, PaigeB quickly packed up his camp site in a park forest where he had been living for the past year, and into the basement in my new house. The basement was an unfinished concrete slab with an empty storage room that was the ideal place for PaigeB to stay at. It was dark and damp, not all that different from camping in the park, but at least he had a roof over his head, and he no longer had to sleep with one eye open. Once he had 'moved in,' I went down to room to check in on him, and I could tell immediately that he had nearly forgotten how to live indoors: his shoes sat just outside his bedroom door, much like one would leave their shoes outside the tent so not to track in dirt and the like; and his bags were always packed so that he could bail at any given moment if need be.

You didn't need a shrink to see that there was something a little off with PaigeB, so I decided to probe his brother Matt for some answers to my inklings. At first, Bender just made jokes, "Oh, he's just fucking with you. He's really a super genius, you know, like one that's so smart he's become a recluse because he can't function properly in society."

Ultimately, I got a lot more than I bargained for when Bender finally stopped joking and got serious, "Well, I suppose you wanna know the truth about my brother huh?"

"Well yeah asshole, I've only been bugging you for the last couple of weeks about it. What's the story there?" I asked.

"Alright…" he said as he walked into our kitchen, opened the fridge, and grabbed two beers. "Lets sit out here," he said, gesturing towards our front porch. "Here," he said, handing me a beer as we both sat down. The sun was directly above us, shining down on our heads creating a glow that was almost like a halo shining off the sweat on our foreheads.

"Thanks," and I opened my beer. "So, start from the beginning, like when you were kids," I pulled out a cigarette and lit it.

"Sure, sure, Let's see…" he scratched his head as he stared at the fresh beer in his hand. "He's almost ten years older than me, so I really don't have too many childhood memories with him in them, but from what I do remember about him was that when he came around, he was like a Dad to us in a lot of ways. You know, since our real dad died when I was about six. That meant Ren, the middle brother, was eight years old," pausing to drink from his beer which I mimicked. "Anyways, he would take us to the ice-rink after school for hockey practice, my brother, and he'd skate with us during open ice and even play pickup games with us. If it wasn't for him, Ren and I would never have never played hockey."

"Is he any good?" I asked, intrigued because at the time I had just begun playing hockey myself.

"Oh yeah man, he was fucking great, that is, until the operations. He could skate circles around most guys at that rink, and I mean fast as…" he tried to answer as I interrupted him.

"Wait, wait, wait, operations? You never told me anything about that shit before," I sat up straight in my chair leaning forward so the sun was out of my eyes.

"I didn't? Oh man!" he said as he sat up further in his seat. "OK, so when I was about um… now let me think about this for a second…" he looked up in thought. "Now ChanceB, PaigeB's first kid, was born when I was what… uh… six," Bender said, thinking out loud. "So PaigeB was twenty when he had ChanceB, and it was the year after that when PaigeB started to get these really horrendous headaches. Now he's a tough guy, but these things had him on his knees, I mean he was bed ridden," he paused to take a drink of his beer, so I took the opportunity to chime in.

"Damn they must have been something then huh, the headaches?"

"Yeah man, it was really hard to see him like that," he shook his head. "The headaches only happened every once in a while for the first six months, but then, suddenly, he started getting them on a daily basis. He started missing too many days of work, so they fired him. Finally, he had one that lasted over a week, and the tough guy that he is, he refused to see a doctor. He finally conceded and went to the emergency room, but only at the bequest of his wife, and only after laying in bed in total agony for eight days," he said before stopping to take another drink.

"Oh man, what was it, a tumor?" I asked.

"No Swartzenager, it wasn't a tooma" he said with his best Swartzenager impression, which was quite pitiful really. "Now I know you're thinking it was something worse than a tumor, but it wasn't. See at the time, our Mom was a Nurse at the teaching hospital on the hill, OHSU, so PaigeB, not having any insurance, got some kinda family deal through Mom. At first they couldn't figure out what was wrong with him, but after a battery of tests they finally decided to give him an MRI. Now you gotta keep in mind that this was the early 80's, so the reason they waited so long was because the machine that does MRI's was a newer piece of equipment and it was super expensive to use, even today the thing costs like $1,000 to have your head scanned. The MRI's revealed some kind of anomaly in his head and a whole group of doctors were baffled as to what it was exactly," drinks. "So they scalped the guy and dug around inside his head, you know, exploratory brain surgery."

"Jesus, so what was it?" I was on the end of my seat clutching my beer so hard I thought I might break the bottle.

"Hold on, hold on, I'm not quite there yet," he said as he smiled cynically and letting out a little laugh. "You see, they didn't do just one, they did two exploratory brain surgeries, and keep in mind these weren't just minor surgeries, these were a big deal each time! He came out of the first one just fine, at least that's what they said. A few weeks later the tests came back, and wuddaya know, they still didn't have a clue what was wrong with him."

All I could muster in response was a "Wow" before he continued.

"It was just a few weeks after he'd recovered from the first surgery that they had him under the knife for the second," Bender said with an ever growing air of anger about him.

"And this was all at your Mom's hospital?" I inquired.

He laughed slightly as he confirmed my question "Yeah," pausing to grasp his disgust in its entirety. Resent. "So here's the really fucked up part, well…" he paused to better articulate his point, "I guess not so much fucked as it was sad. Anyways, after PaigeB was out of the hospital from surgery number two and back on his feet, shit really started to go south for him. You see, at first, we, and by 'we' I mean my family, plus his wife, and even his co-workers, started to notice that PaigeB just wasn't the same guy anymore. Eventually, it came to light that PaigeB was dyslexic, and not just regular old fucked up dyslexia, he had a super rare case of extreme dyslexia. And on top of that, his personality did a five-forty. He went from a family man, working a blue-collar job, to a divorcee and living on the streets within a year." He sighed before he took another swig of his beer, finishing it off.

"Holy fuck man, that's awful!" I said at a near yelling decibel as I followed suit, slamming the remainder of my beer.

"Another?" Bender inquired, as he raised his empty bottle and shook it.

"Definitely," I answered, handing him my empty.

"K, give me just a sec here," he said as he got up and went to the kitchen to fetch us a couple more beers, and I went to the pisser.

Back in our seats, "So, what the fuck, did they ever find out what it was?" I was really anxious at this point. A bit of a silence followed as Bender sat there and stared at the cold beer in his hand as he spun it around. "After the all the tests they finally realized that all he had was Lyme Disease," sighing heavily.

"Hold up, you get that from ticks right?"

"Yup, and it's curable by common antibiotics. Granted, this was in the early eighties when the disease was new, but they really fucked him up with those surgeries. I mean his wife left him within six months, he lost job after job after job, he kept getting kicked out of living situations, and ended up on the street."

"The same street he's been on until just a few days ago when he moved in here, huh? Shit, that's fucked up!" I said.

"You're telling me…"

Everything I thought PaigeB was had changed during that conversation, and to say he was under a new light was a bit of an understatement. His image was thus ingrained upon my mind by the force of a sun, and I had become deeply intrigued by what the man had been, what he became, and who he was from day. Morph. As a result of his condition, I was confronted by a different version of PaigeB each day, and though he often told the same stories, each occupant told it in a distinctly fresh way. Adapting.

238

I didn't fully grasp just how profoundly the surgeries affected him until one night when I was at home alone, or at least I thought I was alone. While watching a movie in my bedroom I began to hear a loud slamming sound coming from the living room directly below me. At first I didn't pay it any mind, thinking one of the Matts had arrived and began hanging pictures on the wall or something of that nature, but after five minutes of constant banging, it started to get on my nerves. It sounded as though someone was hitting a stud in the wall with a hammer over and over again. Agitated, I stormed downstairs to tell whoever it was that they were annoying the hell out of me, and they needed to shut the fuck up. When I got there, I found PaigeB sitting in a rocking chair, slouched over the right arm, with a stream of saliva pouring from his mouth to a large pool on the carpet below him. Rather than rocking forward, he was rocking from side to side with a vacant look on his face. He was rocking so hard that his head was slamming into the wall where he had made a sizable hole. Thanks to various horror stories I had heard from friends and family that had been in the same situation, I knew immediately that he was suffering from a seizure.

When PaigeB was in one of less violent twitching bouts, I grabbed him by the ankles and yanked him out of the chair as far from the pool of drool as I could. I rolled him on his side, put a towel under his head, and sat nearby watching him and the television for nearly an hour before the seizure finally subsided.

I was sitting on the porch one day, not too long after the hole-in-the-wall-seizure, smoking cigarettes, drinking beers, and talking to Bonzai before he left for class when PaigeB came strolling up with a puppy, a black lab to be precise.

"Say there, who's your friend?" I asked him as he led the dog up our front path.

"Shit I dunno, I think he's gotta a tag on his collar," he said as he stopped to bend down and read it. "Here, read it for me," waving me over.

I walked down off the porch, took a hold of the collar, and read out loud, "Rex…" and laughter prevailed. "Where the hell did Rex come from huh?" I demanded to know from PaigeB.

Before replying, PaigeB produced a feeble little laugh in an attempt to convince us that he too thought the name was funny, though we all knew he had no idea what we were laughing at. This often got him in trouble because he would mistake people's laughter for attacks on him and his condition. "I was on my way here and saw the little guy chained up in his front yard. Not a regular chain, but a really fucking short chain, and right next to him was his piece of shit owner sitting in a lawn chair. The old fucker was trying to train him or some shit, but his idea of a training tool was a two by four, and he was whacking the hell out of him," he said as he swung his arm towards Rex. The poor dog whimpered at the sight of PaigeB's imitation of the beatings he had endured for god knows how long. "Oh, sorry boy," PaigeB said as he got down on one knee and hugged the dog. "Anyways, I pushed the old fart down, told him what I thought of him, and took the dog."

"Good for you for rescuing him man!" Bonzai said as he scratched the dog's neck.

Just then Bender walked out and asked, "What's with the Dog?"

"Your brother was just telling us how he took it from the owner who was hitting the shit out of him with a two by four. Fucked up huh?" I turned to Bender.

"Damn, I guess that means we got ourselves a new roommate then huh?" and a good roommate he was.

_____

A few days after Rex's rescue, we were sitting on our front porch smoking cigarettes and drinking beers once again, however this time, we had a puppy hanging out with us. We spent the better part of the last two days trying to come up with a good name for the black bastard, but we weren't having any luck finding one we all agreed upon. After a third day debating names, it was I who finally came up with a name that we all liked: the Ancient Egyptian God of the Underworld known as Osiris, and from that day forward he was known by that name.

He proved to be a pretty unruly little pain in the ass, which was no doubt a by-product of his abusive upbringing. He wouldn't listen to most commands, and as time went by we gave up trying to train him altogether. He was also more curious than a cat, unfortunately, he didn't have nine lives like his feline counterpart, which would ultimately catch up with him…

_____

On a cold October night, the Matt's, PaigeB, and I all ate mushrooms and since it was so shitty outside, we decided to just hunker down in the living room, and watch movies while we tripped. While we were in our own little world, Osiris snuck into the bathroom, jumped up on the toilet seat, and grabbed a bottle of aspirin off the edge of the sink. He took the bottle into Bender's bedroom where he ripped it open and ate nearly twenty aspirin. By the time we realized what had happened, our trips were in full swing, and the poor dog was whimpering, throwing up, and pissing all over the house. We called an emergency Veterinarian hotline and asked them if he'd be ok and if there was anything that we needed to do. They told us that just three aspirin can be lethal to an adult dog, so we needed to get him to a Vet A.S.A.P., or else he could die within a few hours. Being as fucked up as we were, we came to the conclusion that it wasn't a good idea for any of us to take him in, so we called our boss' girlfriend, a big lover of animals. Within twenty minutes she was at our place to get Osiris who she rushed to the vet.

An hour or so later she returned with a bag of charcoal that we were supposed to mix with his food for the next week to help soak the poison up out of his system. For the rest of the night, as we sat around the living room tripping on mushrooms, Osiris would walk across the living room with a really sad, scared look on his face as he whimpered and pissed across the carpet as he walked by every five minutes or so.

Even though he was new to the family, it was still pretty scary to see him like that, but I'll be damned if it wasn't funny as hell to watch him as he filled the house with piss. Within the week, Osiris had made a full recovery, and once again, he was up to his same old mischievousness. There wasn't a safe shoe, pillow, or plate of food in the entire house.

For PaigeB and I in particular, the porch was our sanctuary, a place where we would sit for hours, drinking, smoking, and swapping stories. Even though he would tell me the same stories over and over again without realizing it, PaigeB was hands down my favorite roommate to sit out there with because his stories were truly the best. From the first time I met PaigeB, I sensed there were amazing tales behind the forty year old man's sixty seven year old face. I got him to start from the beginning, at least the beginning of the more interesting times from his life.

He had grown up as a pretty rebellious kid, likely the result of his parent's divorce when he was just twelve, and later the death of his father when he was fourteen.

At one point, he had gotten into so much trouble while living with his Mother in Portland that she sent him to live with his grandmother in Long Beach, California. Grandma had lived in her home since the late 1940's, and over the years, the neighborhood had become progressively worse, until it was considered within the invisible borders of what had been deemed the ghetto. Sending a young white kid to live in a neighborhood where black and Latino gangs ruled the street was a cruel trick to get her son to straighten up, however, PaigeB not only survived the two years he lived there, he did so in style.

The first few times he walked down his grandma's street, he was harassed by a group of gang-bangers that were about his age. At first they just yelled threats at him, threats he thought would never come to fruition until one day when he had to walk by them to get to school and they pulled a knife on him. PaigeB grabbed the kids arm, swung him around and in an instant had the knife to the kid's throat. The others backed off, so PaigeB let the kid go, handed him his knife, and continued to walk to school. Surprisingly, he was pretty much left alone after that. He had established a reputation for himself as the quiet guy not to be fucked with. It was surprising because most street gangs like the one he had encountered don't take kindly to disrespect, and acts of retaliation were commonplace, so it was kind of shocking that they just left him alone, like some 80's movie where all the guy had to do was beat up the bully once and then all the bad guys would leave him alone for the rest of the movie. It just wasn't realistic, but the fact that they were the ones that had done the disrespecting, and PaigeB was just sticking up for himself. No matter how badly the kid that had pulled the knife wanted to jump PaigeB, the gang simply just wouldn't allow it. They saw PaigeB as a badly white kid in a world where he was the minority. Respect.

One of my favorite stories from PaigeB was from this time in his life, when he was still living with his Grandmother. He had met a girl, MelissaS, at his school and he had asked her out on a Friday night date. On the Tuesday before the date, whilst on his way over to a friend's house after school, he saw a brand new Ferrari Berlinetta Boxer parked on the street at the foot of the Hollywood

Hills. When he walked up to get a better look, he realized that not only was the door unlocked, but the keys were in the ignition. Score, he thought as he jumped in, started it up, and drove off. Being somewhat of a flashy kid, combined with the fact that he wasn't the brightest bulb on the chandelier, it was no surprise to hear that he drove the thing all over town, unimpeded, for nearly a week. He parked it in the lot at school when in class, and even right in front of his grandmother's house when he was home, not the smartest choices, but hey, I imagine he became quite popular with his classmates that week. However, it was obvious to him and his friends that he wasn't going to be able to keep the thing forever, and eventually he'd have to ditch it.

One day, on his way out of school, the phone in the car started ringing, something PaigeB had never seen in a car before. Excited to be getting his first call in a car ever, the idiot picked up the phone, and it turned out to be the owner of the car, a Mrs. J.P. Anderson. She pled with PaigeB that if he were to return the Ferrari to her in one piece, she would promise not to press charges. Mrs. Anderson went on to say that her other Ferrari was in the shop, and this was her only means of transportation at the moment, so she needed it back a.s.a.p. PaigeB just laughed and hung up.

When Friday rolled around, he barely made it through the school day in anticipation of his date that evening. When he got home he changed into some really fresh early eighties gear that I'm sure had more neon than a construction site. He sat around watching TV, waiting for seven o'clock to roll around so he could leave to pick up his date. When seven came, he jumped in the Ferrari, and headed to MelissaS's house. When he arrived, I'm sure the girl's parents thought gold mine at the sight of the brand new Italian machine. She, on the other hand, wasn't too impressed, she had no idea what kind of car it was, how much it was worth, and she could care less once he told her. They went and had a nice dinner and after that, they went to a few clubs where they danced until late that night. He dropped her off, getting a kiss before she departed, and drove home feeling pretty good about himself.

The next day he was supposed to pick her up and go to the mall where they were going to go and hang out, a funny thing kids still do to this day, hang out at the mall, Ha ha ha! At the sound of his 10 a.m. alarm, PaigeB got up, got dressed, and walked out his front door to find that the Ferrari was missing. Rethieved? He assumed it got towed by the cops after they ran the tags through their stolen vehicles database, after all, what the hell would a brand new Ferrari be doing in that neighborhood? He wasn't too worried about it coming back to bite him in the ass, thinking he had done a pretty good job of making sure the car didn't have any of his prints in or on it, or anything else tying him to it. It didn't matter though, it wouldn't be his prints that got him caught…

After 'missing' his ride, PaigeB arrived to class unfashionably late, and he found himself with a detention slip in hand by the end of class. Detention was served after school, which meant he'd be there until the moon & stars came out. When he made it to detention, he was pleasantly surprised to find that he'd be sharing the classroom cell with MelissaS. Turns out she was late for class today as well. They whispered small talk at first but were quickly reprimanded by the detention monitor whose strictness was only overshadowed by the large stick up her ass. So that the old bag couldn't hear him, PaigeB lowered his voice even more as he told her about how the car had been taken, and the girl suddenly became visibly upset. So much so that she wouldn't look back to PaigeB for the next twenty minutes which threw him for a loop since she didn't give two shits about the thing when they were joyriding around in it.

"Psst, MelissaS," he spat, quietly beckoning her repeatedly to turn around and speak to him. He did this so many times that he must have looked like a lawn sprinkler.

"What?!?" she finally yelled back as she swung around in her chair pinning him down with her fierce, bitch-face stare.

"Hush you two!" hissed the old viper from the front of the room, "and turn back around there missy," she continued as she pointed at MelissaS. She quickly turned back to face the front, rolling her eyes as she did so. Detention was nearly over so PaigeB decided not to water her lawn any further, preferring to do it at full volume once they were released. When they were let out of detention, PaigeB spotted MelissaS walking hurriedly away from campus just as fast as her high heels and tiny little skirt would allow. He caught up to her and asked why she was so miffed about the Ferrari being taken and she went on to explain that it was because she had left a brand new Boyz II Men cassette tape in the car which she had borrowed from her friend, a notorious, back-stabbing, gossipy cunt. So naturally, she was afraid of what would happen when she reported the lost tape to her.

"That's fucking ridiculous!" PaigeB roared with laughter.

"It's not funny you fucking asshole!" she yelled at him.

On the following Saturday, there was a knock on the door at PaigeB's house. "LAPD, we'd like to speak with a Mr. Bender!" a cop shouted through the door.

"Can I help you?" PaigeB said from behind the screen door as he held back his grandma's yapping lap dog.

"Are you Mr. Paige Bender?" the taller of the two cops asked as he referenced a little notepad.

"What's this about?" handing the dog off to his grandma who had come to see who was at the door, and when she saw the policeman at the door, she shook her head at her grandson, and took the dog from him.

The cops gave him some bullshit story about looking for a missing kid, and they were able to get him out onto the porch where he was supposed to look at a stack of pictures. Instead, they placed him under arrest. PaigeB had already built a reputation for himself with the local cops as a tough kid that hated cops, so no precaution was too great or meaningless when it came to hauling in the lumbering six and a half foot tall man-boy. "… For Grand Theft Auto Shitbird! What'd ya think we were arrestin ya for?!?" the talkative cop yelled in his ear. "Yeah Shitbird!" The other cop finally chimed in.

The night MelissaS had found out about the car being towed, she called various impounds around the city looking for it. She eventually found the lot where the Ferrari was towed to, and the operator was more than happy to give her the address so she could come down and retrieve her cassette tape. When she got there, a squad car, occupied by the same exact cops that had arrested PaigeB, was waiting for her to arrival. They spoke in sarcastic tones to her at first, struggling to keep from busting up laughing at the sheer stupidity of the girl, all of which she was oblivious to which made it all that more amusing to the cops. When they produced the tape an officer said, "Oh, is this what you're looking for?" and without much effort they got her to tell them how the tape got in the car and who was driving. She gave up PaigeB without even realizing what she had done until the taller cop asked her if she realized that she could go to jail simply for riding in a stolen car as a passenger, "knowing it was stolen and not reporting it, tisk, tisk young lady." The reality of what she had done hit her like a ton of bricks, and she pictured PaigeB in handcuffs yelling and cussing her name, a much graver situation than some stupid little friend of hers fretting over a cassette tape.

PaigeB was convicted of Grand-Theft Auto and sent to the Klackimat Detention Center for Boys, a notoriously rough place in southern California. Thankfully, he was big, and he had his street wits about him. Wits he was at least afforded in his youth, wits that would later escape him in a sudden turn of events that would leave him dumb and numb in a matter of a few hours. In stitches.

————————————————

Tired of supporting his older brother with money, food, and shelter, Bender made the decision to ask PaigeB to move out and find somewhere else to live, however, before he had the chance to confront him, PaigeB had already packed up and left. Bender and I got home late one Saturday night to find PaigeB's dungeon completely void of all of his effects.

About a month later, while waiting for a bus, I saw PaigeB pushing a shopping cart full of cans down the street towards me. He came up to me and spoke as if he had seen me earlier in the day, as if he hadn't disappeared without explanation a month prior. I greeted him and asked as many questions as I could think of before the bus came, or before he lost his patience with our conversation as he often did with nearly every activity. When I asked where he had been living, he chuckled before replying that he had erected a tent in a heavily forested area in Forest Park, far from prying eyes, far from any trails or ranger stations. Forest Park, one of the largest urban park in the U.S., covers over 5,000 acres of forested hills west of downtown Portland, making it an ideal place for the city's homeless to camp out at.

There was even a father and daughter duo that had called the park home for over four years that had a book written about them and their time living in the park. Once they were discovered by local authorities, they were relocated to a farm just outside the city where they lived with another family. One night, not long after their upheaval, they disappeared, never to be heard from again.

After my encounter with PaigeB on the street, neither Bender nor I heard from him for months thereafter, and we began to fear the worst, but before our fears could get the best of us, nearly five months after his abrupt departure, we finally received a postcard in the mail from him. He had hitchhiked and rode his bicycle across America all the way to New York. It was a city he had lived in years before, a city which he loved dearly. While he was still living with us, PaigeB had told me stories about his days as a bike messenger there, and he even showed me a clipping from the New York Times covering the Fastest Bike Messenger Race in New York with a large picture of him with his arms outstretched to the sky as he rode over the checkered line painted on the street finishing first in the race. We were happy to finally hear from him, but we were disappointed to find no return address or phone number to call. Unfortunately, we knew this meant that it would be months before we would hear from him again.

Six months later I was living in my own apartment downtown, and Bonzai and Bender had both moved into their own separate apartments as well, though they both had roommates. I got together with each of them quite frequently after we had moved out of our house together, and on one such occasion, Bender arrived pale and very solemn looking. I at once knew that something was seriously wrong, "Is everything alright man?"

"No man, not really," he murmured in a cracking voice which sounded as though he was suffering from a knot in his throat.

I released him, pulled out the chair to my right, and inquired, "Here, sit down. So what's going on?" Before I let him answer I thought of something important that needed to happen first, "Wait, wait, wait… First, we should get you a drink."

With saddened, swollen eyes from crying, Bender peered over towards the bar, catching a glance from the bartender who immediately knew her presence was required at our table. Even though she was across the room from us and hadn't even made eye contact with Bender for more than a second, the concerned look on her face as she approached indicated her recognition of the agony behind Bender's eyes. "Can I get you something sweetheart?" she asked in a sympathetic tone.

"Whiskey please, straight up," he nearly whispered, which he followed with a cough as he adjusted himself in his seat.

"You ok here hun?" she asked after turning to me.

"I'm fine…" but before she started to walk away, I realized I'd probably be there a while, so I changed my mind, "Wait, wait, you know what, I'll take the same as my buddy here, in fact, make them both doubles, and put those both on my tab will you please?"

"Nah man, I can pay…" Bender said, but I cut him off.

"Too late, I got it," I said as I nodded to the waitress who was already continuing on her way to the bar. "But what the fuck man, what's going on?" I inquired finally.

"He's dead," he replied coldly.

"Who? Who's dead?" I asked, even though I already knew exactly who it was. Something inside me screamed a name loud and clear, PaigeB.

"My brother, PaigeB… He froze to death in the Hudson," he replied, pausing just as our waitress set his drink down.

"What?!? He froze to death, what the hell happened man?"

After taking a long drink he continued, "Well, he was found frozen, clutching one of the pylons holding up the pier in about three feet of water, and it was in February so the water was near freezing. Apparently, there's some question as to exactly how he got down there though," Bender replied.

"Ok, wait up, start from the beginning and tell me the whole story," I implored.

He shook his head up and down before continuing, "My mom was the first to find out, but it wasn't until a month and a half after he was found that the cops were able to track down any of the family. Apparently, he was going by an alias, and he was telling everyone he was from Seattle. You see, when PaigeB got to New York the first time, you know, like ten or fifteen years ago or whatever. Anyways, he had nowhere to stay and no work, so he went to some pretty bad guys asking for help," he said before taking another drink.

"Pretty bad guys, like who, what guys?" I asked.

"Mafia, Italians I think," he replied, taking another long drink of his whiskey.

"What? How do you know about his connection with the mob?" I asked.

"This guy, some friend of PaigeB's from New York contacted my mom and told her, and like I said, this guy told my mom that as soon as PaigeB arrived in New York he had gotten involved with the mob. And by involved I mean…"

"Doing jobs for them?" I interrupted.

"…Exactly, but to be more specific, he was part-time muscle…" he said before I interrupted him again.

"So what's this friend's story? How'd he find your mom?"

"…I guess he was his closest buddy there that he had met when he lived there the first time. He knew PaigeB was from Vancouver and not Seattle, but I think he thought it was Vancouver, B.C. I guess he found out that the cops took forever finding my mom, and he felt super bad that PaigeB was cremated before my family could claim his body, so he apologized profusely for his inability to help the cops. He just felt really bad about the whole situation, but more importantly, he felt conflicted about the circumstances surrounding his death," Bender paused to let it set in before he led me into the next part of the story.

"Circumstances, what circumstances are you referring to?" I requested.

"Well, I ended up talking to a friend of PaigeB's from New York, and provided a lot more information about PaigeB and his death than the cops were giving us. He told me about how PaigeB had been working for the mob, but he said it wasn't likely the mob had him whacked. His buddy, who's name I can't remember by the way, thinks it was

246

more likely some disgruntled, piece of shit, gambling addict that PaigeB had leaned on pretty hard for a mob bookie, one of his many assignments as a thug. I guess the guy owed something like ten grand to the bookie, and PaigeB had been beating the guy up once a week for a month trying to get him to pay up. It had gotten to the point where PaigeB was gonna break the guys knee caps if he didn't pay up soon, but PaigeB never got the chance. This friend of his drew the conclusion that this guy was afraid of getting his kneecaps broken, so he offed PaigeB. This was just one of many theories however," Bender continued.

"Before you go into the other theories, what exactly do the cops know for sure about his death?" I asked.

Sighing deeply, Bender took another long drink before continuing "So you remember him always bragging about all the bike races he won in New York?" he asked me.

"Yeah, like all his tales, he must have told me those racing stories at least four times apiece," I said chuckling.

"You too?" Bender laughed, "Well he'd won yet another race, and according to his buddy, it was the big race that the bike messengers put on once a year where the winner gets the title, 'Fastest Bike Messenger in New York,' and I guess it's totally sanctioned and recognized by the city, bike shops, big bicycling corporations, all that shit. The last time he won, he ended up in the paper again, pretty crazy right? So after the race they always throw a big party, and this year it was on a boat," Bender went on before I interrupted once again.

"A boat huh? How big?" I asked.

"Pretty big I guess. It's this old turn of the century boat that's permanently docked on the Hudson. I guess PaigeB got super drunk and his buddy said the last he saw of PaigeB was when he was leaving the party. PaigeB was wasted pretty early on during the party, and he was barely able to walk, but his buddy swears he saw him leave the boat. My brother was found clutching a dock post just below the party boat, and the cops believe he simply fell off the side into the shallow freezing water, where he froze to death in a pretty short period of time," Bender replied.

"But the buddy thinks that's bullshit huh?" I asked.

"Exactly, he thinks that gambling guy PaigeB had been whoopin on followed him to the party, and threw his ass off the far side of the boat where there were no party-goers. Honestly though, I really don't know what to believe. I mean for all I know he could have had a seizure that threw him off the boat."

"Bummer man, bummer," I said before polishing off my drink. "So when's the funeral?" I inquired.

"There won't be one. My folks are too broke, but," he said, emphasizing there was something else afoot, "a bunch of his bike messenger friends and LonnyB (Bender's other brother) are all meeting up at the Ash Street to pay tribute to PaigeB this weekend. You should definitely come and share some stories about him," he said imploring me to accompany him to the bar.

"Of course man, I'm there. Just let me know what time and maybe you and I could meet up at another bar around that area beforehand and grab a beer before we head over there?" I asked him.

That weekend we met with PaigeB's friends, and both Bender and I were surprised to see such a large turnout. It wasn't that we thought of PaigeB as an unpopular guy, it was just that he didn't function like most people, so Bender and I were really impressed to see so many people come and share their favorite memories of PaigeB. It was tough, really tough, but in retrospect, it was exactly what PaigeB would have wanted, especially over a standard hole in the ground funeral.

Two months later, a New York Homicide Detective contacted PaigeB's mother to let her know that they had received information that led them to reopen the case as an unsolved murder, and to this day there have been no arrests. Cold-case.

---

26. Pizza to Go

I got the job without an interview because I came highly recommended by a couple of girls I knew that worked there. Pizza Schitza took it on faith that I'd make a good worker based on two years parlor experience, plus the girls that referred me were the store's two best workers. It was the last time they hired someone without an interview, and it would become the worst reference those girls would ever give for the rest of their working lives.

For the most part my coworkers were ok folks, with the exception of a certain douche bag whose name I never cared to remember. In fact, he was such a douche, I simply referred to him as The Douche, a name I called him to his face the first day I worked with him. The name stuck and everyone, even the forty-something year-old manager, called him The Douche. Why such a douche bag? Let's just say he favored brightly colored Polo T's with the collar popped up, and he used the word 'bro' a lot.

The other kids were typical high school stoners that spent more time in the walk-in refrigerator smoking pot than they did making or serving pizza. Anytime we'd have to go to the back to retrieve something from the walk-in, or even anywhere near it for that matter, we'd stop by the cold box and hot box it. I smoked so much damn pot at that job, and to be honest, my memory of working there is hazy at best, but I'll do my best to recount the best parts.

―――――――――――――――

My fondest memory from that job was when I got super stoned and decided it would be funny if I got all dressed up in the company's mascot, a big yellow cock. Don't ask me why a pizza place had a rooster as their mascot, but they did. When I reached the curb of the main boulevard our store was on it took me a few minutes to realize there were no cars or people as far as the eye could see in every direction. Imagine a big stoned rooster scratching his head on the side of a deserted road trying to figure out if he was actually there, or passed out in the walk-in dreaming all of this, when all of the sudden a line of five cop cars came flying up to him. The lead car pulled up to the curb just in front of me, and I thanked my lucky stars I was wearing a huge rooster head, otherwise the cop would have seen my bloodshot eyes and the ridiculously confused look on my face as I came to grips with reality at the very second he rolled down his window and said "Uh, hey there… chicken… hey uh, chicken guy, have you seen a guy wearing all denim with long brown hair and a beard come past here in the last ten minutes or so?" I just about pissed myself trying to contain the laughter.

"Uh, sorry, no bearded Canadians today sir," I said with a big, hidden, shit-eating grin on my face.

"Ok, thanks chicken guy," the smiling cop said as he made ready to depart.

Before he could pull away I asked him, "Why, what happened?"

"Some guy robbed the jewelry store at the end of the block here. If you see the guy, call 911 immediately, ok?"

"Gotcha," I replied. As soon as the cop left, the other four cars behind him followed suit, and I ran inside to tell my co-workers what happened. They laughed so hard I didn't have to pay for my own weed for the next week. Legend.

There were two owners of the franchise location I worked at, but only one of them ever came around the store, and I hated him from the get-go. He had a thing for little boys and he liked letting me know this little tidbit about himself way too often. I resented the hell out of him and all his creepy little comments, gestures, and ass slaps. It's not that I have anything against homosexuals, but I do have a problem with people who use sexuality to intimidate others. Uncomfortable. Everyone at work knew that he had a 'thing' for me, yet not a single one of my chicken shit coworkers, managers included, were willing to bear witness and have my back if I went to the state with my complaint.

I contacted several attorneys in the area with hypothetical's describing my predicament, and each said that my case was weak without any witnesses to corroborate my accusations of verbal and physical sexual harassment. For my co-workers, the fear of losing their priceless pizza parlor careers was apparently enough for most of them to claim ignorance when it came to our rights as employees, and I believe that they justified their weak constitutions by telling themselves that I must have been full of shit when I had told them I had researched my rights as well as what I claimed the conclusion of such a complaint would likely be. The fact that they simply wrote me off as an office joke and failed to not only help a fellow co-worker out, but also to embrace the rights that were so obviously in my favor, sincerely bugged the shit out of me. However, what got under my skin the most was the thought that if we let this asshole get away with this kind of behavior now, how many other times has this happened before, and how many more times must it occur in the future? Just how long would it take until it wasn't just slaps on the ass anymore? Rape? I want it to be known that I was by no means feeble, however, I would prove that I wasn't necessarily the brightest pizza cat either.

One of the girls that gave me a reference, CarrieS, also happened to be a girl I was screwing at the time. Our relationship was built on twenty dollar bags of weed and seeing how long we could fuck for, which wasn't a bad deal for an eighteen year-old kid. We had no plans of calling each other anything that ended with 'friend,' rather, we referred to each other as 'buddies' which was perfect at the time because we were both screwing any hot piece of meat that came our way. Tenn.

The two of us became instantly famous at Pizza Schitza for getting caught fucking on the roof of the place by a manager, and believe it or not, failing to lose our jobs. This was just one among many crazy incidents that the two of us were a part of, most of which aren't worth mentioning. One that is well worth mentioning, one that made us legendary, was when I took an entire family's order while she remained hidden under the counter giving me the meanest blow-job I have ever had in my life. One second she would be giving me the most gentle, sensual mouth fuck, and the next she was raking her canines in long, fast swiping motions along my manhood that nearly gashed my way into the emergency room. To this day I laugh when I think of the

look on the poor Dad's face I was serving that I swear recognized
the familiar look of cock pains in my eyes as I coughed, winced, and
nearly collapsed in tears before their order was filled. For the
finale I thanked them with what must have sounded like the most
insincere, reluctant "thank you" that they had ever been the
recipients of.

My relationship with CarrieS wasn't the healthiest of relationships,
and she really treated me like shit most of the time, but I really
didn't care because I knew I didn't, and never would, love her. It
was a relationship built on sex with utter apathy toward one another
regarding anything but the sex. The only thing that kept us
'buddies' was the undeniable, primal draw to each other's fuck.

The fun really began about six months after I started working at
Pizza Schitza when CarrieS told me about her plan to rob the place.
She expressed how disgruntled she had become, and I not only
empathized with her, I wanted to take part in the 'great pizza
parlor robbery.' I had not only failed to get my boss to stop
harassing me on my own, I had also failed to convince a single one
of my twenty-something co-workers to stand by me and a principal,
and take the bastard down. More than anyone, I wanted to get the
asshole back.

After berating and manipulating CarrieS, primarily through copious
amounts of ethereal orgasms in rapid succession night after night, I
was finally able to convince her to include me in her plans to rob
our employer. CarrieS and I combined her rough plan with my fine
tuning to create an infallible plan. At first she provided just the
skeleton which held its genius in its simplicity, and I provided the
skin which convinced us both that we could not fail. A smart thief
knows never to be cocky, and to always question every step of the
design whether you're the mastermind, sole thief, or someone
recruited for their particular specialty. For instance, serial
burglars, like most serial criminals, very rarely change their
method of operation (M.O.), and the reason for this is simple: why
change your M.O. if it has worked so well for you in the past? If it
ain't broke, don't fix it. The only drawback to same M.O. serial
crimes is if you leave any evidence behind at a crime scene then
they will have no problem tying you to all the other similar crimes,
ones you likely committed. So it pays to treat each crime, or in our
case, each burglary, as a work of art, not a lithograph of a
popular, selling piece.

CarrieS had created a pretty genius plan, but it lacked the
integration of theory as well as the consideration of certain
unpredictable variables. What-ifs. There's almost always something
that goes awry, some variables you hadn't counted on, so it was my
job to consider any and all such variables. I regarded the human
element as the most important variable to consider when planning any
crime. CarrieS agreed to spend at least a few nights after work with
me brainstorming any and all logical possibilities that might occur,
as well as creating solutions to such problems, and incorporating
the varying plans of action into our general plan of attack. It
would ultimately be the human element that led to the plans demise,
but it was one I failed to consider altogether until it was too
late.

It was a week before I graduated high school and the weather had finally started to clear up and let the sun out. It was early June, and because the weather had become so nice, there were a lot more people out and about on the streets that week and that meant business was good for Pizza Schitza. So good in fact, I decided it was finally time to put my plan into action. When I told CarrieS that I thought it was time, she was reluctant to reply. She stood silent for a moment before looking in my eyes and saying "Look, I'm sorry but I'm out, I just can't do it. Call me chicken, call me whatever, but you're not going to convince me to take part in this. Don't worry though, your secret's safe with me." I was floored, after so much time planning and preparing, how could she just walk away? I grew angry and replied, "Well fine then, I didn't need your help anyways." I shook my head and left her there. The plan had called for two people, but it could work with just one, it would just be a lot riskier. I had four days to get the new plan in order before the fiscal week was up and the restaurant's safe would be emptied by the Manager when he came on Monday morning to take everything to the bank. It was Memorial Day weekend and the banks were closed that Monday, so I had one extra day to prepare. That also meant one extra day of cash added to the safe. Smiles. By Sunday night, my rough estimate of the safe's holdings were somewhere around $5,500 to $6,500 cash. It was on.

———————————

Sunday night, closing time, I was nearly finished with my nightly closing duties. The site manager ChuckE, who was the only other employee working with me at the time, was performing his closing duties as well, duties that included: counting up the cash and receipts in each till; slowly entering the day's sales data into bookkeeping software on the computer (a prehistoric box that had somehow travelled through time from the Ice-Age to secure a place at the pizzeria as number one pain in my ass which it seemed it was destined never to relinquish); placing the day's cash and receipts into the small safe that was bolted to a shelf under one of the many countertops out front; checking my work off the Closing Duties Checklist; and finally, he performed one last walkthrough the restaurant before locking all the exits. Just as he finished the latter, I grabbed my backpack and coat, and walked out the front door ahead of ChuckE, who locked the door behind us. We smoked a cigarette together, one which I intentionally smoked very slowly so that ChuckE would be finished before me, and therefore he would hopefully leave before me. Instead, he waited for me to finish my smoke as he continued to make small talk, much to my chagrin.

"Well ChuckE, I gotta roll. I'm meeting my girl for a late dinner at Takashimi. She loves the sushi shit," I said as I pulled my keys from my pocket.

"Wish I could say the same, but I'm going home to play video games. Lame huh?" We said our goodbyes, and I climbed into my Chevelle. I honked the horn as I tore off down the street headed in the opposite direction of ChuckE.

What ChuckE didn't know, was that while he was in the bathroom, just after locking all the doors, I furtively unlocked the back door for my reentry later that night. That way, when questioned the next day, he would say he was positive he had locked all the exits. Also, thankfully, ChuckE had near obsessive compulsive tendencies when it came to using the bathroom, and he was known to spend a longer amount of time than an average person would washing his hands. I used all the extra time to go into the back office and turn off the security camera VCR. To my surprise it was already off, and I would later learn that they only ran the recorder when the restaurant was open.

I drove just a few blocks from the pizzeria, parked my car, and waited there for twenty minutes just in case ChuckE returned to work for something he had forgotten. I used this time to go through my inventory of items I would use during the heist: three pairs of latex gloves; a pair of black socks, black paratrooper pants with multiple utilitarian facets; a black long sleeved shirt; an extra backpack; three large sealable freezer bags; and a crowbar. I returned to the Pizzeria nearly thirty minutes after leaving, parking my car five blocks down so that it wouldn't be seen in the immediate area if a coworker or boss happened by the place and wondered why my car was there so late. Wearing all black and carrying my bag, I slipped in the back door and proceeded to carry out the rest of the plan CarrieS and I had so carefully devised. All I could keep thinking was that I couldn't wait to see the look on her face once this was all said and done. I went straight to the office where the safe key was kept where I emptied my backpack's contents on the floor, put on a pair of gloves, took the key to the safe, and opened it up. "Cha-Ching!" I nearly shouted as I emptied the cash, checks, and receipts into my bag. "Man, is she gonna regret not being here," I said out loud as I thought of a pissed off looking CarrieS.

Once I had emptied the safe and locked it shut, I returned to the office to place the key back in its hiding spot. I retrieved the crowbar off the floor, and went back to the safe to begin prying off the shelf with the crowbar. It was only held down by two screws so it came off quite easily. I wanted to make the whole thing look as far off from an inside job as possible, so I took even further steps to assure this. I brought the crowbar with me outside where I worked on the lock of the door until it appeared as if it had been compromised enough for someone to have gained entry. I then went back inside where I placed the safe in my extra book-bag and returned to the office where I placed everything else I had brought with me into the other bag before I proceeded to the exit. It was all over within seven minutes, one less than I had planned for.

When I left, I went straight to my friend KirbyO's house and snuck into his backyard via the alley running behind his house. I dug a shallow hole between a tool shed in the corner of their yard and the fence I had just hopped. I figured that this was the perfect place to store some of the loot because it was well hidden, and KirbyO had no ties to the Pizzeria. Before I had made my way to KirbyO's yard, I had parked my car in the alley behind his house and counted out all the cash. I had split the cash into thirds and wrapped them up with rubber bands. After the hole was dug, I grabbed one of these thirds and placed it into one of the freezer bags I had brought, placed the bag into the hole, and filled it with dirt. One down, two to go, I thought as I jumped back over the fence.

I then went to a nearby lake where I threw the safe and the crowbar into a deeper section of the water. Once I had dumped that evidence, I drove home. My parents were out of town for the weekend in Tahoe, so it was no problem for me to dig a hole in our backyard where I buried yet another third of the cash in a freezer bag. The last third I would keep on me to spend. The easy part was over, now came the hard part, waiting for the investigation to come and go, and hopefully it would go unsolved.

I woke up early the next day to my cell phone ringing and ringing over and over again. I had left it sitting on my desk across the room from my bed, so I wasn't exactly too elated when I had to get up out of bed and finally answer the damn thing. It was work, we had been robbed, surprise, surprise. They needed me to come in right away and do a short interview with the police. I agreed and rushed down there with a compelling look of shock and awe on my face. The interview went like this: it was a normal night; nothing out of the ordinary to report; everything was locked up before we left; ChuckE and I left at the same time; and I had been with CarrieS all night. All of this was corroborated by ChuckE, and they would surely interview CarrieS who had agreed to be my alibi. The two investigators thanked me for coming down and told me they would call me on my cell if they needed to speak with me again. I wished them luck and left the restaurant a free man, and a free man I shall remain. I've done it, I've pulled it off! At least that's what I thought…

The next day was my high school graduation. My father had flown in from Florida to attend, but my step-mother couldn't get out of an annual conference that her company put on, so she stayed behind in Florida. My graduation was short and we were out of there within a few hours. Looking at the pictures from that day, through my half smiles and guilty eyes, it's easy to see a definite agitation flushed over my face. I remember being slightly nervous that day, but if I knew what was to come, I would have looked a lot less at ease. My father was only in town for a few days, so we tried to cram in as much time together as possible during his short stay.

A few weeks prior I had finished installing the engine I rebuilt into my 72' Chevy Chevelle, and my Dad had expressed an interest in taking a ride in it. So right after the graduation ceremony, my dad came over and we hopped in the Chevelle. The interior left something to be desired, and my dad joked about it as we began a short drive around my Mom's neighborhood. What he didn't know was that I had lost my license a few weeks earlier for having too many speeding tickets. The suspension was only for a month, and it just happened to be when my dad was in town. Fortunately, he didn't ask why we didn't leave the neighborhood. Unfortunately, as we pulled onto my Mom's street on the return lap, I noticed a local cop in my rearview mirror. Just as I pulled up and parked the car in front of my mom's the cop pulled up behind me with his red and blues lights running. My dad and I were already getting out of the car by the time the lights were going so we slowly walked to the back of my ride and waited for the cop to get out of his.

"Mr. ThomasJ, how are you today?" the cop asked as he got out of his squad car.

"Fine, what's this about?" my dad and I said in unison, which was followed by a shared glance accompanied by a short laugh.

"ThomasJ, you know you're not supposed to be driving, right son? Suspended license, remember?" he reminded me.

This caused my dad to step a bit closer to the officer, fold his arms, and look at me with a slight hint of fatherly disgust, "Really?" my father asked.

"Yes, but that isn't why I'm here. We need you to come down to headquarters and answer some more questions regarding the robbery," the cop contemptuously said as he stared down upon me as I tried to be act as chill as possible in front of my father. The cop all but said 'we got you motherfucker!' My worry lie with the fact that my father had to stand there next to his ostensibly guilty son as the asshole cop's austere tone charged, convicted, and sentenced me right there on the street. My best move was to remain as indifferent to his insinuations as possible, and try to display a disposition that showed concern for the restaurant in order to counter this sudden barrage from behind the badge. Without moving his head, his eyes shifted to his notepad which he scanned quietly before continuing, "but you can find your own way to the station right?" he asked.

"Wait, wait, wait, will he need an attorney?" my father interjected.

"Dad, it's ok, I have nothing to hide. I'll just go down there and answer their questions. It's really not a big deal," I said, trying to sound as blasé as possible. The efficacy of my disposition over officer McDouchebag's was apparently enough to put my dad's immediate uptightness to rest, at least for the time being. My father sighed as he perked up of his eyebrows, and the shrug of his shoulders was all I needed to understand how he felt, "Ok son."

With that the cop leered back at me with a halfcocked smirk as he flipped his notepad shut, got back in his patrol car, and sped off down our neighborhood street with no regard for the abundance of children playing about. It wasn't until he was at least three streets down that we finally heard his siren as he continued to speed through my mother's neighborhood which we could clearly hear for at least another six block distance before his siren was silenced, and the sound of his screeching tires and revving engine were too far off to be heard. Thankfully, this was the icing on an odious cake that the cop had baked for us, a cake that led my father to think more in terms of how ridiculous that cop was, versus my possible guilt. At the very least, it had bought me a little time. Hours, moments, just seconds from the eleventh hour. Miniscule. Minute. Infinitesimal. Over. Done with. Mourning. Forgotten. Now!

A few hours later I had gone down to the police headquarters at city hall, which happened to be just a few short blocks from the pizzeria. Because it housed the local government of a fairly young municipality, it was unlike most city halls in that it was a newer building. Stale. It lacked all the intimidating Greco-Roman nuances of a typical government building, deficient of the physique to intimidate its guests like the large, imposing entranceways of an older city hall. The kind with the tall whitewashed columns, and doors big enough to allow an entire bus to drive through, all of which are reminiscent of a greater time, a time in history that was dominated by giants, greats that include the founders of law, order, and civil infrastructure. I lumbered inside and over to the front desk which was a large circular island sitting in the middle of the main lobby in front of the elevators. There, behind the desk, sat portly woman in an officer's uniform who I told my name to, and explained that there were a couple of detectives that were expecting me, a pair of cops whose names had escaped me. I wouldn't have been surprised if the stereotypical desk piggy had snorted out every word of her response, however, she replied in a predictable manner just the same: a high pitched, bitchy voice, with the mentality that she had to deal with assholes like me all day long, so that somehow justified her in treating every person who walked through those doors with utter disdain. She told me that I needed to take a seat and someone would be with me momentarily. I sat my edgy ass down on one of the numerous leather couches my tax dollars had apparently paid for. The cushy seating brought to mind the dilapidated chairs at the Portland Police headquarters I had sat in earlier that year. I thought to myself, at least the big city kept it real. At least I was quite comfortable for someone facing a second round of questioning for a crime I was most definitely guilty of.

Though I had a very limited knowledge of law enforcement, one based solely upon the common sense of a troubled 18 year-old boy, I knew as well as anyone with at least some street smarts, and no delusions of invincibility, that a second round of questioning was anything but a good sign. I gave myself a fifty-fifty chance of leaving that police station without being given at least one charge of the felonious variety, and I don't believe I was being pessimistic, rather, I felt I was being realistic about a very serious situation. The other %50 was the smart assed kid in me smiling behind a tiny pile of money, and they're counting on my naivety of the judicial system as it pertains to an adult, I was sure of it. A thousand versions of how the questioning was going to go played out in my mind. I had sweat so many bullets by the time my name was called out from a corridor behind me that I thought the nearby metal detectors would surely pop.

My first mistake was followed by the second and then the third in such rapid succession that I might as well have skipped all the bullshit, and handed him a signed and notarized confession from the get-go. First mistake: as I arose from my tanned hide perch and approached the detective in the corridor, I sighed deeply. Tell. Mistake number two: my eyes were glued to my shoes as if they were being humped by a dog that was on fire. The third and final blunder: I failed to make any eye contact whatsoever with the mustached detective as I followed him through the adjacent corridor to the one leading away from the lobby. This, of course, was right after I overlooked shaking the man's hand in the lobby. I might as well have said, "Hey there Mr. Officer, I'm the guy who robbed the Pizzeria. Let's just get this over with as quick as we can, ok? Cuffs please?" What I didn't know, however, was that it made little difference at all how nervous, or how cool I appeared because they already knew I was guilty. They simply needed to make their case foolproof by obtaining a confession, so it was time for them to put the real pressure on.

I followed the cop to a set of elevators were we went up a few floors in unsettling silence before I was led to an interview room. For nearly twenty minutes I sat in the tiny interview room while, I assumed, the detectives sat behind the two-way mirror which took up three-quarters of the south wall, watching me, waiting, allowing me to tear down the walls I had built up around myself, tear at my mind, but I wasn't doing anything like this, rather, I just tried to look as unconcerned as possible. Bricks and mortar, lies held together with ill conceived notions of justified retribution for harassment from a prick of a boss. After that first twenty minutes of sitting in silence I had come to terms with what I had done, and I truly believed that I was justified in my actions. Though I could have been the bigger man, understand it or not, my reasoning was mine, and I didn't need anyone's empathy or endorsement. No matter how they set about trying to make me believe that I was %100 in the wrong, I would always believe that Pizza Schitza, especially that piece of shit pervert boss, deserved every bit of misfortune that came their way.

One of the best pieces of advice I've ever received was from my step-father. More of a warning really, he told me "Son, you'll learn this for yourself as you get older, but it's good to hear it from someone with real experience with it: when it comes to sex, drugs, money, or the prospect of going to jail, people get weird. I mean, people will cheat, lie, dishonor, and throw away all loyalty when it comes to those four things. So please, just try to remember that whenever you find yourself in a hairy situation involving one of those four." My stepfather has proven to be so right on with that piece of advice that it has saved my ass time and time again, but unluckily for me, it was a discussion we had a few years too with regards to this robbery. Like they say, there's no honor among thieves, which is quite similar to my step-dad's feeling that people get weird when jail time is staring them in the face, and to further that notion, there's really no honor among businessmen either because people get weird about money. CarrieS and I were business partners as well as thieves, and unfortunately for me, she got weird. For no real reason whatsoever, not to save her own skin or any other motive other than to save herself some time, she gave me up. During her routine interview with the police, she told them everything, though she conveniently left herself out of a possible conspiracy charge. Apparently, coming to the station was a waste of her precious time.

To say the least, I was fucked.

I thought of you this week, and I couldn't help but worry a little about you. I tried calling, but your phone was disconnected, and I still haven't received a second letter from you…???

Well Ms. Caribou, I hope to hear from you at some point soon, but most of all, I hope this makes it to you, and that you enjoy my stories. Until next time,

With love,

TommyJ

A few weeks after my fourth letter was sent off, I received Caribou's second letter, a letter I felt was long overdue, but hell, at least she was making an effort right?

TommyJ-

TommyJ, TommyJ, TommyJ, surprised? I'm sorry it took so long, I was honestly planning to write this for the past couple of weeks now, but I just couldn't find the time. I've been so so busy! Proud? I would hope so? But really, I am sorry, I must apologize for not being quicker with this letter. Rest assured, I have received all four of your letters, as I had my mail forwarded to my new address, which by the way, is on the front of this letter. So please send all correspondence to the new address if you would honey, thanks.

I wasn't just putting off writing this letter by being lazy or from lack of interest, truth be told I've been trying to figure out what story to tell you. I've had the hardest time picking a story because, well, I didn't want it to seem like I was trying to one-up your stories I know how competitive you boys can be, though you don't seem like the competitive type, are you darlin? But alas, I don't even think I have a story that'll come close to some of the crazy shit you've been through, so I thought it'd be cool if I gave you a glimpse into my life and tell you all about what's been going on lately with me.

You know that day-time soap opera Living Our Days as the World Turns? Well I'm sure you don't, but there's this really hunky guy who plays a doctor who is screwing his patient's wife, who also ends up being his cousin, but he doesn't know it yet. But anyway, the real life actor and I hooked up, and not just once, I've been seeing him long enough for him to give me a key to his place. Crazy huh??!??!! Needless to say, the guy is loaded, and he's been spoiling the hell out of me. Sugar, let me tell you, it's a dream come true. Like you always used to say, I'm living the dream. I guess that isn't so much a story as it's just an update of my life. Kind of lame as far as story-telling goes, I know, but I'm really excited about this one.

On a similar note, I have decided to start my own book, a kind of lady of the night memoir, slash instruction guide to the world's oldest occupation. It's almost a safety manual as well as a get-rich-quick kind of scheme if you think about it. Only catch is that you have to suck a lot of dicks to get on top, tee hee! Since I credit you as my main influence for writing it, I'd be honored if you could read the thing as soon as it's finished and give me some pointers. Please, please, please do this for me!?!? I'd forever be in your debt, and of course when I become famous, I'll attribute all of my success to the great TommyJ. Just let me know in your next letter which I look forward to receiving as soon as you can get the time to write. Well Honey, I hope you're well and we'll talk soon.

Best Wishes,

Caribou

Though a little disappointed that I got such a half-assed letter, I was happy to get a letter nonetheless. I let a few weeks pass before I began writing the next installment, and I took my sweet time completing it. I was nearly out of stories so I knew this would likely be one of the last letters I'd be writing her, at least for a while.

Dearest Caribou-

How's my favorite call girl? Sounds to me like you're doing the best you've been in years, congrats!

I'll cut to the chase since I'm making this a short one today. My grandfather, the last living grandparent I had left, dropped dead of a heart attack this week. His funeral was today and I was asked by my family to be one of the pallbearers which I reluctantly agreed to do. Don't get me wrong though, I was honored to place him in the crypt next to his wife, my Grandmother, who passed some years ago, but I gotta be honest with you, I hate funerals. Now I suppose it's the traditional way of saying goodbye, but I have my own way and it doesn't include such a stiff procession, no pun intended. We all have our own way of saying goodbye, and I think that's why I don't want my family to have a funeral for me when I die, as long as everyone who gives a shit takes the time and says goodbye however they choose to. Save my family money, my friends time, and I think it's a more intimate way of releasing someone into the unknown when you do it in your own way, on your own time. Though I also suppose you could do both, have a funeral and say goodbye on your own.

Anyways, I've been to way too many funerals for someone my age, but I guess that should be expected of someone who lives in the city and knows too many people. I've been to something like two dozen funerals for family and friends over the years, yet I'm not even thirty yet!

I won't dwell on this too long as my intent is not to bum you out, but my grandfather's death brings to mind a story he once told me about the peculiar death of a great, great, great, etc. Grandfather of his, mine as well I suppose, so ours. I'm not feeling all that up to writing my normal lengthy letter, plus, frankly, I'm running out of stories. So, I've decided that this letter shall contain just the single tale from my recently deceased Grandfather, and as always, enjoy.

---

27. Father in the Foreground

I called my grandfather EarpB, my step-father's father, on the
telephone one weekend, and we made plans to go out for lunch the
following day. I picked him up from the front of his apartment
building downtown just afternoon, and we headed for Jake's. Jake's
Bar and Grill was one of his favorite lunch spots, a restaurant that
occupies the first floor of the Governor's Hotel on 10th Avenue,
which was also downtown. We arrived at the front of the restaurant
where we pulled up to the valet station and I handed my keys to a
young guy about my age along with a five dollar bill.

Grandpa and I decided to sit in the bar area, so we didn't have to
wait to be seated by a hostess. Once drinks were ordered and we had
decided upon what we wanted to order, I began asking my grandpa all
sorts of questions about his family's past, and he was curious to
know why, exactly, I was interrogating him about the family,
seemingly out of the blue. I explained to him that I needed a story
for my next letter in a series that I had been trading back and
forth with a friend that lives in L.A., but he didn't have "anything
you kids would be interested in. Hmmm," he scratched his chin,
"nothing really comes to mind." I had to probe into his childhood
and even his parents' and grandparents' lives with the hopes that if
we dug around enough, we'd be able to stir something up, and if I
was really lucky, I'd get a particularly epic tale out of him. I
really just needed to get him talking.

After a few drinks, just before our lunch came, I asked him about
his father's side of the family which I had learned from my step-
father, was known to have a few Gunslingers from the Wild West. This
side of the family was a group of Americans that went back many
generations, but other than that, I knew very little about their
history. All I had to mention was the west, and I could see a light
go on behind my grandpa's eyes. He proceeded to recite a tale his
grandfather had told him about the circumstances surrounding the
untimely death of a great, "and maybe even a few more greats,"
grandfather of his, LouisB III.

––––––––––––––––––––

Overtaken by smallpox, my Great-Grandfather LouisB (many greats ago)
was read his last rites, and his family prepared for his burial. He
left behind a wife and four grown children, and a plethora of
grandchildren. It was the mid 1800's and the place was a frontier
town in Montana with a population of just around three hundred. A
small scale epidemic of smallpox had wiped out nearly half of the
town's population over the last three months. Embalming wasn't
widely practiced at this point so the funeral was scheduled for the
day after his death so the body wouldn't rot and fester. The
ceremony was seen over by the town Pastor, attended by his widow, my
great-grandmother, their four children, some of the grandchildren, a
few town folk, and was finished within less than twenty minutes.
Since the epidemic began, and they were burying nearly five people a
day in the town cemetery, the Caretaker of the cemetery decided to
employ a tactic used during the great Plague of Western Europe for
saving lives of people who were mistaken for dead and buried alive,
which involved tying a string to a bell that hung outside the grave
with the other end of the string going down a tube which was
installed next to the coffin so that if a person were to awake after
their burial, they could ring the bell simply by moving their arm
which the string would be tied to. They did this for my great-
grandfather's burial, and one would have thought that it was a

blessing that the bell was there for LouisB to ring when he did, in fact, awake six feet underground in a coffin. However, it was quite the opposite, it became his damnation.

Eight hours after the last bit of dirt left the shovel and was patted down upon his grave, my great-grandfather regained consciousness and found himself confined within a tiny, dark space, and short of breath. Despite the fever induced hallucinations, it didn't take him long to realize that he must have been mistaken for dead, and he was thus buried where he now lie, underground, in a coffin. The revived LouisB knew from the numerous funeral services that he had been to weeks prior to his own that there were bells being connected to the corpses, so he immediately began to search around for the string that was connected to the bell hanging above his own grave, and it didn't take him long to find that it was tied around his wrist. Unbeknownst to LouisB, however, in the haste of the cemetery's Groundskeeper to close up the cemetery and secure a seat at a card table in the town's saloon, he had neglected to secure the bell to the side of the tombstone in order for the bell to be heard if it were in fact rung. Rather than ring, the bell was drug across the freshly turned dirt of my great-grandfather's grave and stopped over the hole which the string was housed by the hole that ran six feet to the coffin, the hole that supplied LouisB with oxygen. The string was tied to the bell in such a way that the bell slipped over the hole's opening, sealing off the air supply. I can only imagine the look of sheer terror that washed over my great-grandfather's face as he held the slack of the bell's string and what little source of light he had disappeared. The image of a sick man shuddering in the dullest silence imaginable made me shudder myself as I sat across the table from my own grandfather, ErapB, as he continued the story. LouisB, EarpB went on to explain, "had literally sealed his own fate." Realizing the bell was suctioned over the string's hole, he panicked, and began to pull at the string with great force until it finally broke off, leaving the bell atop the hole.

In a panic, hyperventilation set in and it didn't take long for his oxygen to run out. Very soon after, death took over. "Not so saved by the bell, rather the contrary," grandpa EarpB pointed out.

When the Caretaker of the cemetery, the Groundskeeper's employer and only coworker, returned to the cemetery to begin his work for the day, he found the Groundskeeper hovering over my great-grandfather's grave with a perplexed look on his face. When confronted, the Groundskeeper explained that he had found the bell over the hole where it still sat, but he swore he had secured it to the side of the tombstone with the string attached to it, and the other end attached to the corpse. When the Caretaker lifted the bell from its perch atop the hole, there was a great gasp of air down the tube into the grave indicating that all the air in the casket had somehow been depleted, and he knew immediately that something had gone terribly wrong. Both men staggered back from the grave at the raspy shrill, gasping for their own breath as if the grave itself had stolen the air they had been breathing. Quickly regaining his wits, the Caretaker ordered his mortified employee to begin digging.

"…and make great haste, as if it was your soul behind the shovel and your flesh and bones in that grave!" The two men had the casket exposed within a few moments, and despite the near freezing temperatures and brutal cross winds, each man displayed his laborious speed through transparent undershirts. Frightened by what the opened casket would surely reveal, neither man was quick to open the lifeless box, so they both stared at its dirt stained lid, afraid to make eye contact with one another and reveal the true terror in their eyes. The pangs of sorrow and guilt were too great for the Groundskeeper to bare any longer and so with a few swift moves of his crowbar, he had the lid off the coffin, revealing LouisB and the look of sheer terror thus eternally affixed to my poor great-grandfather's face.

"That was not the same look of the man I buried here yesterday Groundskeeper," the Caretaker said as he took a step back from the coffin. His sharp tone was accompanied by a stern look of sharp brows and piercing eyes which commanded an explanation.

To which the Groundskeeper replied, "I, I, I…" realizing his murderous blunder, he was at a loss for words. Suddenly, breaking the silence that followed the Groundskeeper's failed attempt of an explanation, both men gasped simultaneously upon an even grizzlier discovery. The Caretaker produced a small handkerchief from his pocket which he placed over his mouth as they looked at LouisB's hands which were bloodied and missing nails which could be seen still hanging from the inside of the lid where he fleetingly clawed for his life during his final moments.

Without an answer, the Caretaker turned to the Groundskeeper and continued, "Well, what do you have to say for yourself, hmmm? Did you or did you not affix that bell to his tombstone? Were you even at your post in the yard last night, or will I find out from Mr. LazloG that you were gambling last week's wages away at one of his saloon's card tables?"

To which the Groundskeeper replied, "I, I, I…" stammering yet again.

"Worthless, you are a damned fool!" the Caretaker shouted as he began to walk back towards his horse that stood tethered to a tree next to the road.

The Groundskeeper knew the Caretaker meant to not only fire him, but make the true account of LouisB's death known to the Sherriff as well as the whole town. Ruin. The sorrow and guilt was quickly washed away by malice and rage, and the Groundskeeper had barely come to grips with what he had done by the time he was dragging the lifeless body of the Caretaker to the dugout grave. With a few quick jerks back and forth, the Groundskeeper had jarred the pickax loose, and removed it completely from the back of the Caretaker's skull.

"Wait, what? The Groundskeeper killed the Caretaker too?!? No way!" I tried correcting my grandfather as another round of drinks arrived at our table.

Laughing at the genuine disappointment in my voice, my grandpa went on to explain that just as the Caretaker began to mount his horse, the Groundskeeper had run over with the ax and smashed his boss in the head, killing him instantly, at the same time saving himself from, at the very least, immediate incarceration. The Groundskeeper then raised the casket from the grave with superhuman strength, after which he rolled the Caretaker's body into the bottom of the grave, which was followed by the casket with LouisB capped inside back into the grave over his employer, and finished the job by filling the desecrated grave with dirt. As he was nearing the last shovel full of earth, he realized he now had a person's sized mound of surplus dirt still lying next to the grave which he would need to dispose of as well. It would be this very pile of dirt that he left next to the grave while he was retrieving a wheel-barrel from the utility shed that would lead the Scotland Yard boys to suspecting, and ultimately securing a conviction of the Groundskeeper for the deaths of two men. For whilst he was away at his tool shed, my great-aunt had come to the grave to lay flowers down and pay respect to her fallen brother. Due to bad weather, her arrival to town was delayed by over a day, causing her to miss the funeral service entirely. She bore witness to the small mound of dirt that still lie next to the grave which she found slightly odd, seeing that a full day had passed since he was buried, and one would think they would have cleaned up the site by then.

It was a few days later when she was questioned by the Sherriff concerning her visit to the Cemetery and the disappearance of the Cemetery's Caretaker, and it was revealed that her noting of the unkempt grave site would give the Sherriff cause to exhume the grave since this was also the general area where near fresh blood was discovered.

The Sherriff, a long-time friend of LoiusB's, had attended the funeral, and from what he remembered about the service, there wasn't a mound of dirt next to the grave. He also recalled that it had been filled up and patted down flush with the surrounding lawn, and the site had been meticulously cleaned up.

"What better place to bury someone you don't want found than a grave in a cemetery?"

Within a short period of time, the investigators had fashioned a noose for the Groundskeeper's neck, and he would have a grave of his own.

––––––––––––––––––

Again, sorry for the short letter, I'm just not feeling it today. Though I must admit, telling these stories to you, writing all of these letters and getting some of this shit off my chest, has been quite therapeutic for me. I suppose I've found solace in the idea that at least someone out there knows all this about me, and I know my secrets are safe with you.

I'll continue to send letters from time to time, but I can't promise more than one story at a time since I have very little left to write about, but I will try to write you nonetheless.

Best Wishes - XOXO

TommyJ

––––––––––––––––––

28. Dragnet

As I arrived home from yet another boring day at work, I noticed a Ford Crown Victoria parked across the street. It was unmarked, but it had government plates which made me a little weary, but I really didn't put too much thought into it since there was no one in it. I figured that whatever they were up to didn't involve me, and I assumed they were likely the IRS or the Census Bureau over at a neighbor's place. Even though I was on the straight and narrow these days, I still felt slightly weary was because I knew there were things in my past that had a good chance of catching up with me. I tried to put it out of my mind, but I found it impossible as I sat in my living room watching TV. I decided I should do some chores, hoping it was enough to occupy myself, and my mind until I had completely let go of my paranoia.

After ten minutes of cleaning and organizing my place, my fears were fulfilled when the doorbell rang. Great, I thought, my guess is there are two suits out front, and I was right. Through the peephole I could see two federal, men-in-black looking blokes, and even though it was overcast with periodic showers and no sunlight whatsoever, they were both wearing sunglasses. Suits. Before I opened the door the Crown Vic came to mind, and I thought that's weird, I wonder why the thing was empty when I came home. I mean, where were these guys at when I got here? Were they talking to my neighbors about me, or were they snooping around my place, possibly bugging the joint? All I really knew for sure was that I was in some serious shit. The real question was, how bad is it gonna stink? I turned the handle and swung the door open.

"Gentlemen, how may I help you?" I asked in the most chipper, cheesy tone I could muster.

"Thomas Jordan?" asks the taller one, stiff as a board.

"Depends, what're ya'll sellin?" I was all smiles, smart-assed smiles to be exact.

"We just have a few questions for you Mr. Jordan, but it may take up a bit of your time. May we come in?" the stiffer, shorter one asked me.

"And who may I ask is we?" knowing very well what the answer would be, and I must admit, I sweat a few bullets just then.

"I'm Agent Smith with the U.S. Marshals Service, and this is Agent Johnson with the Drug Enforcement Administration…" the taller one said, and before he could go on I interjected.

"Smith and Johnson, huh?" smirking. "Well, I suppose I don't really have a choice here do I? Either we do this here, or you'll just cuff me, take me to a federal building downtown where you'll make me wait hours on end before you finally question me in a small, dark room. Then you'll hold me for twenty-four hours on some bullshit charge which you'll drop just before the twenty-four hours is up and you'll release me, that is, if I don't piss you off. Yeah, um, no thanks, I'd rather not go through all that, so please, come in," I said as I stood to the side beckoning their entrance with a slow wave of my hand, which they obliged. "Can I get you two a water or something else to drink?" I asked as I shut the door behind them, figuring it's likely in my best interest to be polite, at least for the time being.

"No, thank you," they both said in unison as they surveyed my place.

"Here, I must apologize, I have yet to purchase a dinner table set, so let's have a seat at the bar," and again, I motioned for them to follow me. We walked down the small set of steps leading to my living room where I had them each sit in a wheelchair I used as barstools for my wet bar, which sat just three feet off the ground. I walked to the other side of the bar and sat on a stool where I could look down upon them from. From my perch they looked completely out of place, and even more uncomfortable, as they both fidgeted in their wheelchairs, trying to find more relaxed positions. I was surprised they didn't just decide to stand, but it was fine with me because it was so hilarious. "So…" I said holding my palms up, almost as if to show I had nothing to hide.

"Mr. Jordan," Agent Johnson said as he pulled out a notepad from his inside coat pocket, "we're here to ask you some questions about an individual you were previously associated with some years back. Let me first ask you what your relationship is to a Ms." The agent said as he paused to refer to his notepad, "Katie Ingalls?" all eyes on me, intently.

"Katie Ingalls? I don't believe I know a Katie Ingalls. Should I?" I asked perplexed.

Flipping through his notepad and landing on a page after a few seconds, Agent Johnson answered, "You may know her better as Caribou, which is more of a nickname than an alias really, but you already knew that," he smiled, which surprised me, I figured these two for real stiffs.

"Oh, so that's her name," and then it hit me, how the hell did they know I knew her? How did they know about the nickname Caribou? And exactly what kind of legal trouble was she in that required both the DEA and the US Marshals Service. "Yeah, I know her. She's a friend of an old roommate I met quite a long while ago. We've stayed in touch on a personal level, but that's about it. She had mentioned some legal troubles, but she never told me what it was all about. I presume that's why you're here?" I asked, sounding genuinely concerned. I was beginning to think maybe she'd become some kind of snitch, hence the abrupt move to L.A. Though I didn't believe I was in any imminent danger, otherwise, why would she mention her legal issues?

"You're uncharacteristically fidgety Mr. Jordan. Do you have anything to be nervous about?" Agent Johnson asked.

"Fidgety? No, I'm fine. Just one thing though, how do you…" I said trailing off before asking how he could have known how I *usually* acted if this were supposed to be our first meeting? Midway through asking them I realized that it was quite possible that this wasn't the first time they had seen me. Maybe they'd been watching me for some time even. "Sorry, sorry," I shook my head as I gestured for my guests to hurry up their little visit, "go on please." I felt my face flush over as I caught myself gasping for air as if the room had very little left to offer. I quickly recovered my composure as I prayed my momentary lapse with reality hadn't led my guests to draw any conclusions about me.

"We're not actually here to talk about Ms. Ingalls," DEA Agent Smith interjected as he pulled out a stack of envelopes from his briefcase, and for some reason I wasn't too shocked when I recognized the writing on the front of the top envelope as my own. "We're here to speak with you about a Mr. Reggie Jones. It appears from your letters here that you two have a relationship going back as far as five years ago, and it looks like you two had conducted quite a bit of business together, leading us to believe you two were close."

My heart fell through the floor at this point, "Wait up a second, what exactly is this all about? Am I in some kind of trouble here? Do I need a lawyer, I mean shouldn't you be reading me my rights right about now?" I asked.

"Well, if you want a lawyer, then yes, we could take you downtown, put you into a small room, and leave you there, but I guarantee it will be much longer than twenty-four hours," Agent Johnson said. "You're not in trouble, yet, that all really depends on you, and your level of cooperation. It's simple, you answer our questions, and it's likely these letters will just, I dunno, disappear, understand?"

"Yes sir," I said softly, sounding somewhat defeated.

Agent Smith went on, "We're not here to bust your balls Mr. Jordan, what we are here for is to discuss Reggie Jones. When would you say was the last time you spoke with him?"

"Who?" I asked, almost whining out the word.

Adjusting in his wheelchair which almost forced a laugh out from deep within me, Agent Smith sneered in my direction. "Don't get coy with us son, you know exactly who we're talking about," he said as he waved the stack of envelopes at me.

"Oh, you're referring to the person I wrote about in a few stories to Carib… um, I mean Katie Ingalls, a man I referred to as 'ReggieJ'?" I smiled.

"Yes Mr. Jordan, that Reggie Jones," growing impatient.

"Well now I never said I knew a Reggie Jones, I both said and wrote ReggieJ. That could be a million different Reggie's from Portland, and on top of that, who says any of those stories are even true?" I asked, and by this point I was very worked up.

"We already know who Reggie Jones is, and what he's been up to in Portland over the years. Then we come across these letters…" and I thought, yeah right, came across them huh? "… Which are also from Portland, and there are striking similarities between your stories about 'ReggieJ,' and the information we have on Reggie Jones. How do you explain this, Mr. Jordan?" Agent Johnson asked snidely.

"Let me save you guys a lot of time: yes, I know a Reggie, but I don't know his last name, and I haven't seen or heard from him in over five years. Even if there was any truth to those stories, you can't use those letters in court, too many holes need filling, and I'm assuming you've had an eye on me for some time now, so you must know, I lead a productive life. I'm no criminal," I answered, trying to appear as genuine as possible. Though I was being completely honest, I tried to remember certain signs, or tells I had studied that cops look for during interrogations in order to determine if people are telling the truth or not, and it was really coming in handy while looking down upon the two suits.

The two agents looked at one another before Agent Johnson said, "About five years ago the DEA wrapped up an international investigation into the smuggling of Cocaine over the U.S./Mexican border by a Juarez based Drug Cartel, and your buddy Reggie Jones was their Pacific Northwest connection, a kind of Kingpin for Portland and Seattle. At the culmination of the investigation, we arrested Reggie Jones and he was shipped off to a federal prison in Colorado to await trial." This explained why he didn't appear on the inmate roster for any Oregon county when I searched their databases the week he disappeared so many years back. "His trial took several years to make it court, and once it was there, it took just under a year to be complete. He was convicted of multiple drug related federal crimes and sentenced to twenty-five years in prison. He was set to be transferred to a Maximum Security Federal Prison in Indiana, but somewhere during the transfer process, he up and disappeared from the federal prison in Colorado," hesitating before he continued, Agent Johnson went on, "Like a ghost, the guy just disappeared. This was just nine months ago." Now I understood why there was both the US Marshals Service and the DEA was involved: one had put him away, and the other was trying to put him back. I also realized that they were really stretching for any leads by this point if they were nine months behind him, and they had come knocking at my door.

"I'm really sorry, I wish I could help you guys, but I'm just a normal guy trying to lead a normal life. I don't know what else to tell you," I said raising my palms again to show I really had nothing for them. The letters kept going through my mind, and I couldn't help but wonder how they had obtained them. The more I thought about the letters, the more I realized that they couldn't necessarily be linked to me. I wouldn't call myself a paranoid person, but when I decided to write Caribou these tales of sex, drugs, and crime, I thought it was best to make sure I couldn't be linked to the letters physically so I took certain precautions: I never put a return address on the envelopes; I used glue to seal the letters rather than lick them, hence leaving no DNA traces; I never used anyone's full name, including my own; I always sent the letters from the post office and not my house; and I used a generic word processing program so there couldn't be any handwriting comparisons done. Though I knew this, I felt that it was best to keep it to myself, and the only time I would tell anyone about these precautions I took would be if the feds actually did come after me. At that point I would obtain an attorney's services and he or she would be the only one I would tell.

Agent Smith handed me his business card, followed by Agent Johnson's card before they both stood up. "Well, if for some reason you do hear from Reggie Jones, please contact us right away, either one of us," Agent Smith said, finishing our short talk. I then led both agents back to the front door which I opened for them.

"So, um… What will become of the letters," I asked with a smirk on my face.

"You really didn't supply us with anything we could use," Agent Smith said, as he looked over to Agent Johnson, "but, I think we'll just hang onto these for now. You never know when they might come in handy for us in the future," he said with a smirk of his own. "You've managed to somehow change your life around for the better, but something tells me it won't stay that way forever, though I have been proven wrong before. My advice, stay clean, you got too much going for you now," and the agents walked toward their car.

What a dick, I thought. "Take care gentlemen," I said as I shut the door. Needless to say, there wasn't going to be anymore letters to Caribou, at least not with anymore stories. That's for sure.

Oh Ms. Caribou-

How ya been huh, staying out of jail I hope? Unfortunately, I don't have any stories for you this time, or ever again for that matter. I had a visit from two federal agents today, one from the DEA and the other from the US Marshals Service, and you'll never guess what they had with them, my letters to you. If you received and read my letters, then you'll know that they contain extremely sensitive information that could be used to launch an ugly little investigation or two into me and my less than perfect past.

For the time being I think it's best if we just cut off all communication between us indefinitely. That means I don't want to know what your legal troubles are, how the feds got their hands on my letters to you, or anything else for that matter.

Maybe someday we can meet up and have a little chat, maybe even have a few laughs about it all, but for now, not even the slightest chuckle will escape these lips. Until we speak again…

TommyJ

---

29. So Much Left to Play

After revealing most of my deepest, darkest secrets to a near
perfect stranger, I found it almost poetic that this stream of
consciousness, this coming to terms with a life well lived, one that
some might even say was lived too fast, was abruptly brought to an
end by a prison break, a prostitute, and the federal government. I
knew Caribou had attempted to give me and my stories up for some
sort of deal, but, strangely, I was neither bitter nor angry about
it.

I sit in my room switching my gaze between the copies I had made of
the letters I sent Caribou, the two feds' business cards, and the
sunset I can see out of my bedroom window just a few feet from where
I sit. The pinks, grays, oranges, reds, and blues all seem so close,
so tangible, so very malleable, like I could almost reach out and
change the entire landscape with the wave of a hand. Even if I
could, I wouldn't change a thing, it is too beautiful. I stand, pick
up the stack of letters, and just stare at them. I walk down the
hall and into my office where I wrote each and every one of my
letters to Caribou, stopping in the doorway to peer in, looking upon
each item that had a hand in creating those letters: my laptop, a
stack of envelopes, plain printing paper, my printer, the desk, and
the chair I sat in. I take a seat and realize I'm both a great liar
as well as a bad liar, and I laugh softly. My laughter is
nevertheless cut short by a light breeze that catches my cheek and
brushes my hair to one side. I look to the window of my office where
two of the four panes of glass that make up the upper half of the
window were broken out just yesterday. I have yet to board them up.
For nearly an hour I exchange looks with the empty holes as well as
the remaining panes as I become lost in the sunset as it melts away.
Time has stamped the two remaining window panes with wavy scars and
yellow stains which cloud and distort the images outside. Images
that barely make it through, images that are scarcely a recollection
of what they truly are. Through the old panes of glass darkness
creeps over the sun allowing my distorted reflection to stare back
at me, however, the withering creature I see before me is not so
different from the man I truly am. I sense the old soul within me
staring back, attempting to assay the many lives and times we've
spent together. I breathe deeply and tell myself, have a stab at
this...

The End

Author's Contact Info

Thomas E. Jordan
PO Box 1285
Boring, OR 97009
lowrentthebook@gmail.com

www.ingramcontent.com/pod-product-compliance
Lightning Source LLC
Chambersburg PA
CBHW031104260626
47172CB00001B/213